KINGDOM *forgotten*

THE RISE AND DEMISE OF A MORMON ISLAND KING

D1073750

LAURIE LOUNSBURY

To my wonderful daughter, Lexi, whose steadfast support, encouragement and belief in this book made it all possible. I couldn't have completed this daunting project without her.

And to my son Tom, to whom I will be eternally grateful for inspiring me to write this.

PREFACE

This is the story of James Jesse Strang, self-proclaimed prophet and king of a group of Mormons who settled on Beaver Island in the mid-1800s.

James Strang is a real person, and Beaver Island is a real place in northern Lake Michigan, currently occupied by about 300 year-round residents, many of whom are Irish and have connections to the island's earliest Irish settlers found in this story.

To the best of my knowledge through my research, all of the facts in this book about James Strang are historically true, except for the places where I have Strang interact with fictional characters. Many of the speeches and dialogue in the book were spoken by Strang; in a few places I paraphrased or shortened his original speech for clarity.

Having said that, bear in mind that this is a work of historical fiction, and fiction is defined as "fabrication, invention, and concoction." In other words, I made stuff up. Whenever I had real characters interacting with fictional characters, I tried to keep the dialogue as true as possible to what I thought the real characters might say, but it was made up, nonetheless.

My intent with this book is to bring to life a fascinating period in American history that is largely unknown, and incorporate the perspective of the people who were not Mormons but lived in close proximity with the Mormons of Beaver Island while Strang was in power.

I learned the story of James Strang from an eighth grade history class assignment. I was flabbergasted by what I learned. When I asked my teacher, Mr. Bibby, why this fascinating slice of American history was so unknown, he replied, "Maybe the story of Strang hasn't been written in a compelling way that would make people want to read about him."

I never forgot those words. I hope Mr. Bibby would be pleased with what I've written.

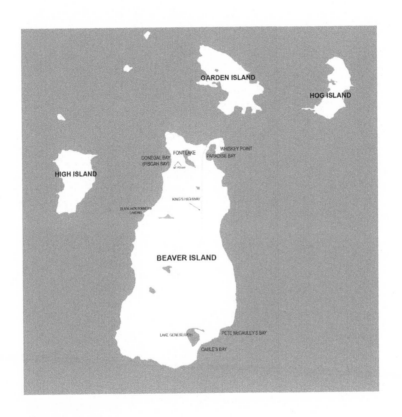

Part I

BEAVER ISLAND MEETS
JAMES JESSE STRANG
1848

CHAPTER 1
MAY, 1848

"You're back," Lucy said bluntly.

She didn't mean for it to sound like a personal affront, but the initial look he gave her suggested he took it that way. She wasn't judging the man who had just stepped off the dock, although she did take note of his short stature. She didn't care about his formal, yet well-worn attire that was out of place on Beaver Island. His red beard could use trimming, but was still presentable. His close-set eyes were the color of a burnished copper half-penny, peering intensely from below a high forehead. His eyes met hers in a look that turned from hostile to amiable as quickly as thunder follows lightning during a nearby summer storm. She wasn't naïve; she didn't think it was her keen mind that changed his attitude. She didn't keep her brains tucked in the front of her calico dress, where his gaze had momentarily flickered.

The man staring at Lucy was easily recognizable. Living on a remote island in Lake Michigan, there weren't that many faces to see, and she rarely forgot a single one of them.

She'd first seen the man one year ago, when he landed with a small, straggly bunch of people from Wisconsin. She'd watched him help his people set up tents and build little shanties on the south shore of Paradise Bay. There couldn't have been more than six or eight of them, all dressed similarly in drab, practical clothes made of coarse brown muslin and wool. The women had frightened yet determined looks on their faces while they stoically organized the smattering of belongings they'd brought with them: cookpots, iron frypans, butter churns, copper kettles, wooden spoons, blankets, bees-wax candles and lanterns. The men dug right into the business of pitching tents, gathering firewood and hunting for food. When they first arrived, Lucy had seen this man depart four days after his arrival, leaving the rest of his fellow travelers to fend for themselves over the long, cold winter. She'd seen how they gazed – first at him, and then at the island – with a mixture of fear and faith.

"Yes, of course I'm back," the man said with a touch of arrogance. "And might I ask who I'm speaking to?"

"Lucy. Lucy LaFleur. I own the boarding house over there." She pointed north, where her two-story, whitewashed home sat overlooking the harbor.

"It's a pleasure to meet you, Mrs. LaFleur. I'm James Strang. I've heard about your lovely home. I would be honored to have the privilege of staying at your home tonight, if you have a room available."

"I do," she said cautiously. His voice was a deep, rich baritone and he was using it now in a most cajoling manner. It was like listening to music that was lightly coated in weasel fat.

"Then I shall be up to see you shortly," James said. "I just have to wait and gather my things after they've unloaded the boat."

"Until then," she said, and turned to continue on her way to McKinley's store.

Lucy carefully picked her way around the muddy holes in the road, lift-ing her skirt a few inches off the ground to keep it dry. She stepped up the two wooden stairs to the porch; the gray, weather-beaten boards creaking with each step. When she got inside, she found Pete McKinley behind the counter, stocking shelves with cornmeal, flour and sugar.

"Afternoon, Lucy," Pete said, shoving a strand of gray hair off his fore-head. "What can I do for you today?"

"Afternoon, Pete. I need some lard, corn meal if you have it, sugar, and I think I'm out of coffee."

"Coming right up."

"Pete, what do you know of Mr. James Strang? He'll be staying with me tonight, and I don't remember much about him other than that curious band of people he brought to the island last year. Some religious thing, wasn't it?"

"Yes, that's right," Pete said. "Mormons. Driven out of Illinois, then persecuted in Wisconsin, so they say. Strang is apparently the head of their flock, and thinks Beaver Island is a good place to rebuild."

"Did those poor folks survive the winter? I've not seen hide nor hair of them," she asked.

"I believe they did. Made their way to Luney's Point. Patrick and his wife took pity on them and helped them farm a piece of land. Set 'em up in those old, abandoned fur trapper cabins."

"I'm glad to hear they made it. The winter of 1847 will definitely go down as one of the worst we've had."

After gathering her goods, she stepped down from McKinley's store porch and headed home. It was a short walk, but heavy mud tugged at her feet after the May thunderstorm they'd gotten the night before. Soon she was climbing the stairs onto the wide front porch of her home. Reflexively, she looked up and down the porch, imagining the children who should have been gathered there, playing dominos or checkers, faces stained with blackberry juice. Antoine had wanted a very wide porch to accommodate a very big family. Lucy straightened her shoulders for the thousandth time and walked in the front door. Alone. *Oh Antoine,* she thought, *why, oh why, did you have to leave me?*

From the kitchen window, Lucy looked out at the lake, loving and hating it at the same time. Delicate ripples danced along the surface, courting its admirers. It was aquamarine near the shore, and then transitioned into indigo blue in the deeper part of Paradise Bay. But she knew all too well that the guileless calm could become a razor-torn canvas of raging fury in a matter of minutes, tossing ships here and there the way a child in the throes of a temper tantrum casts away playthings.

She stopped looking out the window and finished making supper for her new guest, who had made his way to her home after collecting his belongings from the boat that brought him to Beaver Island.

After wiping her hands on her apron, she carried a plate of food and set it down in front of James, who was seated at her kitchen table. It wasn't her best effort for pleasing the eye, but it was perfectly fine food. The pan-fried whitefish, boiled potatoes and white bread looked a bit like misshapen white clouds on the earthenware plate.

James immediately started blessing his meal. Lucy had little patience for the tom foolery of Christian prayers, so she left him to his business and went back to tending the woodstove.

When he was finished praying, James spoke to her. "Could I bother you for some water?" he asked.

Lucy guessed it was thoughtless of her not to have brought him something to drink, but she just never knew what white men wanted. Some thought all water was poisoned, and would only drink beer, and others thought alcohol was poison and would only drink water. The latter category of men was in the minority. The water on Beaver Island was as pure as a spring leaf bud, but a lot of the people she met came from big cities where, she was led to believe, clean water was hard to come by. She brought him water in a copper mug and set it down in front of James' knife point. *You can call me a heathen, a red skin, a squaw, or whatever you choose, but you can't call me ill-mannered,* she thought to herself. The McKinleys had done a fine job of teaching her the manners and mannerisms of white folk after Antoine disappeared. She had spent a month in anguished grief after losing him, never leaving the house, barely eating. The McKinleys had brought her food and nursed her through the worst of her grief. Then they gently suggested she use her large home as a boarding house for visitors to the island. Without a husband to support her, she knew she needed to do something to provide for herself. And, she thought at the time, having other people around might take the edge off her hollowness. The McKinleys then taught her everything she needed to know about the expectations of white people.

With that training in mind, Lucy thought perhaps she should make polite small talk, so she asked the odd little man what brought him back to Beaver Island.

"I was visiting family in New York; now I'm on my way back to my home in Wisconsin." Something about the way he said it made her think it was mostly true, with a bit of a lie tucked in there like the clean tip of a dirty handkerchief poking out of a pocket.

Sensing her skepticism, he added, "I was also doing mission work for the Latter-Day Saints."

She'd heard of the new religion that was building momentum in parts of the country. She read newspapers whenever she could get her hands on them.

"So you're a missionary?" she asked politely.

"I'm the new leader of the Latter-Day Saints," he said, tipping his brow upward slightly. "I was rightfully chosen to be Joseph Smith's successor. Brigham Young is the renegade impostor, dragging those poor, deluded followers across the country to some God forsaken wilderness out west."

She was about as interested in Brigham Young and Latter-Day Saints as she was interested in the mouse droppings behind the kitchen cupboard. Actually, the turds interested her more – they could lead her to the rascally mice that were getting into her grain sack.

"So, where are you headed now?" she asked, not really paying attention.

"Home, to Voree, Wisconsin. A lovely place. It's hard to imagine living anywhere else, but this place is calling out to me. Or, more accurately, I should say that God called me to this place." His deep, coppery eyes, set so close together, now gazed very penetratingly at her.

"Pardon me?" she asked.

"Two years ago, I was traveling back to Wisconsin from Buffalo and my boat sailed past here. It was then that I recognized it as the place God had told me to seek for my people. An angel gave me a vision of a place surrounded by pristine waters, abundant with fish, a place of ample farmland, fields and forests. So here I am," James said.

"An angel gave you a vision? How does that work?" The things these white people came up with; it was astounding to her.

James appeared offended. "As I said before, I am the leader, rightfully named by the late Joseph Smith, founder of the Church of Jesus Christ of Latter-Day Saints, to lead my people to a safe place where we can follow our doctrine and prosper in peace. As such, God, through his angels, gives me visions and tools to help me along the way."

"I see," she said, not seeing at all and caring even less.

"I don't know if you do," Strang said, unwilling to accept her doubtful look. "Back in Wisconsin, I was directed by an angel to take my flock to a place of rare beauty. As soon as I saw Beaver Island, I knew I'd found the place."

"You mean you're going to live here? Permanently?" She couldn't imagine how this fragile-looking man could withstand a winter on the island. The only thing that looked sturdy on him was his head of wavy, dark red hair.

"Yes, permanently. And as we build our community here, we want to incorporate our culture with yours. I have always had great admiration for the Indian people."

Lucy was doubtful about his proclaimed admiration for her 'people,' so she gave him no response. She hadn't met many white men who admired Indians. Most of the white men she'd encountered were either trying to trick or kill her people. But she decided, in her usual pragmatic manner, that if he was going to be sending new people to the island, that meant more business for her, and she didn't want to offend the person who would be bringing her new boarders.

After an awkward silence, James swallowed the last bit of fish from his plate. She picked it up and took it to the washbowl on the sideboard. Lucy looked out at the lake again. Still lovely and calm. But it was mid-May, and she knew it was quite possible to get a late blast of snow and sleet at that time of year. Weather on the island could turn from nice to nasty without any warning. Like her mother, she could sense when a change was coming just by facing the lake and letting the breeze brush against her face.

There was definitely a change coming to the island, and it didn't feel good.

⸺ ◆●◆ ⸺

As Strang stepped off Lucy's porch and looked out at the harbor, he remembered his trip to Beaver Island for the first time, two years ago.

That year, Strang had to scrounge passage on fishing boats and freighters. This year, he was coming back to the island in style after a very successful mission trip to New York. The *Niagara* was the newest of the palace passenger ships to steam from New York to Michigan, then on to Wisconsin and Chicago before heading back east. It had made its maiden voyage the year before. His pockets bulged with money donated to him by new converts to his Mormon faith. James was nothing if not an eloquent speaker who could move people to do things they wouldn't normally consider, like donating their hard-earned money to someone who promised them a better life. Now he remembered well the thoughts he'd had of this place back then as he'd sailed in sight of it the first time.

"Divine." Then a small smile came over him. "Perfectly divine. Divine Perfection. I must remember that for my next sermon."

He knew it was going to be perfect long before he set foot on the island, when he'd seen it from the deck of a side-wheel steamer traveling from New York to Wisconsin. At that point, all he could see was a dot. A series of dots, actually, green and sandy; hardy little souls jutting from the deep blue waters of northern Lake Michigan.

The dots had names. Peculiar names to a man like James: Squaw, Whiskey, High, Garden, Gull, Trout, Hog and Beaver.

His description of Divine Perfection, as he thought of it, wasn't based on the miles of hardwood trees surrounding him. They were essential for building dwellings, but he gave them no more than a passing glance. Nor was it based on the fishing boats lining the harbor, where men pulled vast nets of fish onto the shore. That would put food on the table and money in people's pockets, yet they didn't warrant more than a moment's notice of his time.

It was the remoteness of it all that made it perfect.

Walking on the road that ran along the harbor, James could see his dream becoming a reality in this place. The harbor was deep and very well-protected, a horseshoe-shaped bay with a narrow entrance on the south side. It was an ideal stopping point for steamers that needed to take on cordwood, which was abundant on the island. Looking inland, he saw vast forests of pine, beech, oak, maples and birches. Dark, primordial areas were swampy and crowded with cedars. The forests gave way to fields that were ideal for farming. The beaches glimmered with unspoiled, fine-grain sand.

It was an isolated spot 20 miles away from the Pine River outpost, which was the nearest point on the mainland, which also meant it was 20 miles away from naysayers, doubters, persecutors who disbelieved him. Twenty miles away from the feckless and faithless who didn't trust him to be the prophet of his people. This was where he would stake his claim for the title of Mormon leader. This is where he'd show Brigham Young that he had the better, brighter vision for the future. While Young's followers were starving and freezing to death on their brutally long westward odyssey to the territory of Utah, his flock would be settled and thriving on Beaver Island.

The island was hardly well-developed. It had a general store, a cooper shop, trading post, a livery, and of course, a tavern. The spirits served in the tavern would have to go, James thought, but it could continue as a gathering place and purveyor of food for the Mormon bachelors who would no doubt follow James to the island. Young men would be fools not to pull up roots in the East and move to Strang's island utopia, where he'd promised that everyone would be given free land by the church. He'd also promised that money-making opportunities were everywhere on the island. He promised widows and plain-faced young women that they would find a spouse and happiness here. No one would do without and everyone would prosper if they followed the Mormon rules according to Strang.

Following the rituals established by Joseph Smith, Strang had no difficulty recruiting new members. American citizens were hungry for a new religion. They had grown weary of the heavy robes of priests and the somber sermons of the Old World religions. They wanted something fresh and exciting that befitted the brave new world they lived in, and the Mormons delivered it in spades: Secret gold plates buried on a hillside in Palmira, New York, discovered by an innocent farm boy named Joseph Smith; an angel named Moroni who gave Smith sacred seer stones to translate the Egyptian hieroglyphics into English; a return of the gold plates to the angel Moroni, so that mere mortals wouldn't be tempted to steal the valuable plates, thus leaving behind no tangible evidence with which to dispute Joseph Smith's story.

Add to that the revelations and visions given to Smith by the angels, and the Mormon religion was intoxicating to Americans starved for a new belief. Strang picked up where Smith left off, creating his own tale of visions from angels and brass plates from an angel, buried in Wisconsin and discovered by Strang, that only he could translate. New converts to the faith loved hearing Strang's stories about angels and revelations. It convinced them that they had joined the one true religion, because God spoke directly to his Mormon prophets.

As Strang wandered about Beaver island, reminiscing about his progress with the Latter-Day Saints, he accidentally ran into a strong young man who was bent over, emptying bilge water from his boot.

"Hey, watch where you're going!" the man said.

"My apologies, my good man," James said. "So sorry you got in my way." James gave a quick tip of his top hat to the man he inadvertently jostled.

Feckin' dandy, Will MacCormick thought to himself. *I'm in your way? I live here!* He watched as the stranger made his way slowly along the road, keenly observing activity around him.

Will went back to the boat to check it once more and make sure it was secured for the night. His catch had already been packed in salt. His gill nets were drying on reels in the mild sunshine.

"Willie, care for a pint with me at Cleary's?"

It was Teddy Duffy, Will's cousin and fishing partner, returning from the fish processing house. He was coated with a faint spray of salt.

"Don't see why not," Will said as he joined him.

The two men walked the short distance to Cleary's and took seats at the bar, each ordering a pint from Roald Cleary.

"Did you get a look at the new fella who came off the *Niagara?*" Will asked his cousin. He'd seen Strang disembark the day before and head up to Lucy's house. Even though Strang was short, there was something about him – the top hat, the dress clothes, the intense brown eyes – that made him stand out.

"Nope, wasn't even around when the *Niagara* docked. What about him?"

"Some kind of self-important dandy is all. Ran into him a while ago. Or he ran into me, truth be told."

"Probably is a dandy if he's traveling on the *Niagara,*" Teddy said. "Maybe one of those rich land speculators. Doubt if he's doing anything here except waiting for the *Niagara* to refuel."

Ted and Will engaged in a spirited debate with Roald about the coming summer season. Roald was positive it would be a short, cool summer due to the early and frequent calls of the katydids.

"That's malarkey," Ted said. "It's going to be a long, hot summer. I heard the toads at Barney's Lake singing like mad." Will just sat back and smiled complacently. All that mattered to him was that summer was coming, and that meant warm weather for fishing.

The two men finished a few more pints before wobbling out of Cleary's. As the sun set behind them and lit up the harbor with deep pink light, they caught sight of Tom Bennett's boat, riding low in the water and listing to one side. It looked like the lines tying it to the dock were the only things keeping it from sinking.

"Bennett better fix that boat of his before it keels over," Teddy said.

"I'd better get home before I keel over," Will replied.

CHAPTER 2

MID MAY, 1848

The newcomers arrived, first in a trickle, dribbling one by one off the boats that came into the harbor, then in a steady stream, and finally a gusher like a good smelt run.

Lucy watched warily as Strang spent the next week greeting new converts who followed him to the island. By her count, at least 30 new members had arrived from New York. Among them were Millicent and Archie Donnelly, who stayed at her boarding house while they looked for a place to stake their claim.

Archie and Millie were completely mismatched physically and perfectly matched temperamentally. Archie was tall and muscular, with an oversized head covered with dark hair and bright blue eyes that crinkled around the edges every time he smiled, which was most of the time. Millie was a tiny little thing, nearly two feet shorter than Archie, with coppery hair and soft green eyes. Lucy worried that a strong breeze could knock Millie over; a November gale would probably carry her away. Neither of them had a spare ounce of fat on them, the result of the potato famine they'd left behind in Ireland.

Millie was immediately taken with the place. When their boat pulled alongside the dock in Paradise Bay, the sunshine skittered on the water and the tender young leaves on the maple trees were vivid green.

"This place reminds me of Árainn Mhór," Millie told Lucy in her thick Irish brogue, referring to the Irish island that had been their former home.

It was a fine day, so Lucy walked with Archie and Millie and a few other new arrivals as Strang gave them a tour of the harbor.

"Over here we'll build a tabernacle," Strang told his flock of followers. "Then we'll build a school right next to it. Right there, in town, we'll have a print shop where we can make a newspaper. It's extremely important to be informed. And it's equally as important to spread the word to others about us." Strang smiled sincerely at the group.

"Where are we going to live?" one man asked.

"Yes, where is the free land you promised?" said another.

"There's available land as far as the eye can see," Strang told them. "Farmland, timberland, take your pick."

"Who owns it?" the first man asked.

"We do," Strang replied smoothly. "God has consecrated this land to us."

One of Lucy's black eyebrows shot up into a sideways question mark when he said that, but she bit her tongue. She wanted to see what other tall tales he was going to tell these people.

Lucy knew that James wasn't telling the truth. Patrick Kilty, working for the U.S. government, had surveyed the entire island two years ago, and the government was in the process of splitting the land up into tracts, which would soon be offered for sale. During the long process of surveying the 13-mile long island, Kilty fell in love with the land and moved there with his wife, Lavinia. Pat told Lucy he explained all of this to Strang, who immediately expressed interest in buying land along the harbor. But until Kilty and the government parceled the land into tracts and officially offered it for sale, much of the land was up for grabs. Squatters' rights prevailed, to Strang's way of thinking. The government, as Kilty had explained, allowed people to stake their claim to land, make improvements, and then they could buy it from the government when the land was officially put up for sale.

As they toured the island with Strang, Archie was astounded at the number of strong, tall trees growing in stands all over the island.

"They don't grow like this in Ireland," he said as he looked in amazement at the towering trees. Maple, oak, spruce and red pines, along with beech and cedars, grew thick on the island. Archie had been a builder in Ireland. He wanted to return to the business of working with wood and stone, turning them into something that would nurture and protect families from the harsher elements of nature.

Strang concluded his tour and left the settlers to pick their plot of land. He purposely caught up with Lucy, so she had no choice but to walk with him back to her house.

"This fresh air certainly stimulates the appetite, doesn't it?" Strang said.

"I breathe it all the time, I can't say one way or the other."

"Well, it certainly has made me hungry."

Lucy got the hint. When they were back in her kitchen, she pulled out a loaf of fresh baked bread she'd made that morning. Stewed tomatoes, canned last summer, she put in a pan, along with whitefish.

"Whatever you're cooking smells wonderful," Strang said.

"Then have a seat and I'll serve you some."

Strang seated himself at her pine kitchen table, its surface scratched and worn from years of butchering animals and chopping vegetables. He looked around the kitchen, with its clean, whitewashed walls made of chinked maple logs. Black iron skillets hung from meat hooks on one wall. The little wood-burning stove was blackened with use. A pile of firewood was neatly stacked in a bin next to the stove. A wooden pail of water – a smaller, open topped version of a beer barrel – sat next to it.

Lucy spooned the whitefish and tomatoes onto a plate, then cut a generous hunk of bread from the loaf and placed it in front of him. Then she turned back to the stove to get something for herself.

"Won't you join me?" Strang asked, almost bashfully.

She hesitated, and then nodded to let him know she could do that, although it wasn't her first choice. She would have preferred to eat alone. She fixed herself a plate of food and sat down across the table from him.

"I've been wanting to talk to you," Strang said after swallowing his first bite. "You seem to be an integral part of this island, and I was hoping you could give me some insight to the people here." He spoke with a tone that carried a trace of humility.

"I can try," she said. She looked at his coppery eyes and saw warmth that she hadn't noticed before, as if the copper had become molten.

"I guess I should start by saying I don't want to upset any of the people living here. I want to incorporate our ways into the rhythm of life here that currently exists."

"That's good to hear."

"I do want to build something good here, something lasting, something that will lift people up and inspire them to be the best versions of themselves. I want to create a community that can be an example to people all over the country – even all over the world – that shows what is possible when people work together for a common good."

His words, his tone, were so different than they'd been when she first met him. She suddenly found herself thinking of him as tender and thoughtful – even inspirational. Maybe it didn't really matter if he believed he was a prophet and angels guided him from one place to another. If his goals were noble, perhaps the means to get there were unimportant.

"So what would you like to learn from me?"

"Could you tell me about the people who live here now? Where they came from, and what they do?"

"Well, there's the Anishinaabe Indians who have been here as long as anyone can remember. My mother is Anishinaabe. She married my father, who was a fur trapper and trader from Canada. We lived on Garden Island."

"And your father?"

Lucy's face dropped and she averted her eyes. "He died when I was young. He was on his way to Mackinac Island with a load of furs, and his boat went down."

"I'm so sorry," James said. He started to reach out as if to take her hand in his to comfort her, but then realized it would be inappropriate. His hand went back in his lap.

"That's the way it is in these parts. That lake can turn on you as fast as a fox on the run." Lucy stopped talking and pushed a bit of fish around on her plate.

James sat quietly while she collected herself.

"I just want you to know I think your people are wonderful. Noble. The Book of Mormon calls you the Lamanites, the lost race of noble ancestry. I plan to treat your people with the respect and care you deserve."

Lucy didn't know quite what to make of that. Lamanites? Never heard of such a thing. Her people, as he referred to them, came from right here. Their oral history, handed down from one generation to the next for hundreds of years, told her as much. But if he planned to treat them respectfully and not encroach on their way of life, she was glad to hear that.

"And the other people living here?" he asked, moving the conversation along.

"There aren't many, but there are the fur trappers, most of them are French-Canadian, and then there are the fishermen, they seem to come mostly from Ireland and England. And some of the business owners are just plain American, as far as I can tell. Just like you."

"I hope the other women on the island are just like you – kind and lovely," James said.

Lucy blushed. She couldn't remember the last time she blushed. She looked at his eyes. They were smoldering seductively, like burning tobacco. She felt like he was examining her soul, the way a sailor studies the horizon for signs of fair or foul weather. It unnerved her and pleased her simultaneously.

CHAPTER 3
MAY, 1848

Will MacCormick's father, Dolan MacCormick, was sitting on the front porch of their one-story home on the south shore of Paradise Bay, whittling. He watched as steamers pulled alongside the long pier to unload passengers and take on wood, enjoying the sight of a busy harbor while also keeping an eye out for his son Will and nephew Teddy to return safely with a boatload of whitefish.

Where does the time go, Dolan thought to himself as he carefully ran his sharp knife blade along the length of the wood he was carving. *Seems like yesterday when I got here with little Will. Now he's a grown man and I'm turning into an old man.*

Dolan's physical appearance belied his 49 years of age. The strong muscles in his arms were prominently visible underneath his aging skin, like firm young bodies under a worn bed sheet. He still had a full head of hair, dark with streaks of gray, and bright eyes that always saw the glass as half-full.

The front porch, where Dolan sat with the chair tipped back on two legs and his feet resting on the porch rail, was the best feature of the small house, occupied only by Will and Dolan. Made of wide pine boards, it spanned the whole length of the house. Dolan built his home the way his wife Agnes would have wanted it, even though she never lived to see it. Will's mother Agnes had been taken by the swamp fever when he was just a baby, during the time Dolan helped build the Erie Canal.

When the canal was finished, Dolan never looked back at the rolling hills of Oneida County in New York, where he and Agnes had started their married life. It was too painful a reminder of the life he could have had with his beloved wife. He took his young son and went west by water. It seemed logical that he, a man who helped enlarge the impressive canal that connected New York to the Great Lakes, should avail himself of the new passageway to start a new life.

After traversing the entire length of the canal, Dolan and Will boarded a sailing vessel in Buffalo, bound for Detroit. From there, they boarded a steamer headed for the main northern islands of Lake Michigan – Mackinac and Beaver Island.

Upon their arrival at Mackinac Island, they were greeted by fur traders who were drunkenly hooting and hollering, and fishmongers who were elbowing and bellowing.

"How about this, Will? Looks like there's plenty of opportunity for work here." Will shrieked with a cry that scared the dock rats back into the water.

"Okay, on we go. Up next is Beaver Island." Sailing to Beaver Island was a smooth trip. The lake had quieted itself after a storm, just like Will, who had gnawed on his knuckles until his fitfulness passed. The warm sun was starting to disappear on the horizon, morphing from a yellow ball into a sinking peach when they arrived at Paradise Bay. Will was sound asleep.

There wasn't much to see on Beaver Island. A few shanties along the harbor, a cabin or two set back from the water's edge, a small trading post, and a lot of trees beyond the shoreline. But Dolan was seeing the beautiful, well-protected harbor and the sun setting through the birch leaves.

Dolan's first project after roughing out a small shanty on the island was to build himself a boat. With the tools he'd brought from New York, he fashioned himself a small sailboat with a single mast. For Will, he built a wide seat and looped rope around thick bands of fabric so he could secure Will on their outings. By the time he completed the boat, Will was no longer a baby and Dolan was ready to go exploring by boat.

Staying close to the shore, Dolan explored the coastline of Beaver Island in his boat. After he rounded Whiskey Point and headed west, he could see Garden Island to the north. On one such excursion, Dolan saw smoke rising from campfires along the shore of Garden Island. The lake, like Will, was in a good mood that day, stirring up no fuss in the light breeze. Pulling on the sheet of his sail with his right hand and pushing on the tiller with the left, he brought the boat about and headed toward Garden Island.

There were six campfires burning, tended to by Indian women with long black braids hanging down their backs. Tripods made of green hickory branches formed an open air teepee over the fires. Criss-crossed over the low fires were cedar branches, freshly cut and soaked in the lake. Over the branches hung strips of duck. Dolan's mouth started watering when he was close enough to smell it.

He beached his sailboat upwind of the fires and helped Will out, keeping a firm hold of his hand. Now a toddler with sturdy legs and chubby feet, Will was always ready to lurch forward into an unsteady run, not caring that the sprint usually ended with him face down in the dirt.

As the two of them approached, Dolan leaned over to Will and said, "Do you suppose they speak English?"

"I do," answered a young woman. Dolan was taken aback. He was still far enough away that he thought he would be out of earshot. She must have remarkable hearing, he thought.

She was a powerfully built woman with eyes set wide apart and a long, straight nose that turned down slightly at the end. Her black hair was severely parted in the middle and fixed in two long braids on either side of her large ears. She looked nothing like Agnes, who was petite and pale-skinned, with fair hair and powder blue eyes. Dolan had always thought of Agnes as a small porcelain figurine, pretty and fragile and needing to be handled with the greatest of tenderness.

This woman was clearly the opposite of Agnes. Lithe muscles ran the length of her long, brown arms. Her dress was held up by wide leather straps that stretched across her broad shoulders. She had a skinning knife hanging from her neck, affixed to a twisted leather thong.

She was barefoot. The white sand hid her toes, but he could see the beginning of her muscular legs before they disappeared under the mid-calf-length tunic. The only parts of Agnes that didn't look like they'd been carved from delicate ivory were her ankles. Agnes had the thick ankles of an

Irish peasant woman. The ankles Dolan found himself staring at now were strong and slender.

"Hello, I'm Dolan MacCormick, and this is my son, Will," Dolan said awkwardly.

"How do you do," the woman said, without offering her own name. "What brings you here?"

"I was sailing along Beaver, and I saw your campfires. Just wondered what was going on, I guess. And then the smell. Whatever you're doing smells most appealing."

"We're smoking duck," she said. "Before you know it, the cold will come. We like to be well-provisioned before it happens."

"How did you learn English?" Dolan asked, his curiosity overcoming his manners.

She smiled at him for the first time. Her teeth were large and white, framed by straight, rosy-brown lips. "My father works occasionally as a guide for trappers. They often stayed with my family."

"Is your family still around?"

"Mostly. My father's out fishing right now. My mother died from the cholera sickness. She was a medicine woman, but her powers weren't strong enough to combat such an illness."

"I'm so sorry." Dolan looked down at the sand.

"It's all right. I also have my older brother, Otto."

"So your brother is named Otto, what are you called?" Dolan asked timidly.

"Giiwedinokwe."

"Gee wedding oak way," Dolan said slowly, trying to repeat it correctly.

She laughed. "You can call me Gwen. That's what Pierre always called me."

While Dolan was talking to Gwen, Will was getting increasingly bored. When he sensed his father was raptly paying attention to the woman and not so much to himself, he made a break for it, pumping his little legs rather comically, as he scampered toward the fires.

"Will!" Dolan said sharply, taking off after his son.

Gwen sprang after the child like a deer bolting at the sound of thunder. She caught him in seconds, swept him up in one smooth motion and carried him back to Dolan.

"Thank you," he said as he took the squirming Will from her arms.

"Happy to," she said. "But shouldn't he be home with his mother? Seems a bit precarious to take a child his age in a boat like that even on a calm day. If the wind picks up even a little bit, the lake between here and Beaver will get choppy enough to swamp you."

"He has no mother. We lost her, just like you did yours. But it was swamp fever that took her."

Gwen remained quiet; she just looked at Dolan with her black, penetrating eyes. He found it discomfiting to have her gaze steadily at him.

"Life isn't always kind, is it," she said. "So that means you're raising this papoose by yourself?"

"I am. At least I'm trying to. But I'm getting worried. As you said, the cold is coming soon, and I don't know how to take care of this little fella when the time comes. I haven't found my livelihood here yet."

"What have you been doing for food and shelter?"

"I built a shanty when we first arrived. And I built wooden traps for small animals, and we've done a bit of foraging for fruit. Lavinia Kilty has been kind to us and given us potatoes and yams from her garden."

"Do you know how to fish?"

"I do, but I have no equipment here and no money to buy it."

"I'll ask my father and brother to help you. Can you come back here tomorrow at first light if the weather is good?"

Dolan was thrilled at the prospect of getting into the fishing business. "I can, but what about Will?" Dolan said.

"Bring him along. I'll tend to him."

"I am humbled by your kindness, Gwen. I don't know why you should want to offer such generosity to a stranger."

"It's our way of life," she answered simply. "And I don't want that little boy of yours starving to death this winter."

Sitting on his front porch now, Dolan fondly remembered that first meeting with Gwen. He was drawn to her as strongly today, 23 years later, as he was then. Maybe part of the attraction was the continual pursuit of her and never quite catching her. Gwen gently but persistently refused to marry Dolan, no matter how many times he asked. And she just as persistently refused to move into his home on Beaver Island, choosing instead to stay with her people on Garden Island.

"My people need me," she told him time and again. "I'm the medicine woman. I can't abandon them. My mother handed the healing arts down to me, and I must continue it."

"We need healing over here too, you know," Dolan told her, knowing all too well it was futile. "And I need you."

"You know I love you. But don't ask me to leave my home and my people. That is something I cannot do."

Dolan was inextricably bound to Gwen and her brother. For decades, he fished with her brother Otto, continuing to do so after their father passed away. Dolan was considered an honorary member of their tribe, since he spent so much time on Garden Island. He was content among the Indians, as was Will. Otto and the other male members of the tribe had taught Will to fish and hunt. Dolan taught his son how to build. And together they had built a very nice life. He fervently hoped nothing would change that, but he knew that the only thing that was predictable in life was change.

CHAPTER 4

MAY, 1848

When James woke up, Lucy was already bustling in the kitchen, frying eggs and bacon on the woodstove and slathering bread with bacon grease. It was a cool morning after a cold, rainy night. At times, the rain had turned to sleet. But this morning the weather seemed to be improving.

Lucy saw James looking out the window, searching hopefully for a break in the clouds.

"Give it about an hour, and the sun will come out and it will warm up," she told him.

"How can you know that?"

Lucy smiled, a small twinge of condescension in the corners of her dark, oval eyes.

"I've lived here my whole life, Mr. Strang, I know the weather patterns. For the past three days, the wind has been out of the northeast, bringing high winds and bad weather. We call it a nor'easter, or a three-day blow. This morning the wind shifted, it's now out of the southwest. That will bring sunshine and warmer days."

James was impressed. "So it will be a good day to go exploring?"

"If that's what you want to do. For myself, I'm going morel mushroom hunting and going to pick a passel of wild onions."

"I have no idea what you're talking about," James said with a smile.

"Morel mushrooms are delicious. They only grow for a brief time in May. It takes a combination of a good rain and warmer weather to make them pop. This should be a good day for it."

"And the wild onions?"

"Wild onions are delicate and abundant. I'll cook with them while they're fresh, then pickle the rest to have over the winter. Same with the morels. We'll eat some now, but dry the rest for the winter."

She saw the look on his face, and asked the question he was waiting for.

"Do you want to come with me?"

"I would be honored," James replied eagerly.

The two set off toward the woods about 20 minutes later. Lucy was wearing moccasins on her feet and an Indian tunic. James hadn't seen her dress in her native garb, and was delighted with what he saw. The tunic went to just below her knees, so he had a view of her long, firm legs. Her black hair was braided and hung down to the middle of her back. Around her neck she had a small knife, and over her shoulders she carried two large burlap knapsacks – one for morels, one for wild onions, he presumed.

They walked along the lake for about a half-mile, then turned into the woods, where the ground was damp and fallen cedars were rotting in their path. As they entered the woods, the sun came out. Lucy's prediction had been correct.

Lucy slowed her pace as she scanned the ground. Her steps were silent in her moccasins. If mushrooms and onions had ears, they would never hear her coming.

"There," she said, pointing to a spot on the ground where dead leaves covered the earth.

"What? I don't see anything," James said, bending over to take a closer look.

In one clean move, Lucy bent with her knife and sliced at the base of a mushroom James hadn't noticed. She held it up to him.

"What an odd-looking fellow," James said, studying the mushroom that looked like a tall, skinny teepee with a lot of pockmarks in it. "Reminds me of the dunce caps our teachers made us wear in grade school." Lucy laughed at his remark, which pleased him enormously.

"Perhaps to you it looks odd. To me, it just looks delicious."

"Are there any more?" James asked, still staring at the ground.

Lucy laughed again. "They're everywhere! You just have to train your eyes. Here, watch."

She bent down and used her knife to brush dead leaves out of the way. Suddenly James recognized one of the funny mushrooms – and then another, and then another. Suddenly, where he couldn't see any of them a moment before, he was seeing them everywhere.

"That's amazing! It's like a trick of the eye. Is there any secret to picking them?"

"It's best to cut them at the base, leaving some of the root behind so they'll grow back next year. We also give them a good shake."

"Why do you shake them?"

"I'm not sure," Lucy said. "That's what I was taught to do. Maybe it leaves some of their magic behind to sink back into the earth."

James pulled a knife out of his pants pocket and bent to help Lucy cut and gather mushrooms. She had laid her sacks on the ground. Now she filled one of them with mushrooms with James' help. She crawled along the dirt, her tunic riding up on her legs. James couldn't help but stare.

When the sack was filled, Lucy slung it over one shoulder.

"On to the wild onions. They're much easier to find." They turned south and walked along a path that was lined with slender green leaves.

"These are wild onions. Two leaves on each plant." She stuck her knife into the ground near one plant and loosened the soil around it until she was able to uproot it. She then held it up, brushed soil off the base and showed James the slender, wild onion.

"Wonderful!" he exclaimed. "Wouldn't it be easier to just bring a shovel into the forest and dig them all up at once?"

"No, we pick a few here and a few there, so they will always reproduce."

After an hour of carefully loosening the soil around the plants and pulling them out of the ground, they had filled Lucy's bag.

Lucy led James out of the woods and down to the lake, where the sun was shining brightly and warming the day. Lucy slipped off her moccasins, took the bag of wild onions and waded into the frigid lake water. She emptied the sack of onions into the shallow water. With her knife, she swiftly cut off the leaves and roots, then washed them in the water until a clean, pearly white bulb appeared. She worked quickly, tossing the clean bulbs back into the knapsack. James was fascinated. She was squatting in the water, maintaining her balance on the sandy bottom and working skillfully. It was a beautiful sight.

Lucy carried the full bag of mushrooms and James carried the onions. They walked slowly back to her house, enjoying the sunshine, warm air and a soft breeze that wafted out of the southwest.

"You're a woman of many talents, I can see," James said. "I've told you about me, but I know almost nothing of you. Tell me what it was like to grow up in this wonderful place."

"You sure you have the time? Once I get started…"

"Please. I have all the time in the world for you." James smiled and sat down in the sand. "Come and sit and tell me all about you."

Strang found this woman captivating, even though she was a Lamanite. Mormons believed Lamanites had been cursed with dark skin as a result of displeasing God when they didn't accept the teachings of Jesus Christ. They also believed that if the Mormons succeeded in converting the heathens to Mormonism, their skin would turn white again. Strang knew there was a time and a place for revealing certain parts of his religion. Strang envisioned what this wonderful woman would look like with pale skin as he listened to her story.

CHAPTER 5
MAY, 1848

In her own words, Lucy told James more than she thought she ever would tell anyone. There was something about the way he listened so intently, hanging on her every word. A man who listened was a rare man indeed, and it prompted Lucy to divulge her life story.

Lucy LaFleur told James about her happy childhood, growing up on Garden Island with her Indian mother and French-Canadian father. Life could often be harsh – the late autumn storms were unforgiving; the winters long and bitter – but spring always came, unstoppable with the smell of new cedar growing in swamps, tadpoles in clear cold ponds, and wet earth ready to give way to summer blooms.

She loved all of it. Loved the sight of huge November waves building up far out on the lake, then pounding onto the shore like mighty warriors returning home after a victory. With winter came the season of silence and snow, jackrabbits bounding across white fields and making easy dinner targets of themselves. Spring usually came late, and brought with it timid little green buds on trees, determinedly hanging on and waiting for the summer sun to ignite.

Then there was summer. Although Lucy had never traveled farther than the other islands in the archipelago, she couldn't imagine any place in the world that could be as beautiful as her home on Garden Island in the summer. After the silence of winter, summer was the happy newborn cry of cicadas, katydids, crickets, bullfrogs, white-throated sparrows and loons all vying for their spot on the soundwave spectrum.

And that filled just one of her five senses. The feel of warm, silky sand under her feet, the wash of gentle waves up to her knees, the smell of lilac and pine, the taste of ripe raspberries and blackberries, and the sight of an early sunrise out the back door and a late summer sunset out the front window made her world a perfect childhood home.

But like a milkweed pod slashed by a bear's paw, all the silky strands of her life floated into reality when her father died. Her mother was stoic about it.

"Life is shorter for some than for others, Lucy," her mother told her. "And many folks go through this life never knowing what true love and devotion feels like. Your father gave that to us, and it can never be taken away from us – ever. So be thankful for what we had, and what we still have."

As an only child lacking the guiding influence of a father or even a big brother, Lucy sought out her own male role models.

Black Jack Bonner and her uncle Chief Peaine were as different as a rascally river otter and a majestic 12-point buck, but she loved them both.

Chief Peaine was her mother's half-brother, a man of intellect and honor who easily won the respect of his people. Although he tried to steer Lucy into the work better suited to a young Indian woman, he could see she wasn't going to be dissuaded from learning the skills typically reserved for young men. After a few weak admonitions and protests, Chief Peaine took Lucy with him and taught her how to run a trap line for jackrabbits and fox, and how to shoot deer. He taught her how to swing an axe and split wood. She displayed the patience and quietness necessary for hunting, and was an excellent shot. It took her no time at all to learn how to field dress a deer and drag it home on a travois made of cedar branches and leather strips woven into a net.

Lucy didn't neglect the female side of life; she learned how to skin animals, tan hides, smoke fish, sew and cook from her mother.

By the time she was sixteen, she had discovered Black Jack Bonner on Gull Island, a prominent member of the Irish fishing camp. Looking half-child, half-woman and all mischief, Black Jack didn't turn her away when she confidently paddled her birch bark canoe up to the camp. When Jack learned she was the Chief's niece, he treated her with a mixture of cautious respect and camaraderie. He took her out gill-netting on calm days, enjoying her company in confines of an otherwise boring, small boat.

Black Jack Bonner also taught Lucy a wide variety of colorful words that didn't exist in her native language. She learned to use them all correctly, because it made Jack roar with laughter whenever she did.

"That feckin' deer fly just bit me on the arse!" she would say, and Jack would laugh out loud at the sound of salty words flying out of Lucy's wide, pretty mouth.

Sometimes, on calm summer evenings, she would linger on Gull Island with Jack and the other fishermen until the sun was no more than a glimmering line on the west-facing water.

"Black Jack, can I have some of what you fellas are drinking?" she finally asked.

"I don't know, little Indian princess, your people don't do well with the firewater."

"Aw, please? I'm only half Indian princess," she wheedled.

"I'll give you some of our stuff, but you stay away from the firewater they sell to the other Indians on Whiskey Point. That stuff is poisonous."

"Why do they sell you one kind of spirits and another kind to my people?"

"Because your people don't know any better," Jack said bluntly. "That stuff is loaded with cayenne pepper and tobacco and god knows what else."

The French-Canadian half of Lucy was apparently the side where she got her drinking capabilities. By the time she was 18, she could keep up with all of the Irish fishermen, and outlast many of them. By the time she was 19, her mother started lecturing her about the dangers of spirits.

"I don't care, mother," Lucy told her. "I can throw 'em back with the best of them, at least that's what Black Jack says!"

Lucy shared all of this with James while she sifted sand through her calloused fingers.

"Sounds like you had a wonderful upbringing," James said.

"I did, with the exception of losing my father when I was young."

"And you lost your husband as well?"

Lucy's face sank when he asked about her husband, Antoine. It still hurt her to remember him. She'd never gotten closure on his death; never got to give him a proper burial.

"He was a fur trader, like my father," Lucy said. "French-Canadian. He built our house.

"My father died when he was sailing to Mackinac Island with a load of furs. A storm came up out of nowhere and his boat went down. It was October, and my father thought it was too early for harsh weather. He was wrong.

"My Antoine was going to sail up to Mackinac with a load of furs one sunny autumn day and I begged him not to. I made him stay and promise not to go up until the lake had frozen solid and he could run his furs up to the island on his dog sled. I thought that would be much safer.

"When January came, Antoine was certain the ice was plenty solid for him to make the run. Others had already made several trips to the island with smaller loads.

"He left on a clear day with a large, heavy load of furs. It stayed sunny all day, and the next day too, which is unusual for January. I assumed, with such good weather, he would easily make it to Mackinac and back within a couple of days.

"Three days later he wasn't home, and a terrible blizzard moved in. Some of the men wanted to go look for him, but they couldn't see 20 feet in front of them, so they knew they had to wait. A week went by, and the blizzard finally let up.

"They headed out on small dog sleds, looking for him. They found nothing but a huge pressure crack in the ice about 10 miles out."

"What's a pressure crack?" James asked. His only experience on Lake Michigan was when it was water, not ice.

"When the lake freezes, ice expands, and in some places cracks form where the ice buckles up to make room for itself.

"The theory is that Antoine got swallowed up in a pressure crack. As his sled moved along, the ice undulated up and down, building a rhythm. When he got to the pressure crack, it probably opened and swallowed him up, just like a minnow getting swallowed by a sturgeon.

"He never made it to Mackinac. He just... disappeared."

"Oh, Lucy," James said, and quickly pulled her to him in a comforting hug. She remained there in his arms while tears welled up. She opened her eyes wide to keep them from spilling onto her cheeks.

Then she broke the embrace and sat back up, straight and strong.

"The next spring when the ice went out, one of his dead sled dogs washed ashore at Cross Village. That confirmed our fears. He was gone."

Lucy looked down at her hands in her lap, utterly quiet. There was no more to say.

"I hope you don't blame yourself, Lucy," James said.

"Of course I do! I should have let him go in the fall by boat, but I was so afraid after what happened to my father – "

"Exactly, Lucy, you didn't want to lose him the same way you did your father. Anyone would have felt the same. It was a cruel act of nature that Antoine was lost, it sounds like. Absolutely not your fault."

"That's what everyone tells me, and yet, I can't help thinking, if only…"

"Life is filled with 'if only' moments, where we wonder how different things could be 'if only.' Such as, if only I'd met you before I was married, when you and I were single…"

Lucy was taken aback. She had no inkling that James was attracted to her in that way.

"Stop that, James. I'm sure you're very happy with your wife and your children. Don't talk that way again."

With that, Lucy stood up, collected the bags and started walking briskly back to her home. James had no choice but to follow like a yard dog that got its nose rubbed in its own mess.

Later that night, after eating a dinner of whitefish with morel mushrooms and wild onions cooked in butter, James was settled into his bedroom, presumably sleeping. Lucy couldn't sleep. They had said almost nothing to each other during dinner, making no effort to overcome the awkward silence. Lucy pulled a wool blanket around her shoulders and went outside to sit on her front porch step. She sometimes wished she had rocking chairs and tables on the porch for times like this, but those luxuries were beyond her means.

She sat and listened to the magical sounds of spring. The toads were madly singing their mating song. Although she couldn't see them, she knew what they looked like – little men proudly puffing out the skin beneath their chins and thrumming the sound of their mating call. The females would play hard to get for as long as they could, but eventually the males would pounce on them and mate. Particularly attractive females would find themselves floating in the shallow eddies with two or even three males attached to her, all trying frantically to continue their lineage.

The crickets were singing too, a lively range of melodies compared to the steady monotone of the toads. It was a symphony of nature that she loved. Every now and then a white-throated sparrow would call out to his future mate, singing his same three notes, repeating the last note 10 times in quick succession. On top of that came the plaintive call of a loon to its mate. It was a sound that mirrored the ache in Lucy's heart when she thought of Antoine.

The sky was a clear black blanket studded with stars, so bright they looked like they were within reach.

She was so immersed in the beauty of the evening that she didn't notice James coming through the front door.

"May I join you?" he asked. He was in his nightclothes, with an old wool robe wrapped around his small but fit body.

"Of course," Lucy said. What choice did she have? It would have been rude to tell him she just wanted to be by herself while she listened to nature, but then she realized she actually welcomed his company.

"I've been thinking, Lucy, and it made me unable to sleep," James said. "I want you to find a new man so you can be happy. A woman like you deserves a second chance at love and happiness."

He carefully took her hand in his. It was a friendly gesture, not the actions of a man hoping to take advantage of a woman.

Lucy responded accordingly.

"You're a kind man, James," she said, gazing directly into his eyes. "I don't know if it's possible for me, but I will always keep my heart open to the possibility."

"I'll be bringing lots of eligible men to the island," James told her. "I will keep an eye out for a man who is worthy of you."

Lucy's eyes were closed as she listened to the sounds of the spring night. Curled fans of black lashes rested on her prominent cheekbones. Her eyes opened wide, quite suddenly.

"I am grateful to have you around, James," she told him in a firm, but friendly voice. "You have brought a new dimension to my life, which I am enjoying. I'm glad you found Beaver Island."

"And I'm glad I found you," James said.

Lucy pulled her blanket tighter around her shoulders and stood up.

"It's time to go to sleep," she told him. "I'll have breakfast ready for you first thing in the morning."

"I'll look forward to it," he replied, while trying to think of something to say that would make her stay with him on the porch. But he knew it wouldn't happen. She was a woman of courage and dignity, and wouldn't linger long on the porch with a married man. It made him want her all the more.

And oh, how he wanted this woman! Wide eyes the color of moonless night surrounded by thick black lashes. Skin as smooth as coffee with cream. She was moonlight and fire in a black night.

He was opposed to polygamy, and had promised his flock innumerable times that polygamy would never be a part of their faith, but he suddenly understood why Brigham Young, and Joseph Smith before him, had chosen to allow multiple wives. James wanted to take Lucy as a wife, in addition to his first wife, Mary. He wanted to take care of Lucy and protect her and love her. And yes, he wanted to hold her close and feel all of her skin next to his. He couldn't deny that. But he knew it would never be.

———◆◆◆———

The following morning Lucy was up before James, preparing a breakfast of fried potatoes and venison sausage. They made polite conversation as they ate, and when they were finished, Lucy cleared the plates from the table.

"What are your plans for today?" Lucy asked James.

"I'd like to get to know the island better, walk around, explore and see what other natural treasures this island has to offer."

"Would you like a guide?" Lucy asked.

James was thrilled with the suggestion.

"I'd love nothing more than to have you show me around."

"On one condition," Lucy said, and James' eyed her warily. Lucy laughed. "Don't look so panic-stricken. I just want you to tell me more about how this whole religion of yours got started. You must have some interesting stories about that."

They walked along the shore of Paradise Bay, then cut inland and headed to Barney's Lake. When they reached the shore of the inland lake, Lucy turned and looked straight at James.

"So? Tell me a story," she said, like a child cajoling its mother to tell a favorite bedtime story.

James thought for a moment. He wanted to amuse and entertain her, not scare her off. He decided not to bore her with his early introduction to the Mormon faith.

"As you know, we Saints do a lot of mission work in the east," James began. "We have one fellow, a truly devoted man of God, who was in New York City, doing mission work with our founder, Joseph Smith. This man's name is Lorenzo Hickey. I'm sure you'll meet him someday as he plans to move to the island as soon as possible."

"Go on," Lucy said.

"Lorenzo was walking in the theater district of New York City when a man grabbed him and tried to rob him. The man threw snuff in Lorenzo's face, causing him to have a sneezing fit. The hooligan then tried to grab Lorenzo's billfold while he was sneezing, but Lorenzo was too quick for him, and grabbed him by both arms and held him until he was done sneezing.

"According to Lorenzo, he said to the man, 'Sir, I have no idea why you are resorting to thievery as a means to support yourself, but I'm guessing it's because you're down on your luck, perhaps out of work.'

"Lorenzo guessed correctly. The man was an out-of-work actor, bumping aimlessly around the city, living like a heathen, drinking copious amounts of liquor and living the life of a lost soul.

"Lorenzo told the man it was divine intervention that their paths had crossed. He learned the man's name was George Adams, and he took him to a tent revival where Joseph Smith was preaching. The man was immediately taken with Smith and joined the church. To this day, that man is one of our finest apostles."

James thought the little heartwarming story would move Lucy, but she remained quiet, looking down at the path.

"I guess I should add that George wasn't much of an actor," James continued. "The way the story goes, he let out a tremendous fart when he was playing Richard the Third in New York City. All the people in the first three rows of the theater nearly fainted from the smell."

Lucy laughed, a big, boisterous, laugh, and that pleased James.

James knew to end on a high note. He didn't bother to tell Lucy about George Adams' other talents. While working with a third-rate traveling theater company, Adams learned some magic tricks that never failed to dazzle the less-educated spectators. He could make objects disappear with a sleight of hand. He could make inanimate objects burst into flames and evaporate in a cloud of sparkles. It was nothing more than basic chemistry and distraction, but had remarkable effects on the people who came to hear the Mormon missionaries. People desperate for a better life practically begged for signs to give them a reason to believe. Throw them a little razzle dazzle, Adams learned, and they will believe anything you tell them.

Part 2

IN THE BEGINNING
1840 – 1846

CHAPTER 6
FEBRUARY, 1844

As ceremonial baptism water was being dribbled on James Jesse Strang's head by none other than Joseph Smith himself, he had just one thought – if we waited 20 minutes we wouldn't have needed the baptismal water. It's about to rain and this tabernacle has no roof yet. It was slightly irksome to James to be baptized in an unfinished building. He had hoped for something with more pomp and grandiosity, as befitting the occasion. James Strang was a lot of things, and vainglorious was definitely one of them.

Ever since he was a young, sickly child, Strang had grand aspirations of being a powerful man. His mother doted on him, nursing him through many childhood illnesses and constantly praising his brilliance. She was always telling him what a great man he could be, in an effort to assuage his feelings of inadequacy for his small size and poor health. Strang believed every word.

By the time Strang was 19, he was already trying to figure out how he could court and marry Victoria, the heir to the British crown. He had dreams of power and royalty. When those far-fetched plans failed, he focused his attention on the strife in the national government, hoping a revolution could lead to his rise.

"If our government is overthrown, perhaps some masterful person may form a new one. May I be the one to do it!" he wrote in his diary.

But there was no revolution, and Strang found himself trying other paths to fame and power. He became a lawyer, hoping it would lead to a career in politics and a position as a powerful senator. As a gifted writer, he wrote for newspapers, hoping his voice in local affairs would lead to his rise.

None of his dreams panned out. He found himself married, living with his wife's relatives in Wisconsin, utterly stalled out on his dreams when his brothers-in-law inadvertently led him down a new path. They convinced him to go with them to Nauvoo, Illinois and meet the leader of their new religion, Joseph Smith. As a self-proclaimed atheist, Strang traveled there with skepticism but after he took one look at the thriving city of 11,000 people, mostly Mormons, he was hooked. The church had its own militia of 4,000 men. Strang saw the potential the church had for him. If Smith, a backwards hayseed from upstate New York could achieve all this, Strang thought, then he planned to hitch his wagon to Joseph Smith's star and shoot right past him someday.

Joseph Smith embraced James after the baptismal ceremony had concluded. He then signed and dated James' baptism certificate, carefully writing Feb. 25, 1844 on the dateline. In spite of a rough start as an uneducated farm boy, Smith had started a new religion little more than a decade ago that had spread its wings and flown westward from New York with the speed of Icarus. James wondered if Smith's religion would meet a similar fate to that of Icarus. If so, all the more reason for James to join the flight quickly before it all went up in flames.

"You're a fine man, James, I know you will play an important role in the Mormon Church," Smith said to James.

"I will be humbled and honored to do so." James bowed before Joseph, reached for his hand and pressed it to his lips. "You are the prophet who has saved my meaningless life. Truth and light evaded me. Now I have a purpose, and I will devote my life to following that purpose."

George Adams and Lorenzo Hickey had returned from their mission trip out east and were the first to congratulate Strang on his conversion to Mormonism.

"We are blessed to have a man of such knowledge and passion joining our church," Hickey said sincerely.

George Adams wasn't feeling quite so sincere, but he knew he had a role to play. "Welcome to the Church of Latter-Day Saints, Brother James," he said with a show of respect.

Strang stuck around Nauvoo for awhile, soaking up as much of the Mormon religion and customs as possible. A walk through town showed him that Nauvoo wasn't quite the idyllic city he had been initially led to believe. Non-Mormons were openly hostile to the Saints, as they called the members of the church. They made no effort to steer their horses around Mormons who walked down the road, forcing them to jump out of the way, often landing in ditches filled with rainwater. Some stores, owned by Gentiles (as the Mormons referred to the non-believers) wouldn't even sell them any goods. The Mormons, in return, scoffed and turned their noses up at the Gentiles who stumbled out of the local saloons.

In his second week in town, Strang had the opportunity to hear a Mormon missionary speak at a tent revival outside of Nauvoo. The missionary was a string bean of a man with very erect posture and waxy skin. His loud, piercing voice made Strang feel like he was being battered around the ears with a porcupine.

"The purpose of the Mormon church's system of government is to set aside at will the laws of the United States and of all other secular governments," the missionary said, his voice rising with passion. "A man is not an honorable man if he is not above the law and above government!"

The crowd inside the tent gave him a loud, enthusiastic 'Amen.'

"The law of God is far more righteous than the laws of the land," the speaker continued. "The laws of God are far above the laws of the land!"

Strang met with Smith one evening to discuss the inflammatory speech he'd heard.

"I'm afraid wherever we gather we will be persecuted," Smith told him. "It's the way of the world, James. People fear what they do not understand. And fear leads to hatred. The Gentiles hate us because they fear us. And they fear us because they haven't seen the light.

"We are God's Chosen People," Smith went on. "As such, God wants us to take what we need to strengthen our cause," he said, glossing over the fact that Mormons stole whatever they needed or wanted with little fear of legal repercussion.

Smith and his missionaries had preached many times that God had given the earth and all its bounty to the Mormons. *The Mormons call it consecrating; the government calls it commandeering; and the rest of the world calls it stealing,* Strang thought to himself, finding it all a bit amusing.

"Might I suggest making a move to Wisconsin?" Strang said in one of his private talks with Smith. "Where I live now, there are miles and miles of excellent farmland and forests, just there for the taking. It's near the shore of Lake Michigan, which is convenient for travel. It could be an ideal post for the church."

"That's very intriguing," Smith said. "Why don't you write me a report about the possibilities after you get back home? I'll need to know how much acreage is available, the cost per acre, current population in the out-lying areas, and access to roads and rivers."

Strang headed back to Burlington, Wisconsin alone, but not before Smith made him an elder in the church. He did the same for George Adams and Lorenzo Hickey, because they had served him well, although Smith could tell they would never measure up to Strang's cleverness and charisma.

With his baptismal certificate in his coat pocket and the title of elder in his mind, Strang headed back to Wisconsin. *Not bad for two weeks' time away from home*, Strang thought. He couldn't wait to get home and tell his wife Mary the news.

CHAPTER 7
JULY, 1844

"Joseph Smith has been assassinated!" George Adams delivered the news to Strang as soon as he could, after traveling from Nauvoo, Illinois to Burlington, Wisconsin in a horse-drawn wagon across summer-hardened dusty roads. He was breathing heavily and Strang could smell the stale whiskey on his breath.

"What?! When? How could this happen?" Strang was shocked by the news – and immediately thrilled by what it might mean for his future.

"Just a week ago, I came here as fast as I could to bring you the news. They shot him, right there in the Carthage County jail, where they were holding him on charges of stealing! Killed him dead! Terrible, isn't it?" Adams, the retired actor, was struggling to keep a mournful composure on his face as he delivered the news.

Joseph Smith's death couldn't have come at a better time for Adams. He was on the brink of being excommunicated from the Church due to a few indiscretions on his part. Was it his fault that the ladies were so attracted to him? And he was so attracted to the whiskey that melted his resolve to behave properly?

"This is terrible news for the church. Did Joseph appoint a successor? The church will flounder without a strong leader."

"Well, there are his sons, of course, and then there's Brigham Young, who has always been his right-hand man in the Circle of 12 Apostles, but I don't think Joseph left behind any written instructions on the matter."

"Perhaps we should go to Nauvoo and see what we can do to help." Strang's mind was already spinning, trying to figure out how to get out front in the race to the leadership of the church.

Strang didn't have to wait long before inspiration fell into his hands. He received a letter from Joseph Smith two days later, as he was gathering his things and preparing to head to Nauvoo. The letter was postmarked June 18. Smith was killed June 27. So Smith had written to Strang a mere nine days before his assassination. Had Smith truly been a visionary? Had he seen his death coming and prepared for the worst?

Strang ripped open the letter. It was a response to the report he'd sent Smith about creating a Mormon post in rural Wisconsin. Smith liked the idea, as he said in his letter, and directed Strang to proceed with establishing it.

"We shall name it Voree, which means Garden of Peace," Smith wrote in the letter. "James, you shall be the one to gather the people and plant a stake of Zion in Wisconsin, with my blessing."

After that, the letter went into the mundane details for building Voree.

While reading the dull parts of the letter, Strang had a sudden inspiration. He went to his desk and rummaged through his paper supplies until he found a sheet much like the variety Smith had used for his letter. Then he combed through the large supplies of pens he kept on hand until he found one that matched the nib used in Smith's letter. Then he went to work.

"What are you doing, James?" his wife Mary asked him a few hours later, when she found him surrounded by many discarded sheets of paper scattered around his desk. He had already informed her of Smith's assassination as soon as Adams had left.

"Nothing to concern you, Mary, just catching up on some letters. With Joseph dead, I feel duty-bound to correspond with all the other church elders and prominent members. We must start planning immediately for the succession of a new leader."

Mary glanced at the papers all over. They didn't look like letters to other church members. They looked like the same words, written over and over, in different styles. One sheet had just a couple of sentences on it; another had two or three paragraphs.

But Mary was a good wife who didn't question her husband. He was the father of her children, and a reasonably good provider. Her parents liked him and trusted him. They joined the Mormon Church right after James did, without a moment's hesitation. Mary was more reluctant, but eventually joined the rest of her family in abandoning their Baptist faith and converting to Mormonism.

She left James and went back to the kitchen to start supper. It was unseasonably warm, and she didn't feel much like cooking. She went out the back door to the little vegetable garden she maintained for the family. The tomatoes were coming in nicely, as were the squash and beans. Without warning, she was overcome with grief. She remembered how much her daughter, Little Mary, loved playing in the yard and picking vegetables. What a ray of sunshine she was, and how James doted on her. Two winters ago, Mary the mother was the first to get the influenza, then James, and then Little Mary. James and Mary survived. Little Mary didn't. James had never been the same to Mary after that, as if she was responsible for their daughter's death. He became distant, and less affectionate. And that was cause for worry, because James was a man of very strong sexual appetites.

After making a simple meal of vegetables and cornbread, she called James to the supper table.

He was flush with a new idea. She'd seen that look before.

"Mary, my love, do you remember that day a few weeks ago when I went out into the fields by myself, to collect my thoughts? Do you remember me telling you about a vision I had?"

"No, I don't recall that," Mary said cautiously, masking her suspicion of what might come next.

"Of course you do, I'm certain I told you about it. It was such a lovely vision – more than a vision, really, for I heard beautiful, celestial music all around, yet I'm sure I was quite alone in the field."

"Celestial music, you say," Mary murmured.

"Yes, celestial music, and a compelling feeling that I must go establish our new Mormon community in Wisconsin as soon as possible. I'm certain it was a message from God himself. Or a message from Joseph, by way of the angels."

Mary looked suspicious, as if her husband was trying to feed her a withered piece of venison while telling her it was beefsteak.

"Well, it all makes sense now. On that very day, Joseph Smith was writing a letter to me – a letter telling me to proceed to find land and start our new Mormon community right here in Wisconsin. But that's not all he said in his letter." At that point James straightened up and puffed out his chest, to make himself look as large and powerful as possible.

"Joseph said I am to be the new Mormon leader! Not Brigham Young, as so many believe, but me!"

"Well, my goodness, is that what you want, James?"

"Don't get me wrong, it will be a great deal of work and require tremendous sacrifices, likely for both of us, but if that is what Joseph wanted, I can hardly turn it down." James looked Mary square in the eyes to see if there was any doubt lurking beneath her light brown lashes.

"I'm sure you are just the man to do it." Mary could say that much with a clear conscience.

CHAPTER 8
JULY, 1844

The race was on. Brigham Young, who was president of the Circle of 12 Apostles, said he had the experience to be the new leader. Sidney Rigdon was also a strong candidate, well-liked among some of the Mormons for his stance against polygamy.

And then there was Strang. He arrived in Nauvoo, Illinois, and went directly to the meeting of the church council elders on a steamy July day in the summer of 1844.

"I have a letter from Joseph saying that I am to be the one to lead the church, and we are to plant our new stake of Zion in Wisconsin," Strang said with great authority. "Joseph said we should call it Voree, which means Garden of Peace. As you can see by this letter, there can be no doubt as to who should be the new leader."

Strang handed the letter to George Miller, who was the presiding Bishop at the time. He'd been with the church for a long time, and had often been a confidante to Smith. If anyone knew Joseph's handwriting and style of grammar and punctuation, it was Miller.

Miller furrowed his beefy brow while he read the letter. One caterpillar eyebrow curled downward occasionally and he tugged on his door knocker beard several times while reading.

The envelope was clearly real. Without hijacking the U.S. postal services, it was impossible to forge a postmark. The first page of the letter seemed genuine. From there, George had his doubts. It looked rather like a forgery, but he decided to say nothing. He didn't like Brigham Young and didn't want him to be the new leader.

Brigham Young, who waited impatiently while Miller read the letter, snatched it from Miller as soon as he was done. He gave it the onceover and made his pronouncement.

"There are certain features of style that are unlike any I've ever seen Joseph use," Young said. "Strang has high strains of poetry here but not a word of truth."

Miller's meaty hand darted out and took the letter back from Young as quickly as Young had taken it from him.

"This seems to be a piece of valid correspondence from Joseph, so I, for one, will follow Mr. Strang to Wisconsin, as Joseph had wanted," Miller declared.

Eventually, Young and Strang went their separate ways and spent two weeks lobbying church elders and apostles for the top job.

Strang made an elegant pitch, saying, "Come to Voree. The climate is good. Come, and it will be a place of safety and refuge. Don't be driven into the wilderness by a false prophet, Brigham Young." Strang's smoldering eyes and intensity captured the heart of many followers.

When it was all said and done, the Mormons of Nauvoo were left with a split decision. Some were loyal to Brigham Young and were willing to follow him to the ends of the earth, which was what Utah Territory sounded like. Young made sense when he said the Saints needed to go far, far away, to a place out west that wasn't a part of the United States, so they could live the way God had chosen for them on vast amounts of land not controlled by the government; to thrive, and to multiply so they could become a great, strong church.

Others had good reason to reject Young. He was a believer in polygamy and had already earned the nickname 'The Marryin' Mormon' for having 29 wives. The men were more inclined to go along with the idea of polygamy, but some of the strong-willed women were vehemently opposed to it.

Then there was the matter of getting to the Promised Land out west. It was reported to be a long, arduous trek across undeveloped land – often with no roads, no towns, and almost nowhere to seek shelter or rest if the trip became too taxing. And the threat of Indians scalping them or stealing their wives – even if they had plenty of them – was not a pleasant thought either.

Wisconsin, on the other hand, was practically just around the corner. A week or so of travel on the gentle hills and flatlands of Illinois and southern Wisconsin, and they would arrive at their new home.

With the blessing of George Miller and a few other key members of the church, Strang left Nauvoo with a group of several hundred people and headed for their home in the soon-to-be-built town of Voree. But not before he declared himself to be the true prophet and excommunicated Brigham Young. In turn, Young declared himself the true prophet and excommunicated Strang. And so it was that the Mormon Church became two arms on the same body – the Brighamites and the Strangites.

It took a couple of years of hard work, crude living conditions and many sacrifices, but by April 1, 1846, Strang was able to officially organize the Strangite Church of Latter-Day Saints, complete with certification by the county clerk, the naming of trustees, and documentation citing the church protocols and beliefs. In January of that same year, Strang launched the *Voree Herald* newspaper, which gave him an outlet for his writing skills and proselytizing. *"Truth Shall Prevail,"* was the tagline Strang gave the newspaper. *Yes, truth shall prevail. My version of the truth*, Strang thought to himself.

"Come away to the flowers in the fields and river banks in the forest out here in the open space and here, see the earth and sky mingle, like the greeting of youthful lovers!" he wrote in the first edition of the paper. *"Listen to the pine tree songs, which are chants of praise, and the wind warbles, which are hymns of hallelujah!"* The man had quite a flair for the written word. And with it he attracted many new followers to Voree. Soon the little outpost in southern Wisconsin was burgeoning with new residents.

Part 3

PILGRIMAGE TO THE ISLAND
1848 – 1853

CHAPTER 9
1848

Will MacCormick stopped splicing a worn line on his boat when he saw Tom Bennett making his way to the harbor on foot. He looked a little tired, but even with some sleep-deprived dark half-moons under his eyes, he was a good-looking man. Laughing blue eyes, broad-shouldered and narrow through the hips, Tom was a physical specimen that made women, young and old, take in a quick breath of air whenever they saw him.

"Hey Tom, you'd better do something about that boat of yours, it's listing pretty bad," Will called to him.

"Well now, Will, I ain't a blind man, I can see very well that it's got a little issue, but unlike you, I'm not a bachelor who can spend all my time fixing boats or drinking whiskey. I got a family to tend to."

"I know that, just trying to help. How's Alice doing, anyway?"

"Real good. We just had our third baby last month. Came a little early, so she's a bit on the runty side, but doing okay with Alice constantly feeding her."

"Congratulations on the new arrival! And give my regards to Alice. You want some help with your boat? I've got some pine pitch right here; we could probably patch up whatever hole is letting in water on your port side."

"Thanks, I'd welcome that." Tom looked around the harbor for a moment, and took in the bustling scene of fishermen readying their boats to head out onto the lake.

"Where's Teddy? I thought you two were inseparable," Tom asked.

"He's feeling poorly today. Got the brown bottle flu," Will said of his cousin. "Spent a wee bit too much time on Whiskey Point last night, with Black Jack and Black Pete. I guess they had a nanty narker of a time."

Black Jack Bonner and Black Pete McCauley had little in common except their nicknames and a great fondness for liquor. Jack was a fisherman who preferred to live on Gull Island with other fishermen and fur trappers. He was from Rutland Island, near Árainn Mhór Island off the coast of Ireland, and had a speech pattern that was akin to a squeaky wheel on a pocked road. Black Pete was from Donegal, Ireland. His family had staked out land on the southeast shore of Beaver Island. Black Pete only made the long trip to the northwest corner of the island when the Mackinaw boats were making their scheduled delivery of barrels of whiskey and beer. And naturally, after making the 13-mile trek through swampland, woods and hills, he needed to fortify himself with drinks and camaraderie.

"Speaking of partners, where's your brother? He could be helping you with this boat," Will said.

"Sam's sticking to the land these days. He likes the lumbering. He never did care too much for the water, had a problem with the seasickness. And there's no shortage of trees down his way."

Sam Bennett had found himself a prime piece of real estate on the southeast side of the island. He and Black Pete had a nice little business in the cordwood trade, selling wood to steamers that stopped at Cable's Dock on the southeast side of the island for refueling. Tom and his family had chosen to live on the north side of the island, in a little cabin on Whiskey Point that Tom and Sam built together when they first arrived on the island in 1842.

"Let's take a look at your boat and see what's making her set crooked," Will said. The two of them started walking to the docks when the sound of oxen hooves making sucking sounds on a muddy road caught their attention. They looked around and saw four people – two couples, it looked like – riding in a claptrap cart behind a small, scrawny ox.

"Who in God's name are those scarecrows?" Will asked, referring to the very skinny, ragged-looking people in the cart. Although Beaver Island was 13 miles long and six miles wide, it was still a tiny island when it came to the human population. About 100 people lived there, and they all knew one another by sight at the very least.

"They're Mormons," Tom answered. "Call themselves Latter-Day Saints, or just plain Saints. Came here last year, with some screwball idea that they're going to set up a utopian community on the island."

"What's a utopian community?"

"I guess it's supposed to be an ideal community."

"Don't we have that already? Life here seems pretty ideal to me, although I could stand for shorter winters."

"They got themselves a leader who parked them here last summer. Said he'd be bringing more people to live with them this spring. So I guess any day now, more of 'em are gonna be showing up."

"What are their names?"

"Honestly, I don't know. They keep to themselves. Alva Cable took pity on a couple of them last fall and helped get them through the winter. Now they've cleared some land near him, and they're planting crops. They're even helping to build a road from Cable's Bay to Little Sand Bay."

"Well, I guess the more the merrier. There can't be any harm in having some new blood around here. And I hope they bring some pretty young women with them too – we have a shortage of eligible lasses."

Will had no way of making the connection between the arrogant little man in the black top hat who had bumped into him a week ago and the raggedy people he saw in the ox cart. And he had no way of knowing how he'd regret those words in a few short years.

CHAPTER 10

MID-YEAR, 1848

Even though staying at Lucy's house and enjoying her company was tempting to Strang, he didn't linger long on Beaver Island in May of 1848. He had to get back to Wisconsin before his flock became completely torn apart from inside strife and outside pressure.

He thought he had made a wise choice when he selected the area outside of Burlington, Wisconsin, to become Voree, Garden of Peace, for his following. The land was excellent for farming; a clean, fresh river ran through it; nearby forests provided plenty of lumber for building their town. What Strang hadn't factored in was that the Gentiles in the area were already solidly planted in the countryside, and weren't of a mind to share their fertile land with the Mormons.

Even when Strang returned from an eastern mission trip flush with money, he had a hard time getting the Gentiles to sell him more land. They resisted him at every turn. His flock was finding itself growing more cramped with the arrival of each new batch of converts. The more cramped they felt, the more the divisiveness built up among them.

Strang's brother-in-law, Aaron Smith (no relation to Joseph Smith), was among those who broke ranks with Strang.

"I've had a revelation that James Strang is a false prophet," Smith told the fledgling Mormon community. "He is wicked, and a liar. As one of the first members of Joseph Smith's Latter-Day Saints, I am the better leader."

Aaron then started his own branch of Reformed Mormons.

Most, if not all, of Strang's followers remained true to him.

"Those who stay with me, the true prophet, James J. Strang, will come to know paradise, in this life and in the afterlife," Strang told them. "Those who go with the Pseudoes will know misery, sickness and depression."

As always, Strang was able to whip his followers into a religious fervor. He did it with passionate, fiery sermons that dangled the carrot of paradise in front of them, followed by the stick – instilling fear of eternal damnation.

Strang went a step further, helping his flock plant their crops, hoeing side by side with them, milking cows and chopping wood. It was a hard life, but Strang wasn't about to lose his congregation to Smith. By working with them, he earned their trust and respect.

In the summer of 1848, farming and wood-chopping had to take a back seat when it came time for Strang to attend a church conference in Burlington, Wisconsin. It was to be quite a gathering, with strands of Mormons coming from Michigan, Illinois and Ohio. Many Mormon converts were left to luff in the wind after Smith's death. They needed a man at the helm of their lives, and Strang wanted to be their man.

The conference also welcomed Gentiles seeking a better way of life. It would be a great opportunity for Strang to bring new people into his fold of the church.

He arrived at the outskirts of Burlington the day before the conference was due to start. A large tent was being raised in a field by many men; young ones provided the strength to raise it, while older men provided the experience to do it right. Seeing they needed no more help to get the tent in place, Strang felt free to look about the field, taking in the many small, personal tents already in place along the perimeter. Families were making campfires, women were cooking, men were hauling water from the nearby stream and children were playing catch in the field. The sight of it all warmed Strang's heart.

Strang pitched his own tent away from the rest of the crowd. He wanted to be alone so he could practice his sermon for the next day. It was imperative that he deliver a moving, impassioned talk to win more followers.

The next day, Strang took his position behind a pulpit made of white pine and began to speak.

"My good people gathered here today," he began, his voice rich and melodious, "This is a cruel, harsh world we live in. Evil lurking around every corner in the form of thieves and scoundrels. It is nearly impossible to find work that enables good and decent men to earn a living and support their loving families." He gave a sad, forlorn look to the people listening raptly to him.

"I offer you a better way of life. I offer you the chance to live communally and peacefully in prosperity. Cast your lot with me and live in a place of unparalleled natural beauty… a place surrounded by fresh, clear water where fish swim in abundance. A place of great forests and sandy beaches. A place of rolling farmland and rich, fertile soil. A place where a man can earn a good living through honest, hard work. A place where his wife and children will be safe from the evildoers plaguing the cities around us. A place where each family will have their own snug home, and where neighbors will lend a helping hand in times of difficulty.

"I offer you Beaver Island and the Strangite Latter-Day Saints, a place the Lord has told me is ours for generations to come.

"Bring your tender hearts and your tired souls to me and be reborn with renewed energy and love for one another. Come to me and be baptized into a life of goodness and decency. For anyone who joins me will have my everlasting love and protection."

Strang's speech had the crowd mesmerized. Non-Mormon people living in dirty cities were starving for the life Strang spoke of. They yearned to be away from crowded tenements that fronted onto filthy streets. The men were ready and willing to work hard in a place that offered fresh air and private homes for their families.

When Strang finished speaking, he bowed deeply to the audience, then raised his arms to the heavens above, outstretched and open. "Tomorrow, come unto me and I shall baptize you into our faith. And your life will begin anew."

The next day it was clear that Strang had succeeded in his goal of winning people over to his faith. Dozens of people came up to him and begged to be baptized into the Strangite Church of Latter-Day Saints.

One young girl from southern Michigan was particularly moved by Strang. Seventeen-year-old Elvira Field had never heard such passionate speaking. And when Strang's eyes met hers while he spoke, Elvira felt surges of excitement dance up the nape of her neck. She felt his intense gaze all over her, and it was electrifying.

When the crowd thinned, Elvira broke away from her family and sought out Strang. With a bashful yet flirtatious smile, Elvira addressed Strang.

"I want to be baptized into your religion," she told Strang after his sermon. "I want to be your devoted follower. I want to be by your side as you build your community."

Strang was awestruck by the girl's direct manner of speaking to him. He was also moved. She was so beautiful, so young and fresh. She made him think of a younger, whiter, version of Lucy.

Strang personally baptized Elvira the next day. She wrote her address down afterward and slipped it into Strang's pocket.

"Please, when you are ready, come find me, and I shall go with you," she told him.

On the final night of the conference, Elvira snuck out of her parent's tent and found her way to Strang's tent.

"Elvira, I'm a weak man, and you are a tempting sight for this older man's eyes," Strang said when she climbed into his tent.

"I am yours, James. Take me."

Elvira knew nothing of the intimacies that could occur between a man and a woman, but after Strang started kissing her and touching her hungrily, she knew she was ready to learn.

Strang woke up alone the following morning, thinking about what he'd just done. Elvira slipped out after he'd fallen asleep, not wanting her parents to notice she'd gone missing.

Was that a sin? he asked himself. *How could it be a sin if God sent her to me? Perhaps God wanted me to lie with her to bring religion into her heart. Yes, that's what it was. I needed to have amorous congress with her to bring her into the fold of the one true religion, the Strangite Church of Latter-Day Saints.*

With that thought, Strang easily dismissed any feelings of misgiving. After all, he had just done the Lord's work.

After he dressed, he found the slip of paper Elvira had placed in his coat pocket with her address written on it in a childish script. He was about to throw it out, but then put it back in his pocket. *She might need to be brought to the Lord again in the future,* he thought.

CHAPTER 11
SPRING, 1849

"Have you got the phosphorus?" Strang asked Adams. He was in a fine mood on that lovely late spring evening in New York. The year was 1849, and Strang's plans were right on schedule.

"So when I talk about the angels appearing in front of me and giving me a vision, you light the phosphorus up on that little hill."

"James, I know what I'm doing. We've done this dozens of times. Have I ever failed you?"

James smiled warmly at his colleague. "No, George, you've always done a fine job. Thank you. I won't doubt you again."

James was standing on a makeshift wooden platform – a stage of sorts for his presentation to the good people of Chautauqua County. Candles lined the front of the stage, which his nephew Charles Douglass would light for him just before his performance started.

"I didn't know your brother David had a son," his wife remarked when Strang introduced her to his nephew on the boat trip to New York.

"He's actually David's wife's nephew, her sister's son," Strang explained. "His father died in a farm accident and they thought it would do Charles good to have the influence of a strong man in his life. I offered my help, of course."

Mary found it touching that her husband would take in a gawky adolescent boy who became fatherless at the age of 17. It seemed to Mary that the lad definitely could use the influence and guidance of a man like James. Charles Douglass was a late bloomer, lacking in facial hair or a muscular frame, and struck Mary as a bit effeminate. James would no doubt be a good influence on the boy. It was an act of kindness on James' part that further endeared her to him.

Just before dusk, Charles Douglass lit the candles along the front edge of the stage.

Near the front of the audience were Eliza and Nathan Bowman. They'd heard of Joseph Smith, the founder of the Mormon faith, and of his successor, James Strang. They'd also heard of Brigham Young, who claimed he was the rightful leader of the Mormons, but he was a polygamist, and the Bowmans refused to have anything to do with that. Besides, Brigham Young was out in Utah, and the Bowmans were in New York.

Strang offered his followers a wholesome life among fellow followers, where everyone joined in and helped each other, sharing in their work and then sharing their bounty and the fruits of their labors. Nathan liked the sound of that. His idea of sharing work was to let someone else have the lion's share of the work, with him collecting more than his fair share of the bounty. He was adept at finding ways to shirk work and show up in time for the payday. Unfortunately his last boss hadn't been so keen on the idea of Nathan snoozing under a beech tree while his co-workers chopped wood and split logs. It was the third time in as many months that Nathan had been relieved of his gainful employment.

His wife, Eliza, was losing patience. Eliza was practical and sensible. Nathan was anything but.

"We're going to have to leave New York," she complained to him. "No one around these parts will hire you. Really, Nathan, would it be so hard for you to put in an honest day's work?"

Nathan had chafed at her scolding, but he knew she was right. They would have to leave the area if he ever wanted to work again. Not that he really wanted to work, but he did need to find a way to make a living.

When Nathan read about the Mormons in the Chautauqua Gazette, he was immediately intrigued. Maybe if they started a new life as Mormons, Eliza would quit harping at him. He loved his wife in his own way, but she'd become more shrewish with every job he lost. Her wide gray eyes, that had reminded him of soft sable when he first met her, now more frequently looked like storm clouds.

He could easily convert to this group of Latter-Day Saints if it meant landing an undemanding job that would satisfy Eliza. He was tired of hardship. Tired of farming. Tired of getting up at the crack of dawn to milk and feed cows, as he had done on his parents' farm since he was old enough to grab a teat.

Nathan watched Strang take the stage after a boy lit the candles, which served as footlights.

"He's rather small for such a well-known man, isn't he?" Eliza asked Nathan. "I don't care much for his eyes. Beady-looking, like a feral dog, don't you think?"

"Hush, Eliza, I want to hear what the man has to say."

Eliza was surprised by Nathan's earnest desire to hear a preacher man. She'd never seen any indication from him before that he might want to get himself some religion. And although her gut instinct told her it was highly unlikely, the hopeful side of her prayed that a good dose of religion might make him a better husband and provider.

Eliza tried to concentrate on what Strang was saying, but the evening was warm and she started to feel a little drowsy. Nathan, on the other hand, seemed captivated by Strang's talk:

"And so I tell you, I, James J. Strang, was on the Monongahela River in Wisconsin, on the twenty-fifth day of August, in the year eighteen hundred and forty-six, and had a vision. Angels came to me and lo, they showed me a land amidst wide waters, and covered with large timber, with a deep, broad bay on one side of it; and I wandered over it upon little hills, and among rich valleys where the air was pure and serene, and the unfolding foliage, with its fragrant shades, attracted me until I wandered to bright clear waters scarcely ruffled by the breeze.

"And I felt God near me, and I said, 'What meaneth this?' And He answered and said, 'Behold, here shall you establish My people on an everlasting foundation.'

As Strang finished his speech about the angels and his vision, a brilliant flash of light exploded from a nearby hill. The crowd gasped in amazement.

"And so it is, the angels are with us now, affirming all that I have told you. They have just signaled us with their illumination from the hillside."

After the crowd fell quiet again, a man in the audience shouted out to Strang.

"What about polygamy?" he shouted. "I heard those other Mormons out west practice polygamy!"

Eliza's mouth dropped open and she leaned over to whisper in Nathan's ear.

"I'll have none of that polygamy business!" she hissed.

Strang was ready with an answer for the doubters.

"Brigham Young is a fornicator and adulterer for practicing polygamy," Strang said. "And for anyone who chooses to practice polygamy, I say this to them: May their bones rot in the living tomb of their bodies; may their blood swarm with a leprous, ghastly corruption feeding on their life, generating chilling agues and burning fevers. May their eyes become a crawling mass of putridity!"

The crowd broke into cheers at Strang's graphic and colorful denunciation of polygamy.

"I guess that answers that question," Nathan said.

Strang finished his talk with outstretched arms, beckoning one and all to join him.

"Eliza, I think this is exactly what we're looking for," Nathan said. "Let's get baptized tomorrow and then head west to Beaver Island with Strang."

"Well, I guess nothing is holding us here," Eliza said, although she was feeling skeptical. Whenever Nathan got enthusiastic about something, it was usually a get rich quick scheme that ended disastrously. She weighed her options quickly – stay here alone and let Nathan go to Michigan without her, or jump onboard, literally. She had no family left in New York; her brother and sister had already moved west, to St. Louis, where her brother found work on a paddle wheeler, and her parents had returned to England after deciding America was too rough and tumble for their tastes.

"Okay Nathan, you win. We'll join the Mormons and head to Michigan."

Nathan swept her up in his arms, a gesture of affection he hadn't shown in months. "Oh, Eliza, you won't regret this decision, I promise. I can just tell we're doing the right thing."

CHAPTER 12
SPRING, SUMMER, 1849

The day after his exhilarating tent revival, Strang held a small meeting in the local town hall of Chautauqua for his senior missionaries. Lorenzo Hickey had just completed a mission trip to Philadelphia and was happy to be joining James and his other Mormon friends again in New York. He was lonely after a long, solitary mission trip, traveling without his wife and without his best friend, Increase Van Deusen, a Dutchman who simply went by the nickname Van.

Tired as he was, Hickey was one of the first to show up at the meeting, taking a seat up front along with Van. The two men, both broad-shouldered, rubbed up against each other on the narrow seats. Van had a typically long Dutch face with a prominent chin and thinning brown hair. Hickey was the better-looking, but also the more gullible of the two. From Joseph Smith to Strang, Hickey was a true believer and loyal servant to his prophets. Van had his doubts.

"I have mail for you," Van told Hickey. "I think it's from your wife on Beaver Island. I picked it up for you when I was gathering my own mail at the post office."

Hickey eagerly grabbed the letters, checked the postmarks and started opening and reading them in chronological order. He had only gotten to the second one when he inhaled sharply.

"Good God in Heaven, Van, my wife says Strang has been fornicating with some young woman behind Mary's back! That's adultery!" Hickey's jaw dropped. He couldn't believe the accusation his wife was directing at their prophet, but he also couldn't doubt his wife.

"That is no surprise to me," Van said. "I had a revelation when I was preaching in New Jersey, and it told me that James is an evil man, and whoever follows him will be damned. Now it all makes sense." Van didn't mention the other, darker part of his revelation to his friend, since it hadn't come true.

"I don't know, Van, I just can't believe this. Anne would never lie to me, but James has always spoken out strongly against adultery. I think we should hold judgment until we can talk to him about it."

"Fine, let's go find him. We have time before the meeting starts."

The two men headed out the back door of the hall, where they found James with Charles Douglass.

"Hello, Brother Lorenzo, Brother Van," Strang said. "I'd like to you meet my nephew Charles Douglass. He's helping as my personal assistant on this trip."

Van and Hickey quickly greeted the nephew and then ignored him. They had more pressing matters to discuss.

"Brother James, I am distressed to say that my wife Anne has informed me that you have been fornicating with some young woman on Beaver Island. Is this true?"

Charles Douglass quietly walked away from the conversation, apparently embarrassed by the charge of fornication.

"Of course not," Strang said. "I would never do such a thing. Your wife has a vivid imagination."

"But my wife says she is positive about what she saw – you, with a young woman, on Beaver Island, lying together in a field of clover, having intimate relations!"

"Your wife is lying," Strang said dismissively.

"You're lying," Van chimed in. "I had a revelation about you, and I know you're evil."

"Van," Strang said patiently. "Didn't you also tell me yesterday that you had a revelation about your dear friend Lorenzo, who was going to die in Philadelphia? Apparently that was not the case, as he's standing right here, looking very much alive."

Van's long face grew even longer. "I guess I was wrong about that, but I'm sure I'm right about you."

"Gentlemen. Let's put this nonsense aside and go in for our meeting. We have missionary work to discuss. Come along now." Strang ushered them both back into the hall.

Hickey managed to keep quiet throughout most of the meeting, but at the end, he finally erupted.

"I have just received letters from my wife on Beaver Island that say Strang is guilty of adultery and immoral fornication; the very same abominations that Brigham Young is practicing out west!"

Not one to miss an opportunity for a shouting match, Van quickly jumped to his feet and joined in. "Strang is a liar, a false prophet, and a dangerously wicked man!" he yelled. Then he charged up to Strang, who was much smaller than he, and started pushing him in the chest. "You are guilty! You are guilty," he screamed, spittle flying from his large, crooked mouth and landing on Strang.

Hickey joined Van in the shoving match. Strang was enraged.

"The two of you are to leave the premises and not return until you have gained control of yourselves. I will not tolerate this pernicious behavior."

The two of them left the town hall, but not before Strang gave one loud message.

"We can discuss this like civilized men at our general meeting with the elders tonight," Strang said. "And I'm sure I can give you a satisfactory explanation of this baseless accusation."

Strang sought out Adams as soon as he got out of the meeting.

"I've got to deal with these two before they start an uncontrollable ruckus," he said to Adams. He knew Adams was a man given to inappropriate conduct with women of ill repute and would sympathize with his situation.

"Did Lorenzo produce these letters from his wife? Did he show them to you?" Adams asked.

"Why no, he did not. I see where you're headed with this, George, and I like it. I'll demand to see the letters, and then I can interpret them in a more appropriate manner."

Strang had feared someone might have seen him canoodling with young Elvira Field on Beaver Island. It was a mistake to let her visit him there, but she had insisted, saying her parents were interested in converting to the Mormon Church but wanted to see what Beaver Island was like before making the commitment. While the parents were exploring the island, Strang took Elvira to a secret spot so he could do some deep exploration in the clover. Now it was coming back to haunt him.

But Strang was confident he could get the upper hand in his current dilemma. He had an amazing talent of being able to take written words, right there for anyone to see, and twist them so they could be interpreted in an entirely different light. He could convince people that black meant white and up meant down. Mostly it was a matter of repetition. Say something enough times, say it forcefully, and people will believe.

Strang wasted no time after the evening meeting had convened.

"Brother Lorenzo, would you please show me these letters from your wife, which accuse me of nefarious wrongdoing?" he demanded.

Hickey thought about it for a minute, fidgeting in his seat.

"They are private letters between my wife and me, so no, I won't show you."

The letters contained more than accusations about Strang. They contained bald sexual references about what Anne was looking forward to doing with Lorenzo upon his return. Just reading the words had given Hickey an erection.

"If you won't show them, then how can I justly be accused of such wrongdoing? Where is the evidence?" Strang stared at Hickey. "If I had to guess, I imagine your wife was feeling homesick and missing you," Strang said, switching from a hostile to an amiable approach. "Women have a tendency to exaggerate and make up stories when they are enduring hardships without their husbands around to comfort them."

Strang continued to expound upon the unfortunate habits of women to gossip and tell tall tales when confronted with the hardships of pioneer life.

The rest of the group was quick to take Strang's side, condemning Hickey and his wife instead.

It was hard for Hickey to process. One minute he'd been convinced the accusations his wife made about Strang's deplorable behavior were true. Could it be true that his wife's loneliness was overshadowing her judgment? And now, hours later, he was the one being condemned for speaking poorly about Strang. Adding insult to injury, Strang suspended him from the church for spreading lies about himself. Hickey felt totally dejected. His faith in his prophet had been shaken to its foundation, and his wife's good name and reputation had been besmirched in front of his closest Mormon friends.

Having been suspended from the church, Hickey was not allowed to do any mission work. He suddenly had a huge hole in his life that he didn't know how to fill. Hickey headed aimlessly to New York City without any plans. Whenever possible, he hitched a ride on a wagon or carriage from a kind stranger, but for much of the time, he traversed the state of New York on foot, taking over a month to reach the city. He slept outdoors and in a matter of weeks had gone from a well-groomed man to having the appearance of a homeless beggar. In the city, he drank much, ate little, and slept in alleys. The police picked him up for vagrancy and put him in the county jail. His sad howling and wild prayers for three straight nights earned him a one-way ticket to the lunatic asylum.

The asylum doctors concluded, after one month, they had no real reason to hold Hickey. Praying loudly didn't meet the definition of insanity. In addition to that, they became thoroughly annoyed at their patient's anguished crying, so they released him. Hickey then saw the error of his ways. Right or wrong, Strang was his leader and prophet. He couldn't function without Strang and the church. He desperately needed the structure of church rules and a leader to show him the way.

Fearing the worst from Strang – that his suspension might lead to an excommunication – Hickey wrote to George Adams, begging to be admitted back into the fold. Adams went to meet him and found poor Hickey 20 pounds lighter than he had been at their last meeting; he was disheveled, his hair greasy and beard untrimmed, and his eyes peered out from sunken sockets. Adams pitied him. It was an odd turn of events for Adams; years ago, he had been the man down on his luck, throwing snuff in Hickey's face with the intention of robbing Hickey on the streets of New York; now Hickey was the desperate man in need of help. Adams felt obliged to return the kindness Hickey had once shown him.

"For my own part, Lorenzo, I will gladly welcome you back," Adams said. "Let me reach out to James for you."

"Yes, please do, George," Hickey pleaded. "I have wandered about like a madman, eating grass like an ox, since I took my leave of your company.

Please tell James I love him more than I have ever loved before. I just want to do right and please God."

Strang was quick to let Hickey back into the fold. He reasoned it was better to keep Hickey close at his side than have him wandering about as a loose-lipped, slightly deranged enemy spreading rumors about Strang's unfaithfulness to his wife.

All the while Hickey had been wandering about New York and had been a temporary resident at the lunatic asylum, he had been thinking and wondering about Anne.

When he finally rejoined Adams, he begged for any news of his wife.

"I'm sorry to tell you, Lorenzo, but we learned that Anne has become an apostate and renounced the church. She left Beaver Island, took your three children and went back to southern Michigan, to the town where she grew up. Lapeer, I believe."

Hickey was devastated.

"Oh my Lord, what am I to do?" he asked Adams.

"Find a new wife," Adams said brusquely.

CHAPTER 13
JUNE, 1849

While Strang, George Adams and nephew Charles Douglass criss-crossed the countryside of northwest New York on his mission work, Strang's wife Mary gratefully took the opportunity to stay and visit relatives and friends in Chautauqua.

"And how is James doing these days, Mary?" her cousin Ruth asked over tea. "He has so many responsibilities now! You must be very proud of him."

"Yes, James is very busy these days, with his preaching and his mission work," Mary said dully. Her thoughts were elsewhere. She'd learned of Hickey's accusations claiming James had been cavorting with another woman somewhere in Michigan. She didn't want to believe it, but her mind kept going back to the thought like a tongue to an inflamed canker sore. She knew her husband had a weakness for pretty women. Stories of his entanglements with inappropriate women before he married her had come to her attention. But, to the best of her knowledge, he had remained faithful to her during their marriage.

She always thought James was happy with their marriage, although the early years of making the bed springs squeak on a nightly basis were behind them. She'd grown a little saggy after giving birth to several children, but that was part of life and motherhood, wasn't it? Mary had no false conceit about herself. She was mousy in appearance, with mud-colored brown hair and pale blue-gray eyes that were as close to colorless as eyes could get. Her chin was small and weak. But she had a good sense of humor and a strong disposition that enabled her to follow James across the countryside as he built up his religious following.

"Mary, is everything okay? You seem particularly quiet," Ruth asked. Mary snapped out of her haze.

"Oh, I'm fine, just a little tired. There's so much to do, what with tending to the children and also organizing our home for the move to Beaver Island."

"And when are you moving to Beaver Island? I hear it's going to be a wonderful location for the Strangites," Ruth said.

"I plan to move there as soon as James has built us a proper house."

"Do you think you'll like it there? Do you know any of the people who are already there?"

"Not really, no. I mean, I know some of the men in the Circle of 12 pretty well, like George Adams and Alexander Wentworth, and Thomas Bedford, and, of course, Dr. MacCulloch, but I don't know their wives very well. We've never socialized much."

Mary wasn't about to tell Ruth that George Adams had left his wife in New Jersey while he catted around the country, or that Dr. MacCulloch's wife was a snobby socialite who thought herself above the likes of Mary. Alexander's wife Phebe was a gossipy shrew with a nose like a parish pick axe, and Bedford's wife was nice enough, but dull as a well-used butter knife. Mary figured Thomas married her for her ample bosoms and round behind.

"Well, I'm sure you'll make new friends when you get there," Ruth said, not feeling the slightest bit sure of any such thing. She personally couldn't imagine moving to some wild, remote island in the middle of a lake practically the size of the ocean, where Indians and drunkards apparently lurked behind every bush and under every beached canoe.

"Yes, no doubt," Mary said, secretly sharing some of the very same thoughts Ruth had at the moment.

Where did it go wrong, Mary wondered. *We were so happy in the beginning, before all the Mormon developments. Before Joseph Smith was assassinated. Yes. That was where our lives took a big turn,* she thought. *If only Smith had lived, everything would be so different. We would still be living in Burlington, Wisconsin and James would still be teaching and writing for the local newspaper.*

The assassination of Joseph Smith wrecked everything for Mary. And opened up a host of possibilities for James.

CHAPTER 14
JUNE, 1849

It was Lucy's favorite time of year, when the branches on the raspberry bushes practically dragged on the ground under the weight of the berries.

Lucy worked her way along the path to Whiskey Point, picking berries and dropping them in her basket. While she was picking, she thought about James. He was a regular guest at her house now, staying there every time he visited the island. His house was being built on a parcel of land overlooking Paradise Bay. Archie Donnelly had happily accepted the job offer to build it for James. Her house up the hill looked slightly down on James' property, which was ironic, since she looked slightly down on him, both literally and figuratively.

She couldn't seem to get James out of her mind. How he puzzled her! The whole church business was suspiciously baffling, but James seemed to be quite devoted to it. The people he brought to the island were, for the most part, hard-working, decent folks who just wanted a better life than the one they left behind. There were a few maggots burrowing into the body of the church and curiously, they seemed to have found their way into James' inner circle. Was he blind to their deceit and connivery? That was hard to believe, given his level of intelligence.

And that was the one quality that she couldn't resist – his intelligence. She knew James was married and the father of three children, but still she was drawn to him. He had such a way with words, and could be so charming and clever when he wanted to be.

James could be childish at times, childlike at others. Lucy was drawn to the childlike side, when he was filled with wonder and enthusiasm and boundless energy for his projects. The childishness – the emotional outbursts, temper tantrums, and irrational, dictatorial decisions she could most definitely do without. She could hardly forget the time he angrily and abusively chastised one of his men for failing to pick up the mail on Whiskey Point without imbibing in a quick pint of ale.

"Hello there," a tremulous voice said. Lucy had been so lost in thought that she didn't hear anyone approaching. She looked up to see a young woman with cheeks rosy from the walk in the sun. A smattering of freckles across her turned-up nose made her look even more youthful than she likely was. Wisps of strawberry blonde hair had escaped from the hair clip at the nape of her neck. Lucy guessed she couldn't be more than 19 or 20 years old.

"Oh, hello," Lucy said. "I'm sorry, I didn't know anyone else was out here. I'm Lucy LaFleur, and who might you be?" Lucy asked gently.

"I'm Jane Watson. It's a pleasure to meet you, Mrs. LaFleur." She promptly extended a hand to Lucy.

"The pleasure is mine, and please, call me Lucy. You must be one of the new arrivals to the island."

"I am. My husband Wingfield and I arrived a few months ago."

"Mormons, I am guessing?"

"Yes, we are. I'm hoping we're welcome here?" Jane said it with a hint of nervousness in her sweet young voice.

"Why yes, of course," Lucy answered. "I take it you're out here for the same reason I am – to pick berries."

"Yes, if that's all right," Jane said.

"Then let's get to it."

The women slowly made their way along the path, filling their baskets with raspberries. Jane filled her basket with anything that caught her eye – some wildflowers; a few mushrooms of questionable edibility that Lucy planned to remove from her basket so she wouldn't accidentally poison her husband; and fiddle ferns, which were most certainly edible and particularly delicious when fried in butter.

"Do you mind me asking you about your faith, and how you came to be a Mormon?" Lucy asked Jane after they stopped to sit and rest. She seemed very open and ingenuous and Lucy got the impression she wouldn't be offending her.

"Not at all," she said. "We were living in Burlington, Wisconsin, and then we became Strangite Mormons after Joseph Smith was assassinated.

"So then we moved to Voree, which was a little rough at first," Jane continued. "We lived in tents and practically froze to death that first year, but Prophet Strang was right by our side, freezing along with us, being stoic and keeping us going.

"We realized after that first year, when we got our homes built, that he'd made the right decision. The place was beautiful. Rolling hills and great farmland, the White River running right through town, everything you could ask for. No wonder the angel Enoch told him to bring his flock to that place. But then the trouble began."

"Trouble?" Lucy asked, hoping she didn't sound too sanguine.

Jane chewed a fingernail thoughtfully, apparently trying to decide how much to say. Lucy was fascinated. James had never really shared details of Voree with her, preferring instead to focus on the present.

"Well, there were doubters, you know. The Gentiles who didn't believe in Prophet Strang. They said he was a fraud. They said – " Jane stopped herself abruptly.

"What's wrong?" Lucy asked.

"I'm afraid if I tell you more, you'll laugh at us, like the people in Wisconsin."

"I promise I won't do that."

"Well you see, Prophet Strang was visited by an angel shortly after we moved to Voree. The angel guided the Prophet to a hill on the White River, and told him to dig in a certain spot under an oak tree, where he would find ancient plates that would reveal his purpose.

"The prophet knew how people would react to his vision of an angel, so he took witnesses with him to watch him dig in that spot. And there, sure enough, he found three brass plates, with writing on both sides of them. They were the Plates of Laban, and only the Prophet could decipher them with the aid of an angel. But he was named in the plates as the one true prophet."

Lucy rolled her eyes without letting Jane see. As much as Lucy liked James, this was skilamalink if she ever heard it. A shady business it is, when an angel gives the ability to decipher something solely to the Prophet who's in charge of finding them, so no one else can check its authenticity.

Jane went on, her nervous fingers daddling the hem of her skirt.

"The Burlington newspaper said it was a pack of lies. They said the Prophet was a leader of a gang of thieves who were robbing people under the guise of religious acts."

Aha, Lucy thought, *there it is. No wonder James never told her any of this. It made him look like a charlatan.*

"But you see, the plates proved he was the true prophet. The angel told him where to find them, and the plates also said he was to find a place for his Saints that looked exactly like this place! That's how he came to know Beaver Island would be our new home!"

Jane sat up a little straighter, apparently feeling she had done a good job of vindicating James. Lucy could only help but wonder how a sweet, bright young person could be so gullible. In the same moment she realized that she had been taken – and taken in – by Strang as well.

CHAPTER 15

AUGUST, 1849

Nathan and Eliza Bowman stepped off the three-masted schooner, the *Morgan*, and onto the long pier at Beaver Island. It was a beautiful August day – the type of day that made it possible for residents of Beaver Island to put up with the harsh, bitterly cold days in the winter. Three months had passed since the Bowmans had heard Strang preach in New York. It had taken them that long to gather up their meager belongings and make the trip to Beaver Island.

"Pretty place, wouldn't you say, Eliza?" Nathan asked his wife.

She was looking around the harbor, trying to process the cacophony of hammers and saws building new dwellings, fishermen hollering to one another as they stretched out their nets to dry, oxen clopping on the hard-packed dirt road, white-throated sparrows calling to one another, cicadas humming steadily and small waves whooshing onto the shore. Behind her the crew on the *Morgan* was lowering its sails and they made loud flapping noises as the wind fell out of them. It was sensory overload for Eliza.

"Yes, I guess so," she replied warily. "It's awfully busy, isn't it?"

"Of course it's busy! That's a good sign! It's a thriving new place, just what we wanted for a new start."

"I wish we'd gotten here a little earlier in the season. I wonder how long this weather will last."

"Don't be like that, always seeing bad around the next corner. This is going to be good, I promise you."

"Well, I just want to be sure we can find a place to live before the weather turns."

"We will, I promise."

The two of them were with a gaggle of other new converts to Mormonism, all hoping to find a new and fulfilling life on the island. The long-term goal was clear – Mormon utopia; the short-term goal of finding a place to sleep that night was not quite as clear.

"I think for now we should pitch a tent over there, by the beach," Nathan said.

"What are you going to do for work?" Eliza asked, always the practical one.

"I don't know, we just got here. I want to look around and talk to others and see what might be a good fit for me. I'm sure the Prophet James will provide," Nathan said.

The two of them pitched their tent near the shore of Paradise Bay, then went for a walk to meet others. They barely made it a quarter of a mile before they were stopped by a man of equal height and build to Nathan.

"You Saints?" he asked brusquely.

"Yes, we are, isn't everybody?" Nathan answered the man, who visibly relaxed after Nathan gave him the correct reply.

"No, not everybody," the man said. "I'm Constable Joshua Miller, and also a Saint. Unfortunately there are some rowdy types, some trouble-makers who are not of our faith."

"Is that a problem?" This time it was Eliza who spoke up. "Are they Indians?"

"There's some Indians, but they mostly stay on Garden Island except when they come to Whiskey Point to swap furs for firewater. The others are Gentiles. I don't think they have religion, or at least not one that counts."

His remark made a red flag wave in Eliza's head. She had been a Catholic before her recent conversion to Mormonism. She was not of the belief that there was only one religion that counted and all others were false.

"You folks needing a place to stay? There are some shanties set up on the south shore, for now. We'll help you get settled, don't you worry. We all help one another."

"Thank you, Constable," Nathan said. He had an instant liking for the man. Eliza had an equal and opposite reaction to the constable. Something about him left her mouth tasting like she'd just swallowed curdled milk.

"Plenty of good lumber around here, so you can build yourself a nice home," the constable added.

"I'm not much of a builder," Nathan said, feigning sheepishness. "Just don't have the vision or understanding of how it all gets put together."

"We've got people who can help you. They can teach you how it goes together."

Nathan hoped they would show him how it goes together by doing it for him. If he played dumb long enough, he figured he could get a house built for them without doing too much heavy lifting himself.

"I'll introduce you to Dennis Chidester and Jonathan Pierce. Friends of mine; good, strong builders," Miller said.

"Is that what they do for a living?" Nathan asked hopefully.

"No, they chop cordwood for the steamers. Hard work, but decent pay." Nathan's enthusiasm waned at the words 'hard work.'

"They also work part-time as my assistant deputies," Miller added. Nathan thought being an assistant deputy sounded much better than chopping cordwood. He immediately decided he needed to cozy up to Constable Miller.

There was suddenly a flurry of activity at the dock. A side-wheel steamer had arrived and its passengers were unloading.

"The Prophet's back," Miller said. "And it looks like he's brought company."

CHAPTER 16

AUGUST, 1849

"Let me help you with that, Charles," Strang said as he reached for the young man's valise. Then he took the man's hand and helped him off the boat. It was a strange sight, to see James – the Prophet – helping a gangly man-child with his valise instead of the other way around. Lucy couldn't make sense of it.

Lucy was dressed in one of her favorite, light green linen dresses that had a fine print of white checks. It accentuated her slim waist. She wanted to look good –it had been a long time since she last saw James Strang.

She watched as James and the boy made their way toward her. She admitted only to herself that she missed their conversations. She was sure he would be staying at her home, as was his practice since his second visit to the island.

But who was this boy with him? Too old to be one of James' children. Too young to be a brother-in-law, Lucy thought.

"What a joy it is to see you again, Lucy," James said as he got near enough to be heard over the jostling of passengers and baggage.

"Welcome back, as always," Lucy said. Then she looked away from him and at the boy, who was now standing off to one side of James. He kept his head tilted downward, so she couldn't get a good look at his face beneath the hat, but he had the fresh skin of a young man whose whiskers hadn't made any appearance yet. She wondered how old he was.

"Ah, yes, Lucy, this is my nephew, Charles Douglass," James told her. "He's been helping me all summer, working as my personal assistant."

Lucy extended a hand. "A pleasure to meet you, Charles," she said. Charles shyly took her hand and shook it. His hand felt like a smallmouth bass in hers; quivery and clammy.

"Will you both be staying with me?"

"Yes, if you'll have us. Do you have rooms enough for the two of us?"

"Yes, plenty of room. It seems your flock is very frugal. Not many of them choose to stay with me – most are choosing to pitch tents or build shanties instead of paying for a room in my house."

"I'll have more guests for you soon," James said. "Dr. MacCulloch and his wife are arriving shortly, and I know they'll want to stay with you. Probably the same goes for Alexander Wentworth and his wife."

The three of them made the short walk up the hill to Lucy's home. Charles lagged behind James and Lucy. It seemed like he was making a great effort not to be noticed. Maybe he was just shy.

Lucy was looking forward to one of their after-supper conversations. James could make her laugh with his cleverness, and his enthusiasm was boundless. But this time James begged off, claiming he was exhausted. This surprised her. Even after a long trip, he was always bursting with stories when he returned to the island.

"The boat ride was miserable, rough sailing for much of the trip, so I couldn't sleep," James told her. "And Charles, he got seasick, so sleep eluded him as well."

The two of them did some exaggerated yawning and then made their way up the wooden stairs to their rooms on the second floor. For lack of anything else to do, Lucy tidied up downstairs and went to bed as well.

Lucy hadn't fallen asleep yet when she heard the floorboards upstairs creaking. In the past, she'd heard James snoring lightly, but not much else. This time she heard a steady, rhythmic sound, back and forth on the floor, like a rocking chair might make. Except Lucy had no rocker upstairs. *Maybe James has learned a new religious ritual that he's going to do at night,* she thought. She certainly hoped it wouldn't take too long.

It didn't. When it ended, she quickly fell asleep.

The next morning Lucy woke early. There was a nip in the air, a portent that autumn wasn't too far away. The August days could be lovely and warm, but the temperature dropped noticeably at night, especially on cloudless nights like the ones they'd been having.

She grabbed a couple of extra blankets from the storage bin and went upstairs. Lucy was still in her bare feet, padding quietly down the hall. The door to Charles' room was wide open, so she assumed he was gone.

She assumed wrong. As she stepped in the room she started apologizing for her intrusion.

"I'm sorry to disturb you, but I thought you might get cold at night, so I've got an extra blanket for – "

Lucy stopped dead in her tracks, barely over the threshold into the room. She blinked to make sure she was seeing clearly.

"Do you mind?" Charles said as he snatched up his shirt and held it in front of his private parts.

Speechless, Lucy backed out of the room and closed the door behind her.

CHAPTER 17

FALL, WINTER, 1849

As fall and winter sluggishly made their way toward spring, Strang realized he was going to need more money to finance moving his flock to Beaver Island. And then it came to him. "I've had a wonderful revelation, Mary," James said brightly on a dull winter day.

Mary cringed. Revelations meant James was up to something.

"And what might that be?" she asked with a hint of sarcasm in her tone. James ignored it.

"The angels revealed to me that people who died without the benefit of being baptized into the Mormon Church – which would normally mean they are doomed to spend eternity in hell or purgatory – can now be baptized posthumously! It will be a blessing and relief for the family members who thought their dear, departed loved ones would never be able to join them in heaven!"

"And how does this work?"

"The living may undergo a baptism for their dead relatives. All they need to do is bring a death certificate to me and I can perform the ritual. For a fee, of course."

"Of course," Mary murmured. Now his revelation was making sense. "Did the angel who brought you this revelation tell you to charge money for this service?"

James frowned at Mary.

"I am a very busy man; I am doing this for the benefit of the living, who want to be rejoined with their departed relatives in heaven. I can't be constantly performing good deeds for others without some form of compensation. You and the children would starve to death if I didn't receive compensation for my time and efforts."

Choosing food and shelter for her family over an argument with James, Mary ceased her challenges on the topic.

"Of course, you're right. I'm sure it's a blessing to people to know they will be with their loved ones in heaven."

The dead baptisms were a great success. Dutiful followers scrimped and saved, did without meat or new shoes, so they could have their dead parents baptized. Young couples who struggled to put food on the table came up with the 10 dollars necessary to have their infant child who died of influenza baptized so they could be reunited in Heaven. For James, the influx of cash meant he could buy prime real estate for the church on Beaver Island, if the government insisted on payment for land in the future.

CHAPTER 18

MAY, 1850

"You did what?!" Nathan exploded at his wife, Eliza.

"I invited Huldy to live with us," Eliza said defensively, trying not to flinch in front of Nathan.

"I thought she was living with your brother in St. Louis. Why does she have to come here?"

"She's unhappy in St. Louis. Albert's always gone, working on the river boats, and she's alone most of the time."

"How on earth do you know she's unhappy? It's not like she could tell anyone," Nathan said, as a cruel twist formed at the corners of his mouth. He thought he was being very clever.

"Don't be mean, Nathan. She can't help the way she is. And she can most certainly write letters, which she has done, many times."

Eliza's older sister Huldy was a deaf mute. She was born that way, and Eliza had grown up loving her sister exactly how she was. The family had learned sign language in England, so everyone could communicate with her. Still, it was a rough life for Huldy. She had Eliza's beauty, but living in a world without speech and sound had sapped the vibrancy from her. She had a way of holding herself with a very straight, stiff posture, as if daring anyone to make fun of her. When their parents returned to England, the siblings had to take care of one another. Eliza knew Huldy hated to be a burden, but she could tell from the tone of her letters that she was not the least bit happy living with Albert, who spent his days on the river and his nights in the taverns, leaving Huldy to feel even more alone in an already isolated world without sound.

"How are we supposed to take care of her? I barely make enough to take care of the two of us."

"We'll manage, I'm sure. Huldy needs us."

"Easy for you to say. I'm the one who will be doing all the managing," Nathan said imperiously, as if he slaved for hours on end every day to make ends meet. Eliza knew better. Ever since he'd gotten a job as a deputy constable, he and those other bullies – the Constable Joshua Miller, Jonathan Pierce, and Dennis Chidester — mostly rode around the island looking for people who were guilty of some minor infraction, so they could write them a ticket and charge them a fee for their wrongdoing. Eliza knew Nathan relished what he was doing now.

"When is she getting here?" he asked, resigned to the fact that Huldy was coming.

"On tomorrow's boat from Chicago. I'll meet her at the dock; you don't have to bother yourself."

"Fine. And you find her a place to stay as well. There's no room in our house."

"Nathan! You can't really expect her to live alone somewhere on this island. How will she manage?"

"That's for her – and you – to figure out. I don't want her to disrupt my home life."

In truth, there wasn't much of a home life to disrupt. Ever since they arrived on Beaver Island nearly a year ago, their marriage seemed to be unraveling. As Nathan grew happier with the Mormons, Eliza grew more melancholy. Her hopes for starting a family evaporated as she and Nathan spent less time trying to make a baby. Eliza decided it was just as well. She wasn't sure she wanted to bring a child into this new Mormon world of hers. The whole Saints business seemed like a charade. Nathan was no fool, he probably thought it was a bit of a sham as well, but it suited his lifestyle perfectly, so he was more than happy to go along with the prophet's edicts.

If it weren't for Lucy LaFleur, Eliza didn't know what she would do. She had become good friends with the Indian woman, who was kind, encouraging, and equally suspicious of the whole Mormon religion.

Eliza knew what she needed to do before she picked up her sister the next day. She needed to go talk to Lucy. Fortunately, there was going to be a quilting gathering at Lucy's that afternoon.

After Eliza headed up to Lucy's house, Nathan went to the other side of the harbor, where he busied himself with the business of harassing Mormons and non-Mormons alike. He and his fellow deputies, Dennis Chidester and Jonathan Pierce, reined their horses to a stop in front of Cleary's Tavern.

They spoke to Archie Donnelly, who was chatting with Will MacCormick and Teddy Duffy.

"You ought to know better than goin' in there and consuming spirits with the Gentiles," Dennis told Archie. "It's a sin. The Prophet said so."

"Well now, Dennis, I'm Irish, and where I come from, having a pint of ale with your friends is never a sin," Archie said amiably.

"I don't think it's any of your business who Archie drinks with," Will said, irked with the trio of deputies. Will and Teddy liked Archie, and the feeling was mutual. The two frisky young men reminded Archie of his old pals in Ireland.

"You stay out of this, MacCormick," Dennis said. "It is absolutely our business what Archie does and who he does it with, especially if it comes to drinking."

"Well, fellas, you do what you have to do," Archie said, still smiling. "Write me up, report me to Strang. And while you're at it, you'd better do the same for some of the apostles in the Circle of 12. George Adams and Tom Bedford are no strangers to this tavern."

Archie knew he'd successfully taken the wind out of Dennis's sails with that comment. The apostles in the Circle of 12 were the highest ranking Mormons on the island. And several of them were quite fond of whiskey and ale.

Dennis glared at Archie. "Don't you have a wife to go home to? Unlike these unmarried ruffians?" he said, nodding toward Will and Teddy.

"Millie won't be missing me today. She's up at Lucy LaFleur's with some other ladies. Nathan, I believe your wife is there too," Archie said, his face a gillymug of playfulness.

"It's a quilting circle," Nathan said defensively. "Nothing wrong in that."

"Never said there was anything wrong with it, Nathan," Archie shot back.

"All this tongue wagging has got me parched," Teddy said. "Come on, let's go get us a pint."

Archie, Teddy and Will went into Cleary's, leaving the deputies deflated.

The gathering inside Cleary's Tavern was a typical one. Men who smelled of sweat and fish and sawdust from a hard day's work lined up along the wooden bar, seated on wobbly wood barstools. The bar itself was made of pine that had grown dark with age, beer and chewing tobacco spittle. A few square tables occupied the rest of the space. Behind the bar were plain wood shelves holding a small assortment of spirits. Underneath the counter were oak barrels of beer.

Will's father Dolan was seated at a table with Sam and Tom Bennett.

"Will, my boy! Archie, Teddy, come join us!"

The new arrivals joined the Bennetts and Dolan.

"First round's on me," Dolan said to them.

"Thanks, Dolan, but you don't have to do that," Archie said. He was very fond of Dolan, even though he was from Northern Ireland. Archie concluded that perhaps much of what he'd been taught as a boy about the Northern Irish just wasn't true.

"It's my pleasure. I'm obliged to take care of you young ones while I can."

Will sat down next to his father. Dolan scrutinized his son's face and saw something troubling him.

"What's up? You look distressed."

"Ah, not much of anything," Will answered. "Just a little dust-up outside with those Mormon deputies. They were getting on Archie, telling him he shouldn't be in here with us, taking in a few ales."

Dolan looked at Archie. "Is that true? They giving you a hard time?"

"It's nothing. Just a few bored lads looking for something to do," Archie said.

"I've about had it with those Saints. Hardly saintly, if you ask me," Teddy said.

"I agree," Will chimed in. "I think we need to let them know we're not going to put up with them trying to muscle their way into our turf."

"Calm down, boys," Dolan said. "Let's not be hasty. It's always better to try to get along than to get in a fight."

"If we fought them, surely we would win," Will said.

"Don't be so cocksure, Will," Dolan said to his son. "Those Mormons are very resourceful."

The men paused in silence for a moment, then turned their attention to their beer.

"Cheers, fellas," Archie said, breaking the silence. And he took a good, long drink of his ale.

CHAPTER 19

MAY, 1850

The women gathered in Lucy's parlor room included Jane Watson, Lucy's cousin Gwen, Millie Donnelly and Eliza Bowman. Their chairs were pulled in a circle, so they could all reach a part of the quilt they were sewing. Lucy, Jane, Millie and Eliza were dressed in long cotton dresses with high necks and long sleeves. Gwen was in her traditional Indian garb — a leather buckskin tunic with fringe on the sleeves and hem.

"My sister is coming tomorrow from St. Louis," Eliza said when there was a lull in the conversation.

"How lovely for you!" Lucy said. "Is she coming for a visit, or moving here?"

"She's moving here. I wish it was as wonderful as you make it sound," Eliza said.

"What's not wonderful about having your sister here?"

"Nathan isn't happy about it. He doesn't care much for her; he thinks it will be a burden to have her here."

"Nonsense! Family is never a burden."

"Well, my sister isn't like everyone else. She's deaf, and she doesn't speak. Nathan thinks she's a freak of nature."

Lucy immediately thought of Eliza's vain, selfish husband and got angry.

"I must say, Eliza, your husband isn't always the nicest of people."

Eliza hung her head, feeling ashamed. "I know. He has his faults, but I love him in my own way," she said.

"I'm sorry, I shouldn't have said that. I know you love Nathan. It's none of my business, anyway."

"The problem is… Nathan doesn't want my sister Huldy to live with us. He thinks she'll be in the way. Our house is very small, you know." Their house was a horizontally chinked log cabin, 10 feet by 14 feet, that Nathan had erected with a great deal of help from Chidester and Pierce. Eliza had hoped for a bigger home, but Nathan didn't want to be bothered with spending a lot of time doing the tedious, hard work of building.

"She's welcome to stay here until we find a more permanent solution," Lucy said.

Jane listened to the conversation quietly, mulling over what was being said.

"The church will help take care of her," she said at last. "That's what we do. We take care of one another."

"Archie and I can help too," Millie chimed in.

"Thank you both. You are good women," Eliza said. And she meant it. She didn't have much confidence in Strang's church taking care of her, but she was sure that the kind-hearted Jane and Millie would help however they could.

"Speaking of visitors coming to the island, did you hear that Strang's wife is coming soon?" Jane said, changing the subject. "He told Wingfield yesterday that he plans to bring her and their children here later this month."

"I didn't know that," Lucy said. Finally, she thought, she would meet James' wife. "Then it's going to get very busy around here," Lucy said. "I've received letters from several Mormons who are arriving soon, and plan to stay with me until they figure out their lodging situation."

"Really? Who?" Jane asked.

"Dr. and Mrs. MacCulloch, and Alexander Wentworth and his wife. And George Miller, the constable's father."

"Is George Miller single?" Eliza asked hopefully, thinking immediately of her spinster sister.

"No, I believe he's married, but coming on his own until he can get settled here. I guess his wife isn't the adventurous type. She'd rather have him get them a house and get settled before she'll come."

"That's understandable," Eliza said, wishing she'd done the same thing.

CHAPTER 20
LATE MAY, 1850

The snow didn't stick to the ground, but it made the islanders feel like spring had been cruelly snatched from them. Two weeks ago it had been lovely weather, with spring buds showing their unfurled faces on the trees. Then heavy, wet snow fell from low-hanging, sodden skies and clung to the delicate buds. A nasty wind out of the northeast followed, churning up the lake and leaving the fishermen with little to do.

"My main net is gone," Tom Bennett said to Will MacCormick and Teddy Duffy. They were standing by the harbor, looking out at the whitecaps on the bay. "I know it was right here where I left it, now it's gone."

"You sure you didn't stow it somewhere else?" Will asked.

"Do you think I'm an eegit? Of course I know where I left my net!"

"So what do you think happened to it?"

"I think those damn Mormons stole it, that's what I think!"

The Gentiles on the island had started noticing things were disappearing – Dolan couldn't find his wheelbarrow; Pete McKinley was positive his store had been burgled and sacks of grain had been taken; and Pat Kilty was missing some of his best egg-laying chickens.

"It's that Strang's fault," Teddy said. "He tells his people that God put everything on earth for their benefit, so they think they can take what they want. It's bull shit!"

"Well, I'm not going to put up with it," Tom said. "I got a wife and three kids to take care of, so I'm not gonna have these thieves taking my livelihood away from me."

"What are you going to do about it?" Will asked.

"I don't know. I need to think about it. Maybe I need to drink about it. Anyone want to go to Cleary's with me?"

Teddy never turned down an opportunity to imbibe. "I'm in," he said.

"Sure, why not," Will said.

Cleary's was crowded with like-minded fishermen and fur trappers, all trying to pass the time on a wet, windy day. The bar smelled of wet wool and fish as men elbowed one another to order another pint of ale. After several hours, Tom, Will and Teddy were getting restless.

"Want to go with me to Whiskey Point?" Tom asked, slurring his words a little. "Alice wants me to check on the mail, see if she got anything from her mother."

"Happy to," Will said.

Tom, Will and Teddy slogged through the snowy, wet mud to Whiskey Point, laughing and jostling one another along the way. The copious amounts of alcohol they had consumed prevented them from feeling the icy wind.

When they arrived at Whiskey Point, they walked into the post office, where they found the Mormon deputies Jonathan Pierce, Nathan Bowman and Dennis Chidester sitting around a small wooden table, playing cards. The jocular mood among the inebriated men immediately faded at the sight of the Mormons.

Tom's inhibitions dissolved in direct proportion to the alcohol he'd consumed.

"Did one of you thieves steal my fishnet?" he demanded in a slurred, angry voice.

Chidester's hackles went up instantly. He slapped his cards down on the table and stood up to glare into Tom's eyes.

"How dare you accuse us of such a thing? If your fishing net is missing, it's probably because you're too drunk to keep track of it."

Tom glared right back at Dennis. "I'm perfectly capable of keeping track of my belongings!" He put his hands on Dennis's chest and gave him a hard shove. At that, Nathan and Jonathan sprang to their feet.

"Back off, fool, or you'll be regretting it," Pierce hissed at Tom.

Teddy and Will took up positions next to Tom.

"We're not looking for trouble, we're just here to get our mail, but if you want trouble, we'll give it to you," Will said.

Pierce grabbed Teddy by the front of his shirt and jerked him forward until they were nose to nose. Pierce disgustedly wrinkled his face at the smell of whiskey coming from Teddy.

"You're all a bunch of useless drunks," Pierce said. "You don't deserve to have fishing nets, or anything else, for that matter." He released Teddy with a big shove, causing the smaller man to stumble backward and fall. That was all it took to provoke the others.

Tom threw the first punch at Pierce, who quickly responded in kind. Nathan joined in the brawl as soon as Will tackled Chidester. Within minutes the post office turned into a boxing skirmish, with punches flying and men falling. The Mormons had the advantage of not being inebriated and were soon able to throw the staggering Gentiles out the front door.

The three men who found themselves rolling in the mud outside the post office were incensed. But they were also just clear-headed enough to know better than to take up the fight again. They were outnumbered and unsteady on their feet. Licking their wounds, they headed back to Paradise Bay.

"We'll get 'em next time," Teddy said. He was the drunkest of the bunch, barely able to keep his balance while walking through the icy mud. He shoved a dirty handkerchief into his bleeding nose as he walked.

"We never even got to pick up our mail," Tom said. "That's got to be against the law, right? You can't prevent a man for getting his mail."

"Mail fraud, that's what it is," Will said. "Maybe we should report it to the constable."

"The constable's a Mormon, that won't do us any good."

"Then maybe we should go to Mackinac Island and report it to the sheriff. He's not a Mormon."

By the time the three men finished their discussion, the chill wind had sobered them up. They said their goodbyes, and Will, like the others, headed home. When he got there, he found his father with Gwen, sitting in front of the fireplace where Gwen was beading a piece of breechcloth and

Dolan was reading a newspaper. Will loved Gwen like a mother, since he had no memory of his real mother.

"Goodness, what happened to you?" Gwen asked as soon as she saw Will's left eye, which was almost swollen shut from the blow he'd received from Nathan Bowman. She put down her beadwork and rushed to examine Will's face, which was spattered with mud and blood.

Dolan put down the paper and also rose to greet his son.

"Got into a row with some Mormons at Whiskey Point," Will said. "I'm afraid they got the better of us this time."

"This time?" Dolan asked. "Meaning there was a time before, or you're planning for a time to come?"

"We went there with Tom Bennett, just to get the mail. They started it," Will said, sounding a bit childish.

While Will answered his father, Gwen went to get a fresh cloth, took it outside and soaked it in clean, cold water from the barrel outside. She came back in and dabbed at Will's face, cleaning it, then pressed the cold cloth against his eye and told him to hold it there.

"Why would the Mormons start a fight?" she asked.

"Well, maybe Tom Bennett started it," Will said as he pressed the cloth against his eye. He hadn't realized how much it was hurting until he came in from the cold. "Someone stole his fishing net, and he's sure it was one of the Mormons. They think they're entitled to anything they want. They probably stole your wheelbarrow, Papa."

"We've got no proof of that, son," Dolan said. "Maybe someone just borrowed it and they'll bring it back." Dolan could understand how a poor man might prefer to 'borrow' a wheelbarrow rather than ask for it, choosing to protect his pride instead of admitting his poverty. He hoped his wheelbarrow would come back to him as quietly as it disappeared.

"Tom's not the only one who thinks the Mormons are stealing from us. Lots of other folks are missing things. That never happened before the Mormons got here."

Gwen was thoughtful before she spoke.

"I don't want to spread rumors, but some of my people on Garden Island have heard of such things. I believe most of the Mormons are good people, but I fear a few of them have taken their belief of consecration a bit too far. They may believe that their God put everything on earth for their benefit, but I interpret that to mean that God put the trees and the rivers and the animals and the fish here for them. It shouldn't include other people's property." Gwen tried to remain neutral about the Mormons, but she was growing increasingly distrustful of them.

"I've spoken to Archie about this business of consecration and property," Dolan said. "He said the Mormons believe all personal property should be owned by the church, so everyone can share. I guess it's a good idea in theory, but doesn't work in practicality. And it should only apply to the Mormons, not the rest of us."

"We talked about it on our way back from Whiskey Point," Will said. "We want to go to Mackinac and talk to Sheriff O'Reilly up there," Will said. "We want to put a stop to this before it gets worse. Tom didn't even get to pick up his mail. That's not right."

"Was that before or after the fight?" Dolan asked with a fatherly tone of voice. He loved his son, but could see the bias in his story of the events. And he could smell the stale whiskey on his breath.

"Does it matter?" Will asked defensively.

"It might. I'm not saying who's right or wrong here, I just think we should be careful before we start making accusations."

CHAPTER 21
EARLY JUNE, 1850

When Mary Strang and her children arrived at Beaver Island, she discovered Lake Michigan wasn't the only thing that was riled up.

It had been a nauseating trip, with a strong nor'easter slamming headlong into the schooner all the way from Wisconsin to Beaver Island. The boat rose and fell a good 12 feet every time they crested a wave, which was constantly. Her oldest child William fared the best, seemingly not bothered by seasickness; the next in line, Myraette 'Nettie' vomited almost the entire trip and was totally dehydrated by the time they reached the island; and Hattie, the youngest, rolled out of her bunk and hit her head on the stateroom wall when the boat was broadsided by a particularly large wave, leaving her with a large, dark bruise on her pale forehead.

Mary felt weak and bedraggled when she and her family gratefully stepped off the boat and onto the dock in Paradise Bay. The dock seemed to move and sway under their feet after spending a nearly a week on the *Morgan*. The dock wasn't moving; it was simply an illusion after being in motion on the lake for so long.

As if the weather hadn't been nauseating enough, the company of MacCullochs and Wentworths on the rough journey made Mary feel even sicker. Sarah MacCulloch made no effort to hide her disdain for Mary, thinking she was far above her in society, even though it was Mary's husband who was their chosen leader. Phebe Wentworth was an insufferable gossip, sticking her big, ugly nose into everyone's business.

Upon their arrival at Beaver Island, Mary was looking forward to a long, quiet rest in her new house.

As she weaved off the dock to the shore with her children in tow, she was greeted by jeers and shouts from some rough-looking men standing near the pier.

"Go back where you came from!" yelled one red-faced, blustery man. "We don't want any more of the likes of you!"

"James, what is going on?" she asked her husband as soon as she found him in the crowd of people disembarking from the boat.

"There's been a little trouble with the Gentiles lately," Strang told her as he gathered her suitcases and herded her, along with the children, to their house.

"What kind of trouble?"

"The Gentiles resent us for the community we're creating here. They're just a bunch of drunken bullies. Pay them no mind; I'm sure it will all settle down in time."

Mary was too tired to ask any more questions. She longed for a bed that wasn't heaving up and down on white-capped water.

The house Strang built for them was nice enough, but hardly the palace he'd described in his letters to her. It was two stories tall, with a one-story wing on the right side of it. It was roomy inside, with four bedrooms, a parlor, kitchen and sitting room that Strang planned to use as his office. The exterior had a fresh coat of whitewash and a picket fence running along the front of it.

While the children ran around the house, exploring every nook and cranny, Mary also explored the house at a slower pace, examining the secondhand horsehair couch in the parlor and the new woodstove in the kitchen. It didn't take long before weariness overwhelmed her.

"I need to lie down for a while. Can you watch William and Hattie? Nettie can stay here and rest with me."

"Of course, dear. I'll take them with me back to the boat. I want to walk the MacCullochs and Wentworths to their quarters."

"Where are they staying?"

"At a boarding house just up the hill from us. An Indian woman owns it. I'm sure they'll find it quite adequate."

After Strang got his wife and eldest daughter settled into their house, he headed back to the boat dock. William and Hattie tagged along behind their father, looking right and left at the island that was to be their new home. William, a somber, well-behaved boy, was nine years old and willing to dutifully follow in his father's wake. Three-year-old Hattie darted about like a hummingbird looking for nectar.

Strang had no patience for poor behavior in his children.

"Hattie, stop that! Come here and walk with me and don't leave my side," he told her sternly. "God punishes children who are reckless and wild."

The fair-haired child with a purple bump on her head quickly fell into place next to her father.

When they arrived at the boat dock, the MacCullochs and Wentworths were waiting for Strang. Their belongings had preceded them to Lucy LaFleur's home, thanks to Dennis Chidester and Jonathan Pierce, who had been assigned by Strang to haul the baggage for them.

"Hezekiah, Sarah, how wonderful to see you." Strang took Sarah MacCulloch's hand formally and kissed the back of it. He then shook hands with Hezekiah MacCulloch while clapping him on the back with his other hand.

Alexander Wentworth and his wife Phebe waited their turn to be greeted by the prophet. Although it pained him to admit it, Alex Wentworth knew he ranked below the MacCullochs when it came to Strang's personal feelings about the members of his inner circle. The MacCullochs originally hailed from the high-society side of Baltimore before following Strang to Voree, Wisconsin. Wentworth knew Strang had a low opinion of his family lineage, having come from poor mountain people in West Virginia before finding his way to the slum side of Baltimore, where he had become a member of Joseph Smith's Mormon Church and met the MacCullochs. When Smith was assassinated, Wentworth was living with his wife in Nauvoo. Brigham Young made no secret of his dislike of Wentworth and Phebe, so for lack of a better option, Wentworth followed Strang to Wisconsin. He worked hard to become a confidante to Strang, supporting every word he said and defending him to any challengers. Strang had little choice but to reward him with a position in his Circle of 12.

After Strang greeted the Wentworths with a polite "Welcome to Beaver Island," the five adults and two children walked up the path to Lucy's home. Strang hadn't stayed there ever since his home had been built. He sometimes found himself longing for Lucy. He adored the sound of her laughter when he said something funny, even if he didn't say it on purpose. He missed just sitting close to her and breathing in her scent, which always hinted of musk and pine needles.

"Brother James, I thought the island would be a bit more civilized by now," Sarah said, taking in the sight of the muddy, rutted road and partially built houses along the harbor. No signs of civilization such as street signs or lampposts were in evidence. All Sarah saw was a jumble of cabins, shanties and occasional houses plopped around the harbor willy-nilly. On the other side of the harbor she saw fishing nets stretched out on large spindles, drying in the sun.

There were about 100 Mormons living on the island, but Strang always led people to believe his flock was larger than it really was.

"The weather slowed us down," Strang said, although nothing of the sort was true. He routinely painted a picture of Beaver Island the way he envisioned it; a lovely little place with stores lining the street that curved around the harbor; a printing press and newspaper office overlooking the bay; a tabernacle and school to the south; and tidy homes surrounding the commercial area. That was the future Strang saw, which was not what it was in the present.

"Of course, I understand," Sarah said obsequiously . She was enamored with James Strang, and had been ever since she first heard him speak in Baltimore. A woman of high society like Sarah typically didn't attend the crude tent revivals on the outskirts of town, but her keen imagination had been intrigued by the new Mormon religion she'd heard so much about. When she heard Strang speak for the first time, she was captivated by his strong, melodious voice and articulate speech that demonstrated a large vocabulary; clear signs that he was a man of intelligence and fine upbringing. When he spoke of angels giving him visions and revelations, and then a flash of angel light illuminated the nearby hillside, she was hooked. Clearly the man had a connection with God that couldn't be questioned. While others swallowed Strang's prophesies and visions hook, line and sinker, Sarah swallowed the fishing pole too. She convinced her husband Hezekiah to convert to the new religion with her. Dr. MacCulloch, a man possessing exceptionally mediocre medical skills, was always interested in joining any group that might lead to new connections, which inevitably led to new patients.

"This is my home," Strang said with no small degree of pride as they walked past his picket fence. "You are welcome here anytime."

They continued up to Lucy's home and walked up the steps to her broad front porch. "Didn't you tell us the woman who runs this boarding house is an Indian?" Dr. MacCulloch asked. "This doesn't look like an Indian house, although I guess I don't know what one would look like."

"She's half Indian, half French-Canadian. Her uncle is the Indian Chief in these parts."

"Does that make her Indian royalty?" Sarah asked, hoping she was about to meet an Indian princess. After growing up in the high social circles of Baltimore, Sarah had her doubts about moving to Beaver Island. She found the idea of knowing an exotic Indian princess enthralling.

"I guess it puts her in good stead in the northern Michigan islands," Strang replied. "I don't think it makes her a princess."

Hearing the knocks on her heavy oak front door, Lucy swung the door open and greeted her guests. Strang made the introductions while Lucy carefully avoided looking directly into his eyes. Ever since the morning she walked in on Charles Douglass and found him naked, she'd been unable to speak to Strang. His children lingered on the front porch, not sure if they were supposed to go in with the others or wait outside.

"And who might these two be?" Lucy asked with a nod toward the children.

"Those are mine," Strang said. "William and Hattie. I assure you, I didn't strike her to make the bump on her head. The rough trip on the boat caused that."

Lucy looked at the two children. The boy was slender, with pale skin and his father's reddish hair. He politely did a little bow and said, "How do you do?" to Lucy.

"I do very well, thank you, William," she answered, giving him a big smile.

"Hello, Miss," Hattie said, grabbing the edges of her dress and performing a clumsy curtsy. Lucy laughed. "Hello, Hattie. Welcome to Beaver Island."

"Isn't there a third child?" Lucy asked Strang.

"Yes, Myraette – Nettie, but she's at home resting with her mother. The trip made both of them quite ill."

Then Lucy looked back at the little girl. Hattie had penetrating eyes and light brown hair. Lucy guessed she must take after her mother, with the exception of her eyes, which stared boldly at her. *That she got from her father,* Lucy thought.

CHAPTER 22
JUNE, 1850

A few weeks after getting herself and her children settled into their new home, Mary set out to explore more of the island. She unknowingly wandered up the path to Lucy's house, and saw the Indian woman walking toward her. Mary suddenly realized she probably didn't belong on the path, as it didn't seem to lead anywhere but to the white house ahead.

The Indian woman was upon her before she could think of an excuse to be walking in that direction.

"Hello there," Lucy said as she approached Mary. "May I help you? Are you lost?"

"I'm not sure I'm lost, but I am new here," Mary said. "I'm Mary Strang. I just recently arrived." Mary smiled.

"I'm so happy to meet you, Mary," Lucy said. "I'm Lucy LaFleur. I run the boarding house up the hill. I know your husband." When Lucy said the last sentence, she noticed that Mary's demeanor changed.

In fact, Mary wondered at that moment if James had behaved inappropriately with this woman. She remembered the rumors she'd heard about James fornicating with some woman in Michigan; she wondered if this was the one. But there was something about the poised, elegant Indian woman that made her dismiss the thought.

"I'm happy to meet you too. I don't know many people yet, here on the island."

"Where were you headed? Am I keeping you from something?" Lucy asked.

"No, I was just sort of roaming around, getting the lay of the land," Mary said, feeling embarrassed.

"I was headed to McKinley's store for provisions. I have quite a few guests at my house now, all of whom I need to feed. But could you come up later for a cup of tea?"

"I'd like that very much," Mary said. "If it's all right, I'll walk with you to the store. I don't think I need to explore this path anymore."

"Of course, but you're welcome to walk this way anytime. I always enjoy company."

The two women made small talk about the weather and new arrivals to the island while they walked. As they came around a bend in the path to go to McKinley's, Lucy's keen eyes spotted a small figure walking toward them. The figure froze, did an about-face and darted away behind the store. Mary saw the figure a split second after Lucy did.

"Charles! Oh Charles!" Mary called. "That's James' nephew. I wasn't aware he was on the island," Mary said.

"I guess he didn't hear you," Lucy said after Charles disappeared.

"He's an odd little fellow, I must say. Always sticks to himself, even though I've tried to include him in our family activities," Mary said.

"Yes, I would agree that he's odd," Lucy said.

"Oh, you've met him? Maybe it's just his age, a phase he's going through. He's no longer a boy, yet not really a man," Mary said.

"Something like that," Lucy said, biting her lip so she wouldn't say more.

The two women stepped onto the porch steps of the store just as Black Jack Bonner was departing.

"Black Jack, how are you?" Lucy asked. "This is my new friend, Mary Strang."

Black Jack gave Mary a peppery look. "You're related to the prophet?" he asked gruffly.

"Yes, he's my husband." Mary paled.

"Too bad for you," Jack said. "Gotta skedaddle, Lucy, things to do." With that, Jack turned and walked away.

"He's usually a lot friendlier, Mary, I'm sorry for that."

"I take it things aren't as perfect here as James has been telling me," Mary said.

"There have been some problems, probably just growing pains of the island's new mix of people," Lucy said evasively. She didn't want to burden Mary with the troubles that had been brewing lately. The poor woman had just arrived.

Pete McKinley didn't wait for Lucy to make introductions, choosing to ignore the woman with Lucy. "You know what those Mormons have been up to now?" he said angrily to Lucy. "Black Jack told me they stole one of his men's fishing boats off Gull Island. They saw it happen, plain as day, well, except it was night."

"Uh, Pete, this is Mary Strang, James Strang's wife," Lucy said. "She arrived a couple of weeks ago."

Pete's storekeeper manners took over and the anger drained from him.

"Sorry ma'am and a pleasure to meet you. It's just that there's been a bit of thievery going on around here, and I'm afraid it's some of your people," Pete said. "Just a few bad apples, I suppose," he added.

Mary blanched. It was happening all over again. The disharmony between Gentiles and Mormons, the accusations of stealing. She had hoped things would be different here, but it didn't look like it.

"I'm very sorry, sir," she said politely. "I'll report it to my husband. Hopefully he can take care of it."

Lucy picked things she needed off the shelves and put them on the counter for Pete to ring up. He tallied the amount and wrote it on a tab he kept for Lucy in the top drawer behind the counter. She paid him monthly to make things easier for both of them. She loaded her goods into her knapsack and started to walk out of the store, with Mary by her side.

"I'll see you soon, Mary. I'm counting on you coming for tea. Later today?" Lucy said before she turned to head up her path.

"I'll be there in a few hours, thank you."

The women parted company, with Lucy heading uphill and Mary headed straight ahead to her new home.

◆•◆

Within the hour, a handful of men were gathered at McKinley's store, Black Jack in the center of the men.

"I'm sure that sacks of flour have gone missing from my store," Pete said. "You all know I'm good about keeping track of inventory."

"I lost my best fishing net," Tom said.

"My wheelbarrow never came back," Dolan said sadly.

"Our calf is gone, and I know for a fact she didn't just wander off. I had her tied up and corralled," one of the men from the southern end of the island said.

"This has to stop." Black Jack was visibly angry, something the others rarely saw on the face of the usually jovial man.

"We can't tell Constable Miller, he's a Mormon. He's probably guilty of thievery too," Tom Bennett said.

"It's high time we head on up to Mackinac and tell the sheriff there. Weather's good, I say we sail up there tomorrow." Black Jack looked around at the circle of men to see if they were in accord.

They all nodded yes or chimed in with words of agreement.

"Then it's settled. Let's leave at first light from Gull Island. That way the Mormons won't suspect anything."

"I'll sail over to Garden Island today, with Will and Teddy," Dolan said. "The rest of you can head to Gull Island as soon as the wind is up tomorrow, and we'll meet you there."

Dolan thought it would be best if they didn't all head over to Gull Island in one noticeable group of boats. Plus, he wanted to spend a night on Garden Island with Gwen. It had been weeks since he'd been with her, and he missed her terribly.

There was a light wind at dusk when Dolan, Will and Teddy headed to Garden Island, making the short trip in no time. The three men secured the boat on the beach, battened down the sail and then walked up to Gwen's cabin, where she lived with her brother Otto. Dolan hugged her longingly, as if he hadn't seen her in a lifetime.

"My goodness Dolan, it's only been a few weeks," Gwen said, smiling up at his face.

"A few days is too long for me to be away from you," he said, kissing her.

Will and Teddy greeted Gwen the way grown boys would greet their mom, with playful jostling.

"Have you had supper? I have some duck I roasted earlier," Gwen said.

"We'd never turn down a meal," Will said.

The three of them tucked into a meal of roast duck, corn bread and fiddle ferns cooked in duck fat. Dolan told Gwen about their plans to head to Mackinac Island with the rest of the men. As they talked, Otto came in and joined them at the table. He was all ligaments, tendons and muscle, his skin the color of cherry tobacco. Straight black hair hung down to his shoulders. His black eyes and straight, sharp nose gave him an air of intensity and intelligence. Dolan told him of the Mormon thievery that was happening.

"I've seen and heard of such things," Otto said.

"You have? You never told me," Gwen said.

"Some of our canoes have gone missing," Otto said. "But who is going to believe an Indian? I didn't want to start trouble. But now that it's started, I'd like to see it get finished. I'll go with you tomorrow." It was a declaration, not a question for permission.

"Then we'd better get some sleep. It's going to be a long day," Dolan said. He wasn't really thinking about sleep at the moment. He just wanted to be in bed with Gwen.

CHAPTER 23
JUNE, 1850

Mary followed behind Lucy as she picked raspberries from her bushes and plucked mint leaves from the plants that grew in abundance along the edge of her house.

They went inside and Lucy boiled water for tea, adding raspberries and mint to their cups. After they settled into their chairs at the kitchen table, Mary took a sip of her tea.

"This is delicious, I never would have thought of putting mint with raspberry," she said.

"I don't know if it's an Indian tradition, but there's plenty of mint and raspberries around here, so we've been making it this way for as long as I can remember."

All of this was so new and foreign to Mary. She'd never known any Indians, and had been fearful of living in close proximity to them, but now could see that her fears were groundless, if the other Indians were like Lucy.

"How are you settling in?" Lucy asked.

"The children seem to love it here," Mary answered. "All this room to roam around, and it's not like they can get too far – it's an island, after all."

"True, but it's a big island. You still need to keep an eye on them. Are they finding other children to play with? I think some of Tom Bennett's children are about the same age."

"We haven't met many other families yet, other than the couples who are staying here."

"Oh, so you know the MacCullochs and the Wentworths? And George Adams?"

Mary's nose wrinkled slightly at the mention of her fellow Mormons.

"Yes, I traveled here with them. I hate to sound mean, but Alex's wife Phebe can't seem to stop talking."

Lucy laughed. "I've noticed that too. It makes my head hurt to hear her going on and on like a demented blue jay. What do you think of the others?"

"I met Thomas Bedford and his wife yesterday. She is nice enough, but boring. And Sarah MacCulloch, well, she seems to think she's better than the rest of us, just because she grew up in Baltimore. Her parents were quite prominent there. I can't understand why she would want to give all that up to live on an island."

Lucy laughed again. "I must admit, I think I'd rather drag a rotten board around the island than spend much time with Mrs. Bedford or Mrs. MacCulloch." Lucy went on. "I have friends who you might find more to your liking, Mary. But they're not all Mormons."

Mary was feeling relaxed and calm and, dare she even think it? Happy, sitting here with Lucy, drinking tea and laughing for the first time in a long time.

"I would love to meet your friends, Mormon or not. I know James thinks we should stick to our own kind, but I haven't always seen eye to eye with him on a lot of his Mormon beliefs and… how shall I say it? His 'experiences.'"

Lucy was surprised to hear James' wife say that. She had assumed the prophet's wife would be completely in his camp, dutifully following his every word.

"What, exactly, do you mean by his 'experiences'?" Lucy asked with restrained curiosity.

"You won't tell anyone, will you? James would be furious with me, and when James gets angry, it's not a pleasant sight."

Lucy knew this to be a fact, but she didn't tell Mary of her first-hand knowledge on the subject.

"Of course not. We Indians are known for our silence." She gave her a wry smile.

"His visions, his revelations, as he calls them. I think he makes them up to suit his fancy. But he speaks so passionately, so eloquently, people just want to believe him. I want to believe him, but I just can't, not all the time."

"I found some of his claims to be hard to swallow, but I thought it was because I'm half-Indian, and I don't follow any Christian beliefs, Mormon or otherwise."

"You're half-Indian? What's the other half?"

"French-Canadian. My mother is the Chief's sister, and she married a Canadian fur trapper. There used to be loads of fur trappers in these parts, but they are becoming more scarce as the human population grows and the animal population dwindles."

"So the Indian chief is your uncle? That must make you an important person, even though you're a woman." Mary didn't say it in a condescending manner; she was simply stating things as she knew them. Women were never really powerful. They supported powerful men, but they never had their own power.

Lucy knew what Mary was saying, and took no offense.

"Actually, in our culture, women can be quite important and powerful. My mother's cousin, Agatha Biddle, is the Chief of the Mackinac Island tribe. We have women who are chiefs. And my own cousin Gwen is the medicine woman on Garden Island. That is a position of honor and prestige."

"I'm starting to think I'd rather be a member of your tribe than a member of the Mormon tribe," Mary said jokingly. But it wasn't entirely a joke.

As the two women laughed, the front door opened and the sound of voices traveled to the kitchen. It was Sarah MacCulloch and Phebe Wentworth. The new arrivals were unaware of Lucy and Mary in the kitchen. They sat down in the parlor and continued with their stream of conversation.

"And that simpering little Jane Watson," Phebe was saying. "She's such a gullible little thing! She actually believes the Indians are equal to us!"

Lucy started to do a slow burn in the kitchen, but she held completely still, as did Mary.

"The Prophet is quite taken with the Indians," Sarah said. "He seems to think they're from some noble lost tribe from ancient biblical times."

"I think he's just taken with our boarding house hostess," Phebe said. "She's reasonably attractive, for a half-breed."

"I understand the Prophet stayed here quite a few times on his visits. Maybe he has designs on the Indian woman," Sarah said, ignoring Phebe's insulting remark. "George Adams says the Prophet has an inappropriate fondness for women."

Mary blushed violently at Sarah's statement. Lucy saw it, and put her hand over Mary's and gave her a supportive squeeze.

Lucy, who could move with the stealth of great blue heron stalking a perch in shallow water, suddenly rose and made quite a clatter with her wooden chair and teacup. Mary followed suit.

The two of them walked into the parlor and feigned surprise at the sight of the other women.

"Hello, ladies," Lucy said amiably. "I trust you're finding your way around the island?"

Phebe, in particular, looked at Lucy with fearful consternation that she'd been overheard. Her eyes went over to Mary, who was staring back at her.

"Yes, it's lovely," said Sarah. "We're very happy to be here, Lucy."

"It's Mrs. LaFleur," Lucy said, still smiling at them, hiding her anger. "I still like to honor my late husband." She did not want to be on a first name basis with these women.

"Of course, Mrs. LaFleur," Sarah said. "I'm so sorry for your loss." Sarah was still fascinated by Lucy, still thinking she must be some sort of Indian princess if she was the chief's niece.

"It's been a decade since I lost him, but thank you. Now, if you'll excuse us, I was just going to show Mary around a bit, take her to the Anishinaabe ceremonial grounds on Mt. Pisgah." This was all a surprise to Mary, but she went along with Lucy, acting as if they had planned this outing days ago.

"Oh, I would love to see that!" Sarah exclaimed. "May I join you?"

"I'm afraid you're not dressed for it," Lucy said, looking down at Sarah's elegant, pointed-toe boots that laced up the inside. They appeared to be made of pale kid leather.

"I could change," Sarah said, for once actually regretting her beautiful, handmade footwear.

"I'm afraid we don't have time," Lucy said dismissively. "We have many things to do today."

Mary held her head up imperceptibly higher as she followed Lucy out the front door.

After they closed the door behind them and headed down the path, Mary put her hand on Lucy's arm.

"Are we really going to an Indian ceremonial ground?" she asked.

"No, it's a bit of a hike and then a steep climb and Mary, I don't think you're ready for that yet." Lucy smiled gently at her. "Most white women would have trouble making it on foot."

"I take no offense, Lucy. I completely understand. But oh, how I will never forget the look on Sarah's face when she thought she was being left behind and missing something important!"

Mary had that sweet, impish smile on her face again, the one Lucy found herself liking very much.

CHAPTER 24

LATE JUNE, 1850

"It's just for a short while, Elvira," George Adams said.

He had arrived at Mackinac Island the day before with 19-year-old Elvira.

"I don't like it here," Elvira said. "I want to be with James." She was swatting at deer flies that had joined them at their rickety wooden window table at a popular local tavern.

Outside, above the window, a sign bearing the name 'Jillet's Tavern' was actually hanging properly over the door, attached to the roof line by two rusty hooks affixed to the corners of the sign. In the spring, fall and winter, when the wind streaked ferociously across the island, the sign was more commonly dangling precariously by one corner. Many a man had been conked in the head by the sign when it twisted and bucked in the wind. Most were relieved when a gust of wind tore the sign away completely and sent it into the ditch by the side of the road, making their passage into the bar a much safer experience.

"All in good time, my dear. You know James has everything carefully planned. But you can't be on Beaver Island with his wife and children living there."

Elvira pouted. "My birthday is coming up soon, I want to celebrate with James."

"And you will, I assure you. Now, let's get you checked into the lovely little boarding house I just happen to know of. The Pink Pony, it's called. Mrs. Pinkham runs it. She'll take good care of you and keep you company."

Elvira pictured Mrs. Pinkham to be a dreary old lady whose company she wouldn't enjoy, but she was in no position to object.

"All right George, if I must."

Mrs. Pinkham, it turned out, was not a dreary old lady. She was a woman who appeared to be in her thirties, wearing a too-tight, bright green dress that was cut so low in front that the top half of her bosoms were exposed. Elvira was shocked. The woman's cheeks looked too bright and rosy to be natural; the same held true for her full red lips.

"Mrs. Pinkham, how lovely to see you again," Adams greeted her with a dramatic bow.

"George, how nice to have you back!" Mrs. Pinkham gave him a lascivious smile.

Elvira started to put the pieces together. She knew that James and George traveled frequently together on their mission work, and had no doubt found it necessary to stay at Mackinac Island occasionally on their journeys to the eastern part of the country. It looked like Mrs. Pinkham was obviously one of George's sexual conquests. Everyone knew George was a philanderer except his wife, who remained in their home in New Jersey and saw her husband only when he came back east on mission trips.

Elvira was too young to see the irony of her thoughts: that Adams, a married man, was a philandering sinner and her beloved James, also a married man, was a saint. Different sides to the same coin.

"I must take my leave of you both, I have business to attend to in town," Adams said with another overly dramatic bow.

"We'll look forward to your return," Mrs. Pinkham said with a wink.

Adams returned to Jillet's to conduct a further examination of the female opportunities in town. Mrs. Pinkham was enjoyable, but, he thought, why order the same thing off the menu every time he returned to a place that offered fresh new dishes?

Adams seated himself near the back of the bar, where he had a good view of everyone coming and going out the front door. He calmly ran a hand over his wavy hair and ordered himself a pint of ale along with a shot of whiskey.

A large group of men were sitting at two tables pulled together, close to where Adams was seated. He immediately recognized a few of them from Beaver Island. He angled his chair so they couldn't see his face. The Mackinac Island sheriff was with them.

"We've got to put them on notice," one of the Beaver Island men said. "I think, as soon as we get back, we should let them know we aren't going to stand for it anymore."

"As if their thieving wasn't enough, they're crowding in on our livelihoods," said another. Adams recognized him as Will, one of the young men who fished every day out of Paradise Bay. The shorter, stocky one must be his fishing partner, Ted.

"They are?" asked one of the Mackinac Island men. "How so?"

"They're taking up fishing and logging. I don't want to see Beaver Island get fished out the way Mackinac has," Will said.

"And I'd just as soon not have them cutting into my lumber business," said another man. "I've got a good thing going, cutting cordwood for the steamers. Those Mormons already built their own saw mill and they're clearing the woods as fast as their axes can swing."

Adams listened carefully to the conversation, temporarily forgetting his desire to bed a new woman.

One of the older men from Beaver Island was thoughtfully stroking his chin. He finally spoke.

"We've got the annual Fourth of July celebration coming up soon," he said. "How about if we invite all our Mackinac Island friends over to join us in the festivities? With enough of us, I believe we can stand our ground and state our case. They'll listen if we're united."

"Great idea, Dolan! Let's stand our ground with plenty of rifles and ammunition," said the stocky one.

"Teddy, we don't want a war on our hands, we just want to make our voices heard, loud and clear. I'm thinking a unified front with large numbers should do the trick."

A lone Indian man, sitting silently with the rest of them, finally spoke up.

"I can bring our people from Garden Island to help," he said. "We had to fight hard enough to keep our land after the treaty of 1836. I'm not about to give up ground now to another batch of white interlopers."

"I'm sorry about that, Otto," the man named Dolan said. "It was a dirty trick the government played, but you won in the long run."

"Yes, but it wasn't easy. I vowed never to let anyone take our land from us again. Or our belongings."

"I think we have a plan, then," Dolan said. "Sheriff, can you round up your people and bring them over for the Fourth of July?"

"We can," he said.

"Come to Whiskey Point," said Black Jack. "Seems like a fitting place to hold our celebration."

"Don't forget to bring the beer," Teddy said with a grin. "It's as important as weapons."

Having concluded their business, the men continued to drink and talk. Adams lost interest when one of the men went on and on about his newest daughter, who was the spitting image of his wife Alice, whoever that was. Adams paid his tab and slid out the front door, unnoticed by the group of men. He turned left and started up the dirt road that led to the French Outpost, another one of the watering holes he'd discovered on his last trip to Mackinac. It was not as conveniently located as Jillet's, but the competition wasn't as stiff. The fur traders who frequented the place were typically dirty and smelled of body odor and dead animals. Adams, with his clean-shaven face, well-tailored clothes and trimmed fingernails, was the preferred choice of most women.

CHAPTER 25
JUNE, 1850

The dry weather had turned the wagon ruts on Beaver Island's main road into hard ridges, making a simple walk challenging.

George Adams silently cursed the gritty dust clouds that kept rising and clinging to his white silk shirt every time a filthy ox cart clattered by him as he walked to Strang's home.

"Did you get Elvira settled in?" Strang asked Adams after he greeted him at the front door and escorted him into the parlor.

"Yes, everything is fine with regard to that. She's staying with Mrs. Pinkham."

"Thank you, George. I appreciate your help with this delicate matter."

Strang smoothed his vest and pulled out his pocket watch, indicating that his current business with Adams was concluded.

"There's more, James," Adams said. "It was most fortuitous that I was on Mackinac when I was. I learned something that will be of great interest to you."

Strang tucked his watch back in his vest and looked at Adams with new interest.

"Really? What might that be?"

"I was in a tavern on the island, just to get something to eat, of course, and I overheard a group of men from Beaver Island talking with the Mackinac sheriff and some of the locals there." Adams now paused for dramatic effect. The actor in him couldn't resist stretching his moments in the spotlight.

Strang had little patience for Adams theatrics. "Go on," he said curtly.

"Anyway, I heard these men complaining about Mormon consecration. They are planning something here for their Fourth of July celebration on Whiskey Point. I'm not sure if it's going to be an attack on us or a show of force. I think we should be ready for both."

Strang rubbed his beard as he processed this information. The Gentiles had been getting increasingly vocal in their complaints about the Mormons. He knew it was a potential uprising in the making. And he'd learned enough from his experience in Voree and Nauvoo that this type of uprising had to be squelched immediately. He'd come too far and done too much to have Gentiles ruin his plans for Beaver Island.

"Thank you, Brother George," Strang said. "As it happens, I'm planning to go to Mackinac myself tomorrow; I'll look into this."

"I think you need to do more than look into it," Adams said. "I think you need to take action, make plans."

Strang was way ahead of him.

"Oh, I have a plan hatching even as we speak. I'll get what I need to resolve this little matter." Strang's tone of voice told Adams that he wasn't going to be privy to whatever Strang was planning. It irked him.

Strang could see that Adams was not content. "George, I need you to stay here and continue working on our plans for Proclamation Day. You're my right hand man for the big event. You need to oversee the construction of the platform at Font Lake. Everything must be completed in the next couple of weeks."

Adams wasn't mollified with that. "All the work for Proclamation Day is well underway; my oversight isn't needed," he said. "I know the lay of the land on Mackinac Island. I think I should go with you."

Strang softened his look. He stood, walked around his desk and put an arm around Adams' shoulders. "Walk with me, Brother George," he said as he led him through the front door and out into the street. Adams complied, like an oversized lamb being guided by his trusty sheepdog.

"It's more than just getting things ready for Proclamation Day, George," Strang said in a low, urgent voice. "Look about you, see what's happening on this island," he said. "Trouble is brewing from without and within." Strang gave Adams a conspiratorial wink, then continued. "The Gentiles are plotting against us, as you so cleverly learned. I cannot leave this island unattended. I need one of my most trustworthy men to keep an eye on things. And you are that man, George. You must be my eyes and ears for me while I'm gone. There is no one else I can trust with such oversight."

Adams chest puffed with pride.

"Of course, Brother James, I should have seen that," he said.

"Now I need you to start immediately, infiltrating the Gentiles and seeing what else you can learn of their plans to hurt us."

"I'll get right on it, James, I promise."

Adams walked back through town on the rough road, with no intentions of getting right on anything until the dust literally settled. He prayed for a light rain to fall that night to tamp down the dry earth. He was tired of having dust ruin his lovely clothes.

After Adams left, Mary came out of the kitchen, where she had been baking bread. Her face was slightly damp with sweat, her cheeks pink and her skin the healthy color of someone who had been soaking in fresh, northern air and sunshine. Her apron had a smattering of flour on it. In that moment, Strang found her attractive; something he hadn't truly felt for Mary ever since he'd met first Lucy, then Elvira.

"Mary, dear, something has come up and I need to make a trip to Mackinac Island tomorrow," he told her. "I wish it wasn't so, I'd rather be here with you," he added as he took her hand.

"What is it, James? Trouble of some sort?" Mary was no fool. It was obvious that trouble was brewing on the island. The summer air was dense with the smell of raspberries and rancor.

"Not trouble, really, just need to take precautions so there won't be trouble down the road."

Strang was deliberately evasive.

"I won't be gone long. I think the *Vandalia* is in port, heading to Mackinac tomorrow. I'll catch a ride on it."

"Whatever you say, James." Mary slipped her hand from his and walked back to the kitchen, where the children were waiting to eat. Strang felt a surge of anger at her casual dismissiveness. He deserved better from his wife. The anger dissipated when he remembered that the problem would soon be resolved.

No rain fell overnight, leaving parched ruts in the road. Strang woke early and made his way to the *Vandalia* as she loaded on cordwood. It was early, but already the day was warming more than was typical for a June day.

On his way to the dock, he spotted Hezekiah and Sarah MacCulloch, and it gave him an idea.

"Hezekiah, just the man I'm looking for," Strang said, although it wasn't true until he actually spotted the man and revised his plan to include the wealthy doctor.

"Brother James, good to see you. What can I do for you?"

"Will you excuse us for a moment, Sarah? Church council business, I wouldn't want to bore you with that."

Sarah, who was dressed in a delicate silk dress and carrying a parasol to protect her from the bright summer sun, could take a hint, so she moved on.

"Hezekiah, I'm headed to Mackinac Island on the *Vandalia* today, and was hoping you could come along. I could use a man with your powers of persuasion and influence." Strang hoped his flattery would work its magic.

MacCulloch was looking for a pleasant diversion. Life on the island had already proved to be somewhat boring and confining for a man such as himself, accustomed to attending plays and operas and drinking champagne with people of his ilk. He kept his drinking hidden from Strang, but he doubted Strang would put up much of a fuss if he ever got caught. The height of his social status and the weight of his wallet were too valuable to a man like Strang to be punitive with him.

"I'd be delighted to join you! How long will we be gone? I'll go pack some things now."

"No more than a day or two. Pack lightly, and quickly. The *Vandalia* leaves in an hour."

The two men were onboard and sailing out of Paradise Bay one hour later, leaning on the guardrail, enjoying the fresh breeze and looking out at the lake. The occasional clouds overhead threw shadows on the blue surface of the water, making the lake look like a blue canvas dabbed with heavy brushstrokes of periwinkle.

"So what is our mission?" MacCulloch asked bluntly. He knew Strang was always a man with a plan, and didn't take rides on boats just to enjoy the breeze.

"I've learned that the Gentiles are planning some trouble for us during their Fourth of July celebration," Strang replied. "I've got an idea of what we can do to squelch their plans quite emphatically."

MacCulloch was intrigued. "What might that be?"

"You know the fort on Mackinac? Fort Michilimackinac?"

"I'm somewhat familiar with it."

"They have cannons. Lots of them. What do they need all those cannons for? The fight with the British ended decades ago. The only battles taking place at the fort now are with the poison sumac and ragweed that are fighting to take over the grounds."

"Are you suggesting we consecrate a cannon?" MacCulloch was dubious about the prospect of this.

"I don't think consecration will be possible, but I think we could buy a cannon."

"Do you have the means to make such a purchase?"

"It would be a stretch for me, I must admit. But you have the financial capability to acquire one, I should think." Strang smiled as he said this.

"Ahh," said MacCulloch, now seeing why Strang wanted him along on this venture. "Perhaps we could persuade the ordnance officer to 'unofficially' part with a cannon. For the right price, of course."

"My thoughts exactly."

After a pleasant sail, the men disembarked at Mackinac Island in the early afternoon. They both looked up at the imposing fort. Sturdy logs, with their tops carved into dangerously sharp points, were tightly bound together vertically, forming the barricade around the fort. Strang guessed it must have been at least 20 feet in height. No one could easily scale such a barrier. Strang could only see the rooftops of the buildings within the walls; some appeared to be made of cedar shake, others looked like they were thatched with strips of wood, likely cedar or hickory.

"Shall we?" Strang asked MacCulloch as he gestured toward the fort.

"No time like the present," MacCulloch replied, and fell into step along Strang.

When they arrived at the fort, they were surprised to find it completely abandoned. The stone rampart and the heavy gates beneath it should have been closed and guarded. They were wide open.

A boy who looked to be about 13 years old passed them, kicking a rock back and forth along the road.

"Young man!" Strang called out to him. The boy stopped and turned.

"Where is everyone? Where are the soldiers who guard the fort?"

The boy looked at him as if he was asking for directions to the sky.

"Never came back after they went to fight in the Mexican war," the boy said. "Guess they liked the weather down there better. Or they died."

"There is no one here then?"

"An old sentry comes by every day, first thing in the morning and again in the afternoon. He'll probably be by soon."

"Thank you, lad," Strang said. The boy continued on his way, no longer casually kicking the rock. He wanted to make his escape before the strangers asked him more dumb questions.

Strang and MacCulloch entered the fort and surveyed the grounds and buildings. Some buildings were made of chinked logs rising vertically, others were half-logs laid horizontally.

"I wonder where they keep the cannons," MacCulloch mused, thinking perhaps they would be able to consecrate a cannon for themselves after all. This thought pleased him. More money to spend on recreation for the two of them while they were on Mackinac.

The two men peered into unshuttered windows, seeing nothing much of interest. Most buildings were empty, save for a few benches and tables.

"Who goes there!" a voice rang out behind them.

Strang and MacCulloch turned to see a weather-beaten man in uniform. He looked to be in his late forties. Either the harsh weather or long days in taverns had taken its toll on him. Deep wrinkles fanned out like rivulets from a stream around his eyes and mouth.

"Allow me to introduce myself," Strang said smoothly. "I'm James Jesse Strang, Prophet of the Mormon community on Beaver Island. This is our esteemed Doctor MacCulloch. We've come in search of your help."

"What's a Mormon?" he asked.

"We are a non-violent group of believers in Jesus Christ of the Latter-Day Saints," Strang said. "We are building a peaceful community on Beaver Island. But all is not peaceful, that's why we're here, seeking assistance."

The sentry seemed not the least bit impressed with Strang's explanation; nor did he seem put off by it.

"What kind of assistance? There are no soldiers here anymore," he said.

"We don't need soldiers; we simply need to be able to protect ourselves with perhaps one good weapon. Actually, we don't plan to fire it at anyone; we just want to fire warning shots if needed."

The sentry looked suspicious.

"Who's attacking you?"

"No one yet, and we'd like to keep it that way. There are some bad men – pirates of sorts – and bad Indians, living on Beaver Island. We fear they have vastly more weapons and fighters than we do."

"Damn Indians," the sentry said. "Nothing but trouble."

"Yes, indeed, my good man, that's why we seek your help."

"What is it you want?"

"A cannon. You must have cannons around here that are no longer of use. As you pointed out, there are no soldiers here, and no war going on. Perhaps you could spare us a cannon to help in our quest to protect our wives and families from Indians?"

"We do have some cannons in the munitions building," the sentry said. "But that is official U.S. military ordnance. I'm in no position to relinquish it without orders from my superior officer."

"It's getting late in the day," MacCulloch said, jumping into the conversation. "How about if we retire to one of your fine taverns and discuss this further? It would be our honor to pay for your refreshments."

The spray of wrinkles next to the sentry's eyes curved upward, as if a favorable breeze caught them and turned them north.

"That would be most kind of you," he said. "By the way, I'm Sargent Chamberlin. Charles Chamberlin. Most folks call me Charlie."

"A pleasure it is to meet you, Charlie," Strang said as he shook his hand.

At Jillett's, Strang called out, "Three whiskeys for my friends and me," to the barkeep. "Make mine a scotch whiskey."

MacCulloch's chin nearly fell on his shoelaces when he heard this. He'd been quite pleased with himself for figuring out a way to imbibe without bringing the scorn of Strang upon him. But he'd never seen Strang consume alcohol. He was delighted with this turn of events.

When the drinks were placed in front of the men, MacCulloch pulled a fat billfold from his coat breast pocket.

"Allow me," he said, making sure Charlie saw the large number of bills in the leather billfold.

Strang and MacCulloch painted a picture of Beaver Island for Charlie, talking about the community they were building where everyone worked and shared their bounty. They spoke of Indians getting drunk on Whiskey Point and threatening their women during the day; they told tales of armed pirates stealing their valuables while the industrious Mormons were out logging, fishing or working their crops.

With every glass of whiskey purchased by MacCulloch, the stories became more vivid, and Charlie became more enthralled. By the time Charlie downed his fourth whiskey, he was practically ready to move to Beaver Island and become a Mormon.

"For sure you need a cannon," Charlie said. "I'm your man. I can help you. But I'll be putting myself at risk," he said, dangling the bait.

"We can see that," Strang said. "And that is why there will be recompense for you and your services. Do you think $10 would be sufficient to get a cannon to the dock tomorrow morning?" As Strang said it, MacCulloch withdrew $10 from his billfold and laid it temptingly on the table.

Charlie eyed Strang and MacCulloch, licking his lips at the $10 now lying on the table.

"It's a start," Charlie said. "You're gonna need cannon balls too." He waggled his fingers at MacCulloch, with his palm up. MacCulloch extracted another $5 from his billfold.

"Then there's the matter of gun powder," Charlie continued. His fingers waggled again. MacCulloch put three more dollars on the table.

"I can't possibly move a cannon by myself," Charlie said. "We'll need to take it apart and get a mule to haul the barrel, at the very least. Maybe you fellas can roll the carriage to the boat. And the cannon balls weigh 12 pounds each. How many of those are you gonna want?"

MacCulloch and Strang gave each other a knowing look.

"Would $30 cover all the costs of this project?" Strang asked. Charlie beamed.

"That, and a couple more whiskeys ought to do the trick," he answered.

One hour and three more whiskeys later, the men completed their deal with handshakes all around.

"I can clearly see you are good men," Charlie said, who couldn't see anything clearly through the whiskey fog that had settled into his brain. "I shall slee you tramorrow," he slurred before making a wobbly departure.

After securing passage on the barque *Morgan* for the next day's trip, the two men parted company as well. Strang was headed to the Pink Pony to pay a surprise visit to Elvira, and MacCulloch was headed back into town for much needed food, and less needed whiskey.

After a vigorous night with Elvira, Strang was sated and feeling weak in the legs the following morning. MacCulloch met him in front of the Pink Pony and they ascended the hill together, albeit slowly. MacCulloch's head was aching and Strang's legs were threatening to give out.

When they got to the fort, they found Charlie waiting for them. He looked none the worse for wear, but his looks had already been worn down to the nubbins long ago.

Charlie was holding a mule by a rope tied around its neck. He led the men to a storage barn in the far corner of the fort premises and pushed open the creaky barn door, leading the mule inside with the other.

Charlie pulled a heavy tarpaulin off an object to reveal a small cannon.

"It's an 1841 Howitzer," he told Strang and MacCulloch. "Barrel weight, 220 pounds. Firing range, up to 1,000 yards, depending on how much gun powder you use." Charlie smiled proudly, as if he'd made the cannon himself. "We'll load the tube on the mule, then you fellas can roll the carriage to the boat yourselves."

Strang and MacCulloch paled at the thought of rolling the carriage, with its iron-rimmed wooden wheels, down the steep hill. Charlie fastened a cradle-type of saddle on the mule, which would hold the barrel on its back.

MacCulloch was relieved to see that the military had devised a pulley system that could hoist the barrel from its seated position on the carriage to the mule's back. All the men had to do was pull on ropes and swing the barrel into place.

The rusty carriage was another matter. MacCulloch nearly got himself run over by the carriage as it pitched fitfully down the cobbled road to the dock. Strang bruised both of his knees and scraped his hands trying to stop it from rolling into a ditch.

After a long battle with the headstrong carriage, the three men arrived at the loading dock for the *Morgan*.

"Can we purchase that barrel cradle too?" MacCulloch asked Charlie. "I think we're going to need it when we get back to Beaver Island."

Charlie grinned and put out his hand. "That's the most expensive part, of course," he said. "It'll cost you $20."

MacCulloch pulled out his billfold and withdrew four five-dollar bills. "You're a true gentleman and protector of the innocent," he said, the sarcasm in his voice oblivious to Charlie, who pocketed the money.

After the barrel, cradle and carriage were loaded on the boat with the help of deckhands who were generously bribed to keep quiet about the cargo, Charlie and the mule went back up the hill to fetch the cannonballs and gunpowder. He returned 30 minutes later with a crate of nine cannonballs and a tin box of gunpowder.

Back on Beaver Island, Strang solicited the help of Miller, Chidester, Pierce and Bowman to move the cannon to a safe hiding place. Strang swore the men to secrecy after explaining his Fourth of July plans. They practically salivated at the thought of what was to come.

CHAPTER 26
JULY, 1850

It was shaping up to be a Fourth of July to be remembered. On the third of July, boats started arriving from Mackinac Island, laden with people, beer, whiskey, pistols and rifles. They set up on Whiskey Point. By that evening, nearly 100 revelers were in full swing, drinking and shooting guns at the stars in the sky. They missed the stars, but occasionally hit an owl or gull that was in the wrong place at the wrong time.

"What a revolting way to celebrate the founding of our great country," Strang said with disgust to his men. They were gathered at the site of what would become the print shop for Strang's newspaper. The foundation had been laid and the frame was starting to rise.

With Strang were George Adams, Dr. McCulloch, Constable Joshua Miller, his father George Miller, Tom Bedford, Alex Wentworth, Dennis Chidester, Jonathan Pierce and the newest member of Strang's closest allies, the handsome Nathan Bowman, who had proved himself to be a dedicated enforcer of Strang's rules of law.

"Shall we go break up the party?" Miller asked, itching to flex his legal muscles against the Gentiles.

"No, let them have their debauchery tonight. Tomorrow they will learn who's in charge around here," Strang said.

At the same time, but on Whiskey Point, Tom Bennett and Dolan MacCormick were sitting away from the crowd, talking quietly.

"One of Strang's henchmen came to my boat the other day, checking out my catch," Bennett said. "He told me I needed to pay 10 percent of my profits to the church. I'm not a Mormon, why should I tithe to their religion?"

"That is troublesome," Dolan agreed. "That's why we need to stand up to them tomorrow. I'd like to invite their leaders to Whiskey Point tomorrow so we can discuss this calmly. If there are hundreds of us speaking in unison, I think we can resolve this."

"I think you're a dreamer," Bennett said. "I would like to be optimistic and believe you're right, but I have a bad feeling about these Mormons. Seems to me they want to take over the island. There must be 200 of them here already and they keep on coming."

Gwen, dressed in a beaded tunic with fringe at the bottom, joined them. Her black hair was braided and hanging down her back, practically extending all the way to her waist. She had been sitting with Tom's wife Alice, helping her with their three daughters, but when they lay down for a nap, Gwen saw an opportunity to leave Alice and join Dolan.

Dolan looked over at the gathering, which was growing rowdier by the hour. Teddy Duffy was staggering about while he did a sloppy version of an Irish jig, waving a gun in the air. Will was on the ground laughing at him. Black Jack Bonner and Black Pete McCauley were apparently holding a drinking contest, challenging other men to match them pint for pint.

On the edge of the gathering, Lucy LaFleur and another woman were laughing and talking.

"Who is that woman with Lucy?" Dolan asked Gwen.

"If you can believe it, it's Mary Strang, the prophet's wife," Gwen said.

"My stars, what is she doing here?"

"She and Lucy have become friends. She's a lovely woman. I've spent a few afternoons with her myself."

"Very interesting. Maybe she can appeal to her husband to find a peaceful way to coexist with us."

"I don't know about that," Gwen said. "I don't think her husband knows she's here. He would frown on it, no doubt, her mingling with us."

"I'm surprised she would risk the wrath of her husband to be here."

"I don't think their marriage is on the strongest of footings," Gwen said. "I think Mary finds solace and happiness with Lucy. And I think Lucy is happy to have a new friend."

"Well, I've seen ducks make friends with wharf cats, so who am I to question it?"

The carousing went on until the moon was starting to fade in the sky. Whiskey Point became quiet, except for the sound of inebriated snoring and raccoons pawing through the detritus scattered on the ground.

As if by command from the United States government, the Fourth of July dawned as pretty as a picture of freedom in a glorious land. The sun rose into a pure blue sky and quickly warmed the air.

By noon, more women arrived at the point to join their men, carrying baskets of corn bread, pork, beef and fruit pies. They wore bonnets and light linen dresses. Blankets were spread on the ground and makeshift tables were erected. It was a perfect day for a celebration.

Dolan put two fingers in his mouth and whistled to get everyone's attention.

"I think the plan should be to enjoy our picnic on this fine day, then walk over as one large group to the Mormon gathering. I understand they're having a celebration of their own today, which is natural. This country belongs to people of all religions, so they are entitled to have their own celebration without interference from us. We simply need to stand up for our own rights, and what better day to do that than today? This is a celebration of the freedom we enjoy in this great land. Freedom to pursue our own way of life, whatever that may be."

Dolan's little talk received clapping and lots of people shouting "Hear, hear," while nodding their heads in affirmation. Then the eating, drinking and celebrating began in earnest.

On the other side of the bay, the Mormons were holding a much quieter celebration. Archie and Millie Donnelly could hear the laughter float over the harbor, and Archie secretly wished he was on Whiskey Point with the Gentiles instead of staidly praying over dull food and non-alcoholic beverages with the Mormons. Millie was content to sit with Jane Watson and Eliza Bowman and talk of nice homes and babies; things they all hoped to have in the near future. Eliza's sister Huldy sat with them, but had no such hopes. She sat without saying anything. She relied on Eliza to relay the conversation with sign language, but sometimes Eliza couldn't keep up or forgot. Huldy felt more alone than ever, sitting in the middle of a group of women to whom she couldn't relate. After a while, Huldy signed to her sister that she needed to stretch her legs and take a walk. If she had to *feel* alone, she preferred to actually *be* alone.

When Huldy first arrived on the island, she stayed briefly with Lucy, but the young, enthusiastic Mormon couple Jane and Wingfield Watson were quick to offer her a room with them. They believed she should be living with the Mormons. Eliza wasn't so sure about that, but she trusted Jane and Wingfield, so she went along with the plan. It shamed her that her own sister wasn't allowed to stay in her home. She became increasingly resentful toward Nathan because of his selfishness. She kept her resentment to herself, allowing it to show only when she was in bed with Nathan, where she rebuffed his romantic advances.

Eliza knew things were growing frustrating for Huldy, since the Watsons didn't know sign language. Instead of trying to make herself understood, Huldy simply withdrew farther into her own world of silence. The thought of it made Eliza's gray eyes grow soft with sorrow.

Huldy set off on a path that led to a small inland lake about a mile from the harbor. She'd learned from Eliza that it had been named Font Lake by Strang, and it would be used for baptisms in the future. The remaining women continued to talk, taking little notice of Huldy's departure. They also didn't notice that a small number of their men had taken their leave as well. The women were completely unaware of the cannon hidden nearby.

Back on Whiskey Point, Dolan whistled again to get everyone's attention.

"Perhaps we should start our walk to the Mormon gathering now, and then we can get back to the business of celebrating after we've secured our peace agreement with Strang," he said.

The group started out as a straggling line, then formed up into a mass of moving humanity. As they neared the end of Whiskey Point, they heard a loud boom and saw an explosion of smoke in the air.

"What the hell was that!" Tom Bennett said.

Black Jack was near the back of the group, standing near the shore, when a cannonball landed in the shallow water.

"They're shooting cannonballs at us!" he roared. "The feckin' zealots are shooting at us!" He had no sooner gotten the words out of his mouth when another cannonball sailed onto Whiskey Point and landed on the beach. It was followed by another that splashed into the harbor.

"Are they trying to start a war with us? I'm not backing down!" Bennett yelled, pushing forward.

Dolan grabbed him by the arm.

"Wait a minute, Tom. We're no match for cannon fire. We need to give this some thought."

"I'm done thinking, I'm ready for action!"

"And what are you going to do? Stuff an empty whiskey bottle in their cannon? We can't stop them with what we have."

Another cannonball landed in the harbor while they spoke.

"Let's go back and move everyone to the far side of the point. Their cannonballs can't reach us there," Dolan said.

"Are we giving up? I don't want them to think we're giving up!" Bennett was red in the face and ropy veins were swelling on his neck. "They're shooting at our families!"

"From the look of it, I don't think their cannon can shoot this far. I think they're just trying to scare us," Dolan said. "I think we need to take our stand against them another day. The closer we get, the more likely it is they could actually hit us with one of those cannonballs."

As Dolan started turning the crowd around to steer them back to the far side of Whiskey Point, Bennett made a break for it.

"Tom!" Dolan shouted. Bennett ignored him, and continued running up the road.

Dennis Chidester and Jonathan Pierce were chortling as they loaded another cannonball into the cannon. They didn't see Bennett until he was five feet away from them.

"I'm telling you bastards, you keep that up and I'll come after all of you," Bennett said, his voice a low growl.

"Don't you get it yet, Bennett?" Chidester scoffed. "You're outnumbered, outgunned, and out of luck here. If you don't like it, leave!" He glared at him, his flinty eyes smoking like a spent revolver.

"Only way I'm leaving this island is when my soul goes up to heaven, a place you'll never see."

Bennett had no way of knowing how soon his soul would be departing.

———— ◆◆◆ ————

Being deaf, Huldy Cornwall was oblivious to the booms of the cannon. She continued to amble along the path to Font Lake as it narrowed to a footpath barely wide enough for one person. She liked the feel of green bushes that extended into the path on either side of her, like friendly bits of nature reaching out to touch her arms in sympathy.

When she arrived at the lake, she noticed men building some sort of platform on the north side of the lake. Huldy headed around the lake in the opposite direction, staying close to the shoreline. She saw the imprint of deer hooves and rabbit feet in the wet sand. When a barely noticeable footpath branched away from the lake, she followed it. It was overgrown with brambles.

About 100 feet in, she discovered a small cabin. No more than eight feet by 10 feet, it could accommodate just one person. The overgrowth, the cobwebs on the windowsill, and moss on the door latch assured her that it was abandoned.

The front door had rusted slightly ajar; Huldy pushed hard on it, and then stepped in. Animal droppings, no doubt left by a battalion of mice, speckled the planked wood floor. A small wooden table was in one corner, with one chair by its side. It had a fireplace and an ample supply of firewood stacked next to it. A wooden frame on the other side of the room looked like it once held a mattress for a bed. All that remained of the mattress were a few soiled strips of cloth, corn husks and feathers.

Huldy went back outside and sat down on the small stoop outside the door. The sun was getting lower in the sky, and it shone on her face through the lacework of oak and pine branches. *I think I have found my home*, she thought to herself. *Now I just need to convince Eliza to let me move here.*

CHAPTER 27

JULY 5, 1850

The mood on Whiskey Point the following morning was a somber one. Men rose with aching heads and bloodshot eyes. The womenfolk had left them to their folly the night before and returned to their own homes to sleep.

Teddy sat up groggily and surveyed his surroundings. Tom Bennett was up and gathering his belongings. He'd already made coffee over a campfire and extended his tin cup to Teddy.

"I need to get back to Alice and the children," he said. "I shouldn't have stayed here last night, but..."

"Yes, I know. But you needed to get drunk."

"Seemed like the only thing to do. Was planning on drinking to celebrate, ended up drinking to drown my sorrows. Or anger. Something needed to get drowned."

Teddy gratefully took the coffee and drank.

"I thought Beaver Island would be my home forever, what with the good fishing and all, but now I'm having doubts," Tom said.

"Can't say as I blame you."

"Maybe Cross Village would be the better choice. We've got family there. Well, Alice has family there. I guess they would count as my family. But my brother Sam is here."

"You'd really leave here?" Teddy asked, clearly dumbfounded at the thought of leaving the only home he could remember.

"Don't want to, but if it comes to that because of these damn Mormons, then I will."

About 100 yards upwind of Bennett, Black Jack Bonner was also waking up with a head that felt like an overripe pumpkin. He rubbed the grit out of his eyes and saw Black Pete McCauley next to him, sitting and staring at the low sun.

"That's it for me," Black Jack said. "I'm heading back to Gull Island and steering clear of those Mormons. I don't need to be worrying about cannonballs flying past my head all the time." At the moment, his head felt very much like a stray cannonball had hit him right between the eyes.

"I think you have the right idea," Pete said. "I'm going to go back down to my side of the island. Aren't too many of them down there. Like I always say, if you can't beat 'em, stay the hell away from them."

"You've never said that in your life."

"I'm sayin' it now."

"So much for standing our ground," Black Jack said.

"Maybe someday, but today ain't the day, for sure," Black Pete replied.

The two men parted company; Pete on a buckboard and Jack on a boat. All the others on Whiskey Point were following suit.

Lucy saw the men slowly scatter from Whiskey Point. She was standing on her front porch, dressed in a light cotton dress. Her apron was tied around her waist. It was getting too warm out for her to bother fussing with her thick hair, so she had tied it loosely with a blue ribbon on one side of her face.

She was seething mad from yesterday's escapades. Shooting cannons at innocent people! What was James thinking? Surely he knew it was happening; it was coming from the Mormon gathering, and it was hardly one isolated shot that could accidentally be overlooked by the man who claimed he had control over everything his people did.

Her anger got the best of her. Lucy stomped down her porch steps and headed to Strang's home down the hill. When she got there, she banged loudly on the front door.

Strang answered the door and let Lucy in. The children were staring at Lucy with great curiosity, wondering what the tall Indian woman was doing in their home.

Strang told the children to go play outside so he and Lucy could talk. She was grateful for the privacy, and it took some of the anger out of her. She watched as he gently ushered the children out of the room.

For a second she couldn't believe Strang could have known about the cannon fire. He was a loving father and a husband. He couldn't be capable of such an act.

"Did you know your people would be firing a cannon at the people on Whiskey Point yesterday?" she asked, giving him the benefit of the doubt.

"Very little happens on this island that I don't know about, Lucy," Strang said.

"So you did know? You knew they were going to shoot a cannon at us and you allowed it?"

"They weren't going to hit anyone; we didn't use enough gunpowder to reach Whiskey Point."

"Says you! One did land on the beach! My God, James, you knew this was going to happen?"

"Of course. And I knew the Gentiles were planning to attack us before we made plans to shoot our cannon. Why, they were shooting their guns and rifles the night before the celebration. We heard it. We thought they were already shooting at us."

Lucy had to admit to herself that the drunken men on Whiskey Point had discharged their weapons with joyful abandon for much of the night.

"The Gentiles had no intention of attacking you; they wanted to talk to you about figuring out a peaceful working relationship between all of you. But you've ruined any chance of that, shooting a cannon right at them!"

"In military parlance, it's known as firing a shot across the bow. It was a warning shot, nothing more. We just want the non-Mormon community to know we won't tolerate any abuse or attacks."

"And we won't tolerate any more of your consecration and arm-twisting to live by the rules of your religion."

Mary came up behind them, with a calm look on her face.

"Lucy is right," Mary said. "We must let others live the way they want to, without interference from us. There's plenty of room on this island for all of us."

Strang turned to stare at his wife. He was shocked to hear her defy him. Had she fallen under the spell of the intractable Lucy?

"Mary, this is too complex for you to understand," he said dismissively. "There are many issues at stake here. It's our moral imperative to stand our ground against heathens and non-believers." When he said the word heathen, he leveled his gaze at Lucy. He wanted to hurt her with his words, just as she had hurt him with her effrontery.

"I don't think it's complex at all," Mary said, amazed at herself for standing her ground. "We can live our way, they can live theirs. Neither side should attempt to influence the other."

"We will discuss this later, Mary," Strang said, turning toward Lucy again. "Lucy, have you gotten what you came for? The answers you sought? If so, then please take your leave."

"You'll regret this," Lucy said. "You have the power to fix all of this. You could be a real leader who binds people together instead of driving them apart. But you're choosing divisiveness. It won't end well." She turned and walked toward the door, but not before speaking to Mary.

"In our culture, you could have been the leader, Mary. You would have made a good one." Then Lucy quickly slipped out the front door. Strang slammed it behind her.

Strang turned back to Mary, ready to chastise her for her impertinence.

"The children are waiting for breakfast, James; I have no time for talk." She also turned her back on Strang, leaving him gape-mouthed at her audacity.

Proclamation day can't come soon enough, Strang thought. *Three more days of this wrangling, and then it will be over. Everyone on this island, including my wife, will know who's in charge.*

Part 4

BUILDING A KINGDOM
1850 – 1854

CHAPTER 28

JULY 8, 1850

Elvira woke with the sunrise on her 20th birthday in the home of Dennis Chidester, where she had been ensconced since her secret voyage from Mackinac Island to Beaver Island two days prior. Chidester was there to guard her and keep her out of sight until the big event began.

At Font Lake, George Adams put the finishing touches on the wide platform that would serve as a stage. An enormous wooden chair, with an intricately carved back that was at least six feet tall, was placed in the center of the stage. Archie Donnelly was pleased with the chair he'd built for Strang, although he was baffled by why a man would want such a chair. It looked far too grand for regular use.

Adams surveyed the stage, making sure the heavy, dark red curtain was securely fastened from the rope that ran between two log poles on either end of the stage. It hung behind the big chair. The curtain parted in the middle, which would allow Strang to easily make his appearance from backstage.

Behind the curtain, out of sight, was a trunk of Adams' that he used for his theater costumes. Only he and Strang knew what it contained at the moment. He opened the trunk and checked the items one more time to make sure everything was there. Pleased with what he saw, he closed the trunk again. In one hour, every Mormon on the island would see its contents as they were meant to be seen.

On the other side of the lake, Huldy was tugging her sister Eliza's arm eagerly, pulling her along the narrow footpath. Huldy had talked Eliza into leaving early for the Proclamation Ceremony so she could show her something before the ceremony started. Now they were turning away from the lake and following a barely visible path. Eliza couldn't imagine what Huldy wanted so desperately to show her.

They emerged from the path onto a small, sunny patch of ground where a little cabin sat. Gone were the overgrown brambles, the cobwebs and the moss on the door latch – Huldy had spent many secretive hours cleaning and preparing the cabin for this moment.

She signed to her sister: "What do you think? This is my new home!" Huldy wasn't asking permission, she was stating a fact.

Eliza signed back: "You want to live out here, all alone in the woods in this little shack? You can't be serious."

Huldy pulled her arm and opened the door latch in succession. "Take a look inside, it's perfect for me," she signed.

Eliza stepped into the cabin and was impressed with what she saw. Huldy had done a good job cleaning. She'd prevailed upon Lucy to help her acquire a few needed items, which Lucy gladly loaned her. Now the little cabin had a mattress on the bed stead, covered with a cheerful quilt of orange, yellow and pale green. On the floor was a deerskin rug. The little wooden table had a red clay vase of wildflowers on it. There was an additional side table against a wall with a white ceramic wash basin on it. The stone fireplace had been cleaned of its cobwebs and charred wood, the round stones scrubbed and freed from a layer of smoky grime.

"You've done a good job with this place," Eliza signed. She looked at her big sister with admiration. Huldy relaxed and smiled, her beauty rising from within along with her contentment.

Huldy signed: "I'm glad you like it. Then it's settled, I will live here. But you must tell no one. Only you and Lucy know about it. Lucy told me it was an old fur trapper cabin, long since abandoned and forgotten about."

"Why the secrecy?" Eliza signed.

"I don't know, exactly, but I don't trust your Mormons. I want to keep my location a secret from them."

"If you insist," Eliza signed. "I don't know that it matters. I doubt anyone could find this place without a guide."

Huldy smiled at that. It was exactly how she wanted it.

"We'd better get along to the ceremony now, Nathan will be angry if I'm late."

"Follow me. There's a new path I cut that will take us through the woods and back to the main path to Font Lake," Huldy signed.

Huldy led her sister through the woods on a tiny path, hopping over fallen logs and ducking easily under low hanging branches.

Eliza followed dutifully, again impressed with her sister's skills. What she lacked in hearing and speech, she made up for in dexterity and determination. Sometimes she envied the way her sister was. Being shunned by people due to her disabilities had made her strong and independent. Eliza felt weak and needy by comparison. So needy she'd settled for a man like Nathan, who was good-looking on the outside but had the inner constitution of a mealy pear.

They arrived at the clearing next to Font Lake, where dozens of benches were neatly lined up in rows in front of the stage. The air was fragrant with the smell of freshly cut pine that had been used to make the benches.

Nathan and Chidester were standing at attention on one side of the stage; Pierce and Constable Miller were on the other side. *Whatever was stowed on the stage must have great value to require four guards,* Eliza thought. *Or maybe whatever is going to happen will require four guards.*

Mary Strang and Lucy LaFleur were sitting in the front row near the right side of the stage. Eliza was surprised to see Lucy there. She and Huldy joined them on the bench.

"Lucy, thank you for helping my sister with her new home," Eliza whispered to her. Lucy said nothing, just gave her a smile and a pat on the arm. The less said about it the better, Eliza could see. She changed the subject.

"What brings you here today, Lucy? You're not a Mormon."

"Mary invited me," Lucy said. "I don't know what is going to be proclaimed today by James Strang, but I imagine it might be of interest to Mormons and non-Mormons alike."

Eliza could see the merit in that. With Gentiles, Indians and Mormons sharing space on the island, whatever affected one group would no doubt affect another group. It was like throwing rocks in Font Lake from opposite shorelines. Sooner or later the concentric rings of ripples made their way to the middle and overlapped.

Within an hour, over 300 Mormons were gathered in the clearing. There was a shortage of benches, so most stood and crowded as close to the stage as they could get. The benches closest to the stage had been reserved for the members of the Circle of 12 – Sarah and Hezekiah MacCulloch, the Wentworths, the Bedfords, the Watsons, Constable Miller, his father George and his wife, Lorenzo Hickey, and about 20 other high-ranking Mormons. The rest of the benches had been filled on a first-come, first-serve basis.

George Adams parted the dark red curtains and stepped to the front of the stage. He looked magnificent in his black pants, white silk shirt, grey silk vest, and a short black cape trimmed in red wool that matched the curtain behind him.

Adams was in his element, alone on a stage with hundreds of people giving him their rapt attention. He cleared his throat and began speaking – or emoting – in a theatrical stage voice.

"Gentle Saints gathered here," he began while spreading his arms to the audience. "The Lord has blessed us with a beautiful day today, one of many we enjoy here on Beaver Island," he said. Adams proceeded to ramble on about all the blessings the Mormons enjoyed on the island, under the capable leadership of Strang. The people in the audience nodded their heads dutifully, although Adams was starting to bore them. When Adams saw that he was losing their attention, he got down to business.

"The reason for this gathering today is to share great news with you, but first you must understand the teachings of the Bible." Adams looked at the audience and was pleased to see their attention had perked up. He continued. "We, as Saints, believe that David was king in Israel, and that he was chosen by God, and that the Bible tells us of more 'kings and priests to enter our world on earth.' We believe that kings are below prophets, and that King David and King Solomon were anointed by prophets because the 'less is blessed of the better,' prophets being better than kings. We believe that James J. Strang was chosen by God to be a priestly King, subordinate to his office of Prophet, and that he is of the lineage of David. Indeed, even Joseph Smith taught that a literal kingdom would be restored, and we know now that James J. Strang is to be the fulfillment."

Adams paused, looking at faces in the audience to see if they were following what he said. Strang had written the speech, and Adams thought it a bit confusing, but he went along with the Prophet's desires. As he looked out, he saw a lot of puzzlement. People were either waiting patiently for more talk that would clarify the opening statement, or whispering to the person next to them, no doubt asking if they understood. Adams decided to do what he did best – go off script.

"Therefore, in accordance with the Book of Mormon and in accordance with the words of God, James J. Strang will not only be our prophet but our King as well. As King he will lead our people as a gentle and generous king who protects and seeks justice for all the persecuted Latter-Day Saints.

"So now I ask you all to stand up and pay homage to your King of Beaver Island."

The people who were seated now rose, still in a mild state of confusion. Backstage, Strang had opened Adams' trunk and donned the contents within. A moment later Strang stepped through the curtain that Adams held parted for him. He was wearing a full-length red cape trimmed in white fur. On his head was a tin crown with colored stones pasted on the front of it. He carried a scepter turned from an oak burl.

"Welcome and bow, or curtsy, to your King James!" Adams ordered, and then turned to demonstrate. He bowed a deep, long bow to Strang.

Lucy didn't bow or curtsy. She looked at Mary, her mouth agape. "King?" Lucy asked. "He is crowning himself king of the island?"

"I had no idea this was in the making," Mary said. "He always dreamed of royalty and fame – I guess now he's given himself the royalty. I dread to think how he'll earn his fame."

Strang held the scepter up in his left hand.

"I will stretch out my arm over the lakes and fields and flowers of our home here," he began. "Beaver Island shall be a stronghold of safety to my people, and they that are faithful and obey me I will give them great prosperity, and such as they have not had before, and unto Beaver Island shall be the gathering of my people, and there shall the oppressed flee for safety and none shall hurt or molest them." Strang spoke with a mixture of legalese and preacher. His rich baritone voice carried easily to the people standing in the back of the clearing.

Strang continued. "I have received a revelation from the angels that great calamities are coming on the church, and if some among us scatter, the ungodly of the world shall swallow them up; but if they gather unto me,

I will keep them under the shadow of my wing, and anyone who threatens the safety and well-being of my people shall be purged from the island, for I will do it. But dark clouds are gathering, because the angels have spoken to me of troubles ahead."

The speech was both impressive and frightening. The Saints suddenly had a king and the king had been warned of trouble ahead by none other than angels. And if any of them tried to leave the island to avoid the trouble, they would be swallowed up by evil forces.

"I have had another revelation, delivered to me by the Angel Gabriel," Strang went on. "We are going to bring polygamy and spiritual wifery to the island," he announced.

A gasp went up throughout the crowd. Polygamy was one thing Strang had railed against time and again in his sermons, calling polygamists twisted snakes and amoral beasts who would suffer the buffetings of hell.

"The Angel Gabriel showed me that polygamy will liberate and elevate our women by allowing them to choose the best possible mate based upon any factors deemed important to them—even if that mate is already married to someone else.

"Rather than being forced to wed corrupt and degraded sires due to the scarcity of more suitable men, a woman of our faith can marry the man she sees as the most compatible to herself, the best candidate to father her children and give her the finest possible life, no matter how many other wives he might have."

Eliza grabbed Lucy's forearm and squeezed it. "This is exactly why I didn't want to become a Mormon," she hissed. "We heard Strang speak in New York and he promised that polygamy would never be a part of his faith." Her fists clenched and unclenched repeatedly as she spoke.

Lucy was frozen. It was all too much to process. James had just crowned himself king of the island, and now was telling the women they could marry any man they chose, even if he was already taken.

Strang pulled a rolled piece of parchment out of the deep pocket in his robe and unrolled it. He began reading:

"In other proclamations, I deem that Paradise Bay will now be called St. James Harbor. Our community, which is growing rapidly around the harbor, will be the City of St. James. We will welcome with open arms and warm hearts any and all people who wish to join our faith and live according to our rules. We will thrive and become one of the most highly regarded, bountiful, blessed places in Michigan, nay, in the country and in the world."

Quite a few Mormons cheered at this. Strang then seated himself on the handsome wood chair, looking small in comparison to the magnificent seatback that towered behind him. In that moment Archie realized why Strang wanted such an imposing chair. It wasn't a chair he wanted, it was a throne.

Adams took center stage again.

"There is one more thing," Adams said to the audience. "It is my honor and privilege to introduce King James' new spiritual wife, Elvira Field Strang." With that, he pulled the curtain aside again and Elvira, wearing a pale blue dress that was overlaid with delicate white lace, emerged onto the stage.

Mary gasped in horror. It was Charles Douglass who stepped forward from behind the curtain. She had no trouble recognizing the nephew's soft chin and dark eyes. But Charles had let his dark hair grow since Mary last saw him, and had transformed into a young woman with breasts, a small waist and slim, curved hips. Mary fell back onto the bench and would have toppled to the ground if Lucy hadn't caught her.

A stunned hush fell over the rest of the crowd, until someone finally shouted, "That's Charles Douglass! That's your nephew!"

The crowd started buzzing. "I knew there was something off about that boy," MacCulloch said to his wife.

Lorenzo Hickey realized in that moment that his wife Anne had been right about Strang in the letters she'd written to him, the very letters that had caused him to be suspended from the church and made him so distraught he ended up in a lunatic asylum. Strang *had* been fornicating with a young woman, and the young woman was the person Strang had been passing off as his nephew. Anne had fled the island after discovering Strang's adulterous behavior and when Lorenzo returned to Beaver Island he had been unable to find her. Now Hickey had no wife and Strang had two of them. Yet he'd come to see that he needed the sanctuary and support of the church. What was he to think now? While Hickey pondered this, the audience grew vocal.

"You can't marry your nephew!" One of the new converts yelled. "Is she even a girl?"

"We didn't sign up for polygamy," said another.

Strang raised his oak burl scepter and waved it at the crowd. "I am a mere servant of the Lord, and I am doing as I've been told to do by His messenger the Angel Gabriel. I was told by the angels to disguise Elvira as a boy only for her own safety as we traveled through a country beset with evildoers. I am powerless to oppose His wishes. Since I have also been given a revelation about a great calamity that is coming soon, it is imperative that I follow the Angel Gabriel's instructions. If you all know what is good for you, you will do the same."

The crowd fell silent. They greatly feared the burning flames of Hell and the buffetings of Satan that could be their fate if they disobeyed God's wishes. It was really not a choice at all; they would do as their prophet commanded so as to avoid a vividly terrifying punishment.

After the crowd calmed down, Strang took Elvira's hand. "I trust you all will welcome my new wife to the island, and will make sure she is happy and accepted. And I hope you will all wish her a happy birthday. She turned 20 today."

Elvira curtsied and then smiled smugly at the audience. Like it or not, she was their new queen.

Mary struggled to regain her composure. "Did you know about this?" she asked Lucy sharply. "You acted peculiarly that day we saw Charles Douglass in town."

"I had no idea James was going to do this," Lucy said. "I knew that Charles was really a girl – I discovered that quite by accident when I went to his – or her – room to deliver extra blankets – but I thought James was keeping a concubine that he would eventually cast aside. I certainly didn't condone his behavior, but this? I'm not clever enough to have imagined this."

"You could have told me," Mary said. Her face was drawn tight with anger. "You could have spared me the public humiliation of learning this today!"

Lucy looked down at her lap, embarrassed by her duplicity. "I'm so sorry, Mary," she said quietly. "I wanted to spare your feelings. I was hoping the situation would resolve itself."

Mary softened slightly with Lucy's apology.

"James was spending a lot of time alone with Charles Douglass on mission trips," Mary said. "Now I know why. He was fornicating with a young girl."

The color rose high in Lucy's cheeks, this time not from shame, but from jealousy. She was feeling jealous of the petite little Elvira, who now stood next to James, holding his hand.

"I think I'm going to be sick," Mary said and put her head between her knees for a moment. Then her head popped back up as a new thought entered her mind. "Oh no, do you suppose James is going to bring her into our home? I will *NOT* accept that!"

"I don't blame you one bit for feeling that way," Lucy said. "But do you have a choice? He's the king now, and your husband. I don't envy you." Lucy tried to imagine being in Mary's position and the thought of it made her want to slap him.

King James was oblivious to their conversation. He had stepped down from the stage with Elvira and was shaking hands with the men and wives in his circle of 12, who, after recovering from their initial shock, were congratulating him on his royalty and new wife. Some of the men gave Strang knowing winks and sniggered as he passed by.

Adams clanged a cymbal he'd stolen from the orchestra pit in New York City to get the crowd's attention. "We shall follow the King in a procession to the tabernacle for a celebration. Please fall in line."

Strang stepped off the stage and started up the path to town, followed by Adams and the rest of the circle of 12. The remaining members of the congregation followed accordingly.

All but Mary Strang and Eliza Bowman.

The two women went with Lucy back to her home. They were too stunned and angry to take part in any celebration.

They took seats in Lucy's kitchen, around the worn wooden table. Lucy put a pot of water on to boil for tea. Then she went over to a cupboard in the corner of the kitchen and opened the bottom door. She pulled out a bottle of scotch whiskey. Antoine had loved scotch. He never drank excessive amounts, but enjoyed the mellow warmth that blanketed his brain when he sipped it.

"I think this is called for, under the circumstances," Lucy said as she set the bottle in the middle of the table.

"We don't drink spirits," Mary said.

"Well, maybe you should," Lucy said.

"I'm with Lucy," Eliza said. "Why should we follow Mormon rules when the rules keep changing? It's like trying to play hopscotch while someone keeps redrawing the lines. I don't know when to jump or where to land."

Lucy took three cups from a cupboard and poured a healthy shot of scotch in each. She set one in front of each of them.

"Drink up. It will make you feel better, Mary. Actually, it will make you feel worse, but not until later."

Eliza gulped her scotch quickly, then made a face. Mary sipped hers timidly. Lucy shot hers back and put her empty cup on the table.

"I never saw this coming, ever," Mary said, holding her head in her hands.

"Nor did I. I must confess, Mary, I got to know James fairly well before you came to the island. At first I was put off by him. Then I found his enthusiasm infectious, and his wit and humor were most welcome to my quiet home. But then he seemed to change right in front of me, like a preying mantis changes its colors to blend into whatever nature surrounds it..."

"I know. That's James. He says one thing on one day and the complete opposite on another day. He will change his positions and speak of revelations that are tailor-made to suit his needs."

Eliza poured more scotch into her cup.

"How could you live with such a conniving, two-faced man?" she demanded of Mary. "I gave up my whole life in New York to come here. Your husband spoke movingly about how wonderful things would be here, and he said in no uncertain terms that he would never follow the sinful ways of Brigham Young and allow polygamy!"

Mary drank more of her scotch. "You think I'm pleased with this? He told me the same thing for years! And now I'm the one who has to deal with a second wife in my midst. At least you don't have that burden to carry, Eliza. Oh Lord, how am I going to do this?" It was a rhetorical question, and she looked for the rhetorical answer in the bottom of her cup, which she drained in two quick swallows.

"One day at a time, that's how," Lucy said. "You are his first wife, which, in my opinion, makes you his only legal wife. You have power over him through that."

The women lapsed into a muted silence and drank more scotch. There were no words to say, only heavy thoughts and feelings to deal with.

Out of sight and out of mind was Huldy, who had quietly retreated to her new home in the woods. She hadn't needed a sign interpreter to tell her what happened at Font Lake. Strang appearing with a crown and royal robe made it clear he was to be their king. The little woman who joined him in a fancy dress that looked like a wedding dress held his hand and stood by his side, smiling. The look of disbelief and anguish on his wife Mary's face explained it all.

Huldy sat at her little table and thought about the future. She didn't know what it would hold; she was just glad she would be isolated from most of the Mormon developments.

Huldy couldn't hear the celebration going on in town at the unfinished tabernacle. The Mormons were dancing to the lively tunes of fiddle players, celebrating Strang's coronation. There was a feast waiting for them, which had been arranged by Phebe Wentworth and Ruth Ann Bedford. Lanterns hung from tree branches and poles, allowing the celebration to go on into the evening. While Strang didn't allow spirits, he was very much in favor of celebrating with dancing and music, which he found to be uplifting, especially when the celebration was all for him.

Strang noticed his first wife's absence, but didn't concern himself with it. *She's in shock, but she'll come around,* he thought. *She is my wife. She must obey me just as I must obey God. And God has declared to me that this is how we are meant to live.* Then he swept Elvira into his arms and danced her around the room.

CHAPTER 29
LATE JULY, 1850

The morning after Proclamation Day, which also became known as Coronation Day, Lucy headed over to Pisgah Bay to clear her mind. She took off her moccasins and sat in the sand where she had once sat with James after picking mushrooms and wild onions. That had been a very good day. This one was quite the opposite.

She buried her toes in the warm sand. It always gave her a sense of peace to sit near the shore, sifting sand through her fingers and looking at the lake, but that day it wasn't working. When she heard twigs snapping on the path to the beach, she turned to see Strang emerge from the cedar trees.

"I thought you might be here," Strang said to her as he sat down next to her, uninvited.

"You're the last person I want to see right now," Lucy told him coldly.

"Lucy, I need to explain," Strang said, but she stopped him before he could continue.

"There's nothing to explain. I figured out you were an adulterer, a promiscuous man who cheated on his wife the day I discovered Charles was actually a woman. Now I come to find out you're a sly-witted horned beast, shoving polygamy down the throats of your followers just so you can justify your carnal appetites. It's a disgrace."

"It's not a disgrace, it's spiritual wifery," Strang said defensively. "Mary is my first, legal wife, and Elvira is my second, spiritual wife. And I was opposed to spiritual wifery, very much so, until I was visited by an angel who told me differently."

"Oh for the love of all that is decent, drop your story about angels coming to visit you and telling you how to live your life. I don't believe a word of it."

"That, perhaps, is because you're not a believer," James said contemptuously. "If you believed, you might hear them for yourself."

"What I am hearing right now is more crap than an ox could produce in a week of eating spring rye!" Lucy was shouting but she didn't care.

"Lucy, lower your voice. You're behaving in a most uncomely manner."

"I will not tolerate your podsnappery! You think your stories of angels and visions and revelations from god make you better than me? You are sorely mistaken, James. I speak the truth. You wouldn't know the truth if it stepped on your head." Lucy gave him a searing look that would have peeled the skin off a rabbit if one had hopped in between them.

Strang suddenly slid close to Lucy and grabbed her by her upper arms. He pulled her even closer, so that their faces were no more than six inches apart. She could feel his breath on her face.

"You want truth, Lucy? Here's some truth for you! You're the one I love! You're the one I wanted to marry! But you would never accept such a thing. You can't understand how a man can love his wife and love another woman as well. Elvira would never have turned my head if you had loved me. So in some ways, this is your fault!"

With that, he suddenly released his grip on her arms, pulled her body next to his and kissed her. She didn't resist. He kissed her more deeply, exploring her wide, warm mouth.

Lucy found herself allowing the kiss, enjoying it, getting lost in it. She hadn't been kissed by a man since Antoine died, which was a decade ago. It felt delicious to be held and kissed in such a passionate way. She returned his passion with an open mouth and welcoming tongue.

Then she came to her senses, slowly but surely. She broke the embrace.

"That will never happen again, James. And none of this is my fault. Don't try to blame your shameful behavior on me. I'm not some silly, love-stricken girl who will fall for that trick. You can't hold me accountable for your lustful feelings."

She gazed at him steadily while she spoke, and it unnerved him.

He longed to hold her and kiss her again, to sop up her passion like dry bread in a soup bowl. But he knew she would rebuff him. She was like a polarized magnet to him – sometimes he was drawn to her, then sometimes she repelled him, depending on whether or not his moral compass was pointing true north.

—◆•◆—

With the speed of a lightning bolt splitting a tree in two, word of the new king and his royal proclamations ripped through the island community.

Mary Strang tried to hold her head high, but the weight of her husband's announcements made her feel like someone had put a boulder on her head.

To her relief, James hadn't moved Elvira into their home; instead, he created a private room for her on the second floor of the newspaper print shop. Mary didn't want to think about what went on there, but at least it wasn't taking place right under her nose.

Strang's Circle of 12 Apostles grew emboldened by the king's new proclamations. They mounted a large wood sign at the entrance of the harbor, prominently bearing the name "St. James Harbor." The locals who had unofficially called it Paradise Bay for their entire lifetimes were ill-equipped to do anything about it. Strang had a posse of his own men guarding the sign round the clock. Another sign was posted by the side of the road, directly across from the main dock where newcomers disembarked. It said, "Welcome to the City of Saint James."

George Adams left on a mission trip the day after the coronation, and returned a month later with a new young wife, Louisa Cogswell, the wealthy widow of a prominent man from Baltimore. Adams told everyone the sad story of his first wife Caroline, who had been stricken ill with consumption and died in New Jersey.

"He sure didn't waste any time finding someone to fill the void next to him in bed," Lucy said to Mary one day. Lucy had a particularly low regard for Adams, who she believed to be a moderately talented fraud.

"I'll miss Caroline. She was a good woman," Mary said. "We spent quite a bit of time together back east when our husbands were doing mission work." In the month since Strang's coronation and ensuing royal proclamations, Mary had resigned herself to the polygamous situation she found herself in. She couldn't see any way to fix or improve it; the deed was done.

Louisa Cogswell Adams was one of the few Mormons who was well-liked by the Irish fishermen. She was young and pretty, with her cheeks rouged and her lips stained bright red. Her pert figure was on display with her dresses that fit tightly down to her hips. She played cards and drank with them in their shanties. Rumor had it she did more than play cards with them. Her behavior was not that of a well-born widow from Baltimore, which suited the Gentile fishermen just fine.

Phebe Wentworth, whose nosiness was in direct proportion to the size of her sniffer, was one of the few Mormon women who liked Louisa, mostly because Louisa fed her a steady diet of gossip. One morsel was just too delicious for Phebe to keep to herself. She hustled up to the Strang house, knowing the king was not home at the time. She found Mary talking to Lucy outside, leaning on the picket fence.

"Sorry to interrupt, and you know I hate to be the bearer of bad news," Phebe began.

Lucy and Mary knew nothing of the sort was true. Phebe loved to be the bearer of bad news – it was good news that bored her.

"What is it, Phebe?" Mary asked.

"I was talking to Louisa Adams, George's new wife, just trying to be friendly and make her feel at home, and, well, she told me something I think you should know."

Mary waited, not saying anything, which was most annoying to Phebe. She wanted Mary to beg for the information. Phebe finally plowed ahead.

"We all know about your husband's new revelation about polygamy, and we know about, er, his, uh, new addition to your family – "

"Phebe, I have no desire to discuss our private business with you, so please come to the point, if there is one."

Phebe tilted her tuberous nose upward defensively.

"It would appear that your husband has designs on Peter McKinley's daughter Beth. He wants to take her as another wife." Phebe smiled a wicked, salacious smile.

"Pete McKinley's daughter Beth!" Lucy said. "She's just a child, no more than fifteen years old!"

"Yes, well, I guess our king is staking out his claim for her."

"I don't believe a word of what you say, Phebe, and I certainly don't believe anything that comes from Louisa Adams," Mary said. "Go away, and keep your nasty rumors to yourself."

With a grunt, Phebe sashayed away, hips swinging and nose leading the way.

"I just don't believe that, not one bit," Mary said to Lucy.

"I don't either," Lucy agreed. "From what I've seen, James has been too busy with mission work and building the tabernacle; he couldn't possibly have time to go courting." Out of respect for Mary, Lucy didn't mention the hours she knew James spent in the private room above the print shop with Elvira.

"He'll be home tomorrow. If there's any truth to it, I intend to find out immediately and put a stop to it."

When Strang returned home the following day, he looked exhausted. Boat travel and mission work was taking its toll on him, along with trying to keep things calm and orderly on the island.

Mary approached Strang with the gossip she'd heard from Phebe.

"There is not one bit of truth to that!" he exploded. "Louisa Adams is guilty of slander against me, her king and prophet, and I'll not have it! I will put her on trial for that!"

Wasting no time, Strang called upon his deputies, Chidester, Pierce and Bowman, to help him. He told them of the false accusation that had been leveled against him.

"Find out everything you can about Louisa Adams. Find out why she would spread such a lie about me!"

George Adams was away on business on Mackinac Island, which made it easier for the three deputies to do their snooping. That evening they saw Louisa enter a Gentile cabin and heard her laughing with whomever was inside with her. Peeking through the window, they saw her soft, plump legs up in the air, completely naked. And they saw the strong, freckled back of an Irishman in between those bare legs.

Knowing the woman was fully occupied and in no position to go rushing home, they went to Adam's house and started going through drawers and cupboards. They found a valise that no doubt belonged to Adams, and they helped themselves to the contents inside.

The men took the letters and papers to Constable Joshua Miller, who was better at reading than they were. By the light of his lantern, he began reading the documents.

"Here's a letter dated a month ago, from a Mrs. Adams in New Jersey," Miller said, initially confused. "But Mrs. Adams is here on the island, and has been for longer than a month."

"What does it say?" Bowman asked.

"It says, 'George, my dearest, I'm happy to report that I am making a full recovery from my consumption. I miss you very much and look forward to your return. I wish you didn't have to spend so much time on that island of Brother Strang's. Please hurry home to me. Devotedly yours, Caroline.'"

"It would appear that Adam's first wife has made a remarkable recovery from her death that George reported," Chidester said.

"So Louisa Adams is his second wife? But if his first wife isn't dead..."

"Then he's a polygamist," Chidester finished.

"Strang supports polygamy, so I don't see much of a problem here," Bowman said.

"The problem isn't polygamy, the problem is that Louisa is speaking blasphemously about our king, accusing him of seeking a child's hand in marriage," Miller said.

"I think we'd better report this to the king. He can decide what to do about it."

———————◆◆————————

Strang was a man who harbored grudges and sought revenge. He fully believed that wrongs against him must be righted. Sinners should be punished. He was also a man who could wait patiently for just the right time to exact his revenge.

When he spotted Louisa on the road in front of the harbor a few days later, he casually confronted her.

"Louisa, might I ask where you got the idea that I was seeking to marry the young McKinley girl?"

Louisa was taken aback by Strang's forthright approach. In her view, rumors and gossip were to be dealt with behind people's backs, not to their faces.

"Why George, of course," she said, the blush deepening on her already unnaturally pink cheeks. "He told me he saw you speaking intimately with the girl at McKinley's store."

"Yet George drew no such conclusion as you seem to have done, and has said nothing of the sort to me, or to anyone else."

Louisa fidgeted nervously, shifting her weight from one dainty foot to the other.

"Louisa, where did you say you're from?" Strang asked, quickly changing the subject. That made Louisa even more uncomfortable.

"Baltimore. My dear late husband, Alfred Cogswell, was a very successful merchant there. Owned a pharmacy on Broad Street." Her voice quavered even though she was trying to sound calm and authoritative.

"Have a good day, Louisa," Strang said, and turned on his heel and walked toward the tabernacle, leaving Louisa confused and nervous.

Miller and Chidester went to the tabernacle to find Strang, where he was overseeing the construction and trying to hurry the workmen along.

"We found something of interest, King James," they said to him. Strang immediately perked up.

"Let's take a walk," Strang said.

Miller had painstakingly copied every word from the letter Caroline Adams had written to her husband. The men then returned the letter and other documents to George Adams' valise before George returned. Now, as they walked along the shore of St. James Harbor, Miller produced the replica of the letter and showed it to Strang.

"George lied," he said. "His wife is still very much alive, and apparently doing quite well."

Strang took the letter, folded it and tucked it in his inner coat pocket.

"Thank you, gentlemen, you have done good work. When is George due back on the island?"

"Next week, I believe," Pierce said. "Can't stand to be away from that new wife of his, so maybe sooner."

CHAPTER 30

AUGUST, 1850

"Oh my." Mary had nothing else to say as she read the letter from Caroline Adams, her dear, dead friend who was not quite so dead after all.

"What is it?" Lucy asked. She'd walked with Mary to the post office on Whiskey Point to make her feel safe. Some of the Gentile fishermen had taken to bullying the Mormons when they stepped on Whiskey Point, which Lucy found extremely distasteful. The rowdies had heard Lucy cuss and seen her sucker punch a roughneck once, so they steered clear of her and whomever she was accompanying.

"A letter from Caroline Adams," Mary said.

"Oh, how sad. She must have written you just before she passed."

"On the contrary. She's quite well, and venting her spleen about the poor treatment she's suffered at George's hand."

"She's alive?"

"Yes. She says here that she got sick and George abandoned her. She's been writing him letters but he never responds. I guess the scoundrel found that saucy Louisa more to his liking and simply rid himself of Caroline."

"Awful! I never did care for that man. He's not worth the skin on a fart."

"I wonder if James knows. He's already quite angry with Louisa for spreading rumors about him. This will really put him over the edge."

"Are you going to tell him?"

"I think I must. He may have adopted the practice of polygamy, but he certainly wouldn't allow the mistreatment of a first wife. I'll give him that."

Lucy thought the same thing. She found it deplorable that James was now promoting polygamy, but she had to at least give him credit for treating both of his wives decently. It reminded her of white people who trapped and caught rabbits for pets, and then they treated them kindly and fed them well. The rabbits weren't happy with the situation, but they weren't entirely miserable either. Perhaps the rabbits preferred that to the fate Lucy would have given them – a quick death and into the stew pot.

"I think I'd better get back and let James know about this," Mary said, walking quickly out of the post office with the letter clutched tightly in her hand.

"I'll walk you back, then leave you to it. Let me know how it goes."

＋•＋

Strang listened while Mary read Caroline's letter to him, although he already knew from his deputies that Caroline was alive and well.

"That's it," he said when Mary finished. "When George gets back, those two are going on trial with the council of elders. This is unacceptable! Louisa slandered me! She accused me of having designs on a mere child, a 15-year-old girl! Heaven only knows who else heard her scurrilous lies about me! They're going to be excommunicated and cast to the buffetings of Satan!"

"James, I think the bigger issue is how George treated his first wife, not what his new wife said about you." In Strang's heightened state of fury, Mary decided not to mention that she knew Elvira was just barely 17 – two years older than the McKinley girl – when he started canoodling with her.

"The biggest issue is clearly that Louisa spread falsehoods about me and besmirched my good name! I am the king here, and such behavior cannot be tolerated!"

Mary could see Strang was having one of his childish tantrums. She didn't press the issue any further, but she planned on attending the trial with the council of elders.

When George returned a week later, the deputies Bowman, Chidester and Pierce had already unearthed more information about Louisa. The Irishman Teddy Duffy, who had enjoyed copulating with the luscious

Louisa, had no problem talking about her. He reported that when he told her he worried about lying with a married woman, and a widow at that, she told him, "Oh, don't worry, I'm not really married. And I'm not really a widow either. The fellow I lived with back in Baltimore isn't dead; and for the record, I never married him either."

After several whiskeys, she also let it slip that she was a 'working girl' from Boston.

"Working girl?" Teddy had asked her. "What type of job did you have?"

"The type of job I can do lying on my back," she had replied with a laugh.

In short, Louisa was exactly the type of woman that struck Adams' fancy – low-browed, loose and completely unburdened by any of the social niceties that made society women such a bore. He loved her desperately.

When Strang informed him that he and Louisa were going to be called to trial by the council of elders and Louisa might be excommunicated, Adams was beside himself.

"King James, I love Louisa with all my heart, more than I love my life! Please go easy on her."

"It's not up to me, it's up to the elders," Strang said. But everyone knew better. The trial and the council of elders were all show; nothing more than a group of obsequious men licking the boots of Strang in hopes of having favors granted to them.

The trial was held in the unfinished tabernacle; no roof was needed on the dry summer day. Louisa was dressed demurely, wearing a simple brown cotton dress with an unadorned neckline. It fit loosely, hiding her curves and making her less alluring. She also had no false color added to her cheeks and lips. George went in the opposite direction, dressing in his magnificently elaborate King Richard III costume. He hoped it would give the illusion of such grandeur that Strang couldn't possibly dethrone him from his high position in the church.

"You're a common prostitute!" said Lorenzo Hickey.

"You have deceived us about your background," said George Miller, father of the local constable.

"You lied about being married to George. And George, you lied about being married to Louisa. You are sleeping with her outside the covenant of marriage. You are both adulterers!" said Dr. MacCulloch.

Strang stood up. He was wearing the same heavy cloak he wore at his coronation.

"Gentlemen, let's stick with the most insufferable charge. This woman smeared my good name! She spread lies about me and made untoward suggestions that I was seeking the hand of a girl too young for marriage. That is what this trial is about!"

Although Mary wasn't supposed to speak, she couldn't contain herself.

"George Adams abandoned his lawful wife, left her to die, and started cavorting with this woman of ill repute. That is the most egregious of wrongdoings here."

As of one mind, Strang and all the councilmen turned and glared at Mary.

"You are speaking out of turn, Mary," Strang said, rebuking his own wife.

"James – King James – you know in your heart that to abandon your lawful, FIRST wife, is unconscionable." Mary wasn't about to back down on this issue.

"We will consider your words, Mary," Strang said. "You may leave now."

The trio of deputies rose from their seats in the back to escort Mary out. They heard Strang's unspoken message loud and clear; Mary was to leave. If they had to carry her out kicking and thrashing, they would.

Knowing she was outnumbered and out-muscled, Mary left of her own volition.

"Apostles, elders, what say you with regard to the charge that Louisa Cogswell Adams defamed the King of Beaver Island by spreading insidious, unfounded rumors about him?" Strang asked his audience. "With a yea or nay, please vote to excommunicate the so-called Mrs. Adams."

"Yea!" they all called out.

"And now the nays," Strang said, knowing there would be silence.

"Nay!" shouted Adams, flinging his heavy Richard III costume cloak dramatically to the side while he raised his right hand high into the air.

"Brother George – at least for the moment you are still a brother – you are not allowed to vote in this matter. Sit down." Although a much smaller man than Adams, Strang was able to make him cringe from the power of his deep baritone voice and glittering copper eyes. Adams sat down. Louisa was excommunicated.

Adams was on trial next. After much discussion, the council found themselves in disagreement about Adams' charges. Did he truly believe he thought his first wife was dying and would be dead in a matter of hours, as he claimed? Did Louisa Cogswell fool him with her story of being a wealthy widow, or did he know her true nature?

Even Strang was hesitant to cast out George Adams, one of his biggest supporters, out of his church. Who else could prepare the impressive fireworks that dazzled the masses as the sign of angels?

In the end, the council decided to indefinitely suspend Adams from the church and strip him of his high status as an apostle and a member of the council.

"The woman, Louisa Cogswell, must leave the island immediately," Strang said.

"But James, I can't live without her!" Adams wailed.

"Then I guess you must leave the island as well." As much as it pained Strang, an example had to be made of George Adams.

George Adams and Louisa Cogswell packed their things and left Beaver Island in disgrace the following day.

By the time Adams and Louisa were boarding a schooner bound for Mackinac Island, Mary Strang had heard the news of the council vote.

She confronted Strang at supper.

"So you found Louisa guilty of defamation and slander where your name was concerned, but you brought no charges against her for adultery, fornication with Gentiles or lying about her background?"

"Those charges are immaterial." Strang said dismissively. "What does it matter? She's gone."

"And George, you suspended him for adultery but there was no punishment for abandoning his lawful wife?"

"We weren't sure about that."

"You weren't sure? I showed you the letter from Caroline! Your own men showed you a letter from Caroline from some time ago, while she was still waiting for George to return to her! Letters he received, so he knew she lived."

"What's done is done, nothing else matters."

"Well, it matters to me. If you're doling out punishment, it should be for the proper crime."

"Mary, please stop! You don't understand the intricacies of these matters."

"Oh, I think I understand quite well. All that matters to you is you, James." Mary turned and walked away before Strang could respond.

As he watched her walk away from him, he started to think that his first wife was becoming way more trouble than she was worth. *Another problem I have to dispose of,* he thought to himself.

CHAPTER 31

SEPTEMBER, 1850

"You're actually going to pay the damn tax?" Tom Bennett asked Will and Teddy incredulously.

"Dolan says we should. I'm against it though," Teddy said.

"Your father supports this, Will?" Bennett asked.

"You know how Papa is; he just wants everyone to get along. He told me we've been making a good living off fishing, I live for free in his house, Teddy lives in a cabin Papa helped him build, and we don't have many expenses. He said to think of the 10 percent as a business tax, not a tithe to the Mormons."

"Well, I'm not paying it. I've got a wife and three kids to feed. I'm not helping to pay for the tabernacle or newspaper shop or whatever else they plan to build here."

"I can't say as I blame you, Tom, just saying what we decided to do," Will said sympathetically.

The men were preparing their nets and fishing boats while they discussed the tithe, or tax, that the Mormons had recently announced would be charged to everyone on the island. Chidester, Pierce and Bowman – the constable's deputies – would be calling on all the homes of everyone on the island and would be expecting to collect 10 percent of their income.

Teddy and Will loaded the last of the gear into their boat, then helped Tom cast off before getting back into their boat.

"Guess we better get to fishing, and hope for a helluva catch if we have to give 10 percent of it away," Teddy called to Tom as they all hoisted their sails and headed out of St. James Harbor.

"If I get a helluva catch, then I'm spending 10 percent on a new dress for my wife, not the Mormons," Tom replied.

Huldy was up early, as usual, about the same time the fishermen were leaving the harbor. She loved watching the sun rise through the leaves that flickered in the morning breeze. She was serenely contented in her new little home.

Although she wanted to keep her location as secret as possible, Lucy had finally talked her into sharing the location with Archie and Millie Donnelly. Huldy was going to need a lot of firewood to get her through the winter, and plenty of canned goods as well. Archie, a man with a heart as big as his body, was happy to lend his strong back to Huldy. He chopped and split wood for her until the entire exterior south side of her cabin was neatly stacked with firewood.

"You'll probably be needing more than that come the middle of winter, so I'll split plenty more for you this fall," Archie told her. "Right now, I need to keep building while the weather's good." He said the words while making hand gestures to the wood and the sun and the horizon, and Huldy more or less understood what he was saying.

Millie's gift to Huldy needed no words. She and Archie delivered a wheelbarrow full of canned goods to Huldy on a late summer day. Millie loved to can, a chore most women performed to survive, not as a passion. To Millie, the act of canning food was a labor of love, and Millie loved to share vegetables and fruit with her husband and friends in the dead of winter.

Huldy was very grateful to them, and glad she'd taken Lucy's advice to invite the Donnellys into her world.

The Donnellys were leaving just as Eliza emerged from the hidden path. She tried to visit her sister a few times a week, but it wasn't always possible. Nathan was very suspicious of his sister-in-law and was forever trying to discover Huldy's whereabouts.

"Why do you care so much where my sister is living?" Eliza asked Nathan one time when he was pestering her about Huldy. "You didn't want her in our home, now she has a place of her own. You should be delighted."

"I'm a deputy on this island. It's my responsibility to know where the island residents are living, in case of emergency or something."

Eliza let out a sharp laugh. "Oh, please, Nathan, that's nonsense. You don't need to know where everyone lives. I'm not going to tell you where Huldy is because I don't want you harassing her. She has a right to privacy."

Now Eliza took a seat at Huldy's little table and sipped the coffee her sister had given her.

"What's new in town?" Huldy signed. "Is Nathan treating you all right?"

"Same as always, I guess. Busier, now that the king has declared everyone must tithe 10 percent to the church and the deputies will be going around enforcing the law and collecting the money."

"Everyone?" Huldy signed. "Gentiles too?"

"They're going to try to collect from everyone. I don't know how well that will go over with the Gentiles."

"I'm glad I don't earn a living," Huldy signed. "I'd hate to have Nathan pay me a visit and demand money from me." Huldy smiled as she signed her words, to assure her sister she was just kidding. Sort of.

Eliza spent a productive day with her sister. They picked blackberries and thimbleberries, and gathered edible mushrooms and greens.

"I'll take the thimbleberries to Millie, she knows how to make wonderful jam out of them," Eliza signed to her sister as she lifted the sack of berries from her sister's shoulder and left her with the sack of blackberries and greens.

As she left, Eliza thought again how surprisingly wonderful it had turned out to have her sister on the island with her. After such a rocky start, with Nathan refusing to have her at their home, to awkwardly living with the Watsons, Eliza was amazed at how well her sister had adapted.

She was thinking those warm thoughts about her sister when she got home. All the happy thoughts drained from her when she saw Nathan sitting at their table, holding a wet cloth on the side of his face.

"What happened?" she said, lifting the cloth to see his swollen eye and reddened cheekbone.

"That mule of a man Tom Bennett is refusing to pay his tithe," Nathan said. "He managed to land one punch before we took care of him."

Eliza cringed inwardly. "What did you do to him?"

"What we needed to do, that's what! He's surely learned his lesson now."

The next morning, Eliza went to visit Tom Bennett's house, hoping to catch his wife Alice when the children were napping. She didn't know Alice well, since she was a Gentile who preferred to avoid the company of Mormons, but she liked what little she did know of her.

Alice opened the door to Eliza with a grim look on her face.

"What did they do to Tom?"

"Beat him to a pulp, just about," Alice said. "Three against one, hardly a fair fight. He's in bed now, resting. Couldn't go fish today. He's afraid some of his ribs are broken."

"Oh, Alice, I'm so sorry. I really am. I wish it hadn't come to this."

"It's not your fault, Eliza, and I'm grateful to you for coming to check on us. You can tell your husband and the other Mormons that they've won. Tom and I have decided to move to Cross Village. I have people there."

"You're really leaving Beaver Island?" Eliza was suddenly frightened to hear of a decent Gentile family leaving the island.

"Yes. I'm going to leave first with the children while Tom packs up our things. He'll join us later. He wants us off the island as soon as possible. Sorry to say, but he's worried the Mormons might decide to hurt other members of our family if he doesn't cooperate. And there's no chance he'll pay them a cent. He's a proud, stubborn man."

Nothing Eliza could think of to say was right, so she said nothing. She simply took Alice's hand and squeezed it. "I'll miss you, Alice. Have a safe trip."

"Thank you," Alice said. "You take care of yourself, Eliza."

Eliza didn't know that those were the last words Alice would ever share with her.

CHAPTER 32
LATE SEPTEMBER, 1850

Tom Bennett stood on the pier with his wife, Alice, and his three daughters. The youngest, Dottie, was in Alice's arms. Caroline and Catherine were running up and down the pier, greatly excited about their upcoming boat trip.

"Careful girls, you don't want to fall in!" Tom called to them. "That water's plenty cold!"

"Yes, Papa," said Caroline, the eldest at age six. Catherine, running close on her big sister's heels, was four. She almost ran into the back of her sister when the elder child slowed abruptly to a walk. In Catherine's hand was her favorite doll, which she had named May. May was made of dried corn kernels stuffed into a cotton body. Her head was a chestnut with corn silk glued onto it for hair. Alice had made a little bonnet and matching calico dress for May, which was becoming frayed from so much handling by Catherine.

"Papa, did you give May a kiss goodbye?" Catherine asked her father while proffering the doll to him. Tom squatted down so he could be at eye level with Catherine and the scruffy doll.

"Why no, I don't believe I did," he answered. "May, I must bid you farewell for a while. I hope you have a lovely boat trip. I shall miss you very much." With that, he gave the doll a kiss on her head.

Catherine looked down at May. "You're going to be all alone until you can join us, Papa, Maybe May should stay here with you to keep you company." She extended her arm and offered him her beloved doll.

Tom's eyes briefly welled up at his daughter's generous offer. He knew how much she loved her dolly, and to part with her for even a few weeks was a tremendous sacrifice on her part.

"Well now, Catherine, my love, I don't know much about taking care of dollies. I think May would be better off with you, but thank you for the offer." He hugged his middle child close to him and buried his nose in her sweet-smelling dark hair.

"No, Papa, I want you to keep her. You know how to take care of her. You take care of us just fine." The little girl once again proffered her doll to her father. Tom took the doll from her and snugged it to his chest.

"If you insist, my sweet," he said. "I shall take very good care of her." As he tucked the doll in his pocket, his daughter Caroline approached.

"Mama says it's time for us to get on the boat," Caroline told her father. As the eldest, Caroline was the most responsible child, always wearing a serious look on her heart-shaped face.

"Yes ma'am, here we go," Tom said to Caroline. He picked up their suitcases and walked with his two daughters to the gangplank, where Alice was waiting. Little Dottie squirmed impatiently in her arms.

Tom put their luggage onboard, then gathered Alice in his arms, squeezing both her and Dottie, and gave her a big kiss goodbye.

Then he gave Dottie a peck on the cheek and tousled her soft, fine hair. Goodbye, my loves," he told them.

He turned, bent down and hugged his other two daughters to his chest. "Caroline, you help your mother take care of those other two rascals, all right?" He said as he kissed her.

"Yes, of course I will, Papa," she said.

"And Catherine, you be good to your mother and sisters, you hear me?" He tickled her tummy, then gave her a kiss. "Yes, Papa, and you take care of May too."

He watched as Alice boarded the boat with his three little girls, and then walked back to the shoreline to join his brother Sam, who was standing next to Lucy.

Alice and the girls found a place at the railing of the side-wheeler *A.D. Patchin,* an impressive, 226-foot-long steamer with two black smokestacks sitting in front of the side wheels. The boat had two decks and could easily accommodate the handful of passengers onboard. Since it was the end of September, the number of people traversing Lake Michigan was dwindling dramatically. The steamer was loaded with a lot of cargo, a few crewmen, and the Bennett women.

A stiff wind from the east tugged at Alice's bonnet and prompted the girls to cling to her skirts in order to keep their balance. Dottie quit wiggling when the wind hit her tender little face.

As the steamer pulled away from the dock, Alice waved vigorously to Tom, Lucy and Sam. They all waved back with equal enthusiasm.

"I'm gonna miss them something fierce," Tom said to Lucy.

"You'll be joining them soon," she answered. But she said it with more conviction than she felt.

Something about the weather was setting off alarm bells in Lucy's head. She could vividly remember an easterly wind just like this one, blowing across the bay the day her father departed for his last trip to Mackinac. Watching Alice and the children leave the dock, Lucy got a shiver that ran up her arms and into her head. The whitecaps and swells were racing across the harbor as if they were being pursued by murderous pirates. She had a bad feeling and it was clinging to her like a cold, wet dress.

It was dusk when the *Patchin* left Beaver Island, even though it was just late afternoon. The days were growing very short as autumn started marching inexorably down the bleak road to winter. The wind picked up speed as they watched the boat grow smaller on the horizon.

"Brrr! They're gonna have a cold trip, I'm afraid," Tom said. "Gonna be a rough one, too, steamin' right into the wind like that. Good thing Alice and the young 'uns are made of sturdy stuff."

"Come on, Tom, I'll buy you a pint or two," Sam said, pulling his brother's arm in the direction of Cleary's Tavern.

"I never turn down free ale," Tom said, taking one last look at the *Patchin* before turning to head away from the harbor.

While the Bennett men walked to the tavern, Lucy walked home, pulling her collar tighter to her neck, trying to halt the icy fear that was creeping up.

◆•◆

The wind went from gusting to howling at some point in the evening. It shifted from east to northeasterly, a small but important distinction. The slight change in wind direction would make it harder for the *Patchin* to hold its course. Lucy couldn't sleep through it. She lit a candle and tried reading to distract herself.

Tom and Sam worked the following day and the next, loading the big crate to take Tom's things to Cross Village, until the nor'easter eventually wore itself out. Four days after Alice had left for Cross Village, Ned Martin, Alice's cousin, arrived at Beaver Island on his fishing boat.

Dolan saw Ned and was about to greet him when he took note of the grim look on Ned's face.

"What is it, Ned?" Dolan asked his old friend.

"The *Patchin*. She ran aground on Ile Aux Galets. Some of the crew survived, but no one else."

It took Dolan a moment to process the information, and then it came to him. Alice Bennett and her children had been on the *Patchin*.

"Oh God, Ned, I'm so sorry. Does Tom know yet?"

"No. I just got here to bring him the news. Worst news I've ever had to deliver to a man. Don't know how I'm going to do it."

"Want me to come with you?"

"Would you mind, Dolan? I could use the support."

Sam had departed that morning, leaving Tom to the business of tidying up after three days of behaving like bachelors. Tom's head was still aching when he answered the knock on the door.

"Ned! Dolan! Just in time, you can help me pick up the pieces of Alice's dishes that somehow got broke over the past few days." He smiled at them; then his smile faded when he saw the look on their faces.

"Oh Lord, what is it?"

"I'm so sorry, Tom. Alice and the children didn't make it to Cross Village. *Patchin* ran aground at Ile Aux Galets. Only a few of the crew members survived."

Tom turned white and let out an unearthly wail. He sank to his knees and put his head on the pine floor, still wailing.

Dolan and Ned knelt beside him, not knowing what to do. They each put a hand on the widower's back and tried to comfort him. Tom fell over onto his side and curled up in a fetal position. Clutched to his chest was May, the little doll his daughter Catherine had given him. It was all he had left of his family.

"I think I'd better go find Sam and his wife. They need to be with Tom now," Ned said.

"I'll stay here until you get back," Dolan said.

From her front porch, Lucy had seen the sad, final act of Alice's life play out. She saw Ned arrive; saw him speak with Dolan; saw the shocked look of horror splay across Dolan's face; and saw the two of them head up to Tom's house. Lucy's premonition had been correct. She hated herself for that.

With deep sadness and resignation, Lucy went inside and began to make plans for a large Irish wake. She would host it, she decided, because no one knew better than she what it felt like to lose your loved one to the lake.

CHAPTER 33
NOVEMBER, 1850

Tom Bennett was unable to function for over a month after the death of his wife and three daughters. His brother Sam and his wife took him in and cared for him, trying to get him to eat a small bite or drink a little water each day. All Tom could do was lie in bed and cling to the little doll his daughter Catherine had given him. He had managed to take care of the raggedy doll, but not his own family. It made him sick to his stomach.

The once rugged Tom aged significantly in a month. He became gaunt and stringy. His skin had a gray pallor to it from lack of decent nutrition and poor sleep. He no longer cared about his appearance. He had no wife to look good for; he had no reason to live.

Ever so slowly, he came out of his all-consuming despair, but a different man emerged in the place of the old Tom. The new Tom was a bitter and angry man with none of the rowdy humor of his old self.

"I'll see Strang dead by the end of this year," Tom told his friends on a late October day. "I will see him dead if I have to do it myself."

It was too difficult to blame a wicked nor'easter for the loss of his wife and children. Too difficult to believe that Mother Nature would simply snatch his family from him arbitrarily. He wanted an easy target; a target upon which he could heap mountains of vitriol for his loss.

Strang became that target.

"If it weren't for Strang and his taxes, I never would have sent Alice to Cross Village," Tom said repeatedly to his brother and anyone else who would listen. "If it weren't for Strang and those henchmen of his, my Alice would have been here with me during that storm. We never would have made plans to leave."

By early November, Tom was able to attend a wake Lucy arranged for him. As was usually the case with an Irish wake, it turned into a raucous affair, with whiskey flowing and beer sloshing on Lucy's red pine floor. She sloshed and drank along with everyone else.

Quite a few Mormons came to pay their respects, to the Bennett family's surprise. Mary Strang, Lorenzo Hickey, Sarah and Hezekiah MacCulloch, Jane and Wingfield Watson, Tom and Ruth Ann Bedford, Alex and Phebe Wentworth, Nathan and Eliza Bowman, and of course, Archie and Millie Donnelly, all attended to offer their condolences to the Bennetts. The loss of a wife and children overrode all religious differences.

King Strang was noticeably absent. He'd embarked on a mission trip shortly after the *Patchin* went down. Elvira had been beside herself with worry for her husband when he set sail, fearing he might meet the same fate and leave her to raise her child without a father. She was pregnant. According to her calculations, she had conceived the baby the night of the coronation, which made her inordinately proud.

Mary Strang wasn't nearly so concerned about James. She knew Elvira was with child, and it drove her half mad to think of James doting on a new baby, taking some of his love and affection away from her children to devote to the new one. James had only so much free time, and Mary knew the new baby was going to gobble up more than its fair share of those precious hours and minutes. Mary was far more jealous of the new baby than she'd ever felt about Elvira. A husband's attention for herself, she found she could do without; the thought of losing some of his attention for her children was infuriating.

At the wake, Mary enjoyed a pint or two of ale, to everyone's surprise. Phebe Wentworth could hardly contain herself, as she started mentally making a list of people she wanted to tell about Mary's shocking behavior.

Dr. MacCulloch and Thomas Bedford also imbibed at the affair, leaving their wives in a corner to talk about whatever it was they had in common, which was almost nothing. Sarah MacCulloch gave her husband a gimlet-eyed look as he left her with the buxom Ruth Ann, who was about as lively as sodden driftwood. MacCulloch enjoyed the company of Bedford, who was an amiable, talkative young man. Bedford's position in the church wasn't as high-ranking as MacCulloch's, but he was a loyal soldier to Strang and earned the respect of his fellow Mormons. The two of them eventually struck up a conversation with the Gentile Alva Cable, who lived near Sam Bennett on the southeast side of the island.

"So you're going to sell your land on the harbor?" MacCulloch asked.

"Yes, I like living down on the southeast side, and I have a store there," Cable said. "It's too much work to run two stores. That's why I closed the one on Paradise Bay. No point in keeping the land if I'm not going to run the store."

"I could be interested in it," MacCulloch said. He was thinking that the only store in town was run by a Gentile, Pete McKinley. Surely it would be profitable to open up a store run by Mormons, so the Mormons didn't have to do business with Gentiles.

"I'd be happy to talk to you about it," Cable said. "No hurry, with winter coming on. We can figure out the details in the spring."

"I could help you run it," Bedford said. "I have experience in retail." Bedford's only experience in retail had been as a boy, stocking shelves at a local store in his hometown. But he was quick to see an opportunity to improve his lot in life so he pounced on it.

While the men discussed the possibilities of a Mormon store, Huldy entered the house. She was pink-cheeked and glowing from her cold walk in the woods to Lucy's home. Eliza promptly joined her sister and began signing to her. She had no intention of trying to match Huldy up with the newly widowed Tom Bennett in any big rush, but it did occur to her that possibly someday, they might make a good couple. Eliza was always thinking that Huldy would be so much happier if she had a mate. Huldy knew this, and found it extraordinary that her unhappily married sister still labored under the delusion that having a man was a necessity for a happy life.

After hoisting their mugs of ale and cups of whiskey to the memory of Alice and the children many, many times, the wake got into full swing. Alva Cable pulled out a fiddle and started playing; Black Pete McCauley sang along in his lovely Irish tenor, although the words he sang were almost unintelligible with the combination of whiskey and his brogue; Will and

Teddy began doing an Irish jig, locking arms with anyone nearby and drawing them into the dance. Black Jack Bonner stomped his heavily booted foot on the floor to keep time.

Lucy joined in the dance, swishing her skirt from one side to the other, hands on hips and elbows out, dancing around the room. Huldy joined her and kept perfect time to the music. She couldn't hear a note, but she could feel the steady pounding of Black Jack's foot on the floor and it filled her with an impulsive urge to dance. Lorenzo Hickey watched Huldy, who was flushed with the heat coming from many people in close quarters, sway and twirl gracefully. For the first time since his wife abandoned him, he felt a stirring of emotion.

Hickey's steady gaze caught the attention of Eliza, who quickly sidled up next to him.

"My sister is lovely, isn't she?" she asked him.

"Is that your sister? I had no idea. I don't believe I've met her yet."

"I can introduce you," Eliza said. "As soon as this song is over."

"I would be most grateful if you would."

Eliza grabbed her sister by the arm and dragged her over to Lorenzo as soon as there was a pause in the music.

"Mr. Hickey, this is my sister, Huldy Cornwall. Huldy, this is Mr. Lorenzo Hickey." She signed the words as she spoke.

Huldy's face darkened. "I don't want to meet one of your Mormon men, Eliza!" she signed back rapidly.

"Does she not speak?" Hickey asked.

"No, she's deaf and mute. But she makes up for it in many positive ways."

"A woman who doesn't speak and can't hear might not be a bad thing at all," Hickey mused, not realizing he said the words out loud. Hickey wasn't always sure whether or not his random thoughts had escaped from his mouth.

"Please tell her it's my pleasure to meet her." Hickey made a deep bow toward Huldy as he said it.

"Huldy, he is happy to meet you and doesn't care that you're a deaf mute," Eliza signed.

"I don't care if he doesn't care! I don't want anything to do with those men!" Doing without the ability to hear and speak, Huldy had an awareness of human nature that others lacked. While many innocent people joined Strang's church, believing in the concept of communal, happy living, Huldy did not. She had a heightened sense of smell and she smelled a rat whenever she was near Strang.

When she was done signing and rejecting Hickey, she turned away and rejoined the dancing.

"I'm sorry, my sister is a bit shy," Eliza said.

"I understand. I can't imagine a life without sound. It must be lonely."

Eliza agreed with Hickey, but knew Huldy wouldn't feel the same way.

"May I call on her sometime?" Hickey asked.

"I don't know, but I'll try to arrange it," Eliza said.

They both turned their attention back to the dancers. Hickey watched Huldy with a fresh interest. Eliza smiled inwardly, hoping to make a match for her sister.

The wake lasted well into the night. By the time the last person left, Lucy was exhausted and wanted nothing more than to climb into bed. Instead, she cleared dishes and mugs off tables, pulled out a heavy mop and cleaned the floor before the beer and whiskey puddles had a chance to permanently soak into the floor. Sunrise was two hours away by the time she finally collapsed into a deep sleep. She dreamt of Antoine, who now had the company of a sweet young wife and her three precious children at the bottom of the vast, cold lake.

CHAPTER 34
END OF 1850, BEGINNING OF 1851

Strang returned to Beaver Island from his December mission trip in the nick of time, beating the ice formation on the lake by a few weeks.

One of his first tasks was to crank up the printing press at the newspaper office and proudly print the first edition of the *Northern Islander*, the newspaper that would be distributed throughout northern Michigan. The Mormons needed a paper to tell their side of the story. Strang was enraged by the downstate newspapers which, in his opinion, were being very unfair to them, printing inflammatory stories about the Mormons and showing them in a poor light. To Strang's way of thinking, their articles about the practice of Mormon consecration and forced tithing were greatly exaggerated, even if it was true. Strang wanted to right the wrong, as he saw it, with uplifting articles about all the good things the Mormons were accomplishing on the island; and he wanted to punish any Gentiles who were speaking ill of the Mormons.

His second task was to move Elvira into his family home, where she would live with Mary and the children. He gave Elvira her own room upstairs at the end of the hall, as far from Mary as he could manage.

"I can't leave her in the print shop," Strang told Mary. "She'll freeze to death over the winter! That place is too drafty and has only one wood stove downstairs. And besides, now that we're printing our newspaper, there just isn't enough room for Elvira."

"I don't want that woman in my house! She doesn't belong here. And what about our children, James? How are you going to explain this to them?"

"Children are very resilient. They won't mind a bit. Elvira is going to give them a new little brother or sister for them to play with."

Mary harbored cruel thoughts for Elvira, hoping she and her baby would die during childbirth. Every time Mary thought such a thing, she hated herself for thinking it, but it didn't change her feelings.

Somehow, Mary adapted. In time, she even managed to remain civil to Elvira when the whole family ate meals together. But part of Mary's ability to cope relied on her sharing her true thoughts about her husband to Mormons and Gentiles alike.

"Of course James had no 'vision' from angels who told him to practice polygamy," she said to Eliza Bowman and Jane Watson on a dull winter's day, when the women were gathered in Jane's kitchen, washing clothing in a wooden tub filled with water they boiled on the stove. It took the three of them to wring out the heavy, wet clothes and hang them on a line stretched across the kitchen, where they could dry by the heat of the woodstove.

"Wingfield says polygamy isn't all bad," Jane said. "He won't take another wife, he promised, but he can see the virtue of having it available to single women."

"If Nathan takes another wife I don't think I could handle it," Eliza said. "I don't know how you manage, Mary."

"What choice do I have?" Mary said. "I can tell you one thing; watch out for any of James' revelations. They're nothing more than the work of his imagination and ego, making things up to suit his purposes."

Young, trusting Jane was upset to hear Mary say that.

"You can't really believe that," she said. "King James is a wonderful leader. We wouldn't be here without his revelations from angels that led him to this lovely place. I've never been happier than I am now."

"I'm glad you're happy, but it has nothing to do with revelations and angels. And your happiness is coming at the expense of other people's misery. The Gentiles don't seem to be very happy to have us here. What about you, Eliza? Are you happy?"

Eliza stopped scrubbing a shirt on the washboard. "I wasn't very happy in New York. Nathan couldn't hold onto a job there. At least here, he has steady employment."

"But are you happy?" Mary persisted.

"What does happiness mean for a woman? We work like peasants to take care of our men and our homes. We cook, we clean, we wash, we stand over hot stoves canning food, then we do it all over again. I guess I don't really know what it means to be happy."

"You need a child, dear," Mary said. "That's what will bring you joy."

At the mention of a child, Jane blushed deeply. "I wasn't going to say anything yet, but Wingfield and I are going to have a child," she said, touching her still-flat stomach.

"Oh, how wonderful!" Mary said. "I'm truly delighted for you."

"Yes, congratulations," Eliza said unconvincingly. "I hope it brings you all the happiness you seek."

———— ◆◆ ————

While the women chatted and washed clothes, Hezekiah MacCulloch was seated at his desk, writing a letter to his old friend Frank Johnson.

Johnson was a savvy businessman and an opportunist. He also had money. Lots of it.

"Frank, I am missing your congenial company and the bustling city of Baltimore. I'm happy to report that your daughter Phebe and husband Alex are doing well here."

MacCulloch paused at this point in his letter, wondering how truthful he should actually be. He didn't care for Johnson's gossipy daughter Phebe, and her choice of husband had always perplexed him. Although Alexander Wentworth was certainly a physically attractive man – tall, with dark blue eyes, a flat, straight nose, and full lips surrounding a mouth that was unfortunately filled with crowded, crooked teeth – his social background was beneath the likes of Frank Johnson. He was a bumpkin from West Virginia who had managed to marry well when he captured Phebe's heart. Frank's late wife must have rolled over in her grave when Frank consented to the marriage. MacCulloch suspected that Frank was happy to marry his daughter off and be rid of her constant jabbering.

"I must say, Beaver Island has its own unique merits, some of which I believe would be of great interest to you.

"As you have no doubt learned from your daughter, we Mormons are build-ing a community here, and it's going well, but there are certain challenges. There are quite a few non-Mormons on the island; loggers and fishermen for the most part. There is also one store on the island's harbor, owned by a non-Mormon.

"Our people would naturally prefer to do business with our own kind. The Gentile store is thriving as our Mormon population grows. Just think of the money to be made if we were to open up a Mormon trading post – we could probably put the existing store out of business.

"Therefore, I encourage you to make a trip here. There is a wonderful oppor-tunity to start up a store with very little expense. A man who owns land and ran a store right on the harbor has chosen to move his operations to the other side of the island. The store is vacant and the land will be available for sale soon.

"I have already spoken to this man, Alva Cable, and he is amenable to sell-ing his property to us. With your excellent negotiation skills, we could no doubt get the property for far less than what it's worth. I don't think there are any other people with the means or desire to buy it.

"I look forward to hearing your response, and shall pray that it is a pos-itive one.

"Yours truly,

"Hezekiah MacCulloch"

MacCulloch folded the letter, put it in an envelope and sealed it with a wax seal bearing his initial. With little else to do, he decided to walk to the post office on Whiskey Point and put it in the outbound mailbag himself. The mail sled was due to go out as soon as the snow stopped falling.

When MacCulloch arrived at the post office, he found Pierce, Bowman and Chidester pawing through the mail, occasionally plucking a letter out of the bundle.

"What are you doing?" MacCulloch asked.

"King's orders," Pierce said. "Looking for letters the missus wrote to her family back in Voree. We're to pull them out."

"Why doesn't the prophet want his wife's letters to get mailed?"

"He thinks she's writing bad things about him. You know how he gets about that. No one, not even his wife, dare say anything bad about him."

MacCulloch knew all too well how thin-skinned Strang was when it came to criticism.

"Just make sure this one goes out, will you?"

"Sure will," Pierce said as he took MacCulloch's letter and put it in the bag.

MacCulloch left the post office as the snow was letting up and visibility was improving. He looked toward the far end of the point, where he could see Indians exchanging goods with a couple of white men.

MacCulloch walked in their direction, idle curiosity carrying him across the snowy landscape. As he drew closer, he could see who it was – Eri Moore, a recent convert to Mormonism, and Gus LaBlanc, a Gentile. LaBlanc was a red-faced, husky man who was the official mail carrier in charge of driving the dog sled back and forth to Mackinac Island in the winter. Moore often accompanied him on the premise that it was too dangerous a trip for one man to do alone. MacCulloch could see them handing over bottles of whiskey to the Indians while receiving money from them, no doubt earned from the fur trapping business.

For the second time in an hour, he asked the same question he'd asked of Miller's deputies.

"What are you doing?"

Moore looked nervous. LaBlanc looked like he couldn't care less.

"Just doing a little business, Dr. MacCulloch," Moore said. "It's rough work driving the mail up and down from Mackinac on a dog sled. Figured we might as well make a little money before we start on the trip."

"I'm going to have to report you to King Strang," MacCulloch said. "You know he strongly disapproves of selling whiskey to the Indians."

The Indians were from North Manitou Island and spoke almost no English. They stood there in their heavy deerskin coats that went down to their knees, bottles in hand, cash extended toward Moore, who wouldn't take their money. If he didn't accept payment, could he be charged with selling to the Indians?

LaBlanc reached out, took the money and stuffed it in his heavy coat pocket. The Indians turned and walked back to their sled near the frozen shore.

"I don't answer to your king," LaBlanc said. "I only answer to the U.S. Government. And the government doesn't care what I do to earn a little extra cash for my troubles."

Moore was trying to think fast on his feet, something that didn't come easily to him.

"You just saw that, it wasn't me selling to the Indians, it was Gus," he said. "I didn't take any money. You never saw me holding a bottle of whiskey."

"Don't be daft, Eri, I know what you were doing. And, you twit, you already admitted it."

MacCulloch stomped away, acting thoroughly disgusted with Moore and his alcohol transaction. He was very sanctimonious when it came to the sales and distribution of liquor. He was quite the opposite when he was the one procuring it. The hypocrisy escaped him.

CHAPTER 35

WINTER, 1851

Beaver Island was sound asleep under a blanket of heavy snow in February of 1851. Its residents had little to do besides chop wood, trap animals and try to stay warm.

The news that Eri Moore had been selling liquor to the Indians gave everyone something to gossip about. Strang immediately called the Circle of 12 Apostles together to charge Moore with his crime.

Mormons packed the still unfinished tabernacle to watch the trial, which was disappointingly short and swift. Moore was expelled from the church with little fanfare.

"It would be best if you and your wife left the island, Eri," Strang told him. "As a former Mormon, you will be expected to leave your belongings here. They belong to the church now."

Moore's wife gasped when she heard that. The items they brought to the island last spring came from their home in Ohio. She wasn't about to leave her grandmother's quilts and her mother's dishes in Mormon hands.

The Moores left the tabernacle and headed home, but not before stopping to visit Gus LaBlanc.

"We need to leave the island," Eri told Gus. "Probably move to Mackinac Island. Think we could ride with you on the next mail run?"

"Fine by me," LaBlanc said.

"Can you use your big sled? We'd like to take a few of our things along with us."

"Long as you take care of my dogs, get 'em fed, that's fine. Leaving two days from now."

The Moores went home and started packing their belongings.

"Don't say a word to anyone, Peggy," Eri told his wife. "I want to get out of here with whatever we can take, and without any interference from Strang's men."

Peggy simply nodded in agreement and kept on stuffing cherished items into burlap sacks.

They got up before dawn two days after being expelled from the church. LaBlanc's sled and dog team were waiting in front of their modest log cabin. On the sled was a small sack of mail.

Peggy got on first, sitting at the rear of the sled, then Eri and Gus loaded their belongings on the sled in front of her. She was unable to see much over the piles of bags and tool boxes, but she didn't mind. The load in front of her would break the wind and keep her somewhat warmer, so she was content with the arrangement.

Eri climbed on the runners behind Peggy, and Gus stepped on behind him. With a crack of his whip, the dogs bolted forward and trotted through town, gaining speed as they neared the shore. The sled bumped over the mound of ice that built up on the shoreline, and then they were on the frozen lake, headed north. The air was still and cold, and the only sound that could be heard was the dogs' breathing and rhythmic footsteps thumping across the ice.

The quiet was broken by the sound of a gunshot.

"What the hell?" LaBlanc said as he looked back over his shoulder to see where the shot came from. Eri looked as well.

"Damnation, it's the Mormons, they're chasing us!" Eri said.

"Merde! We'll go hide on Garden Island," LaBlanc said. "We've got enough of a head start, I don't think they can catch us."

LaBlanc cracked the whip over his dogs' heads again and gave them a French shout of "Marche, marche," telling them to run. They picked up speed and veered slightly west, so they could slip into the cove on Garden Island, where most of the Indian settlements were located.

The Mormons pursuing them had two sleds with six dogs pulling each one. Two men sat on each sled and a third stood on the runners, driving the dogs. LaBlanc was able to put more distance between them thanks to his sledding experience and team of superior dogs.

LaBlanc didn't slow his team when they reached the shoreline of Garden Island. The dogs leaped over the hump of ice, and the sled followed, becoming airborne for a moment when it flew over the hump. Commanding his dogs with "Gee's" and "Haw's," LaBlanc guided the dogs straight to the home of Gwen and Otto Miigwech. When he got there, he jumped off the sled and pounded on the plank next to the door opening. The home was a typical Anishinaabe dwelling, a wigwam twice as long as it was wide, with a curved roof. The frame was made of tree branches bent into arches, then covered with planks and finally overlaid with deer hides that had been stitched together. A hole in the center of the roof allowed smoke from the fire to escape.

Gwen answered, looking baffled.

"Take care of these people, will you, Gwen?"

Eri and Peggy were frantically pulling their belongings off the sled and dragging them to the door.

"Who are they?" Gwen asked LaBlanc. She'd known the mail carrier for years, since he often stopped on Garden Island on his way back from Mackinac. Otto came up from behind and stood by Gwen.

"Mormons, expelled from the church," LaBlanc said. "Now we've got other Mormons chasing them. I'm not sure what's going on, but I'm not sticking around to find out."

Otto looked at Peggy Moore, who was wild-eyed with fright. He made an instant decision and started to help the Moores carry their things into his home. Gwen, trusting her brother's instincts, followed suit.

Within minutes the Moores and their motley assortment of bags and boxes were all safely inside the house. LaBlanc, with nothing but a sparse bag of mail on his sled, took off, heading back to Beaver Island. He had no desire to drive his dogs all the way to Mackinac Island with armed Mormons in pursuit.

Although they had little knowledge of Garden Island, the Mormons had no difficulty following Leblanc's sled trail to Otto and Gwen's home. When they arrived, they were greeted with the sight of Otto standing in front of the door, a rifle in hand. Otto was a formidable sight even without the rifle. His black eyes glared menacingly at the Mormon posse.

"We're looking for Eri Moore," Constable Miller said. "We don't want any trouble; we just want what belongs to us."

"I'm afraid I can't help you," Otto said. "You'll have to take this up with Chief Peaine. You're on Indian property now." Otto didn't move a muscle while he spoke. He didn't blink. He just held his gaze at the men.

Miller was flummoxed. He'd never been to Garden Island before. He became anxious at the thought of an island full of angry Indians doing battle with his small group of men.

"Come on, fellows, let's get back home. Nothing more to do here." He backed away from Otto, who continued to stare at him. Disappointed over the lack of a fight, his men climbed back on the sleds and followed their own tracks off Garden Island.

By the time they were back on the lake, LaBlanc had already arrived at Beaver Island. He drove his team straight to the post office. The sun was well up over the horizon and the island was coming to life.

LaBlanc pulled up in front of the post office, grabbed the mailbag, flung open the door and heaved the mailbag into the building. He'd accidentally grabbed it by the bottom, so when he threw it, letters sailed out and scattered all over the floor.

Mary, Lucy and Eliza were standing in the post office, watching the scene unfold. Mary and Eliza were hoping to have mail from their families waiting for them. LaBlanc left the building as quickly as he'd entered it.

The women looked at the letters covering the floor and started to pick them up, carefully stacking them in piles on the post office counter.

"What was that all about?" Lucy asked no one in particular.

"Looks like this is the outbound mail," Mary said. "I guess the letters I wrote a few days ago aren't going to Mackinac today." She continued to pick up letters and put them on the counter. Lucy and Eliza did the same.

After they'd picked up all the mail, Mary thumbed through the letters, looking confused.

"None of my letters are in here," she said.

Eliza went over to the pile and sorted through it. "Mine aren't in here either," she said. "I wrote my brother Albert at least three letters this past week."

Postmaster Jim Dorry was behind the counter, minding his own business. He was a greasy little man who always smelled of tobacco. He wasn't a Mormon, but he wasn't a Beaver Islander either. He'd been sent to the island from Mackinac to run the post office.

"Mr. Dorry, has anyone had access to the mail besides you?" Mary asked.

"Well, now, sometimes the constable and his men come here to check on things," Dorry said evasively.

"Check on things? What does that mean?" Mary asked.

"They go through the mail, see what's going out. Sometimes they pull some of the letters out and get rid of them."

"And you let them? Isn't that against the law?"

"I suppose that could be said, but the constable tells me they answer to the laws of God and their king, and those laws rank above the laws of the government." Dorry didn't mention the bribes he received from the constable and his deputies for allowing them to sort through the mail.

Eliza looked crestfallen; Mary looked angry; Lucy looked ready to rearrange his possum face.

"Postmaster Dorry, you have an obligation to uphold the laws of the U.S. Government," Lucy said. "What we have here is a case of tampering with the U.S. mail, and that is most certainly against the law. If I must, I will send someone to Mackinac Island and have this reported to the county sheriff. And you will be held accountable."

Dorry didn't look terribly concerned. "Mrs. LaFleur, the constable and his men have told me they were just following Strang's orders. Mrs. Strang here wouldn't want to see her husband get arrested, would she?" He glanced at Mary and then gave Lucy a smug smile, exposing his pointy, tobacco-stained teeth.

"You don't know what I might want to see," Mary retorted. "Maybe that's exactly what needs to happen."

The three women pulled on their heavy cloaks and started to walk home.

"James must know I write to my family, and more often than not, I complain about him," Mary said. "So James is not allowing any of my letters to get through."

"And Nathan is helping him," Eliza added.

"We need to get word to the sheriff on Mackinac, but I don't know how we can do that," Lucy said. "We need someone we can trust to tell him. And it has to be someone the sheriff up there will trust."

"Let's ask Dolan," Eliza said. "Everyone trusts Dolan."

The women didn't know then that they wouldn't need to solicit help from Dolan. A few days later, LaBlanc went back to Garden Island and fetched the Moores and their belongings, and then hauled them up to Mackinac Island. The first thing Eri Moore did was visit the sheriff and file a complaint about James Strang, charging him with mail fraud. After having picked up the mail with LaBlanc numerous times, he was well aware of what was going on at the Beaver Island post office. He'd never mentioned it while he was a Mormon in good standing. Now that he had been expelled from the island, forced to abandon the cabin he'd built and then hunted down like a bear by Strang's men, revenge was exactly what he wanted.

CHAPTER 36

EARLY 1851

It was a short matter of time before George Adams and Eri Moore bumped into each other on Mackinac Island. They were all staying at the Pink Pony with their wives – Eri's real wife Peggy, and George's pseudo wife Louisa. It was somewhat awkward for George to be near Mrs. Pinkham with the new love of his life, but as a woman experienced in the ways of lust and love, Mrs. Pinkham was gracious to Adams and stoic about losing her former amour to a younger woman. In fact, she quite liked Louisa's energy and bawdy sense of humor.

While the women spent their days swapping stories and doing small chores, the men spent a good deal of time in Jillet's tavern, plotting their revenge against Strang. Both men were indignant for having been ousted from the Mormon Church. They considered their wrongdoings miniscule at best, not worth such severe punishment.

"We both know Strang is breaking about a hundred laws on Beaver," Adams said one late winter day as he hoisted a pint of ale to his lips. His face was pale and soggy, the result of constant gray winter skies and barrels of readily available whiskey on Mackinac.

"You know a lot more than I do, George," Moore replied. "I was new there, barely had gotten myself and the missus settled in before I got booted out."

"Well, there's the mail fraud for starters, and then I'm pretty sure all those Saints are logging on federal land without permission. I don't think the United States government will be quite so tolerant of the Mormon policy of consecration as others might be."

"I never thought about that. Just figured all that land was up for grabs."

"It was at one point in time, but not anymore. There's another thing you probably don't know about. Almost no one does." Adams, ever the actor, leaned in toward Moore, first looking left and right to see if anyone could overhear him. It was quite a dramatic, pregnant pause.

"My goodness, what?"

"Strang was counterfeiting money! That print shop, where they print the newspaper? Well, Strang was also minting fake money. Half-dollar coins." Adams sat back smugly. "I'm one of the only ones who knows."

"Do you have any proof? Any of the counterfeit coins?"

"No, we got them off the island fast as possible. Spent them in other parts of the country, on mission trips."

"Not much we can do about it then, unless the sheriff catches him red-handed in the act of making coins."

"You never know, it's one more thing that will help build a case against Strang."

With little else to do during a wretchedly long winter, the men adopted a letter-writing campaign to their congressmen, detailing the laws being broken by King James. They even wrote to the President of the United States, Millard Fillmore, who paid little attention to the letters from Adams and Moore. The members of Congress weren't particularly moved by the former Mormons' pleas for justice either. Beaver Island was a remote little spot that had little or no bearing on their political future.

It wasn't until Fillmore made a trip to Detroit to visit his brother that his curiosity about Strang was piqued. His brother Charles was an avid news reader and filled the president in on the odd band of Mormons who had taken over Beaver Island, and whose numbers were growing every day. He let his brother Millard know that Strang had voiced his opinions in the editorial pages of the *Detroit Daily News*, and his opinions clearly leaned Democratic.

Hoping to be re-elected in 1852, Fillmore, a Whig, realized a Democrat like Strang could pose a threat to his election numbers in Michigan, a no-toriously fickle swing state.

"I need a meeting with George Bates," Fillmore told his brother. "He's the federal prosecutor in these parts, and he's a Whig too. We've got an election to think about, and I don't want this Democrat Strang costing me the state of Michigan."

The next day a surprised and delighted Bates met with the President of the United States. After the President outlined the situation for Bates, he rubbed his hands together in eager anticipation. Bates was a small man with a big head of auburn hair and an even bigger ego. He hungered to make a name for himself.

"Get your warrants in order," Fillmore told Bates. "Charge Strang with whatever you think might hold up in court. But stay away from the bizarre kingdom and religious stuff. We don't want to be accused of religious persecution."

The latter part was disappointing to Bates. After having read about Strang, he was eager to prosecute him for polygamy, but then realized the president was right. Strang never really committed a crime, since immorality couldn't be considered a punishable offense in federal court. He had never tried to legally marry his second wife.

"You'll move forward with this as soon as the ice goes out on Lake Michigan," Fillmore told Bates.

<hr />

The ice broke up on Lake Michigan in March, and Bates wasted no time issuing subpoenas for George Adams, Gus LaBlanc, postmaster Jim Dorry and Eri Moore to give depositions. Adams and Moore were more than happy to comply, meeting with Bates on Mackinac Island and providing their testimony about Strang's alleged criminal activity. Adams provided a map of Beaver Island to Bates, outlining the places where illegal logging had taken place on the island.

Moore and LaBlanc told Bates about the sled chase, with Mormons shooting at them when LaBlanc was trying to deliver the mail to Mackinac Island. Postmaster Dorry reluctantly confirmed that Strang's men had gone through the mail routinely and plucked out letters that contained potentially damning information about the king. Dorry knew his testimony would probably bring to an end the bribes he'd received from the Mormons. He was saddened by that prospect.

From Mackinac, Bates sailed on to Beaver Island, where he took the depositions of Gentiles to build his case against Strang. Regardless of whether the Gentiles had any concrete evidence of crimes committed directly by Strang, they eagerly testified against him.

It didn't take long for word to get back to Strang that Bates was on Beaver Island and gunning for him.

"It's all ridiculous," Strang told Miller and his deputies. "Bates has no solid evidence against me. These are all trumped up charges, and I'm being persecuted for my religious beliefs, pure and simple."

"I heard he wants to take your deposition as well," Miller warned Strang. "It might be in your best interest to leave here for a while."

Strang thought about it. As a lawyer, he knew that lying under oath during a deposition was a crime; he didn't know what questions Bates might ask him, and his lawyerly instincts told him it would be best to avoid questions that could put him in a precarious position.

"I hear Hog Island is lovely this time of year," Strang said to Miller, referring to the small, uninhabited island a few miles northeast of Beaver Island, which was anything but lovely in the mucky, cold month of March. "Perhaps we should row over there tonight, when it's dark."

Miller smiled. "Yes, I think that would be a fine idea. In the meantime, you may want to secure yourself in the second floor of the print shop. I'll have my men stand guard."

Bates was a day late in his effort to subpoena Strang. When Bates knocked on his door, he was informed by Elvira that her husband had left the island to take care of urgent business elsewhere. Strang, meanwhile, was well hidden on Hog Island, enduring the cold and biding his time.

CHAPTER 37
APRIL, MAY 1851

After a long and bitter winter, spring came to Beaver Island, bringing with it the rebirth of flowers and fields, and the birth of several Mormon babies.

Being a strong, young woman, Elvira Strang had no difficulty whatsoever delivering her baby boy on April 6, 1851, almost exactly nine months after Strang's coronation. Dr. MacCulloch attended the birth, with nothing much to do except catch the baby. A child of 12 could have done the same thing, as easily as catching a melon thrown gently from a distance of two feet. Yet to hear MacCulloch talk about it to his fellow Saints, he let everyone believe that the king's new heir to the throne wouldn't be alive today had it not been for his heroic efforts in delivering the boy.

Elvira named the child Charles James Strang, a deliberate reference to her days of traveling incognito as Strang's nephew Charles. Mary was apoplectic about the name.

"This is a total slap in the face!" she complained to her husband. "It's humiliating. Tell that foolish wife of yours that I won't tolerate that name!"

"I promised Elvira she could choose any name she wanted if it was a boy, and I would choose the name if it was a girl. I can't go back on my word," he replied.

"Really, James? You expect me to believe that? You know very well you can do whatever you want and Elvira will obey your wishes. I suspect you think it's quite clever, naming him Charles."

Although he would never admit it, Strang did think it was clever. It amused him, and brought back memories of deliciously illicit sex that he enjoyed with Elvira before he made her his spiritual wife.

"Let it go, Mary. It's done." Strang walked away, making it clear that he would not entertain any more discussion of the name of his child.

Fine, have it that way, Mary thought to herself. *You want to make a fool out of me? Two can play at this game.*

Jane Watson's delivery of a baby girl three days later was not as easy as Elvira's. At the advice of Lucy, she had been under the care of Gwen. When the labor contractions started, Gwen discovered that the baby was face-up instead of face down, the preferred position for a safe delivery.

"You must get on your hands and knees, like you're scrubbing the floor," Gwen told Jane. "Now, put your elbows on the floor so your hips are higher in the air." Gwen hoped the position might ease the baby away from the birth canal and allow it to turn over on its own.

A very frightened Jane did as she was told. The contractions were driving the baby's head into her spine, causing agonizing pain. She tried to be stoic and keep her yelps and screams to herself, but they escaped from her every so often. Her nervous husband Wingfield paced up and down in front of their little home, worried sick for his wife. Childbirth was mystifying and terrifying to him.

"This is going to cause some discomfort, but I have to do this, Jane," Gwen told her. She inserted a hand into Jane and gently turned the baby, eventually succeeding in getting it properly positioned. After that, it was simply a matter of time before Jane was able to deliver a tiny baby girl.

"Drink this," Gwen told Jane as soon as she laid back, exhausted and perspiring from the delivery.

"What is it?" she asked, taking a cup from Gwen that she had prepared earlier.

"Raspberry leaf tea. It will help you expel the afterbirth without losing blood."

"How do you know all this?"

"My mother taught me. Her mother taught her. We learn a lot through experience and sharing of stories."

Jane drank the tea and felt glad that she'd chosen Gwen to deliver her baby instead of Dr. MacCulloch.

While Jane Watson had endured a painful delivery, she still considered herself lucky. Millie Donnelly had also been with child, but lost the baby within two months of announcing her happy news. Millie would have gladly traded places with Jane. As a good Mormon, Millie dutifully agreed to have Dr. MacCulloch to tend to her. He did nothing to help her through the miscarriage, except to tell her brusquely that losing babies was all part of womanhood, and she just needed to keep trying. He also told her to pray more and live a saintly life. Losing a baby was God's way of punishing sinners.

"Your husband should stay away from Gentiles and spirits," MacCulloch added. "It's probably his fault that God took your baby." Millie was heartbroken. And her normally good nature soured with resentment toward MacCulloch. She vowed then that if she was lucky enough to become with child again, she would seek the aid of Gwen, the talented medicine woman.

Gwen stayed with Dolan for three weeks prior to Jane's delivery, and for an additional two weeks afterward, to make sure mother and daughter were doing well. Dolan loved having Gwen in the house for such a long stretch of time. They were both sitting on the porch on an unseasonably warm, late April day when they heard a commotion coming from the harbor. They could make out Tom Bennett yelling at Constable Miller.

"You'd better go see what's happening," Gwen told Dolan.

"I suppose I should," he agreed, and headed off the porch and toward the harbor.

"What's going on?" Dolan asked, as he stood in front of Tom Bennett and Joshua Miller.

"He's trying to steal my catch," Bennett said with a growl.

"I'm taking what's owed us. Ten percent, as agreed upon," Miller said in a huff.

"I never agreed to that, and I never will!"

"Your boys pay it, don't they, Dolan? They know it's the law."

"Will and Teddy chose to donate 10 percent voluntarily, to keep the peace," Dolan said. "They aren't doing it because it's an accepted law.

We don't agree that it's a law. We only agree to share the wealth with our Mormon neighbors."

"Well, we Saints believe it's a law that applies to everyone on the island. So pay up the 10 percent, Bennett," Miller said.

"Over my dead body."

"That's the way you want it, fine," Miller said.

"Now there, let's all take a step back," Dolan said to the men. "Constable, why don't you let Tom be on his way and I'll settle this matter with you."

"Are you gonna pay for him?" Miller asked.

"Don't you be doing that, Dolan," Bennett said. "I can handle this myself."

"I'm just suggesting that Tom go home and you and I have a little talk about this business in private."

Miller looked at Dolan while he thought about it. Dolan was a highly respected, patriarchal figure on the island. And although his hair was gray, his body was still hard with well-earned muscles from doing manual labor and hauling fishing nets his entire life. He probably had the strength to whip Miller in a fistfight if he chose to.

"I guess I can allow that, for now," Miller said.

"Go on home, Tom," Dolan said. "You still living down at Sam's? Gonna take you awhile to get there, so you'd best be getting on."

Bennett left, but not before glowering at Miller. "This isn't over, I promise you," he said, getting in the last word.

"He's a problem, that one," Miller said to Dolan.

"You don't make it very easy for him to not be a problem," Dolan said with a sharp tone of voice that came unnaturally to him. "Why can't you leave the man alone? He lost his wife, his children, why can't you let him keep his income?"

"Rules are rules," Miller said with a shrug of his shoulders.

"Oh, balderdash! You can decide when and how to enforce rules. You don't go after all the Gentiles on the island. You've got it in for Bennett. I don't know why, but I know it for a fact."

It was true. Miller harbored an intense dislike for Tom Bennett. When he'd first met the jovial man with the adorable wife and precious children, he was consumed with jealousy. Miller was a single man. He was attractive enough in his own way, with a strong face, thick eyebrows and a heavy, rounded chin covered with a beard. But women were repelled by Miller's overbearing attitude. He tried to be on his best behavior whenever he began courting a woman, but sooner or later he would start getting bossy and demanding. He was also quick to criticize and slow to compliment.

Over time, he saw how the women on the island all gazed longingly at Bennett. And he saw how Bennett's quick sense of humor won over women and men alike. He watched as Bennett doted on his wife and bounced his babies on his knees. He grew to hate everything about Thomas Bennett. Miller secretly gloated when Bennett lost his wife and children, believing it brought Bennett a little closer to his own miserable lot in life.

But Bennett had friends and family. In spite of his terrible loss, he still was nowhere near as bitter and lonely as Joshua Miller. And that was a thorn that continued to poke angrily in Miller's side.

"Just leave him alone for a while, okay Joshua?" Dolan wasn't asking. He was telling.

"I'll think about it," Miller answered, knowing it would never be thought about and would never be done.

———— ◆•◆ ————

King James Strang was in a fine fettle. After spending a few cold, wet days on Hog Island a couple months ago, he had returned to Beaver Island to learn that the prosecutor Bates had given up trying to find him. Strang felt confident the whole business of arresting him and charging him with criminal activity would cease without any concrete evidence.

Strang's Mormon community had swelled to a population of over 600 on Beaver Island. Little homes and cabins lined the harbor, with a second row of homes sitting behind the first, up on the gentle hill. Further inland, houses and barns sat next to rows of neatly plowed farm fields. He was looking to expand his kingdom to the mainland, with plans to build posts in Traverse City and Pine River, which was a small outpost on the northwest side of the state of Michigan, about 20 miles from Beaver Island. He was the father of a healthy new son. Elvira's small breasts had swelled into ripe melons as she nursed their hungry boy. It made him lusty and eager to take her in bed, and she just as eagerly gave herself to him.

Mary was his only immediate concern. Her humiliation over the naming of baby Charles had prompted her to unleash a stream of insults and innuendo about Strang. She chose to keep company with non-Mormon women like Lucy, Gwen, and Huldy, the strange sister-in-law of Nathan Bowman.

The whispered gossip eventually made its way back to Strang. Over and over, one of his apostles would have to tell him, "I'm sorry to tell you this King James, but Mary has been talking poorly about you again."

Mary would have to go. That was all there was to it. It would probably cause a scandal, sending his first wife away, but worse problems would erupt if she stayed on the island.

While Strang was sitting in the print shop, contemplating solutions to his marital problem, Constable Miller was working on a way to solve a problem of his own. Miller pounded on Dennis Chidester's door until Chidester answered it and let him in.

"Get Bowman and Pierce, and then round up a posse of strong Saints. We're gonna go pay those Bennett brothers a visit. When you've got 20 or so men, meet me in front of the tabernacle."

Chidester asked no questions, simply did as he was told. Within 45 minutes, the three deputies were mounted on their horses with another 18 Mormons behind them, riding horses or driving buckboards. Dr. MacCulloch joined the pack, feeling bored and looking for something to do. He had just acquired a new Colt Paterson revolver, and was eager to show it off.

"We're going to pay a visit to Sam and Tom Bennett," Miller announced. They have not been paying their taxes. It's time we collect."

Miller now called the 10 percent tithe an island tax. It seemed to alleviate tensions with at least some of the Gentiles, who adamantly refused to tithe to a religion they didn't believe in.

The group of men made their way down the corduroy road that led to Sam Bennett's house on the southeast side of the island. The road had been made by the earliest of the Mormon arrivals, who cut young cedars, stripped them of their branches and laid the thin, six-foot long poles horizontally to form a road that went through the swampy areas of the island's interior. The road could withstand the weight of wagons whose wheels would otherwise have become hopelessly mired in the low-lying bogs.

When the group arrived at Sam Bennett's house, they kept their distance – staying at least 50 feet away from the front door – and formed a loose semi-circle to prevent anyone from making an escape.

"Sam and Tom Bennett, come out now! You're under arrest for refusing to pay your taxes!" Miller shouted.

A moment later, Tom shouted back at him through the open front window. "I'll not pay anything to your church, or your king! I'll only pay what's owed to my country!"

Sam Bennett grabbed his rifle. Tom was unarmed.

"Get back from the window, Julia," Sam told his wife, and motioned for his brother to do the same. Neither obeyed his request, keeping their eyes on the men outside.

"Get off my property, you're trespassing!" Sam called to Miller. "Get off, or I'll shoot!"

With those words, Sam stuck his rifle out the window and pointed it at the sky.

"He's going to shoot us!" Chidester said, and immediately lowered his own rifle and fired at the house. Other Mormons followed suit.

"Stop shooting!" Bennett yelled, setting his rifle down. He walked to his front door and threw it open. "Stop, stop!" he said, raising his hand with the palm out.

Pierce, the largest of Miller's three deputies, was getting light-headed at the thought of being shot at. He was a classic bully who was a tough man when he was doling out the punishment, but a nervous bunny when his own hide was being threatened. He didn't even look to see if Sam Bennett was carrying a weapon. Pierce shot his musket at Bennett, adrenaline racing through his body and making a well-aimed shot impossible. A musket ball smashed through Sam's upraised hand.

Tom Bennett saw the blood spray from his brother's hand and lost what little self-control he still had. He grabbed his brother's rifle, pushed his bleeding brother back into the house, and lowered the rifle at the Mormons as he marched onto the front porch.

Seeing the rifle leveled at their heads, the armed Mormons started shooting wildly. One bullet went straight through Bennett's heart. Chidester's gunshot caught Bennett in the leg. Other bullets embedded themselves in the cabin's logs and splintered wood around window frames. MacCulloch fired several times, but wasn't sure if he hit anyone except possibly one of the Mormons standing in front of him. That hapless fellow was the only Mormon to receive a gunshot wound to the side of his ear, which he survived.

The same could not be said of Thomas Bennett. He dropped dead on his brother's front porch.

It was all over in a matter of seconds. Miller sat on his horse, looking panicked.

"We have to get out of here," he said to his men. Then he turned his horse and galloped through the woods, followed by a posse of confused men who were trying to figure out how a simple arrest went so terribly wrong.

CHAPTER 38

MAY, 1851

When Julia Bennett saw the Mormons flee, she rushed to the porch to check on her brother-in-law Tom first. Seeing there was no hope for him, she ran back to her husband, who was woozy from the loss of blood. She ripped off the hem of her dress and wound the fabric tightly around Sam's ruined hand.

With her arm around his waist and his good arm draped across her shoulders, she helped him off the porch, over to the barn and into the buckboard she used for her rare trips to town. She hitched Tom's horse to the buckboard and swiftly climbed aboard, then cracked the whip over the horse's head, sending him into a fast trot.

"I hope to heaven Gwen is at Dolan's house right now," Julia said to Sam, who was pale and perspiring. "She can fix your hand." It wasn't what Julia was thinking, however. She was fairly sure his hand was a lost cause. She was hoping to save his life before his blood ran out.

Gwen was still at Dolan's house, so she could keep an eye on Jane Watson and her newborn. When she answered the door and saw Julia holding a very weak, pale husband, she immediately hurried the two of them into the house and got Sam onto a bed.

"My stars, what happened?" Gwen asked.

"Mormons came to arrest Tom and Sam for not paying taxes. Shot Sam in the hand." She paused. "Tom's dead."

Dolan walked in then, carrying a load of firewood, which he dropped when he saw Sam's bloody, mangled hand.

"The Mormons shot Sam and killed Tom," Gwen said without further elaboration. She had no time for details. She went to get a bucket of clean water and some tanned leather straps she had stored in a special basket. She grabbed a jar of honey off the sideboard as she headed back to Sam.

Dolan was stunned. He kept mumbling "This is bad, this is really, really bad," over and over. He sat by Julia's side while Gwen worked on Sam's hand, cleaning it, pulling shredded skin back into place, removing bone fragments and smearing honey all over it, then binding it together with leather straps.

"What's the honey for?" Julia asked. She'd never seen Gwen work; fortunately, she'd never had the need for Gwen's medical services.

"Helps with the healing. Keeps the wound clean and protected."

Gwen's ancestors had figured these things out through generations of experimentation and treatment, none of them understanding that honey had proteins that would ward off infection, and trace amounts of vitamins and minerals that would hasten the healing process. Julia assumed it was Indian medicine magic.

Sam and Julia spent the night with Dolan and Gwen. Sam slept fitfully until Dolan gave him a shot of whiskey, which helped him nod off. Sam was still asleep the next day, with Julia by his side, when Dolan and Gwen left the house, headed for the home of King James.

Mary was looking out the window, taking in the sight of a sunrise over the lake, when she saw Gwen and Dolan. She slipped out the front door and walked toward them, meeting up with them about 50 feet away from her home.

"We have bad news to discuss with your husband," Dolan said. "There's been a murder."

Mary gasped, but knew better than to start pestering them with questions. Dolan's lips, drawn tight in an angry line, told her to wait for details.

"Come with me, I'll get James," she said, and hurried back to her home, with Gwen and Dolan right behind her.

Mary let them into her house, and then went to find James. She banged on the door to Elvira's bedroom, knowing that her husband was in there, either sleeping or fondling his heavy-breasted wife.

James answered the door in his bedclothes.

"Mary, you are not to bother me when I'm with Elvi-"

Mary interrupted him. "There's been a murder on the island," she told him. "Dolan and Gwen are here to discuss it with you. Hurry up and get dressed."

Strang wasted no time. He was dressed and downstairs within minutes. He saw Dolan and Gwen seated on a small horsehair loveseat in the parlor. Dolan's feet were tapping on the circular rag rug in front of him. Gwen was looking at the whitewashed bookshelves that lined the wall on either side of the fireplace, and the abundant books with legal names on the spines.

As soon as Dolan saw Strang, he stood up.

"What's this about? Murder, you say?" Strang asked.

"Yes, that's what I say," Dolan answered. "Your men murdered Tom Bennett and shot his brother Sam in the hand. It will probably never work again and he'll lose his livelihood."

"How am I to believe this? I must go talk to my men. There must be a misunderstanding."

"There's no misunderstanding. Julia Bennett brought Sam to us for help. She saw the whole thing. Your man Miller rounded up a posse and rode down to Bennett's to collect your damn tithe. Sam pointed his rifle toward the sky to warn them and your men started shooting at them."

Strang was having difficulty believing that his Saints could be to blame for Tom Bennett's death. The Gentiles were always quick to blame the Mormons, twisting the facts to suit their needs. To him, it sounded like Sam Bennett started shooting at innocent men who were just trying to do their job. And Bennett's wife Julia was covering up for her husband, who no doubt started all the trouble.

Strang strode through town 20 minutes later, on his way to Miller's house. The town was wide awake by then, with fishermen gathered along the harbor's edge and Gentile women clustered in front of McKinley's store, all talking rapidly about the death of Tom Bennett. With each telling, the plot became more murderous and the Mormons became more evil.

"This is all your fault, you king of criminals!" Teddy Duffy shouted at Strang as he walked hurriedly past him.

"You'll pay for this!" shouted Will.

Archie Donnelly was standing with the Gentile fishermen, worried that he might be on the wrong side of the growing divide among islanders. He'd joined the Mormons just to make Millie happy. After losing their baby, even she seemed to be disenchanted with the Mormons.

Strang found Chidester, Bowman and Miller all huddled around a small table in Miller's house. They'd spent the whole night wide awake, shaking from the encounter, and getting their story straight for King James.

They needn't have worried. The quick-thinking Strang had already worked things out in his head, and presented them with the facts as he saw them.

"So I imagine you were just doing your job, asking the Bennetts to pay their tax," Strang said.

"Yes, that's right," Miller said.

"And those hot-headed Bennetts, they started shooting at you, so of course you had to defend yourselves, correct?" Strang asked.

"Yes, that's just what happened," Miller said. He still wasn't entirely sure what happened, since he wasn't the one who fired the first, second or even third shot. He wasn't sure if anyone would ever know whose bullet tore through Tom Bennett's heart.

"Well, this is indeed a tragedy, but an accidental tragedy that could have been avoided if the Bennetts had behaved in a proper manner, respectful of the laws we have here. I'll make sure your good names are cleared of any wrongdoing."

Miller and his men breathed a collective sigh of relief. Strang left them and headed straight to the newspaper office, where he found Wingfield Watson.

"Brother Wingfield, I need you to write an article for the next issue of the paper immediately," Strang said. "We need to set the record straight about what happened to Tom Bennett, may he rest in peace."

Strang told Winfield the details of the scenario he'd created with Miller and his men, and left Wingfield with the additional instruction to "Feel free to pontificate on the drunken nature of the Bennett men and their frequent, alcohol-fueled outbursts against the peaceful Saints. There is blame to be found on both sides."

Wingfield was a solid writer, but not much of a pontificator. He preferred to stick to the facts. Nevertheless, he promised Strang he'd write an article that would hopefully put to rest the accusations of a murder committed by Mormon hands.

When the next issue of the *Northern Islander* newspaper was distributed, the Gentiles knew they were beaten. Many of them knew of Tom Bennett's hatred of Strang and the Mormons. They had all heard Tom said that he would kill Strang. It wasn't an impossible stretch of the imagination to believe that the Bennetts fired first. Even so, Tom's death caused the chasm between the two groups to widen even further.

Archie was the only Mormon standing up for Tom Bennett.

"Julia told me the Mormons shot first," he said to Dolan. "She saw Dr. MacCulloch in the front row of men, shooting right at Tom. He ought to be arrested for the murder. We need to get up to Mackinac and get the sheriff to come down and arrest him. We can't let this murder go unpunished."

The two men planned to make a trip to Mackinac along with Bennett's body, which was being sent to the county coroner on Mackinac Island, but their plans got waylaid when new developments cast the island into turmoil.

Bates took no chances when the day arrived to arrest Strang. He had told President Fillmore that Strang had already evaded him once when he was on the island to take depositions, and would no doubt resist arrest unless they came for him with the full might of the U.S. Government on their side. Fillmore finally agreed to let Bates take the *USS Michigan*, the first iron-hulled warship to ply the Great Lakes, to make the arrest.

Strang was waking up on a sunny June day, thinking he'd handled the Bennett death with superb skill and was feeling quite good about life when, through the open bedroom window, he heard voices heading up the path to his door. He looked out the window to see the massive warship, *USS Michigan*, anchored in the harbor. It was an ominous sight. The *Michigan* was 163 feet in length and had two steam-powered side wheels and three towering masts. As he took in the sight of the ship and its crew of 30 or so armed men, he heard the voices getting closer, and then their owners were knocking on his door.

"Elvira, answer the door please, and let those men in," Strang said to his sleepy young wife. She dutifully rose and pulled on a plain dress and shoes, then went to answer the door.

Strang got dressed in his best three-piece suit and combed his beard and hair. He didn't know what the men were here for, but he wanted to look appropriately decorous when he confronted them.

When he was ready, he headed down the stairs, where he found the men sitting in the parlor alone. Elvira had gotten them settled, and then went to tend to young Charlie.

"How may I help you, gentlemen?" Strang asked politely.

The smallest man with auburn hair and blue eyes spoke. "I'm George C. Bates, federal prosecutor in the State of Michigan. This is U.S. Marshal Charles Knox, and this is the USS Michigan's First Officer Richard Bullock. You are under arrest for 38 counts of treason, federal trespassing, counterfeiting, mail fraud – "

Strang stopped him with one raised hand. "I see you have the arrest warrants in your hand, and I trust they are all legally certified," Strang said calmly.

"Of course," Bates said, feeling quite powerful since he was actually about a quarter of an inch taller than Strang.

"Then I shall not resist arrest," Strang said, much to their surprise. Strang knew he had no alternative. There was a warship waiting for him in the harbor, with military men onboard, ready to spring into action if he refused to accommodate the prosecutor's request.

After being rowed from the dock to the Michigan on the ship's tender, Strang boarded the Michigan with all the kingly dignity he could muster with his hands cuffed behind his back. The cocksure Bates had insisted on the handcuffs. Mary and Elvira watched with incredulity. Elvira was filled with concern; Mary was filled with wonder. She wondered if her husband was going to end up in prison.

Lucy watched the scene unfold from her own front porch. The King of Beaver Island, being escorted to a warship in manacles. She could see Mary and Elvira taking in the same view. What on earth was happening? Lucy lifted her skirts slightly so she could take large strides on her way to the Strang home. Whatever was happening, it was sure to have an impact on island life and Lucy wanted to know.

CHAPTER 39
MAY – JULY, 1851

The courtroom in Detroit was packed.

Gawkers, gossipmongers and more than a handful of newspaper reporters were all in attendance, eagerly waiting to get a look at the man who had proclaimed himself King of Beaver Island.

Also in attendance were many of Strang's followers, who made the trip from Beaver Island to Detroit to offer the king their support.

A coterie of Strang's opposition – the people Strang had unceremoniously cast out of his flock – were also in the courtroom. George Adams was there with his lowbrow lady Louisa; Eri Moore was there, with his wife Peggy; and even Gus LaBlanc grudgingly made the trip in case his testimony was needed.

Chit-chat came to an abrupt halt when Strang entered the courtroom, dressed in a modest dark suit and accompanied by his defense attorney, Colonel Andrew McReynolds, a highly regarded Democrat and a very popular man in Detroit. Strang's red beard was neatly trimmed and his hair combed back off his high forehead. He looked around and gave a self-effacing smile to the crowd and to Judge Ross Wilkins, also a Democrat.

It didn't take long to seat a jury of twelve. It was comprised of 10 Whigs and two Democrats. Strang and the Mormons were Democrats. Bates, like President Millard Fillmore, was a Whig. Bates smiled inwardly as he looked at the jury. He could already see the headlines in the *Detroit Daily Advertiser,* a decidedly pro-Whig newspaper, announcing his victory.

Bates opted to begin with the charge of trespassing on federal land and stealing timber from the U.S. Government. In his opening statement, Bates painted a vivid picture of a beautiful, heavily wooded island in the remote stretches of Lake Michigan. He spoke of Mormons chopping down tall trees and hauling lumber to their own lumber mill, built on federal property without permission.

"Strang has encouraged his people to fell a great number of logs of pine and cedar timber," Bates told the jury. "This timber is the property of the United States, and is of great value, to wit, one thousand dollars."

Strang's defense attorney McReynolds called Phineas Wright, a level-headed Mormon, to the stand. Wright lived on the southeast side of the island, where a lot of the logging had been going on. Wright was an unassuming man with a broad face and burly frame.

"Have you, or any of your fellow Mormons, illegally cut timber on Beaver Island?" MacReynolds asked him.

"No sir, not illegally," Wright said. "We were cutting timber legally because we were improving the land that we intended to purchase."

"So you had every intention of improving the land and then buying it, as allowed by the Pre-emption Act?"

"Yes, if that's what it's called. We were told it was legal to improve and settle the land we planned to purchase."

"Your witness," MacReynolds said to Bates.

Bates was familiar with the Pre-emption Act that allowed citizens to make improvements on land they planned to purchase. And Bates knew that once the U.S. Government offered land for sale, the Pre-emption Act was no longer applicable.

"Surely your leader, the brilliant prophet and king Strang, would be aware of the fact that the Pre-emption Act was no longer applicable after you arrived at the island and started chopping down trees," he said to Wright. "Because the land in question had already been offered for sale."

"I had no knowledge of that, and I have no knowledge of what James Strang knew at the time," Wright said placidly.

Bates tried to bully Wright into admitting he knew what they were doing was illegal. It backfired. The jury, most of whom had never heard of the Pre-emption Act, envisioned a place where, with a little hard work, a person could carve out a nice living cutting wood that the government wanted to keep for itself. They didn't expect a small band of pioneer settlers to understand the confusing wording of some government act. They sympathized with the Mormons.

Strang's lawyer clinched the jury's sentiments when he put Strang on the stand.

"Are there any non-Mormon Beaver Island residents who are logging on federal land?" he asked Strang.

"I believe Mr. Peter MacCauley and Mr. Samuel Bennett are logging, and to the best of my knowledge, they haven't purchased the land," Strang answered.

"So they are doing the exact same thing the Mormons are doing, but we don't see them in court today, being prosecuted, is that correct?" MacReynolds asked.

"Yes sir, that's correct. It's clearly a case of religious persecution, as I have said repeatedly," Strang said, getting his sentence out before Bates could object.

Bates moved on to the mail fraud charge, feeling confident he would have no difficulty convincing the jury of Strang's guilt. He had Adams and Moore ready to testify about mail fraud. He had a deposition from postmaster Dorry and Gus LaBlanc was also ready to testify.

Eri Moore was supposed to be one of Bates' key witnesses. After taking the oath to tell the truth, the whole truth and nothing but the truth, Moore crumbled on the witness stand like day-old cornbread. He recanted his story of being shot at as he, his wife and Gus LaBlanc raced across the ice to Garden Island. He denied that the Mormons had been armed with weapons and had fired at them.

"I think it was just some Indian boys out hunting," Moore said of the gunshots. He was looking down at his shoes while he spoke.

Bates objected loudly. "Witness tampering, judge!" he exploded. "Obviously, someone got to my witness and threatened him! He told an entirely different story during his deposition!"

Judge Roy Wilkins was a patient man but he was growing weary of Bates. "Your objection is overruled, Mr. Bates," he said sternly. "There is no evidence of witness tampering at all. Please sit down."

When Strang took the stand, he explained that the Mormons were in pursuit of Moore to arrest him for selling liquor to innocent Indians. They were not trying to stop the mail from getting to Mackinac.

LaBlanc's testimony was of no use after Strang declared that the Mormons were after Moore, not the mail.

Bates put George Adams on the stand. Adams was so eager to get revenge on Strang that his testimony soared to new heights of improvisation.

"Strang ordered us to go through the mail and pull out letters from his wife and a few other people who were likely speaking poorly of him," Adams said. "He told us to stop at nothing, even kill anyone who got in our way. Then he ordered us to burn their homes and set their farm fields on fire and burn their timber."

Adams' testimony only served to sway the jury further to Strang's side. Adams' overly theatrical allegations against the man who was courteously sitting quietly next to his defense attorney, patiently listening with an earnest, avuncular expression on his face, made Adams look like a fool.

MacReynolds wisely let Strang take the stand again. In a gentle, self-deprecating manner, Strang told the jurors about the hard-working Mormons who just sought peaceful, better lives for themselves and who tried to get along with the Gentiles, to no avail. He explained how he had sought the help of the state and federal government to protect his people, with no results. He described the daily persecution the Mormons suffered, while quietly minding their own business. By the time Strang finished, the jury, the media and the onlookers all had a very different opinion of the charming, articulate king than the one they'd had when he entered the courtroom.

The people who remained on Beaver Island during the trial avidly read the newspapers that were delivered to them by steamers.

Mary and Lucy sat in the post office late one afternoon, reading the *Detroit Free Press* and the *Daily Advertiser*. They were flushed from a long day of farming. Most of the island's male Mormon population had gone to Detroit for the trial, leaving the summer work of planting, weeding, hoeing and pruning to the women. Lucy helped the Mormon women, most of whom she liked. The women tending the fields were not the people causing trouble on the island. In fact, with most of the men gone, island life had settled into a pleasant routine of togetherness and conviviality. The women baked pies and broke bread together. Ironically, it mirrored Strang's original concept for the island. It just required Strang's absence to come to fruition.

"Well I'll be darned," Mary said as she read the *Free Press* account of the trial, her voice filled with perverse admiration.

"What?" Lucy asked. She was reading the Whig newspaper, the *Advertiser*, which had a story that cast Bates in a favorable light and Strang as a crafty leader with a penchant for power and fake royalty.

"He's doing it again, according to this," Mary said. "He's charmed the jury. He's even charmed the news reporters who find him to be, and I'm quoting here, *'A man of strong moral convictions, with a great kindness and generous spirit for his followers.'*"

"He does have a way with words," Lucy said, remembering the early days of her acquaintance with Strang. She really had cared quite a bit for him. Even now, she hoped he would somehow manage to avoid prison time.

"The *Free Press* is predicting James will be acquitted of all charges. They're saying the whole trial was based on trumped up charges by a glory-seeking prosecutor who wanted to make a name for himself."

"The *Advertiser* isn't reporting it that way," Lucy said. "They're saying Strang is a master manipulator who took advantage of gullible people. But they don't say much about the actual charges against him."

"What they're both saying is not very far from the truth, I suppose," Mary said thoughtfully. "I don't think James ever had malice in his heart. But he sabotaged himself with his craving for power."

"Closing arguments are next week, so I guess we'll soon know what the jury thinks of all of this."

As Bates saw his victory slipping through his fingers, he appealed to the President once more. Through a flurry of exchanged telegraphs, the two men had a conversation about the trial.

"These people are polygamists! The jury will be outraged at such immoral behavior. And what about their practice of consecration? They steal in the name of God."

"What they do within the confines of their religion is up to them," Fillmore said, already seeing the case was lost and knowing he would need

Strang's Mormon voting block if he was to win re-election. "And there is no proof of this consecration. They live on an island with a bunch of Indians and Irish. I imagine there's stealing going on by all sides."

"Strang crowned himself king! There are no sovereign kingdoms in the United States of America! It's treason!"

"I think he uses the term 'king' the way the Catholics use the term 'Pope.' He knows he's not really a king, it's just part of their religious terminology."

Fillmore wanted to distance himself from Bates and the case. He had an election to win in a little more than a year. The federal prosecutor's ego meant nothing to him.

Fearing his dream for accolades and prestige was slipping away, Bates decided to ignore Fillmore's directive to keep religion out of the trial. Bates had to prove that Strang's followers would do and say anything for their king, including committing crimes.

He put Dr. MacCulloch on the stand.

"When you joined the Mormon Church, did you take an oath in which you renounced allegiance to all laws, powers, potentates, presidents, or governors with the only exception being the laws of Strang or those of the Mormon Church?"

"I took some sort of oath, but I'm a little fuzzy on the exact words," MacCulloch replied. Then he burped and the courtroom laughed.

Next up was Reuben Field, Elvira's father, who had joined the church after his daughter married Strang.

When asked the same question by Bates, he responded, "There is nothing in the covenant as I interpret it requiring me to violate any law of the United States or of Michigan." Bates decided there was no point in pressing the biased father-in-law of the king any further.

Bates was getting frustrated. He needed to discredit Strang any way he could and make his followers look like fools.

He called Sarah MacCulloch to the stand.

"Mrs. MacCulloch, you are an educated, accomplished lady, born in Baltimore, and reared in the very best society. Can it be that you are a Mormon?" Bates asked her.

"Yes, sir, I have that honor, sir," she said, smiling politely and showing the jury her beautiful, straight white teeth.

"Can it be possible, madam, that so accomplished a lady as you are can believe that that fellow Strang is a prophet, seer and revelator?" Bates said the last words with an incredulous sneer on his face.

"Yes, Mr. District Attorney, I know it."

"Perhaps we do not comprehend each other, madam. What do you mean by a prophet?"

"You know well enough, sir. I mean one who foretells coming events, speaks in unknown tongues, one like Isaiah and the prophets of the Old Testament."

"Madam, how do you know that Strang speaks in unknown tongues and foretells coming events?"

"Because I have heard him, and witnessed those events thus foretold."

"Can it be possible, Mrs. MacCulloch, that you are so blind as to really believe that that fellow who sits there – that Strang, is the Prophet of the Lord, the successor of Him?" Bates felt like he was about to seal the deal with his witness, where she would make a dunce out of herself. He felt he had cleverly backed her into a corner.

Instead, Sarah MacCulloch stood up and shook her fist at Bates.

"Yes, you impudent district attorney, and were you not such a darned fool, you would know it too!" Every person in the courtroom snickered with delight.

After a short recess to collect himself, Bates returned to the courtroom and called George Adams back to the stand.

Adams was eager for another opportunity to perform in front of a packed house. That day, he was dressed flamboyantly in a frock coat with a fancy silk tie that wrapped twice around his neck and was tied in a bow in front. He leaned forward, ready to field questions from Bates and in turn, deliver spell-binding answers for the jury and onlookers. It would serve Strang right to be chopped into mincemeat by Adam's testimony. He was the one who crowned Strang king, and then was so unceremoniously ousted for loving Louisa.

"Mr. Adams, what was your profession before joining the Mormon Church?" Bates asked.

"I was an actor in New York and Boston," Adams replied in a booming, baritone voice. He wanted to make sure the people in the back rows could hear him.

"When you were serving in Mr. Strang's Circle of 12, did you have the opportunity to act?"

Adams was confused. He thought he would be giving a soliloquy about Strang's criminal activities. He didn't know where this was going.

"I decline to answer that question, sir. It has nothing to do with the court."

"I'm afraid you must answer, Mr. Adams," Bates continued. "Now, what position did you hold in this Circle of 12?"

"If you must know, I was an apostle who represented the Apostle Paul."

"And when you met with the Circle of 12 and the other officers of Strang's church, did you dress in costume?"

Adams blushed deeply.

"Yes, sir, when I enacted the part of the Apostle Paul in our church, I did so in my old theatrical costume of Richard the Third." Adams was aghast when the courtroom erupted in laughter at this admission. "I'll have you know I cut quite a striking figure in that costume!" he blurted out.

Bates scored points for making Adams look like a blustery buffoon, but it wasn't enough to offset Mrs. MacCulloch's snappy retort.

Then Defense Attorney McReynolds put Strang on the stand. Strang's closing statement was eloquent and brilliant.

"Like Jesus and his disciples before me, I and my people are victims of religious persecution," Strang said in his melodious voice. "I don't even know if I'll have a family and a home to return to when this trial reaches its completion. Those who hate me are well-armed, vicious wolves and may very well have burned my home to the ground and taken the lives of my loved ones."

Strang read the jury as easily as he read books to his children. He could sense they needed a reason to believe he was a rational, law-abiding man.

"Our lifestyle on Beaver Island is based on 'Divine law,' which governs our personal behavior, but is never above civil law," Strang continued. "I teach my followers to obey rulers and magistrates who are in positions of civil authority. We do not stray from the laws of the country; we simply abide by good moral and religious codes of conduct."

Strang then looked in the direction of the still dejected Eri Moore and deflated George Adams. His voice rose.

"If you think we Mormons are not to be believed in the first place, then why would you believe the words of Mormon outcasts? George Adams is a man so corrupted that he wasn't fit for the lowest position in the church. Are you going to lend credence to his words over the words of decent, moral citizens?"

After closing arguments, Judge Wilkins gave his instructions to the jury, cautioning them to make a decision based on facts, not religious influences.

Deliberation was short. The verdict declared Strang was not guilty on all charges.

The *Free Press* wrote an extensive article about the key aspects of the trial.

"*Without one particle of proof the Mormons were branded as felons and murderers; as being so sunk in infamy and crime, as to be without the pale of human sympathy, or common justice.*

"*The evidence was of the most dim and shadowy nature. Most of it related to anything else than the charge of obstructing the mail, and seemed designed rather as a general expose of Mormon credulity and the peculiarities of the Mormon faith than as testimony upon which a prosecuting officer could seriously ask conviction by the jury. There was little evidence of the obstruction of the mail; but the testimony was full and voluminous upon the question of King Strang's prophetical gifts; upon binding covenants, church discipline and management. That the Mormon defendant was a Mormon was the only crime fully substantiated.*"

Three days later, a triumphant James Strang stepped off the sailing vessel *Wisconsin* and onto the dock at St. James Harbor. He'd been gone nearly two months, and the island was a sight for sore eyes. The harbor was alive with activity – more homes were being built along the shore, extending south toward Luney's Point. The tabernacle loomed majestically from the hilltop, and construction of the schoolhouse next to it was well underway. Strang's vision was becoming a reality.

Elvira, with baby Charlie in her arms, raced to greet her husband. Mary stood back from the excited crowd of Mormons, all waiting to greet their victorious king.

Strang walked down the pier with the posture befitting a vindicated man, head up, chin out, receding hairline tilted toward the sky. He had read all the news articles about himself, and the abundant, favorable coverage of the trial had rekindled one of his age-old dreams; to become a powerful politician.

CHAPTER 40

FALL, 1851

As a pretty young woman, Rose Antoinette Pratt had taken a big gamble in life.

It was an abject failure.

Rose was the eldest daughter of lower, working-class parents, living in a shabby neighborhood of southwest Philadelphia. She had inherited her mother's brains, which were woefully underutilized as the wife of a ditch digger and mother of seven. It seemed to Rose that each baby her mother had after herself was more colicky, scrawny and unappealing than the one before it.

Rose figured out early in her childhood that she wanted no such life for herself. She was smart, wickedly funny, and bestowed with extremely ample bosoms and a tiny waist that gave way to broad hips and a round bottom. She was fully developed by the time she was 13, and boys adored her.

As soon as she could, Rose got a job in a fancy millinery shop where she could come into contact with the higher end of society. Even though Rose had no interest in spoiled rich girls, she befriended them whenever she could. She stroked their egos and appealed to their vanity, complimenting them and cooing over how lovely and clever they were. Personally, Rose couldn't stand them. She thought they were a bunch of simpering fools.

But those girls were her ticket to the boys of high society, and that was what she was after.

It didn't take a smart girl like Rose very long to figure out what boys wanted – sex. She gave them what they wanted in copious amounts, yet always taking care to not make the same mistake her mother had made; getting pregnant at a young age and marrying a handsome but dumb man because it was the proper thing to do. Rose loved her father, but was not blind to his shortcomings. She wanted better.

Rose finagled invitations to society parties, where she was always surrounded by a gaggle of wealthy young men who found her sharp-tongued wit delightful. They were even more delighted when they discovered that her sharp tongue was exceptionally talented when it went exploring around their private parts. Rose kept her virginity, knowing it was a prerequisite for marriage into one of Philadelphia's finer families. She figured out that men were content to leave her virginity intact as long as she pleased them in other ways, which were far less ladylike and definitely more exciting.

Rose flitted from one young man to another, always pleasing them with her bow tie mouth and beautiful white breasts. She happily allowed them to do exploring of their own on her well-curved body.

When she turned 21, she was certain the offers of marriage would start rolling in. All the men she dated told her repeatedly how much fun she was; how smart she was; how different she was from the boring socialite girls who wouldn't let them do more than give them a peck on the cheek at the end of the evening. They all promised their undying love and devotion.

The requests for her hand in marriage didn't come. Undeterred, Rose upped her game, and through trial and error, learned even more about the ways of pleasing men. She was a sexual expert by the time she turned 25. She was sure her skill would put her in the front of the line for well-bred men who wanted a lifetime of sexual pleasure instead of a prissy society girl.

Rose traded sexual favors for the promise of marriage to many a wealthy young man. One by one, the boys who had promised she could have their hearts, went off and married proper girls who came from their same social stratum.

At the age of 28, Rose knew she'd made a terrible mistake.

The working-class boys had no interest in her after having been snubbed by her for so many years. Even so, a few of them made passes at her, mostly in hopes of groping her large bosoms. By the time Rose was 30, the working-class boys lost interest in her as well, and went on to marry young girls from their neighborhood.

When her 33rd birthday rolled around, Rose was a bitter, angry woman; an old maid, still living in her parents' crumbling home with her raucous younger siblings. Her pretty mouth became a thin straight line that turned down at the corners. Scowl lines were forming around her eyes and a knife-sharp, vertical line creased the skin above the bridge of her nose. Even her once-desirable body was losing its firmness and shape. She had to find a way out of her deplorable situation, but for the life of her, she couldn't think of one.

Then Rose saw the small article in the newspaper, announcing a Mormon gathering to be held near her home. The article invited one and all to come and learn more about the Latter-Day Saints of King James Strang, who would guarantee a life of happiness and fulfillment for those who joined him on Beaver Island.

"Women shall have the husbands they want and deserve," the article said. *"No woman should have to settle for a dirty, drunken beast because there is a shortage of eligible men. Our beliefs allow women to have husbands of their choosing."*

Rose quickly decided this could be her ticket to a better life. It wasn't the society life she wanted, but the spigot to that pipe dream had rusted shut long ago.

On the day of the Mormon gathering, Rose dressed in her best linen dress, which was indigo blue and snug, but modestly so. She walked the two miles to the meeting place and entered a large tent when she got there.

In the front of the gathering was a tall man, broad shouldered, with pale, watery eyes. She promptly wondered if he was one of the eligible men. Good-looking enough, though a bit worn in the face, she hoped he was an example of the possibilities.

She took a seat on a wooden chair near the front of the group. She listened as the man explained the beliefs and goals of the Latter-Day Saints on Beaver Island. All his talk about a clean, pure lifestyle in a community surrounded by fields, forests and beautiful water bored her. She wanted to know more about the eligible men.

"We adhere to a practice called spiritual wifery," the man who had introduced himself as Lorenzo Hickey said. "A man may take more than one wife if he can afford to support her properly. This way, decent women can marry a man of good quality, even if he already has a wife."

Rose thought about it for a moment. She had never heard of such a thing, and wasn't sure if she wanted to share a husband with another woman. But the more she thought about it, the more she liked the idea.

Let the other wife do the cooking and cleaning, I'll take care of the sexual needs of a husband, she thought. Even though she'd lost her youthful blush of beauty, she still knew how to please a man in bed, and undoubtedly better than any other woman, she was confident of that.

When the man finished speaking and took questions from the audience, Rose raised her hand.

"If a woman goes with you to this island, how do you arrange a marriage for her? Is it up to the woman to find a new husband?" she asked Hickey.

For a moment, Hickey was stumped. This was new territory for him. He still wasn't convinced polygamy was the proper course of action, but it was too late to protest. He dared not call into question anything his prophet said. Hickey had once lost his bearings after he'd accused Strang of fornication and been suspended from the church. After being allowed back in the fold, he'd discovered his own wife had left him. Now Hickey had only one thing to bring meaning to his life – his Mormon faith. And Strang had made polygamy a significant part of that faith.

"Our Prophet James will provide, I assure you," Hickey said. "He is a man of great wisdom and knowledge. He will make sure that his promise of a husband for every woman will be fulfilled."

Hickey was quite proud of himself for coming up with an answer that would please the surly-looking woman who asked it. *Let it be Strang's problem,* he thought. *He's the one who started it.*

"I'm ready to leave today," an older woman in the middle of the crowd said.

"I'm ready as well," said another.

Rose could see she wasn't the only woman looking for a mate. The competition was already growing and no one yet had even figured out exactly where this island was located. Lake Michigan was all they knew. Rose had never been near a lake.

"I'm ready to make one of your Beaver Island men the happiest man on earth," Rose said loudly, then licked her lips suggestively. It brought smiles to the faces of men in the audience.

Rose then pursed her lips and gave a tight smile to the other women. She had made her mark. Word would travel back to the island about her, and she would get the man of her choice.

———◆•◆———

With the help of a guidebook she purchased at the train station, Rose Pratt planned out her long journey to Beaver Island. She would take a train from Philadelphia to Pittsburgh; from there, a stagecoach to Cleveland; then she could board a steamship that would take her to Detroit; and from there, board a boat to take her to Beaver Island. The tickets were going to cost her every penny she'd saved in her life. Once again, she was gambling with her life; but this time, she had a guarantee. She'd been promised a husband by Mr. Hickey, who even put it in writing for her.

With her tickets and the letter from Hickey clutched in her hand, Rose said goodbye to her family and picked up her small suitcase, ready to head for the train station.

"I'll be fine, mother," Rose assured her mother when she saw the tears in her eyes. "I'll be a married woman. You don't need to take care of me anymore." Rose's father gave her a perfunctory hug goodbye, secretly glad that there would be one less mouth to feed at the Pratt family table. After the short family farewell, Rose Pratt embarked on her new life.

CHAPTER 41

AUGUST, 1851

After reading mostly favorable news coverage of Strang and his followers on Beaver Island, more people who were tired of crowded, dirty city life decided to abandon their roots and move to Beaver Island.

Among them was Frank Johnson, who initially had reservations about making the move. He'd read and re-read the letter from his friend Hezekiah MacCulloch about opening a general store there, carefully weighing the very real risk versus the unknown reward.

There wasn't much to keep him in Baltimore. His wife had died several years ago, shortly after their conversion to the Latter-Day Saints, and his daughter Phebe had married a Mormon, Alexander Wentworth. They had both moved to Beaver Island, leaving Johnson with nothing but a store to run in Baltimore. Johnson realized he was lonely. He'd spent too many evenings alone, going out to dinner, eating rich food and growing a paunch. His light brown hair was thinning as he aged, and his hazel eyes had lost their sparkle.

After Strang's trial, Johnson decided in favor of moving to Beaver Island. He and MacCulloch met with the former store proprietor Alva Cable the day after Johnson's arrival. Johnson was a man who wasted no time when it came to business. Cable was firmly ensconced on the south end of the island with his brother James and wanted nothing more to do with the property he owned on the harbor, which was rapidly being surrounded by Mormon homes. Negotiations were quick and painless. Cable accepted their first offer for his property. He didn't need the money. His business on the southeast side of the island, selling cordwood and supplies to boats whose captains preferred to avoid the Mormon enclave in the City of St. James, was thriving. Cable even included his small cabin that was on the adjacent property as part of the deal. Frank Johnson promptly moved in.

From his storefront porch across the road from Johnson and MacCulloch's new store, Peter McKinley watched as Thomas Bedford, Alex Wentworth and a handful of young Mormon men unloaded dry goods and food staples as fast as the boats could deliver the products. The new Mormon store was rapidly being stocked. They would be open for business long before the weather turned foul.

Lucy stepped onto McKinley's porch and saw him standing at the corner, leaning on the rough-cut wooden porch rail and looking like a man who had lost his best hunting dog.

"Peter, what's the matter?" Lucy asked him.

"I'm afraid it won't be long now," McKinley said. "That store will be open for business soon, and the Mormons will no doubt shop there, not here. I don't know if my business can survive that."

"Now, Pete, you know there are lots of us who will continue to take our business to you," Lucy said. "You'll be fine." But she, too, wondered if Peter could handle the competition.

"More Mormons coming, more of our kind leaving," McKinley said. "It doesn't bode well for my business."

Lucy took the older man gently by the elbow. "Come on, I've got some supplies to buy, so let's go inside. Sell me something I need. Or sell me something I don't need, and I'll find a use for it." She smiled at him, and for the first time all day, he smiled back.

After filling her sacks with more supplies than she would need for a month, Lucy left the store and headed home. She was surprised to see Mary Strang sitting on her front porch steps. She looked forlorn in a drab green cotton dress that was worn thin at the elbows.

"Well, this is a surprise," Lucy said to Mary. "What brings you here?"

"I've come to say goodbye," Mary said as she stood up. When Mary let out a sob, Lucy dropped her bags and gave Mary a hug.

"What do you mean, goodbye? You can't be leaving!"

"James is sending me off the island. I'm taking the children and going back to Wisconsin."

"Why would he do such a thing! You're his wife! His real wife!" Lucy was aghast. She ushered Mary into her home and got her settled in a chair, then went back out to retrieve her groceries. Back inside, Mary was sitting where Lucy had left her, tears streaming down her face.

"I'm so ashamed," Mary said, swiping at her wet face with the back of her hand.

"Ashamed? Angry is what you should be! What do you have to be ashamed of?" Lucy was angry enough for the both of them.

"James said I've disgraced him and undermined the community he's building. And he's right, I did do that."

"You spoke the truth about him, there's no shame in that."

"Well, it felt good at the time, to tell people about his ridiculous visions and revelations from angels, but now it's blown up in my face. Nobody wants to hear bad things about their chosen leader."

"They are a bunch of ignoramuses if they choose to believe James. And they will no doubt get what they deserve someday." Lucy had no idea what she meant by that, but it felt like the right thing to say.

"Couldn't you just stay here and live with me?" Lucy asked. "I've got plenty of room." Even as the words escaped her, she knew it was impossible. Mary had grown stronger during her time on the island, but she wasn't strong enough to be insubordinate to her powerful husband. And certainly not in a community that would side with him.

"You and I both know that can't happen. It's all right. Other than you, there wasn't much here I really liked. My brothers and parents are all in Wisconsin. I'm actually kind of glad this happened. I've missed my home and my family there. And at least James isn't trying to keep the children here with him. I guess that's good news, although it breaks my heart that he cares so little for them that he would send them away with me."

Lucy couldn't tell if Mary was being stoic or truthful. Seeing a small smile form and her pale eyes brighten at the mention of her family in Wisconsin, Lucy decided Mary was telling the truth.

"You know I'll miss you very much," Lucy said. "You've become a good friend to me."

"I feel the same," Mary said "We'll keep in touch. I'll write lots of letters. So if you don't get letters from me, you'd better go see James and tell him to quit meddling with the mail again."

They both laughed, although Mary's was a weak chuckle.

"I'd better go get packed. I'm leaving this afternoon on the *Morgan*. Fitting, I suppose, that the boat that brought me here will take me back home."

Mary rose from her chair, and Lucy rose too. "I'll walk you home," she said.

When they arrived at the Strang home, Elvira was outside with the baby, pacing a few steps back and forth, trying to get little Charlie to stop crying. Mary stepped swiftly around her and went into the home to pack, leaving Lucy outside.

"I understand you'll now be the first wife," Lucy said to Elvira.

"I'll be the only wife," Elvira snapped back. She was clearly frazzled, trying to get the colicky infant to settle down.

"I wouldn't count on that. A man who will cast aside his first wife in favor of a younger woman will no doubt do the same thing when the younger woman is not so young anymore."

Elvira hadn't thought of that. She'd been the pampered, young second wife for long enough that it didn't occur to her James might seek the company of yet another woman.

"You don't know what you're talking about," she spat at Lucy, who remained calm.

"Sadly, I do." Lucy left it at that. She would never tell Elvira that at one point in time, it was she who James had longed for in the absence of Mary, and it was she whom he had hoped to make his second wife.

Lucy stood on the dock to wave goodbye to Mary and her three children as the *Morgan* pulled away. She had hoped to see James so she could give him a piece of her mind, but he never materialized. He didn't even have the decency and courage to bid a proper farewell to his first and only legal wife and his first three children.

The people who had disembarked from the *Morgan* earlier that day were milling around, looking for the people who were supposed to greet them.

Rose Pratt was among them, dressed in a cheerful calico print dress that emphasized her generous bosoms. She stood on the edge of the road, taking in the sights and sounds. She could hear a sawmill somewhere nearby, buzzing through one tree after another. Hammers pounded and work-men shouted. A sign was being hoisted on a large, nearby store that said, "Johnson and MacCulloch, General Store." A handsome young man rode by on horseback. She leveled her gaze at him and deliberately widened her blue eyes.

"Are you looking for someone?" The man asked her.

"I believe a man named Lorenzo Hickey was supposed to meet me here," she said demurely. She liked the look of this man, all tall and handsome. "I'm a brand new Mormon."

"I'm Nathan Bowman, deputy constable," Nathan said, sitting a little straighter in his saddle. "I can go get Mr. Hickey for you if you'd like."

"That would be most kind of you," Rose said, giving him her sweetest smile. Her lips trembled at the effort. She hadn't used her flirty smile mus-cles in a long time.

"I'll be right back, I promise." Nathan turned his horse's head and gave him a gentle kick, steering him in the direction of Hickey's home on the southern shore of the harbor.

When he arrived at Hickey's small, tidy house, he dismounted and tossed the reins on the fence post. He knocked loudly on Hickey's door.

"Lorenzo!" he called out. "You've got a lady at the harbor waiting for you. Did you find yourself a new wife and keep it a secret from us?"

Lorenzo answered the door, looking panic-stricken.

"Oh dear no, it must be one of those women who heard me preaching about polygamy," he said. "What am I to do with her? I promised those Philadelphia women we'd have husbands for them if they came to Beaver Island."

"Well then, find her a husband," Nathan said easily. "She's not too bad-looking for an old maid. Someone will take her."

Back at the harbor, as soon as Nathan was out of sight, Rose's face re-laxed and assumed its more natural, saggy countenance. She tapped her small foot impatiently and glowered at dirty fishermen who looked her way.

When she spotted Nathan walking with Hickey, she once again put on a cheerful face. Hickey didn't look very cheerful at all.

He extended his hand to Rose. "A newcomer from Philadelphia, I see!" Hickey said with artificial enthusiasm. "And you are…"

"Rose Pratt," she answered quickly. "Mr. Hickey, where am I to stay until you've found me, ah, um, my permanent arrangement?" Rose wasn't sure how to use the word polygamy in a sentence.

"I believe there's room at Lucy LaFleur's boarding house, it's just up there." Hickey nodded in the direction of Lucy's. "Nathan, could you carry Miss Pratt's belongings up the hill for her? I've got important business to attend to," he lied awkwardly. The only important business he had to attend to was to find Strang and figure out what they were going to do with the women who came to the island looking for husbands.

Nathan didn't have anything in particular to do that day except ride around and look for people to harass about their taxes and tithing, so he agreed to help Rose.

"It would be my pleasure," Nathan said as he took Rose's suitcase. He gave her a broad smile. He hadn't flirted with a woman in years and he was finding it quite pleasant to do so, even if the woman in question was beyond her prime. As he picked up her bag, he snuck a look at her disproportionately large bosoms and immediately had thoughts about what he would like to do with them.

When they arrived at Lucy's, Nathan knocked on the door and Lucy answered it.

"Mrs. LaFleur, I have a new guest for you. This is Rose Pratt, one of our new Mormon brethren."

Lucy looked at the woman. She had no wedding ring on her hand. She had the worn look of a dog that was once strong and fit, but had been forced to pull a dogsled too many times in hard weather.

"Welcome to Beaver Island," Lucy said. She took Rose's satchel from Nathan and guided Rose into the house. "Thank you, Nathan, I'll get Rose settled in now." It was her way of telling him to leave.

Lucy showed Rose to a room upstairs with a view of the harbor. As always, she tried to make polite conversation.

"I'm sure you'll enjoy your stay here," she said. "The Mormons seem to be good people."

"I certainly hope they are, since I'm planning to marry one of them soon," Rose said.

"Oh, really?" That explained things. The woman must have met another new Mormon somewhere and the two of them had come here to start a new life. "And who has the pleasure of your hand in marriage?"

"I don't know," Rose said without a trace of embarrassment. "I haven't picked him out yet. But I was told that single women like me are welcome to come here and pick out a husband of their choosing, even if the one they want is already married. That Nathan fellow is a fine-looking man, does he already have a wife? Maybe he'd be in the market for another one."

Lucy dropped Rose's bag with a loud thud. "You came here by yourself to find a husband? A man who might already be taken?" Lucy knew she sounded rude, but she couldn't help herself. Her rudeness didn't bother Rose in the slightest.

"Yes. I've got a letter, signed by Mr. Lorenzo Hickey, stating that the Strangite Church of Latter-Day Saints will find me a husband on this island if I don't find one for myself first."

Rose bent down to dig in the satchel that Lucy had dropped and fished out her letter. "See? It's right here. All official, signed by Mr. Hickey. So what about that Nathan fellow, is he married?"

Lucy thought of Eliza, who had struggled for so long to find happiness with Nathan. What would bringing a second wife into their home do to Eliza? But then Lucy realized she was getting ahead of herself. The vain Nathan Bowman would never agree to marrying an old spinster like Rose.

"Nathan is married, I'm afraid, and I have no reason to believe he'd want to take a second wife."

"Well, you just never know now, do you?" Rose gave her a secretive smile. "I might be able to convince him otherwise."

Lucy left Rose to unpack. She went downstairs, where she stood at the window and looked out at the harbor. The island was changing so quickly, she could hardly keep up with it. Should she expect to be inundated by an onslaught of lonely women? Women who had been promised husbands if they converted to Strang's church? It was surreal. She watched as one wave after another crashed on the shore and dissipated, only to be overtaken by the next oncoming wave that crashed with equal force. *Now I know what the sand on the beach feels like,* Lucy thought to herself as the waves kept coming.

CHAPTER 42
AUGUST, 1851

After unpacking her meager belongings, Rose left Lucy's home and walked into town. She was drawn to the store with the large new sign that said, "Johnson and MacCulloch." Rose liked new things. She also liked the man she saw leaning against the porch rail. Nathan Bowman was idly picking a scab on his knuckles instead of helping unload pallets of flour, sugar, coffee and other assorted goods.

"Well, hello there," Rose said with her trademark tilt of the head and quick purse of her lips.

"Hello, Rose, good to see you again," Nathan said. "I was just resting for a moment. Tiring work, unloading hundreds of pounds of groceries." Nathan overestimated the amount of groceries he had unloaded by a factor of about 100. He flexed a muscle to indicate how hard he had been working.

"My goodness, they're lucky to have a strong fellow like you to help them," Rose said breathlessly, making sure her bosoms heaved up and down with her words. It worked. Nathan noticed.

"Mr. Bowman, may I ask you a favor? I'd like to look around the island but I'm not sure if it's safe for a woman like me to be wandering around all by myself. Could you show me around, perhaps, a little later today?"

Nathan looked at the horizon, judging that there wasn't more than a couple of hours of daylight left. "Sure, but we'd better get started. It will be dark before you know it."

That was exactly what she was planning on. Rose smiled and slipped her hand through Nathan's extended arm.

They walked around the harbor, then followed the shoreline toward Luney's Point. Rose had chosen their direction, steering Nathan toward the big stand of trees she saw in the south. Trees meant shadows. Shadows meant being alone with Nathan and out of sight of prying eyes.

When they reached the edge of the forest, Nathan hesitated. "It's getting close to dark, maybe we should head back," he said.

"Oh, but I love the sight of sunset coming through the leaves," Rose said, tugging at his sleeve. "Let's just go a little farther." Rose reached for his hand, and in the process brushed the back of her hand against his groin. That was all it took.

When they were no more than 20 feet inside the forest, Rose turned to Nathan, stood on tiptoe and kissed his neck, then ran her tongue along his neck and under his chin. Nathan had never felt anything like it. It was dark in the woods, only a bit of the fading sunset flickering in the tree branches as the breeze moved them about. He couldn't see Rose's face, but he knew where it was. At the moment, it was burrowing into his shirt, her tongue leading the way.

"Oh, Rose," he groaned as she continued to make her way down his chest. She'd unbuttoned his shirt and her tongue and lips were making their way slowly, sensuously, down toward his navel.

She gently pushed Nathan back until he was leaning against a birch tree. Then she knelt in front of him and unbuttoned his trousers. Nathan was too stunned and excited to protest.

What happened then was something Nathan never dreamed a woman could do, or would do. Within seconds he climaxed, and slid down to the ground where he sat, unable to speak. Rose nuzzled next to him and stroked his nipples. Then, unbelievably, she once again positioned herself in between his legs and did even more unspeakable, filthy, exotic, thrilling things to him.

Nathan never went home that night. He and Rose spent the night in the forest, where she brought him to climax a remarkable four times. He walked, rather gingerly, back with her to Lucy's house at sunrise, not caring if anyone saw them together.

When Rose got back to her room, she rubbed parts of her body with a mixture of rosewater and glycerin that she'd brought from Philadelphia. Her nipples were cracked and sore from encouraging Nathan to suck and bite them. Her bottom was red where she told him to spank her hard for being a naughty girl. But it was worth the pain, she knew. By the time he had his second orgasm, he told her he loved her; by the time he had his fourth, he agreed to marry her.

Eliza wasn't alarmed when Nathan didn't come home that night. He'd often spent the night out, playing cards with the other deputies, or roaming around the island in the dark with them, consecrating items from the Gentiles.

She was mildly surprised when he did come home later that morning in an unbelievably good mood. She couldn't remember the last time she'd seen him so upbeat and happy. *Maybe they consecrated something of tremendous value, and are anticipating King Strang's exuberance when they present it to him,* she thought.

Eliza didn't become alarmed until Nathan stayed out all night for six straight nights in a row. She finally confronted him about his week of staying away from home.

"I can't tell you what I'm doing," Nathan told her. "But trust me, it's very important. I'm doing the work of the Lord and of King James. We will be blessed for it."

Nathan was right about getting blessed for his nocturnal activities. He'd gone to Strang and told him of his desire to wed the frumpy Rose Pratt because she was a good woman who deserved a good man, as she had been promised. Strang was amazed that a strapping young man like Nathan would take on a spinster like Rose for the good of the church. But it was exactly what he had preached about. And here was Nathan, helping Strang make good on his promise of a good husband for all women who sought one. Strang couldn't have been more pleased.

"I'd like us to be married as soon as possible," Nathan told the king. "In a private ceremony. I think my wife Eliza will take the news better once it's a done thing. No point in upsetting her ahead of time."

"I completely understand your sentiments," Strang told him, remembering his own days of hiding his relationship with Elvira from Mary. Better to present women with a fait accompli than with an opportunity to wreak havoc on a man's plans, Strang knew all too well.

Exactly one week after meeting Rose Pratt, Nathan became her wedded husband in a ceremony performed by Strang and witnessed by Miller,

Chidester and Pierce. They couldn't see what Nathan saw in Rose, but they also didn't believe for a minute he married her out of the goodness of his heart. There wasn't a lot of goodness in Nathan's heart, and what there was, he lavished on himself.

Lucy didn't give much thought to the fact that Rose Pratt spent very little time in her home. Lorenzo Hickey had arranged to pay for her room and board; beyond that, Lucy assumed Rose had been caught up in a flurry of Mormon welcoming activities.

Lucy was sweeping her front steps when she saw Eliza Bowman headed her way. Eliza's round gray eyes were twinkling. Her dark blonde hair looked freshly washed. She was wearing a pretty linen dress that flattered her tall, slender figure. Lucy put her broom down and walked to greet her.

"Lucy, could I borrow that blue vase you have?" Eliza asked.

"Of course, come with me," Lucy said as she headed back up the steps. "What's the occasion?"

"I don't know, but when Nathan left the house this morning, he was in a wonderful mood and he told me something big and important was about to happen and I should have the house looking its very best by supper time."

"Well, that's mysterious and exciting," Lucy said. "Want to go out back and pick some flowers for that vase?"

"Yes, please," Eliza said. "Nathan's been so busy this past week, doing something secret for King James. I think he's about to get promoted to some special office in the church."

Lucy found it hard to believe Eliza's ne'er-do-well husband could have actually earned a promotion in the church through hard work. But she couldn't blame Eliza for wanting so desperately to believe her husband was working his way up the ladder to success.

"If that makes you happy, then I'm happy for you," Lucy said.

Eliza left Lucy's home with a vase full of wildflowers. When she got back to her tiny home, she set the flowers on the square table under the window, tied a yellow apron around her waist and began making supper. She fried chicken in heated lard in an iron skillet, and when it was cooked, she pulled the chicken out of the pan and added potatoes and onions to the hot lard, enjoying the sound of the sizzling they made. The small home was soon filled with the smell of fried onions and potatoes. Supper was ready and on the table when Nathan came home.

Eliza was hanging up her apron on a hook near the stove when she heard the door open. In walked Nathan, with a grumpy-looking older woman.

"Eliza, I can tell you my news now," Nathan said "King James has made me an apostle! I am now in the Circle of 12, making me one of the most important Mormons on the island!"

"Wonderful!" Eliza exclaimed but looked confused. "And this woman, who is she? Does she escort the Apostles to and from the tabernacle?" Eliza spoke directly to Nathan, ignoring the woman.

"Eliza, this is Rose Pratt. Rose Pratt Bowman, my new wife."

At that moment, something snapped in Eliza's head. She looked at Nathan, her husband of seven years, and saw a completely different man. It was as if her head had been bound in gauze during their entire marriage and now the gauze had fallen away and she was seeing him for the first time. She looked at his glittering eyes, noticing the greed and joy he felt for his newest acquisition.

"Never. Ever. Will there be a second wife in this house."

Eliza didn't hesitate. She turned on her heel and walked out the door, not bothering to close it behind her. She started running. She ran down the road away from town, toward the forest. She ran and ran and ran, losing her left shoe first, and then the right one. She ran barefoot through the woods, not feeling the scrapes and cuts on the soles of her feet. She ran until it was dark out, and she couldn't see her way in the woods. Then she sat down on a fallen log and wept.

Back at the Bowman household, Nathan saw no reason to waste a perfectly good supper that was already on the table. He sat down and started eating, motioning for Rose to join him.

"Do you think you should go after her?" Rose asked. The food smelled delicious, but she didn't want to lose the wife who would be doing the cooking and the chores on the first day of her marriage.

"King James said it would take her a while to get used to the arrangement," Nathan said with a mouth full of potatoes. "She just needs some time to think about it. She'll be back. Now eat, and then I know what we can have for dessert." Nathan pinched Rose's nipple hard as he said the words. Rose slapped his hand away.

"Not at the supper table!" she admonished him. "For goodness sakes, Nathan, learn some manners!"

Nathan was taken aback. For a week, he had been fondling, pinching, spanking, probing and poking Rose any way he wanted. Now she was his wife and he was being rebuked? This had to be nipped in the bud.

Nathan slapped Rose across the face. Then he slapped her once again for good measure.

"I'll do what I want when I want to do it. You are my wife now, and as the King told you, you are expected to submit graciously to your husband."

Rose kept her head down and said nothing. She contemplated her situation. She was now the second wife to a handsome but selfish man, living on an island in the middle of a freshwater ocean; and the first wife, who was supposed to cook and clean and make life easy for Rose, had run off and left Rose to fend for herself.

Rose started to wonder if she'd just taken another gamble in life that would pay out in dirt instead of dignity.

—————◆◆◆—————

Eliza eventually fell asleep in the woods, a rotting, moss-covered log serving as her pillow. She shivered with cold through the night. When she woke, she ached all over. Her lavender dress was torn and muddy. Her feet were bruised and bloody. Her heart felt the way her feet looked.

And yet strangely, she also felt emancipated. All these years she'd been subservient to Nathan, thinking he deserved her devotion. She'd loved him even when he failed. She'd stuck by him when others didn't. Now she saw him for who he was. A spineless, self-serving snake.

Picking herself up off the forest floor, Eliza looked up to see where the sun was coming from. It was hard to tell through the thick branches, but she was pretty sure she could head west as long as she kept the slanting rays of light on her back. She started picking her way carefully through the brush and saplings, headed toward the one place she knew she would be safe and welcome – Huldy's little cabin in the woods.

CHAPTER 43
SEPTEMBER 1851

Huldy couldn't hear her sister approach her cabin, snapping twigs as she dragged her tired feet to the door. Huldy looked up from her table where she was eating breakfast to see Eliza standing in front of her. Normally beautiful and well-kept, Eliza looked like she'd slept in a burrow with angry porcupines. Her dark blonde hair had fallen out of its bun at the nape of her neck and was snarled, with a few twigs stuck in it.

"My God, what happened?" Huldy signed as she rushed to help her sister to a chair.

Eliza signed back: "Nathan took a second wife in exchange for being promoted to church apostle. Some pathetic spinster. I won't tolerate it. I left. I slept in the woods last night."

Huldy grabbed a blanket from her bed and wrapped it around Eliza's shoulders. She fetched water from the rain barrel outside, took a cloth rag and started washing Eliza's face and hands. A grateful Eliza allowed her sister to tend to her.

"You can live here with me," Huldy signed. "It's small, but we'll manage." When she finished signing, she moved on to her washing her sister's feet, which were torn and crusted with dried blood.

"I don't want to live on this island anymore," Eliza signed back. "I want to leave here. I want to be done with this Mormon life. You can come with me."

Huldy sat back on her haunches, where she was positioned in front of Eliza on the floor. She was still for several moments.

Then she signed: "I know this will sound strange, but I like it here. I don't want to leave. But I don't blame you for wanting to leave."

Eliza put her hand on her sister's cheek. "It doesn't sound strange. This place seems to fit you. But how am I ever going to get off this island? There's probably a Mormon posse out looking for me now."

While Eliza soaked her feet in a bucket of cool water, the two of them rapidly communicated through sign language. Eliza knew that it was frowned upon for Mormons to leave the island. It would be a disgrace to Nathan if his first wife abandoned him. They would try to stop her any way they could. Leaving by steamer would be impossible. She pondered the thought of sneaking away on one of the Irish fishermen's boats, but that would require leaving in broad daylight. And she didn't know if any Irishman was willing to risk his own neck to get her off the island.

"Let's ask Lucy," Huldy signed. "You stay here. I'll go find her."

After living alone in the woods for a year, Huldy had become very adept at slipping quietly and quickly from one place to another without being seen. She took her own route to get to Lucy's home without going through town, choosing instead to skirt around the cedar swamp, through the spruce forest and across a field of tree stumps that took her to Lucy's back door.

She knocked on the door and waited. Feeling like the situation required urgency, she then opened the door and stepped in the kitchen. There she stayed, not wanting to trespass any further into Lucy's home.

Lucy appeared from the front room, and with her was Lorenzo Hickey. It looked like they were concluding a business transaction. Hickey was putting his billfold back in his coat pocket when he looked up and saw Huldy. He immediately stood straighter and smoothed his hair off his forehead.

"Hi Huldy, how nice to see you," Lucy said. "I'm just finishing up with Mr. Hickey, who was paying the bill for one of the new Mormon women in town. I guess she's found a place to live."

Lucy tried to pantomime the meaning of the words she spoke to Huldy, but Huldy didn't seem interested. She tugged at Lucy's sleeve and jerked her head toward the door.

"You need me to come with you? All right, let me finish up with Mr. Hickey."

"If she needs something, I'd be happy to offer my assistance," Hickey said, his eyes never leaving Huldy.

"I don't know about that, Huldy is a very private person," Lucy said. She looked at Huldy and then gestured to Hickey, asking Huldy if he should come too.

Huldy got agitated and shook her head vigorously, all the while pulling Lucy out the back door.

"I guess she doesn't want your help, but thank you for the offer," Lucy told Hickey. "You can let yourself out the front. I need to go with Huldy."

"My offer of help always stands," Hickey said with a quick nod of his head toward Huldy.

Huldy led Lucy along a circuitous path back to her home. Lucy was amazed at the clever path Huldy had found through some of the island's most challenging topography. When Lucy entered the tiny cabin, she was shocked to see a disheveled Eliza with her head in her hands, elbows resting on the table.

"What on earth happened to you?" Lucy said, quickly taking the other chair at the table. Huldy pulled up a three-legged milking stool from the corner and sat next to Eliza on the other side.

"Well, it finally happened," Eliza said. "Nathan has completely given himself over to the Mormon lifestyle. He has been made an apostle in the Circle of 12, and he sealed the deal by taking a second wife." Eliza's tone was flat and devoid of any feeling.

"You must be joking!"

"I wish I was. Oh, Lucy, I can see now what a useless man Nathan is. All he ever cares about is himself. And money. And finding a way to be successful without doing any work. Well, he found it. He married his way to the top level of the Mormon church."

"Who would agree to marry Nathan? Don't take this the wrong way, Eliza, but most the women on the island aren't fooled by his good looks. They know he has no substance." Lucy had never said those words aloud to Eliza before. It felt good to speak the truth to Nathan's wife.

"A newcomer, some horrid woman named Rose something."

"Rose Pratt? That clapper-clawed spinster?! I can't believe Nathan would accept her as a second wife."

"I can't believe it either. Maybe Strang paid him to do it. I don't care. I just want to leave."

Lucy took Eliza's hand and reached up with her other hand to brush some of the tangled hair off her face. "Leave the island? Or leave him?"

"Both. I want to put this all behind me. Start fresh somewhere else. I've been lying to myself about Nathan for too long. When he brought that wretched woman into my home and introduced her as his wife, I suddenly saw everything clearly." Eliza lifted her chin up defiantly. "I deserve better than him."

"I couldn't agree more. So let's get you off the island."

"How? Nathan won't take this easily. It's an insult to his manhood to have a wife leave him. He'll have all his pals looking for me soon, if they aren't already."

Lucy was already getting up from her chair, ready to spring into action. "I'll think of something. Don't worry, we'll find a way. I'll be back soon, when I've got a plan."

<hr />

Eliza wasn't too far off in her estimation of Nathan's plans. He hadn't looked for her the evening she disappeared, choosing instead to stay home and get his second wife properly trained about her wifely duties. On their second night of wedded bliss, Rose had barely swallowed her last bite of the meager meal of bacon and fried cornbread she had clumsily prepared when Nathan roughly grabbed her and dragged her to her feet.

"Take your clothes off," he ordered, and then sat back in his chair to watch her struggle out of her dress and underclothes.

When she was completely naked, he said, "Clear the table. I don't like the sight of a table with dirty dishes on it."

Household chores, Rose thought to herself. *This is exactly what I was hoping to avoid. I need to get that first wife back here as soon as possible.* A breeze floated through the window and hardened her nipples. Nathan noticed it and grinned. She was mad at her own body for making it look like she was sexually aroused.

Nathan got out of his chair and circled behind her. When Rose bent over the table to pick up a plate, Nathan grabbed her and pushed her head down onto the table, where he held it firmly with one hand.

"Time for my dessert," he said while he used his other hand to shove Rose's legs apart and jam himself into her.

Even though Rose said nothing and made no move to escape, her dryness told Nathan she was an unwilling partner, and that excited him even more. He was finished with her in less than a minute.

"Now clean this place up," he said as he buttoned his pants. "I like a tidy home."

Rose glared at him, her mouth pinched closed as tightly as a mule's behind in black fly season. "I think it would be wise of you to go find your first wife, or you might get stripped of your new apostle status," she said.

"Don't tell me what to do," Nathan said. But he was thinking essentially the same thing.

Leaving Rose naked with bruised hips from banging into the table, Nathan saddled up and rode over to Constable Miller's cabin.

———— ◆•◆ ————

Lucy burst through the door of Huldy's cabin without knocking.

"I have a plan," she said to Eliza, who was now bathed and dressed in one of Huldy's dresses. Her hair was clean, brushed and rolled into a bun at the nape of her neck.

"What is it?"

"I went to Dolan's house, hope you don't mind, but I figured we'd need help with this one. Gwen was there. We decided we can dress you up as an Indian and Gwen and Otto can paddle you off the island in one of their birch bark canoes. No one will be inspecting Indian canoes. We'll do it at night, when no one is around."

"Where will I go?" Eliza asked, feeling both nervous and excited at the prospect of her imminent departure.

"South Fox Island is probably the best. Folks are settling there, non-Mormon people. It's a nice place. And if you don't like it, you can catch a boat from there to Waukazooville on the mainland easily. I hear quite a few white settlers are moving there."

"Oh, my, I'm actually doing this." Eliza sat down, feeling overwhelmed.

"Don't worry, Otto and Gwen have friends on South Fox. They'll take care of you. We'll gather enough provisions and clothes for you to manage until you get settled."

"How can I ever thank you?"

"Thank me by getting out of here and finding a happy new life. Without Nathan." Lucy smiled kindly.

"So when shall we go?" Eliza asked. Now that arrangements were made, she was eager to get going before she could change her mind.

"The moon will be full in two nights, which will make it much easier to paddle. If the weather holds, that would be the time to go," Lucy answered.

"All right. I'll be ready."

"Yes, you will. We'll see to it." Lucy squeezed her hand and headed back out the door, leaving Eliza to explain the plan to her sister through sign language.

"Let me see if I've got this straight," Joshua Miller said to Nathan. "You brung home your new, second wife, and the first wife ran off? Can't you keep two wives happy at the same time?" Miller snickered as he said it. He had been seething mad when he found out that his deputy was getting a second wife when he didn't even have a first one. Although after he got a look at the second wife, he wasn't feeling mad so much as lucky.

"Eliza was extremely upset, and King James said to expect that, it's perfectly normal. They just need time to adjust."

"Yeah, like Mary adjusted real good; that's why she got kicked off the island all the way back to Wisconsin." Miller was enjoying himself. He liked having a reason to belittle the handsome deputy.

Nathan was starting to do a slow burn.

"Like it or not, Joshua, I have two wives, with the king's blessing, and I've got to find the first one. You're the constable here, and the king would not be happy if you let my wife get away."

Unfortunately Nathan had a point. Miller was obliged to make sure a scorned, angry first wife didn't escape and spread stories in the surrounding area about the Mormon community's questionable activities.

"Alrighty then, let's round up a posse and start looking for her. You head down to the sawmill, I'll head to the schoolhouse. Men are either sawing logs or pounding them together for the school. We'll meet at the tabernacle."

Twenty men met at the tabernacle, with the promise of at least that many more after sundown. They made a plan to break into pairs in order to cover the most turf possible, then laid out a grid pattern that each pair would search. The men who came after sundown would be assigned spots along the shore to keep anyone from slipping away in a small boat.

The searchers were swift and efficient, but not efficient enough. Huldy and Eliza sat in total darkness in the little cabin as Eliza could hear them tramping through the woods no more than 50 feet from Huldy's home.

The next day Huldy again went to fetch Lucy, taking a different route through the beech groves and prairie grass. Huldy never took the same route more than once in a week, to ensure that a path couldn't be detected. Again, Lucy was impressed.

Back at Huldy's, Eliza reported the news to Lucy. "We heard them searching in the woods, looking for me," she said.

"I'm afraid you're right. I saw them on the beach last night. I took a walk and found that they've posted men along the shore about every 100 feet. This is going to be harder than we thought."

Huldy didn't need to hear the conversation to know what was being said. She signed to Eliza, "I have an idea. We need the help of that nice Mormon man. The one you introduced me to last winter. The one that was at Lucy's house when I went to fetch her here."

"Lorenzo Hickey?" Eliza signed as well as spoke the words. "How on earth could he help?"

Lucy looked at Huldy and then it dawned on her what Huldy had in mind.

"We need a good Mormon to sneak you past the Mormons," Lucy said. "Huldy, that's genius!"

Eliza signed Lucy's words for Huldy, who then blushed and smiled.

"But why not someone like Archie? I like Archie, and he's a Mormon," Eliza said, suddenly nervous to let another person into their tight conspiratorial group.

"Archie isn't much of a Mormon and everyone knows that," Lucy said. "He joined to make Millie happy, and to come here for a fresh start. Lorenzo, on the other hand, has been one of Strang's devoted men since the beginning. And he's guileless. No one would suspect Lorenzo of deceitful behavior."

Within the hour, Lucy was knocking on the door of Mr. Lorenzo Hickey. He answered, looking pleasantly surprised to see her.

"My goodness, I wasn't expecting company, please come in," Hickey said.

Lucy entered the little home and glanced around. It was neat and tidy, unexpectedly so for a bachelor.

"Mr. Hickey, you said the other day that you'd be happy to help Huldy Cornwall if needed, correct?"

At the mention of her name, Hickey's neck flushed.

"Why, yes, I'd be delighted to help. Is she all right?" His flush faded as quickly as it had appeared when he became filled with concern.

"She's fine, but we do need your help. Could you accompany me to her home? I can explain more there."

Hickey was already reaching for his coat. "I'm at your service. Lead the way," he said, following Lucy out the door.

Lucy led Hickey on an equally circuitous path to Huldy's home. The man would never find his way back out of the woods unescorted.

After opening her front door, Huldy gave Hickey a warm smile and a nod of thanks. It made Hickey want to do anything she asked of him. Then he turned and saw Eliza at the little table.

"My stars, you're missing! People are looking for you everywhere! Is that what you need, for me to take you home?" Hickey was confused.

"No, Mr. Hickey, I do not need or want you to take me home. I don't have a home here anymore. I'm leaving."

Lucy could practically see the cogs in Hickey's head turning 'round and 'round, straining to add up one missing woman, one deaf mute sister, one cabin in the woods and one Indian woman in the center of the action. It was a piece of cogitation that was beyond his command.

Lucy spared him any more confusion and carefully spelled out the entire situation to him, including the plan to get Eliza off the island dressed as an Indian.

"I feared this practice of polygamy would come to no good," Hickey said. A part of him cringed to realize he'd been the one who had promised husbands to the women of Philadelphia, allowing the tree of polygamy to bear its bitter fruit. "I am so sorry for your circumstances. Please let me give you some money to tide you over." Without a moment's hesitation, Hickey reached for his billfold and pulled out every coin and paper dollar he had and handed it to Eliza.

"I couldn't possibly take your money, Mr. Hickey."

"Please. You must. You joined the Latter-Day Saints in good faith, trusting that polygamy would never be allowed on this island. I cannot hear the revelations that the angels bring to our prophet, but in this case, I think he heard them wrong. So take this money as my way of making things right for our king's misguided revelation."

Eliza took the money. Huldy touched Hickey by the hand and gave him a smile of gratitude. His heart swelled.

"I just had an idea," Hickey suddenly said.

The three women looked at him with surprise. Hickey was a kind-hearted man, but no one ever mistook him for the type of man who might have an idea.

"Well, I've been thinking this through the way I like to do, trying to picture the scene as it's going to happen.

"Eliza is dressed as an Indian, and is getting into an Indian canoe in the dark of night, with Gwen and Otto.

"I know I'm not the smartest fellow, so I'm asking myself, 'Why would Indians be embarking on a canoe ride at night?' If I was one of the men that Miller has stationed along the beach, I'd be inclined to go over and see why Indians are going on a canoe trip in the night."

Lucy and Eliza were nonplussed.

"Go on," Lucy said.

"So I'm thinking to myself as I see this scene, I'm thinking, what is going on here? Maybe if Gwen had been called to tend to a sick person, maybe she would take a sick person back to Garden Island to tend to that person there, where she has all her medicine woman tools and potions.

"So maybe Eliza shouldn't be dressed up as an Indian at all. Maybe she should be dressed up as Huldy. They look quite a bit alike, you know."

Lucy and Eliza both looked at Hickey with new admiration. The man wasn't dumb, he just had his own plodding way of thinking.

Hickey went on, encouraged by the rapt looks on their faces. "So you put a big bonnet on Eliza, one that belongs to Huldy, and you put her in Huldy's clothes, and she acts all wobbly and sick and vomitus and all, and Gwen and Otto just lift her into the canoe and paddle away. She doesn't need to answer any questions that might be asked because if she's Huldy, she can't talk!" Hickey finished with a triumphant flourish of his hand.

"Well, I do believe that is precisely the plan we need," Lucy said. "Gwen can tell anyone who asks that she suspects it's the cholera, so no one will get close enough to see who it really is."

Hickey beamed. "Can you explain it to Huldy for me?" he asked Eliza. "She should know, since she's the one who's supposed to get deathly ill in the next 24 hours."

On the following night, the little band of conspirators had to wait for the sun to set and darkness to take its place. The moon was full and a shimmering path of moonlight lit the way from Garden Island to Beaver Island.

Otto paddled the birch bark canoe onto the shore, hopped out and pulled it up on the beach. Gwen and Lucy met him there with Eliza, dressed as Huldy, being held up between them as she staggered with feigned illness.

Hickey had taken a position about 50 feet away from Otto's landing point. Dennis Chidester was another 50 feet away.

The sound of a canoe being dragged onto a beach caught Chidester's attention.

"Hickey!" he called. "What's going on down there?"

"Don't know, but I'll look into it." Hickey started walking toward Otto and the women.

"Stop! Wait for me. Whoever it is, they might be armed," Chidester said.

Hickey hadn't anticipated this. He waited for Chidester, trying to think on his feet and having no success.

"Looks like Indians," Chidester said when he caught up with Hickey.

"I believe you're right, nothing to worry about there," Hickey said and started to turn back.

"Hold on, I want to see what's going on." He continued to hike toward the canoe, which was now being loaded with a moaning Eliza. Otto was holding the canoe steady while Gwen climbed in after Eliza.

"Who goes there?" Chidester said as he approached.

"It's me, deputy, Lucy LaFleur, and my cousins, Otto and Gwen. They have a sick emergency to deal with."

Chidester got closer. "Who's in that canoe with them?" he asked, growing suspicious.

"Huldy Cornwall, Nathan's sister-in-law," Lucy replied.

Gwen spoke up. "I was staying at Dolan's when Huldy practically crawled onto the porch. I fear it's the cholera. She's been violently ill." On cue, Eliza leaned over the side of the canoe away from Chidester and made terrible gagging noises. The boat shielded her face from the deputy.

"Well then, get her off the island, she's contagious!" Chidester said, backing away from the canoe.

Otto gave the canoe a hard shove and within seconds it was floating. He hopped in the stern and started paddling, with Gwen paddling in front and Eliza riding in the middle. Eliza's last view of Beaver Island was upside-down, as she continued to hang her head over the gunwale and pretend to vomit.

Hickey watched the canoe get smaller and smaller as Chidester stomped past him, going back to his original watch post position.

"You've been hornswoggled," Hickey whispered under his breath as he passed. He was smiling to himself.

A week later, a very healthy Huldy was seen at Johnson and MacCulloch's new store, buying supplies. And the search for Eliza had been abandoned. The Mormon men didn't know how she did it, but they knew she had outwitted them and escaped.

CHAPTER 44
SEPTEMBER, OCTOBER, 1851

Frank Johnson and Hezekiah MacCulloch sat at a round table in the storeroom in the back of their new store, counting a sizeable pile of money.

"Not bad for a day's work, eh?" MacCulloch said. The money had come from yesterday's till.

"Not bad at all," Johnson said. "I'm definitely glad I decided to come here."

MacCulloch was enjoying his role as storeowner. It involved a lot of prestige and very little work. Johnson had hired his son-in-law Alex Wentworth to manage the store, along with his friend Tom Bedford, and they, in turn, had hired the island's new arrivals to stock shelves and clean. Rose Pratt Bowman had been hired to work the register behind the counter and straighten the merchandise displays at the end of the day. Nathan was pleased to have a wife who brought home her pay each week and turned it over to him. Rose did so, but not before tucking a portion of her pay into her secret pouch under their mattress. She was saving up for a possible escape from the island. She'd created a sexual monster with Nathan, she realized too late. Her sexual expertise and skill became an addiction for Nathan. He wanted it constantly. As a result, she was perpetually bruised and sore.

———◆◆◆———

Across from the store, on the shore of the harbor, Archie Donnelly and Dolan MacCormick were watching a boat on the horizon get bigger as it neared.

"Think that's him?" Archie asked.

"I hope so," Dolan replied.

While many of the island's residents put Tom Bennett's tragic death behind them, Archie and Dolan wanted justice for what they considered murder. They had sailed up to Mackinac in August, bringing Sam and Julia Bennett with them, to report the crime to the sheriff. It had been determined by the county coroner that the fatal shot had come from a Colt Paterson revolver. The bullet found in Tom's heart matched MacCulloch's new weapon.

Sheriff O'Reilly was convinced there was enough evidence, along with two eyewitnesses, to make an arrest. He promised he'd get the paperwork in order and sail down to Beaver Island on September 5.

"It's him," Archie said as the boat got closer. The boat had a burgee flying from its forestay that bore the sheriff's star.

Archie wasn't the only one to see it. Joshua Miller and Dennis Chidester were patrolling the waterfront and spotted it too.

"What's the sheriff's boat coming here for?" Chidester asked.

"I don't know, but it could mean trouble. Let's go get Bowman and Pierce and our weapons."

The four men gathered in front of Johnson's store, where they had a bird's eye view of the harbor. They saw the sheriff's boat pull up alongside the dock and saw Archie and Dolan secure the bow and stern lines.

The sheriff disembarked, along with his deputy. The two men walked toward Johnson's store, with Archie and Dolan trailing behind them.

Miller and his men, leaning on their rifles, greeted the sheriff.

"Morning, gentlemen, what brings you to our island?" Miller asked.

"We have a warrant for the arrest of Hezekiah MacCulloch. Is he inside?"

"What's he been charged with?"

"He is being charged with the murder of Thomas Bennett. Now step aside," the sheriff said, nudging Miller out of his way. He stepped into the store, followed by his deputy, Archie and Dolan.

Miller, Chidester, Pierce and Bowman also followed them into the store.

Johnson was emerging from the back room, where he'd left MacCulloch.

"You MacCulloch?" the sheriff asked Johnson.

"No," Johnson said. "What do you want with MacCulloch?"

"I'm here to arrest him for the murder of Thomas Bennett."

"Not so fast." Miller stepped in front of the sheriff, his rifle in his right hand and his left hand on the holster of the gun on his hip. He was blocking the way to the back room of the store. Chidester, Pierce and Bowman followed suit, positioning themselves alongside Miller, each of them holding a weapon in their hands.

"Now look here, I have a warrant for his arrest, you can't stop me," the sheriff said.

"We most certainly can, this is our jurisdiction. In fact, we'll deal with MacCulloch in our own way," Miller said. "Bowman, Chidester, go get MacCulloch and take him to the prophet's home and put him under house arrest."

Everyone looked confused. The sheriff sensed a standoff, and didn't want to get into a gunfight with the local constable.

"They're not arresting him, he's one of their own," Dolan protested. "They're protecting him!"

Meanwhile, Bowman and Chidester went into the back room of the store, where Johnson was already pushing a perplexed MacCulloch out the back door.

"Take him to Strang's, he'll know what to do," Johnson said. Johnson didn't care much for the king, but he knew he'd protect MacCulloch. The man knew too many of Strang's secrets to let him be arrested by Strang's enemies.

Miller and Pierce prevented the sheriff from entering the back room of the store by casually pointing guns at him. "Sorry, private property, you don't have a warrant to enter that room," Miller said.

With Dolan and Archie trailing behind, the sheriff went out the front door and looked to his right. Far ahead, he saw three men push through the gate on a picket fence and disappear into the home of James Strang.

As soon as the men were safely inside Strang's home, they told the king what was happening. Strang moved to his desk and pulled a gun out of the top drawer. The other men pulled their guns.

The sheriff, Dolan and Archie took long strides to Strang's home, where the sheriff banged on the door. Without opening the door, Strang called out to him, "Do you have a warrant for my arrest?"

"No," the sheriff said. "I have a warrant to arrest Dr. Hezekiah

MacCulloch. I have reason to believe he's in there."

"You're wrong," Strang said. "I'm in here alone, and I have a gun. Unless you have a warrant to search my house, I suggest you be on your way, sheriff. I'm holding a weapon, and I have a right to protect my home and my property."

"We know he's in there!" Dolan shouted.

"You know nothing of the sort, Dolan," Strang said imperiously. "He might have been here, but now he's gone. I have no idea of his whereabouts."

"You're lying!" Dolan shouted again, until Archie put a quieting hand on his shoulder.

The sheriff looked beleaguered. "I'm sorry, but there's nothing more I can do," he said to Dolan. "I don't have a warrant to search Strang's home, and it's for sure he's not going to let me in. I guess I wasted a trip down here."

Dolan and Archie wore matching looks of defeat. The sheriff turned around and headed back to his boat with Archie and Dolan following in his wake.

Pierce had remained behind after the other men spirited MacCulloch away to Strang's home. When Sheriff O'Reilly's boat left, Pierce walked down to the dock and confronted Archie.

"You helped arrange this arrest?" Pierce said. "You're a Mormon. You're supposed to stand on the side of your brethren."

"I stand on the side of justice," Archie replied. "Thomas Bennett was murdered and his killer should pay."

"You're walking on thin ice, Donnelly," Pierce said. "You'd better watch yourself."

Back at Strang's home, Chidester, Bowman and Miller stood in the parlor with MacCulloch and the king. Miller had caught up with them after the sheriff left.

"Brothers, we escaped a run-in with the law this time, but I don't know if we can count on our luck in the future," Strang said.

"What else is there to do?" Miller asked.

"We need to be in control. We need to elect our own people to the county positions. This wouldn't have happened if we had a Mormon sheriff." Strang had been thinking about it ever since his arrest in June. *Power lies in politics,* he thought to himself.

"We'll run our own candidates for all the county seats in the November election," Strang said. "Our numbers are greater than the Gentiles in this county. We should be able to make a clean sweep."

Strang the Prophet was indeed prophetic about the election. All the Mormon men who were eligible to vote, cast their ballots for fellow Mormons. They won every position they ran for. The Gentiles didn't see it coming, and didn't turn out enough voters to hold off the Mormon onslaught.

Joshua Miller's father George was elected county sheriff, ousting the anti-Mormon Sheriff O'Reilly. The one-time murder suspect MacCulloch became the county clerk. Chidester became the postmaster. Pierce became justice of the peace. Strang was elected circuit court judge, township supervisor and county commissioner.

Mackinac Island, Beaver Island, and Cross Village were now completely under Mormon control.

CHAPTER 45

NOVEMBER, DECEMBER, 1851

Lucy missed her friends.

Pete McKinley, with his wife and daughter, left the island almost completely destitute after losing the bulk of his once-thriving business to Johnson and MacCulloch. He couldn't even sell his property. No Gentiles wanted to take over his business in the Mormon stronghold; the Mormons knew once he left, they might be able to consecrate his property for their own without paying a cent.

Lucy particularly missed Mary Strang. They had become close friends in a short amount of time. They exchanged a few letters, with Lucy telling Mary all about the colorful developments on the island, and Mary telling Lucy about the peace and contentment she'd found back in Wisconsin, surrounded by friends and family. There might have been more letters, but Lucy never was sure if Strang was letting all the mail from his first wife get through to Lucy.

While Lucy had never been close friends with Eliza, she missed her too, and often wondered how she was doing. She never got letters from her. Lucy imagined it was because Eliza didn't want her location to be traced through postmarks.

By the end of November, winter had a firm grip on the island. Sodden, gray skies hung low in the sky, blotting out any sunlight. Snow fell like damp flour.

Lucy began to worry about Huldy, whom she hadn't seen since the snow started falling a few weeks earlier. She decided to go check on her.

She put on her deerskin boots and coat, and sat down on her bottom porch step to attach her snowshoes. They were shaped like minnows, made of bent cedar with leather straps crisscrossing from one side of the cedar to the other. In the center of each was a patch of deer hide, stuck in place with pine rosin. Lucy placed her feet on the hide and then tied leather straps around her boots.

She bent her head against the wind and snow and walked to Huldy's cabin, where she saw smoke rising from the chimney. That was a good sign.

She took off her snowshoes, leaned them against the cabin wall and, as usual, she entered without knocking.

She found Huldy seated at her little wooden table, playing checkers with Lorenzo Hickey.

"Lucy! How nice to see you," Hickey said, rising from his chair. Huldy stood up too, and gave Lucy a hug.

"I didn't know…" Lucy started.

"You didn't know Huldy and I have become good friends." Hickey finished her sentence. "Huldy has been teaching me sign language, although I'm afraid I'm not very good at it." He signed the last sentence so Huldy could see what he was saying. She laughed and nodded her head.

"What brings you here?" Hickey asked. "Everything okay?"

"Yes, fine, I was just wondering if Huldy has heard from Eliza. I hope she's doing all right."

Hickey pointed at Lucy's heart, then pointed to the pile of letters Huldy had stacked on a bookshelf. Apparently Eliza had been taking the risk of writing letters to her sister. Huldy handed the mail to Lucy.

"Huldy let me read them too," Hickey said. "Sounds like Eliza's doing fine. She said the Indians on South Fox Island were very kind to her, but she felt out of place. They took her to Waukazooville on the mainland. Although I guess now it's being called Northport."

Lucy quickly scanned the letters, skipping over minor details to get to the important facts. Eliza was doing wonderfully. She was thrilled with her independence. She started mending people's clothes as a way to make friends and support herself, and now had a business of her own as a tailor. She always was good with a needle and thread.

There were men who courted her, and she enjoyed their company, but had no interest in getting married again. Legally, she was still married to Nathan. She was content to leave it that way.

"I'm so glad she's doing well," Lucy said as she handed the letters back to Huldy. "I should get going. I didn't mean to intrude, I just wanted to check in."

Hickey turned his head so Huldy couldn't read his lips. "Please stay for a bit, Lucy," he said. "I adore Huldy, but sometimes it's nice to hear a voice in this home."

Lucy accepted a chair at the table. They switched from checkers to cards so Lucy could join them. They passed the snowy afternoon away playing games and rehashing Eliza's great escape.

When Lucy returned to her own home, it was nearly pitch dark outside, even though it was still an hour before supper time. Lucy made a fire in the kitchen stove and started cooking her meal. She scooped lard out of a tin can and put it in an iron skillet to melt over the heat.

She heard a frantic rapping on the door. When she opened the door, she saw Archie Donnelly looking befuddled.

"I'm so sorry to bother you on a night like this, Lucy, but we have a bit of a situation. I'm not sure if Millie is all right. Could you come?"

"What's wrong with her?" Lucy asked as she went for her coat and boots.

"Probably better if Millie explains it." Archie's cheeks turned redder than they already were from the cold when he said it.

"Ah, female problems, I take it," Lucy said. She walked out the door with Archie and headed to his home on the other side of town, both of them clomping along as quickly as they could in heavy snowshoes.

Millie looked well enough when they got there, glowing from the light of the fireplace. She was sitting in a rocking chair near the fire with a blanket over her lap.

"What is it, Millie?" Lucy asked after taking off her coat.

"I'm with child." Since the last time Millie had briefly been in the family way and then miscarried, her complexion had changed from pale to peachy. She'd put on weight so she no longer resembled a newborn bird with translucent skin stretched over fragile organs and bones. In the four years she'd been living on Beaver Island, her body had made a comeback after the stress and starvation she'd endured during the Irish potato famine.

"I'm so happy for you!" Lucy said.

"I think I've been in the motherly way for about a month now, but just an hour ago I found drops of blood, you know, in my underthings."

While she'd never had a child of her own, Lucy had heard of this happening. Spotting, Gwen called it. Gwen had told her it was quite common.

"Well now, it's good news that you're with child! I hope this time you'll let Gwen take care of you," Lucy said.

"I certainly plan to do that. Archie has been waiting to make a trip to Garden Island to fetch Gwen for some time now, but the weather's been too bad.

"So what do you make of the drops of blood? I'm not going to lose another baby, am I?"

Lucy patted her hand where it was resting on her stomach. "I think not, Millie. I think it is perfectly normal. But the sooner you can see Gwen, probably the better."

Millie looked so tiny under the heavy wool blanket, Lucy wondered how such a small woman could carry a baby to term. But it happened all the time, she knew.

"I wanted to fetch Gwen today, but Millie wouldn't let me," Archie piped up. He was carrying a cup of hot apple cider from the woodstove over to Millie.

"Millie was right. You can't see three feet in front of your face in this snow. You never would have made it to Garden Island."

Lucy left Millie with instructions to take it easy for the next few days and not do anything strenuous. Archie walked her back home.

"She'll be all right, won't she, Lucy?" Archie asked. "She's such a delicate thing, I worry about her getting through this."

"She'll be fine," Lucy said. "Women have been doing this since the beginning of time. And plenty of them are tiny."

Lucy found it touching to see how the immense, strong Archie was beset with worry for his little wife. *They're a good couple,* Lucy thought to herself. *If anyone deserves a healthy baby, it's them.*

When the weather cleared two days later, Archie set off for Garden Island in a borrowed rowboat from Dolan. He rowed with powerful strokes and made it to Garden Island quickly.

He found Gwen's home based on the description Dolan had given him. Gwen was outside, brushing snow off their log pile. She was dressed in typical Indian garb, wearing deerskin boots and tunic-style coat that came to her knees, also made of deerskin. It had a hood trimmed with fox fur. Her dark eyes peered at him through the fluffy fur that hung over her forehead.

"Hi, Archie, what brings you here?" she asked.

"Hi, Gwen. I'm here for you. For Millie. She's going to have a baby! This time we want to do it right, with your help."

"I'm so happy for you! And I'd be happy to help Millie with the birthing process."

"The thing is, she had a little, uh, issue a few days ago. We talked to Lucy about it, and she thought you should come check on Millie."

Gwen knew better than to press Archie for more information about the 'issue.' She knew some men couldn't bring themselves to talk about the female anatomy.

"I'll come today. If you can wait an hour, I can go with you. I've got to visit one of our elders on the island first. She's not doing well in this weather."

"Nothing's more important to me than my Millie, so I'll be happy to wait." The big man plopped right down on the snow-covered ground.

"You can wait inside," Gwen said, laughing.

"Even better." Archie got up and followed Gwen into the wigwam. Gwen gestured toward a chair near the fire in the center of the room and Archie squeezed his large frame into it, after taking off his coat, wool cap and mittens.

"I'll be back soon," Gwen said, and left.

She was back in two hours, having been summoned along the way to look in on another neighbor who had fallen ill. She found Archie exactly where she left him, waiting patiently.

"Let's go see your Millie now," she said, and Archie sprang out of the chair.

It was cold on the lake, but calm. Archie rowed easily through the flat water. When they got to Archie's house, they found Millie inside, humming and knitting.

"Archie, how about if you run along now. You must have work to catch up on after waiting so long for me," Gwen said. Archie got the hint and left.

Gwen gently asked Millie questions about her last pregnancy, wanting to know how far along she was when she lost the baby, and if she had taken any special herbs or medicines to fortify the baby during the pregnancy. Millie answered eagerly, wanting to avoid whatever caused her to lose the other baby.

Gwen asked if she could examine Millie, and Millie obliged, lying down on their bed.

Afterward, she talked to Millie.

"Since you're such a small woman, the distance from your womb to your portal is quite short," Gwen said. "The weight of the baby in your small frame might have caused you to lose it last time. I suggest that this time, when you get to be four months along, you stick to bedrest for the rest of the term."

"Goodness! That's a long time to be in bed. I've got work to do, I have to take care of Archie."

"I can say with great certainty that what matters most to Archie is your health. You've got your Mormon community to help you."

"I don't know about that," Millie said. "They're all pretty mad at Archie for trying to get MacCulloch arrested for Tom Bennett's murder."

"Then we'll find you help some other place. You'll be cared for."

When Gwen was finished with Millie, she walked over to Dolan's house. She knew he'd be delighted with her surprise visit. He was inside, helping Will and Teddy mend their fishing nets.

After hugging her, he reached in his pocket and pulled out several coins, which he handed to Will.

"Enough work for the day, boys," he said. "Why don't you go on over to Cleary's and have a pint or two? It's on me."

Will and Teddy smiled at each other. They knew why Dolan wanted them out of the house.

"Sure Papa, no problem," Will said, giving his father a light, playful punch in the shoulder as he moved past him to get his coat.

As soon as the boys were gone, Dolan took Gwen in his arms again. "Work's done for the day, what shall we do now?" he said, grinning at her.

"We could play cards, or we could split wood," Gwen answered, teasing him.

"Or we could do this!" Dolan swept Gwen off the floor and carried her into his bedroom.

Even though Gwen had ushered Archie out of the house, he actually did have work to catch up on. The Mormon schoolhouse was nearing completion. He wanted it finished by the time the bad weather permanently set in.

Strang didn't pressure him, but he had hinted that it would be nice to have it done by Christmas. Strang envisioned a large Christmas party in the new schoolhouse as the ideal way to christen the building.

By the first week in December, the school was finished. Benches built to seat two students each lay in rows that faced the front of the main schoolroom. Each bench had a wooden desk with a footboard in front of it. Archie had built all of them. A smaller room adjacent to the main room was intended for school meetings. The main room had a large woodstove for heat; the small room had an open fireplace on one wall.

"Wonderful work, Archie," Strang said when he examined the building.

"I'm glad you like it, sir," Archie said. He had trouble calling him King or Prophet.

"There's the matter of my bill," Archie continued. "You promised to pay me the balance due on completion."

"Yes, indeed I will," Strang said. "For purposes of bookkeeping, you'll need to write out a bill for me. Just figure it out, then take 10 percent off for your tithe. You can come see me tomorrow and get paid."

"I'll do that, sir, thank you," Archie said, thinking he'd need Millie's help with this. He wasn't good with percentages.

CHAPTER 46
DECEMBER, JANUARY, 1851, 1852

It was a Saturday in December, the Lord's Day in the Mormon community. All the island Mormons who could slog through the deep snow were sitting in the tabernacle. After delivering a rousing sermon about God testing people's strength during harsh weather, King Strang announced that the schoolhouse was completed and there would be a Christmas celebration in the building to officially christen it.

"All island residents will be invited, as our gesture to unite us in spite of our religious differences," Strang announced. "Everyone should join together to celebrate the birth of our Christ and our new school."

Word quickly spread that Gentiles were invited to the grand Christmas party, but not many of them expressed enthusiasm about going.

Jane Watson, Phebe Wentworth, Sarah MacCulloch and Ruth Ann Bedford were in charge of the decorations. They spent two weeks stringing popcorn and dried berries, and making long garlands to hang in the school. They gathered pine cones and spruce branches to make arrangements on the desks.

"How many people do you think will come?" Phebe asked while she and Sarah were stringing popcorn. Jane had left briefly with her baby, who needed feeding and diapering. Ruth Ann was out cutting spruce branches.

"I imagine 100, at least," Sarah answered. "The snow will make it impossible for some to get here, but the families who live nearby will come."

"Do you think Rose Bowman will come?" Phebe asked. She was filled with curiosity about Nathan's wife. Surely, there was a story to learn – and tell – about Nathan's second wife. She was hardly ever seen about town; the only place Phebe had seen her was behind the counter at Johnson's store. Phebe tried to cozy up to Rose, but Rose remained tight-lipped.

"I don't know and don't really care," Sarah said. "She's a Mormon now; I think she would be expected to attend." Unlike Phebe, Sarah had no interest in Rose. She thought of Rose as being so far beneath her in social status that she wouldn't waste a precious breath saying hello to her.

"I wonder how many of the new women will come," Phebe continued, trying to prod Sarah into a bit of gossip. "There are quite a few new ones here, staying at the Indian woman's house."

"Lucy LaFleur. Her name is Lucy LaFleur." Although they weren't friends, Sarah respected Lucy, even if Phebe didn't.

"Fine. Lucy LaFleur's house. I heard at least three new women are staying there. Women who have come for husbands. I'm actually glad Alex doesn't earn much of a living. King Strang won't let men take a second wife if they can't provide for multiple wives, and my father won't pay Alex enough to afford a second wife. But your husband is quite well off…"

"Dr. MacCulloch will never take a second wife. Out of the question. He doesn't believe in polygamy, regardless of what the king says."

"You can never be too sure," Phebe said, enjoying seeing Sarah get in a lather at the thought of a second wife in her home.

Just as Sarah was about to deliver a snappy retort to the insufferable Phebe, Jane tugged open the front door and swept in, bringing a rush of icy air with her. She closed the door as quickly as she could.

"Where's your little one?" Sarah asked. Jane was rarely seen without her baby in tow.

"Abby is down for a nap and Wingfield is watching her at the newspaper office," she said. "King Strang was also there. And guess what? He's agreed to let me teach the children when school opens after Christmas!"

"You want to teach? Ick. I hated school," Phebe said. Learning was something that never came easily to Phebe as a child. Unless she was learning about other people's private business.

"Yes, I love reading and learning, and I'd love to share that with children."

"I think that's wonderful," Sarah said. "I'm sure it will be very rewarding to impart knowledge to eager young minds." Then she gave Phebe a disdainful look.

Strang's decision to let Jane teach school was unusual. Being a teacher was typically a job reserved for men. But Strang had always supported smart women and believed in treating them fairly. It was one of the many contradictions of the king, a man who believed in polygamy, yet treated women as equals – at least in some unexpected ways.

———◆•◆———

The schoolhouse was a festive sight on the night of the party. Wingfield Watson rapidly fed logs into the woodstove to keep the large room warm. Green spruce boughs, popcorn and berry garlands hanging on the walls, along with candles on the desks, made the room cheerful and bright. Lanterns hung in each corner of the room, casting a flickering yellow light throughout the building. The pine floor was scrubbed and shining.

The snow let up just before the party started, so the turnout was higher than expected. Lucy walked in with a new woman who had arrived on the island that fall; Betsy McNutt, considered a spinster since she had attained the age of 31 without marrying.

When they approached the schoolhouse, they saw that the path to the front door had been shoveled. The snowbanks lining the path had large holes punched in the sides and candles were glowing inside the holes, lighting the path. They entered the schoolhouse to find the party in full swing. A Mormon fiddler was playing dance music and people were dancing around the desks and down the center aisle. Strang was in his element, greeting people and accepting their compliments on the new school.

"Which one is King James?" Betsy asked Lucy.

"The one up front, with the red beard and wavy hair," Lucy said.

Betsy carefully studied him. Although she was past her prime, she was still a reasonably attractive woman with a small flat nose, wide cheeks and a nice smile planted in the middle of her round face. Her dark brown hair was straight and parted in the middle, pulled back at the nape of her neck into a roll.

Jane Watson was chatting to parents, telling them she was eager to start teaching their children. Wingfield jiggled baby Abby in his arms, trying to keep her from fussing.

Elvira was standing next to her husband, greeting people and showing off baby Charlie, who was sleeping with his head on her shoulder, drooling slightly.

Betsy McNutt made her way through the crowd to the king. She curtsied and said, "It is a pleasure to finally meet my king. I've heard great things about you. I can see from this gathering that they must be true."

Strang beamed, took her hand and kissed the back of it. "It is our pleasure to have you in our midst, Miss…"

"McNutt. Betsy McNutt. Although I hope I'll be changing my last name soon." She smiled playfully at Strang.

Elvira caught the look that Betsy was giving Strang and immediately became jealous.

"James, will you hold Charlie for me?" she said, handing the sleeping child to her husband. "He's getting so heavy, I can hardly manage him."

"Is this your child?" Betsy asked. "He's beautiful."

"Thank you," Elvira said, even though she knew the woman was directing her remark to Strang.

Betsy left the king and his queen and circled around the room, introducing herself to the Mormons and making polite small talk as she went.

Midway through the festivities, Constable Miller whistled to get everyone's attention. He cleared his throat.

"I'd like to welcome all of our new arrivals to the island," he said, looking primarily at the single women. "May you all find what you're looking for here; peace, tranquility, prosperity and marriage."

He looked directly at Betsy McNutt. "And who might you be interested in marrying, young lady?" he asked her. He was trying his best to flatter her. She was no young lady, but she was tolerably nice-looking, and he wasn't a very young man anymore.

"There is only one man for me here," she replied in a raised voice. "I shall wait until the King himself requests my hand in marriage."

Miller's face immediately turned down. Strang's face immediately turned up. Elvira's face turned into a grimace.

Lucy chuckled quietly and leaned down to whisper to Millie, who was standing beside her.

"Let's see how he gets out of this one," she said, presuming that Strang would not be of a mind to marry an aging spinster.

"I am honored and flattered, Miss McNutt," Strang said graciously. "If that is indeed your desire, so it shall be."

Elvira's mouth gaped open, but she said nothing. This was a matter that she would discuss in private with her husband after they were home.

———◆•◆———

Rose Bowman chose not to attend the party, as much as she used to like parties. She stayed behind at Johnson's store, preferring to stock shelves and sweep the floor than go to a Mormon gathering. She was a Mormon in name only, as it had been required of her to join the church in order to obtain a husband.

It was turning out to be a poor bargain.

"You're still here?" Frank Johnson said to Rose as he emerged from the storeroom where he'd been taking inventory. "Didn't want to go to the schoolhouse party?"

"Where I went to school, nuns whacked our hands with a ruler if we so much as passed gas or giggled, so it left a bad taste in my mouth for school."

Johnson laughed. "I went to a Catholic school too, I know what you mean. Those nuns were terrifying!"

Rose smiled for the first time in a long time. Her mouth could still be pretty when it was tilting up at the corners.

"I have a bottle of whiskey in the back room if you'd care to join me for a smaller Christmas celebration." There was nothing untoward in his voice, so Rose agreed to it.

They sat at the table where Johnson and MacCulloch counted the money at each day's end. Johnson set the bottle of whiskey in the center of the table and went over to a shelf to get two glasses. He poured a small amount of whiskey in each glass.

"Here's to a Catholic education," he said, raising his glass to Rose.

"And here's to no more bleeding knuckles after a Catholic education," Rose said, raising her own glass.

While sipping whiskey, the two of them talked about their backgrounds and upbringing. Rose was surprised to learn that Johnson was a self-made man who had been born into similar surroundings as Rose's.

"You're lucky you're a man," Rose said. "You could work your way out of poverty. Women are expected to marry their way out."

Johnson studied Rose. When he'd first met and hired her, he thought she was prune-faced and ornery. As he watched her work over the following months, he occasionally saw a look of soft wistfulness slip onto her face. He knew she was quite smart; he'd watched her tally a customer's sales in her head faster than he could ever do. Her math was always correct and the till was always balanced at the end of the day. She'd memorized every inch of the store and could easily direct a customer to the item they were looking for. He decided there was more to Rose Bowman than met the eye.

They finished their drinks and Rose stood up to leave.

"I'd better get going," she said. "Nathan doesn't like it if I'm not home when he gets there."

Johnson helped her with her coat. "May I walk you home?"

"That's all right, I'll be fine. It's better if I walk alone."

Johnson suspected she wanted to walk alone in case they came upon her husband. Nathan was very possessive of Rose, he'd noticed. He didn't allow her to spend free time in town or make new friends. Rose was always either at work or at home.

But then, so am I, Johnson thought to himself as he walked alone to his own little cabin next to the store.

CHAPTER 47

WINTER, 1852

"He's going to do it! He's actually going to do it!" Phebe Wentworth was beside herself with gossipy glee when she barged into Johnson's store.

"Who's going to do what?" Rose asked. She didn't much care for Phebe, but Phebe was one of the few women in town who had attempted to befriend her, so she tolerated her as best she could. Besides, Phebe was the daughter of Frank Johnson, Rose's boss, so she wanted to stay on her good side.

"The king is going to marry Betsy McNutt! He pledged he would at the Christmas party, but no one took him seriously. I mean, he's the king, he doesn't have to marry gnarly old spinsters who come here looking for husbands – oh, sorry."

"No apology necessary," Rose said, shrugging her shoulders. Rose was pragmatic. Truth was truth, no point in denying it. She had been one of those gnarly old spinsters who came to the island looking for a husband, and she got one. Now she wished she hadn't.

"So how did you find out he's going to marry her?" Rose asked Phebe.

"Ran into her at the post office. She said she and Strang will be holding their wedding ceremony in the tabernacle January 9. That's just a week away!"

Phebe sailed out of the store as quickly as she sailed in, nose pointed upwind, coat fluttering behind her. She had a busy morning schedule. There were a lot of houses to call on to spread the news about the king's third marriage.

Lucy entered the store with the usual feeling of awkwardness. She missed Pete's old store and hated having to spend money at the store that put Pete out of business, but there were no other options.

"Good morning," she said politely to Rose.

"Good morning," Rose said back. That was usually the extent of their exchanges. Neither woman cared much for the other. Rose had no reason to dislike Lucy. But Lucy disliked her for how she'd upheaved Eliza's life, so the feeling became mutual.

After roaming around, putting items in her shopping basket, Lucy came to the counter and set the heavy basket down for Rose to add up.

"Could you please put this on Archie Donnelly's account? I'm doing the shopping for Millie, she's on bedrest."

"How do I know that Archie has approved this?"

"Do you want me to go fetch Archie and drag him across town so he can vouch for me?"

Rose knew better than to continue to challenge Lucy LaFleur. If Lucy was lying, she'd find out about it soon enough. And it wasn't as if Lucy would sneak off the island with a stolen bag of groceries.

"That's all right; I'll take your word for it." Rose quickly tallied the items and wrote the amount down on a pad of paper behind the counter, along with the name Archibald Donnelly.

Lucy carried the heavy sack of groceries to the Donnelly house, where Millie was waiting. Archie was out back, splitting wood.

"Oh, I wish I could help you with that!" Millie said from her perch on a day bed that had been set up in the parlor area of their home.

"You stay put, that's your job, tending to that baby," Lucy said.

She took off her heavy raccoon coat with the fox fur-trimmed hood and hung it near the door.

"I'll cook up a few days' worth of food for you and then leave you to your resting," Lucy said.

"Oh, please stay awhile. This resting business is so boring! At least stay for supper," Millie said.

"I guess I could do that." Lucy had no renters to feed at the moment. She turned her attention to the kitchen woodstove and began feeding it the small pieces of wood Archie had chopped and split. He made them small so they would catch fire quickly; he also made them small because he wanted it to be easy for Millie to get the stove started.

Lucy made a venison stew with cornbread, that was nearly ready when Archie came in. He looked rather comical, completely covered with snow and with icicles hanging from his nose. Lucy used a big spoon to scoop out some stew, which she extended to Archie.

"Here, warm up. You look like you need it."

He leaned into Lucy's spoon and swallowed the steaming contents in one bite.

"Oh boy, that hits the spot! Thank you."

Archie slipped out of his wet coat and hung it on the mantel, next to the fire. He put his boots on the hearth to dry. While he was there, he threw a couple more logs on the fire.

When it was time to eat, Millie joined Lucy and Archie at the table. They talked about the things islanders always talked about – was it going to be a long winter, how was the deer population, did they have enough provisions to tide them over until spring – there wasn't much else to discuss.

After dinner, Archie asked Millie to stay at the table with him.

"I need your help writing up the invoice for Strang's schoolhouse," he told Millie. "I've been putting this off for too long now, and we need to get paid. Gotta calculate my cost of materials, what I paid my laborers, and what I paid myself. Then I have to deduct 10 percent for my tithe."

Lucy, who was gathering her things to leave, turned around when she heard this. "You shouldn't take 10 percent off the total, Archie; you should take it only off your personal pay. The laborers can pay their own 10 percent, and you should be fully reimbursed for materials."

"Why does Strang want you to do it this way?" Millie asked. "Before he just paid you for your work, then his collectors came around and took the 10 percent."

"I don't know, but it's what he wants, and what I need to do if I want to get paid."

Archie and Millie spent an hour pulling together all of Archie's scraps of paper, where he'd written down the cost of his supplies and how much he'd paid his workers each week. Lucy let herself out long before they were done.

When the work was finished, they had a clean piece of paper that had three itemized lines: one for materials; one for paid labor; and one for Archie's labor. It didn't occur to them to put his cost of labor on the paper showing the amount before and after the 10 percent tithe. They just calculated what he should be paid after the tithe and wrote it down.

"There, that's done," Archie said, relieved to have the paperwork completed. He hated that part of his job. "Now, my little precious one, let me help you to bed." He kissed his wife on the top of her head, then scooped her up in his big arms and carried her off to the bedroom.

———◆◆◆———

James Jesse Strang married Elizabeth McNutt on January 9, 1852, in a quiet ceremony at the tabernacle. Elvira stood next to them at the ceremony. It hadn't taken her long to figure out she had two choices regarding the newest wife – get along or get thrown out. She didn't want to suffer the same fate as Mary, so she got along with Betsy as best she could.

Strang's wasn't the only new plural marriage on the island. George Miller, father of the constable, took a second wife as well, to the chagrin of his still unmarried son. Several other Mormons took second wives during the winter. It became somewhat accepted that women with no means of support and facing a long, harsh winter, should be taken in by married men. The fight about polygamy was being lost by those who opposed it. Bad weather and starving women trumped monogamy.

Nathan Bowman was one man who had no interest in taking another wife. He was enjoying himself very much with the one wife he had. Rose had opened up a whole new world to him, and he'd discovered he was quite fond of rough intimacy. If Rose protested, he did whatever he was doing even harder. After a while, she figured out that he liked hearing her sounds of pain and protest, so she tried very hard not to make any sound at all. That was fine by Nathan. It brought out the creativity in him. He just found new ways to make her yelp or cry.

———◆◆◆———

"I got paid by Strang, at last," Archie told Millie a week after he'd presented the king with his bill for the schoolhouse. "Should be enough to get us through the winter, then building will start up again." He stuffed the money in a jar on the top shelf of the kitchen area.

"We're going to need every penny when we have another mouth to feed," Millie said as she patted her stomach. She was brimming with maternal instincts. Archie bent low to kiss her on the cheek. Her skin felt like velvet compared to his scruffy face. He didn't shave in the wintertime, claiming the beard kept his face warm. The truth was that he hated shaving, but did it in the nice weather to make Millie happy. She said she loved seeing all of his handsome face.

"Help!"

The cry for help came from somewhere outside. They heard it faintly through the closed, shuttered windows of their house.

"Did you hear that?" Archie asked. "I thought I heard someone call for help."

"I heard it too," Millie said. "You'd better go see what's going on."

Archie pulled his boots back on, his heavy coat, red wool cap and mittens, and then headed out the door.

"Help!" He heard it again, coming from the south, where there were fewer cabins. He broke into a run, peeking quickly into each cabin he passed to see if someone was in distress.

He rounded the bend on the shore and heard it again. When he looked up, he saw Rose Bowman hanging out of a window, bare shoulders exposed to the cold air. He then saw Nathan's hand grab her by the hair and yank her inside.

"What the hell do you think you're doing?!" Nathan exploded as he shoved Rose forcefully back onto the bed. After Nathan had spanked her bare bottom several times, he unbuttoned his pants and pushed them down. In that moment, Rose made a break for the window again and started yelling.

"Oh no you don't," Nathan said. He whipped her around by the arm, then punched her in the eye. It was his first time to punch her; he usually preferred slapping, but he discovered punching felt good too. Rose reeled back and fell on the bed, dazed, unable to move while stars swam in her vision.

When Archie burst in through the door a few moments later, he saw Rose on the bed, completely naked, curled in a fetal position, her purple bottom showing, while she held her right eye. He immediately knew what was going on.

"You feckin' bastard," Archie snarled, right before he pulled his massive arm back and then released it, punching Nathan hard enough to knock him backward, where he fell against the table and then landed on the pine floor.

"You broke my damn nose!" Nathan cried, holding his nose that was now gushing blood.

"I'd like to break your jaw too, for beating your wife," Archie said, making a fist again. "What kind of a man hits his wife?!"

"She's my wife, it's none of your business," Nathan said defiantly as he scrambled back onto his feet.

"She's a woman; you never hit a woman!"

Rose's vision cleared while they shouted at each other. She wrapped herself in a dirty blanket and waited to see what would happen next.

"Rose, put some clothes on, you're coming with me," Archie said.

"She is not!" Nathan said, but moving remarkably quickly for a big man, Archie grabbed him by the neck and forced him against the cabin wall.

"Go on, Rose, I'm not watching. I'll keep an eye on this bastard while you dress. Let me know when you're ready."

Nathan attempted to kick Archie but it was no use. Archie's long arms and considerable height made it impossible for Nathan to reach him. And when he did try kicking, Archie tightened his grip around Nathan's neck until Nathan felt his eyes bulging out of their sockets.

"I'm ready," Rose said. She had dressed as fast as she could in a brown wool dress, heavy stockings and boots. She had her coat and winter hat on too, with the brim pulled down over her right eye so it was difficult to see the damage Nathan had inflicted.

"Where are you taking her?" Nathan finally was able to say after Archie released him.

"None of your business." Archie gently took Rose by the arm and led her out of the house.

"Where *are* you taking me?" Rose asked as she stumbled through the snow.

"Away from here," Archie said, looking around. He didn't know where he was taking her. There wasn't a spare inch of room in his house. He looked up the hill.

"For now, I'm taking you to Lucy's," he said.

Rose stopped in her tracks.

"She hates me, she won't have me," Rose said.

"I don't know if she hates you, but I know she'll hate what's been done to you," Archie replied, tugging at her arm and putting her back in motion.

Lucy answered Archie's knock on her door as she wiped her hands on her apron. She'd finished field dressing a deer she shot earlier, and was now butchering the parts on the kitchen table. She planned to make venison stew for supper and hang the rest of the cuts of meat in her shed out back.

She looked at Archie, then Rose, then back to Archie again. Rose tipped her head back so Lucy could see her eye, which was nearly swollen shut and starting to discolor.

"Come in," she said.

CHAPTER 48
WINTER, 1852

"Who did this to you?" Lucy asked after she, Archie and Rose were seated in her parlor. Lucy had taken a dishcloth outside and broken an icicle off the porch roof, then stomped on it to break it into little pieces that she wrapped in the cloth. She brought the bundle inside and handed it to Rose, who gratefully held it against her eye.

"That feckin' husband of hers, Bowman, the animal," Archie said, answering for Rose.

Rose remained silent. She was afraid to open her mouth. Afraid she'd start crying, and she hated showing any signs of weakness.

"For the time being, you'll stay here," Lucy said. There wasn't warmth in Lucy's voice. She'd never cared much for Rose Pratt, but she couldn't let the woman go back home and get beaten by Nathan again.

"I can pay," Rose said quickly. "I've saved money. I just don't know how I'm going to get it," Rose said, immediately realizing that her money pouch was hidden underneath the mattress in the house currently occupied by a very angry Nathan.

"We'll work that out later," Lucy said. "Go make yourself comfortable in the room you had last time," Lucy said. "Right now, I have to go see someone." Rose headed upstairs, feeling inordinately happy about the thought of lying down on a bed without having to worry about her husband pouncing on her.

"Don't try and talk sense to Nathan," Archie said after Rose left the room, thinking the fiery Lucy might march right over to Bowman's house and attempt to knock some sense into him.

"I have no intention of speaking to Nathan Bowman. Archie, would you please come with me?"

"Of course," Archie said, jumping to his feet.

"Where are we going?" Archie asked as he and Lucy started down the path from her house.

"We are going to speak to King Strang. This type of behavior cannot be tolerated."

They knocked on Strang's door, which was answered by Betsy McNutt Strang.

"My husband is at the newspaper office," Betsy said, with emphasis on the word 'husband.'

Archie and Lucy proceeded down the road to the newspaper building, where they could see a lantern burning in the window and smoke rising out of the chimney. Lucy pushed the door open without knocking.

Strang was seated at the main table in the room, writing. He looked up, surprised to see anyone calling on the newspaper office on such a bleak day.

"What can I do for you?" he asked as he stood up from the table.

"I've come to file a complaint about Nathan Bowman," Lucy said. "Archie bore witness to the fact that Nathan is beating his wife. This is unacceptable to me, and I hope it's unacceptable to you as well."

Strang sat up straight in his chair, and motioned for the two of them to take chairs across the table from him.

"You're sure about this?" he asked Archie.

"Dead sure, sir. I heard Rose calling for help from their window. I went to their house to see what was going on and found Nathan roughing her up pretty bad."

"She's at my house now, nursing a black eye and God knows what other damage done to her at the hands of Nathan."

"You're right, this is completely unacceptable," Strang said, anger starting to show on his high, furrowed brow. "I will not tolerate such beastly behavior. You have my word this matter will be resolved immediately."

Lucy was pleasantly surprised that Strang agreed so readily. She had expected him at least to attempt to defend Nathan. She didn't know that Strang had strong feelings about men who mistreated women. He'd seen it happen in Nauvoo, by early Mormons who treated wives worse than they treated feral dogs. It repulsed him.

Strang sent Wingfield Watson, who was in the back room of the newspaper office, to find Constable Joshua Miller. He also told Wingfield to make sure the constable came back with his pistol. When Wingfield returned an hour later with the constable, Strang had decided on his course of action.

"Joshua, I want you to bring Nathan here immediately. Tell him he's under arrest. Don't let him give you any trouble. Keep your weapon drawn so he knows you mean business."

Miller was speechless. He couldn't imagine what one of his deputies had done to inspire such wrath in the king.

"He has a right to know what he's being arrested for," Miller said, hoping to get some insight to Nathan's alleged crimes.

"Tell him I will personally be delivering the charges," Strang replied. "Now go on."

Miller had no choice but to follow the king's orders. When he got to Nathan's house, he found it empty. He let himself in, noticed the overturned table, the dirty, rumpled bedsheets, and the blood spatters on the floor.

Miller went back out and closed the door behind him. He tried to think of where Nathan might have gone. He saw two sets of tracks in the snow. It wasn't hard to see where one set of tracks went up the hill to Lucy's, and the other set went toward Roald's tavern.

Miller had never set foot in the tavern. He agreed with Strang that liquor was a dangerous poison. But the circumstances were so pressing that he pushed open the tavern door, where he saw a few men seated at the wooden bar. Nathan was one of them, but he was sitting alone at the end of the bar, away from the fishermen who were ignoring him.

"What in God's name has gotten into you?" Miller asked Nathan as he came up from behind him. "The king has demanded that I arrest you!"

Nathan turned to look at Miller, showing his crooked, bloody, swollen nose.

"Archie Donnelly did this to me," Nathan said. "He's the one who should be arrested."

"Well, then, you need to explain that to the king. I'm supposed to bring you in, no questions asked. Come on."

Miller pulled Nathan off his barstool. Although unsteady on his feet from consuming several shots of whiskey, Nathan complied.

When they got to the newspaper office, Miller walked Nathan in the door and then pushed him toward Strang, who was rising out of his chair.

"Thank you, Constable," Strang said in an imperious tone. "You will now bear witness to the charges against Nathan Bowman.

Nathan looked at the king with glazed eyes. He wasn't accustomed to drinking, and the whiskey he'd consumed to alleviate the pain shooting through his nose left him groggy.

"Nathan Bowman, I have it on excellent authority that you have been beating and mistreating your wife, Rose Pratt Bowman. Is this true?"

Nathan weaved back and forth a bit.

"I only did what a man has a right to do with his wife," Nathan said defensively.

"You are wrong there. A man has no right to hit or mistreat his wife. I will not tolerate such behavior in my kingdom. So I ask you again, is it true that you have been beating your wife?"

"She likes it," Nathan said. "She wants me to do it. Sure, I get a little rough, but it was her idea." Nathan shrugged his shoulders.

Strang felt bile rise in his throat. "I am finding you guilty of grossly mistreating your wife. You are excommunicated. You have 24 hours to get off this island."

Nathan snapped into full consciousness at the words. "Leave the island?! It's the dead of winter, where am I supposed to go?"

"I don't care where you go, as long as it is away from here. You may never live among the Latter-Day Saints again."

"But how am I supposed to get off the island?" Nathan whined.

"The lake is frozen. You can walk right off," Strang responded crisply. "If you are not off the island by tomorrow, I will have you locked up for at least 10 years in the Mackinac jailhouse. I'm the judge in this county, and that is the minimum sentence I will give you. Take your choice."

Miller had been watching the conversation carefully, his mouth agape. He had no idea Nathan had been rough with his wife. Miller wasn't a prince among men, but he could never imagine hitting a woman. He was repulsed by his deputy. Former deputy, he realized.

"Come on, Bowman, looks you have some packing to do," Miller said, pulling Nathan toward the door.

"And Constable, keep an eye on him every moment until he is off this island," Strang said. "Report back to me when he's gone." Strang then turned his back on both men, ridding himself of the sniveling Nathan Bowman.

"How long has this been going on?" Lucy asked Rose. They were seated at her kitchen table. The butchered deer meat had been salted and was safely stored in the shed outside, wrapped in linen cloth. Rose was looking down with one eye at the venison stew Lucy put in front of her. The other eye was swollen shut.

"Pretty much since the beginning," Rose said. "It's my fault. I sort of – "

Lucy interrupted her. "Stop right there. I don't want to hear details. It's not your fault, though. It's never a woman's fault if a man strikes her. Some men try to make it out to be that way, but they're just bullying cowards."

Rose looked up at Lucy gratefully. "Why are you being nice to me? You don't like me, I know that."

Lucy had to respect Rose's forthrightness. The woman didn't avoid ticklish topics.

"It's not that I don't like you. It's that I don't like what you did, marrying Nathan Bowman and driving his first wife off the island."

"I did her a favor," Rose said bitterly.

"You probably did. She's actually quite happy now."

"And I'm quite the opposite." Rose fell silent and took a bite of stew. Lucy did the same.

"I was an unmarriageable woman in my home town," Rose admitted to Lucy. "Then along comes this missionary who tells me I can have any husband I want on Beaver Island if I become a Mormon. It sounded too good to be true."

"And it turned out it *was* too good to be true. I don't know how the other families with more than one wife are doing," Lucy said. "Maybe some of them figure out how to make it work. But I cannot see how it could be an ideal situation for anyone, except perhaps the husband."

"It was a husband who made up the rule, so I imagine it's the husbands who benefit," Rose said rancorously.

Rose and Lucy ate in silence for a while, the only sound coming from the wood crackling and hissing in the stove.

"I'm sorry you lost your friend after I married her husband," Rose said.

Lucy looked up at her. She saw a sad, defeated woman in front of her. "It's all right. It's behind us now. And it will be completely behind us after Strang punishes Nathan, as he promised to do."

Rose perked up. "The king is going to punish Nathan? I thought they always protected one another."

"In some instances, I think they do, but not in this instance. I think Strang will dole out a harsh punishment to Nathan. Say what you will about your king, but he does try to treat women fairly and respectfully." Lucy thought fleetingly of the early days of her acquaintanceship with Strang, when he was a loyal friend to her. She missed those days.

"Oh, I do so hope you're right."

It was a bitterly cold day when Nathan woke up in his small house after a restless night. Sleep eluded him after the whiskey wore off and his nose throbbed painfully. Miller had slept in Nathan's cabin, propped up against the door, shotgun in the crook of his arm.

"Joshua, really, you've got to help me. Maybe I could stay at your place until spring comes. I'll lay low, no one needs to know I'm still here," Nathan wheedled.

"No, Nathan. I've got to follow the king's orders. Now get up and get packed."

Nathan was panic-stricken. He had no idea where he was going to go. He'd never been to any of the other islands in the archipelago, because he didn't care much for Indians, who were the primary residents of the out islands. Gull Island had white men on it, but they were Gentiles and probably hated him.

"Where am I going to go? I can't get up to Mackinac in this weather, I'll freeze to death."

"Why don't you head over to Pine River? Just walk down to the south end of the island, then cut straight across. There's sled tracks you can follow. The people on the south end deliver supplies to Pine River in the winter."

"Walk across this lake? That doesn't sound safe," Nathan said, grasping at any excuse to avoid the fate looming ahead.

"You'll make it," Miller said dismissively. He wanted to be rid of Bowman as soon as possible.

Thirty minutes later, Nathan Bowman was dressed in as many layers of clothes as he could wear, topped by a heavy wool coat. He had a pair of old snowshoes he'd consecrated the winter before from some hapless islander who left them propped up against the outer wall of Cleary's tavern. He put those on after he wrapped a wool scarf around his neck and pulled a wool hat on his head.

He slung the leather strap of his knapsack over his right shoulder.

"Bye then, Joshua," he said awkwardly. "Maybe this will all blow over and I'll be seeing you again soon."

Miller looked at him with dead eyes. "Goodbye, Nathan." Then he turned his back on him, having no desire to watch Nathan plod slowly down the shoreline toward the south end of the island.

Rose learned of Nathan's banishment from Frank Johnson the following morning, when she showed up to work. The swelling had gone down and she could see out of the tiny slit that was her eye. There was no way she could hide the purple circle underneath.

Frank Johnson was shocked to see her face, but said nothing about it, not wanting to make her feel self-conscious.

"King Strang wanted me to tell you that Nathan's house is now yours," Johnson said. "As his wife, you're entitled to it."

"Really?" Rose hadn't even thought about the house. She wasn't sure she ever wanted to go back there. She could picture it the last time she was there – dirty, rumpled bedding, Nathan's clothes scattered on the floor, the woodstove grimy with spattered bacon grease, the fireplace filled with ashes that needed to be shoveled out, the table littered with bits of dried food, and the pervasive smell of body odor and brutality

— somehow, she had gotten used to the squalor. Now the thought of it revolted her.

"Well, if you want it, it's yours. You can take your time and think about it," Johnson said.

Within the hour, Jane Watson, Ruth Ann Bedford and Phebe Wentworth entered the store. Wordlessly, they each gave Rose a hug.

"We're here to help you with whatever you need, Rose," Jane said.

Rose was taken aback. She'd never really considered herself a Mormon, and had avoided church gatherings. She barely knew those women. Were they taking pity on her? She hated pity.

"We could get your home ready for you, perhaps tidy up a bit," Ruth Ann said.

"We'll get rid of all his things," Jane added.

"That would be nice," Rose said. "You'd really do that?"

"Of course we will," Jane said. "That's what the church is for. We stand by our members and get through hard times together."

"All right then, thank you." Rose didn't know what else to say.

CHAPTER 49
SPRING, SUMMER, 1852

The rest of the winter passed on Beaver Island the way it typically did – bouts of zero degree weather kept people indoors, burning firewood in kitchen woodstoves and in open fireplaces, trying to stay warm. When the temperatures grudgingly rose above freezing, snow melted and ran in muddy brown streams that sluiced the road diagonally toward the lake. Cold fog typically blanketed the island during the thaws. Then the temperature would drop again, freezing the streams in the road, making even a short walk hazardous.

People got sick. Strang's wives, Elvira and Betsy, both got the influenza, sending Strang into a panic. He'd already lost a daughter to the disease; he couldn't bear to lose anyone else he loved. The two women rested in their respective bedrooms, sneezing and coughing, while Strang delivered hot soup and tea to them, prepared by Jane Watson and Ruth Ann Bedford. He wouldn't allow any of the church women to visit his wives in their bedrooms, fearing visitors might catch the disease. He risked his own health to tend to them, washing their faces with cloths soaked in warm water he boiled himself on the stove. His two wives recovered, none the worse for it, to Strang's relief.

Food supplies dwindled. Canned goods got consumed long before any new vegetables would be growing outside. Blinding snowstorms made even a walk to the store nearly impossible.

With the profits Frank Johnson had made in the late summer and fall, he had stocked his store abundantly in preparation for the winter. But by

April, even his supplies of flour, wheat, rice and lard were running low and there was still two feet of snow on the ground.

Everyone had cabin fever.

Except Nathan Bowman. He had no cabin.

Nathan made it to Pine River in January, after lurking around Cable's Bay on the southeast side of Beaver Island for several days. Alva Cable finally took pity on him and gave him a ride to Pine River on his dogsled when he was running supplies to the mainland.

From there, Nathan scrounged places to stay with fishermen and trappers whenever he could. He often wound up sleeping outdoors in a dirt hollow carved into the side of the bluff. He fine-tuned his ability to hold his liquor by drinking with the rough men who would occasionally share some of their drink with him.

By the time April came, Nathan was firmly entrenched with the loud, filthy outdoorsmen who eked out a living from fishing and fur trapping. He learned how to run traps for them, even though he hated the work. He did it because he hated starving even more.

He traveled on dogsleds with the trappers who headed to Mackinac Island to sell their furs. While in Mackinac, Nathan rewrote his personal history, telling a tale of Strang banishing him from the Mormon Church because Strang had designs on his wife and wanted him out of the way. The more he told the story, the more he embellished it, including a savage beating delivered to him by Strang's men.

It wasn't hard to convince the Gentiles on Mackinac and in Pine River that Strang was a horrible person who deserved their hatred. They were already angry that the Mormons had won every seat in county politics. Stories that put Strang in a bad light were just the fuel they needed to fan the prejudicial flames that had already ignited the community.

By May, the ice disappeared from Lake Michigan and fishing, lumbering and building began in earnest. Archie had accepted a job offer from Dr. MacCulloch to build him a new, two-story home on the north shore of the harbor, near the general store.

Archie was at the lumber mill, watching massive maple logs go through the steam-powered sawmill, cutting the trees into square timbers, four inches by four inches and 16 feet long. With the help of his workers, he loaded his wagon with timbers and prepared to head to the building site. Archie was just stepping onto his wagon, reins in hand, oxen at the ready, when Chidester and Pierce stopped him.

"See you've got a new job," Pierce said.

"Yep, building a new home for the doctor and his missus," Archie replied and once again started to climb onto his wagon. Once again, he was stopped.

"Understand Dr. MacCulloch gave you an advance on your pay," Pierce said.

"Yeah, so what of it?"

"You need to pay your tithe for the schoolhouse. You can use your advance for that."

Archie looked at Pierce incredulously.

"I already paid my tithe! The king asked me to take 10 percent off my bill, so I did. That counts for my tithe."

"According to the paperwork we have, there's no mention of that," Pierce said. Chidester just stared menacingly at Archie. "We've seen your bill. Doesn't say anything about taking 10 percent off your charge."

"Well, I'm not paying you a thing. I'll take this up with Strang." This time Archie climbed on his wagon and didn't look back at the two men while he urged his oxen forward.

"Go ahead," Pierce called after him. "You'll see. You have to pay."

On his way to the building site, Archie stopped at his own home to check on Millie. She was resting contentedly in their main room, propped up in a chair with lots of pillows to support her back. One hand was holding a book and the other hand was resting on her swollen belly. She loved to feel the baby kick.

After giving Millie a kiss, Archie told her about Chidester and Pierce trying to extract another 10 percent of his schoolhouse pay.

"That's not fair at all!" Millie said. "You must go see the king. I'm sure he'll set this straight."

"I'll do that, at the end of the day," Archie promised.

Archie and his workmen had laid large stones from Lake Michigan as the foundation for McCulloch's house. Using rods and lengths of twine, Archie made sure the stones were level before he started laying the timbers in place.

Beaver Island provided Archie with plenty of sand and clay to make the chinking material that he spread between each timber. By the end of the day, the first three rows of timber were in place.

Archie walked down to the lake and rinsed his face, neck and hands with icy cold water before heading to the newspaper office, where he knew he could usually find Strang. The king was there, seated at the long table he used for his desk.

"What can I do for you, Archie?" Strang asked pleasantly.

"It's the matter of my tithe for the schoolhouse," Archie said. "Your men Chidester and Pierce came to collect my tithe. I told them I'd already taken the tithe off my schoolhouse bill for you."

Strang looked perplexed. "Let me see if I can find that," he said. He rose and went over to a file cabinet where he kept his paperwork. After a few minutes of thumbing through papers, he pulled out Archie's bill.

"I don't see any mention of your tithe here," Strang said.

"I took it off the total before I put the amount due on the bill," Archie said.

"But if there's no record of it, I don't know what to do. Do you have your original paperwork?"

Archie knew he didn't. The minute he had finished the bill, he'd tossed all the scraps of paper into the fireplace. He didn't like clutter.

"No, I don't," he said glumly.

"Well, then, I guess this is a lesson for both of us. We need to make sure our paperwork is detailed and clear. I guess you'll just have to pay your tithe and remember to keep better records next time."

Strang sat back down at his table, the matter being concluded as far as he was concerned.

"But King James, this isn't fair – "

"I'm afraid there's nothing more I can do, Archie. Sometimes life hands us hard lessons to learn."

Archie knew it was pointless to argue with the king. He knew anything he said would come out tart as an unripe cherry.

When he got back home to Millie, she could tell by his scowl that things hadn't gone well. He recounted his conversation with Strang for her.

"I've about had it with these Mormons," Archie said. "I'm glad we came here, and I'm glad it was the Mormons who told us about this place, but there's too many things that just aren't setting right with me and this religion."

"I know. It's my fault, I talked you into it. Can we just go back to being Catholic?" Millie needed religion in her life. She needed a God she could pray to, a higher power that she could ask to keep her baby and her husband safe.

"I don't think that's possible, not on this island. But God is God, so I think you can pray to the Catholic God just as easily as the Mormon God. Who's going to know the difference?"

Millie smiled. "Then that's what I'll do. But don't tell anyone," she said, giving Archie a wink.

"Your secret is safe with me," Archie said, grinning back at her.

◆•◆

The last snow of the season fell May 6; a wet, heavy snow that fell in sheets, like rain, except it was white and solid. As quickly as it fell, it melted the following day under a warm spring sun. And just like that, winter was over and spring had arrived.

When Lucy went foraging in the woods in late May and early June, she always picked enough wild onions, mushrooms and berries to share with Millie and Archie. Knowing Millie was confined to bed rest, Lucy made strawberry and raspberry jam for the two of them, then pickled onions and dried mushrooms for them.

"You're too good to us," Archie said to Lucy on a fine June day, when she came bearing canned goods for them.

"You know I love you both, I'm happy to do it," Lucy said.

"Oh! Feel the baby, Lucy!" Millie was propped up in bed, hand on her increasingly large belly.

Lucy went over and placed a hand on Millie's stomach. She could feel a tiny foot kicking, and then felt the swirl of an arm or leg as it moved around.

286

"Goodness, she's a lively one, isn't she?" Lucy said.

"Do you think it's a girl?" Millie said excitedly. "I'd love to have a little girl."

"Gosh, I don't know, that just came out of my mouth."

"I'd love to have a baby girl, as long as she's as sweet and pretty as my Millie," Archie said. He had moved over to Millie's other side and was smoothing her hair off her face.

"Whatever it is, it will be a lucky baby to have the two of you for parents," Lucy said.

A few days later, Gwen paddled her canoe over to Beaver Island to check on Millie and to spend some time with Dolan. As she paddled past Whiskey Point, she noticed how sad it was looking. The abandoned home of Tom Bennett was standing forlornly without a portion of its roof, which had blown off in a winter gale. Pete McKinley's store and outbuildings looked equally neglected without Pete there to maintain his property. Porch railings had rotted and fallen over; wooden window shutters were hanging crooked, suspended by just one remaining bent iron hinge; and heavy snow accumulation earlier in the winter had collapsed the roof of his storage barn.

Gwen paddled to the south shore of the harbor and beached her canoe near Dolan's house. She walked straight to Millie and Archie's house, wanting to take care of business before pleasure.

She examined Millie carefully, feeling her small pelvic structure and the active baby inside. She worried that Millie might have a difficult time delivering the baby, but she said nothing to Millie about it. She didn't want to worry her unnecessarily.

"Judging by your size, I'd say you're going to be having this baby in August," Gwen told her.

Millie beamed. "I guess we'd better start thinking of baby names," she said.

"You do that," Gwen said, giving her a pat on the arm. Then she let herself out the door, leaving Millie to rest.

When she got back to Dolan's house, she found him sitting on the front porch with Will and Teddy. The younger men were mending boat lines that had frayed over time. Dolan was whittling.

Gwen bent to kiss Dolan, and then tousled the hair of Will and Teddy affectionately.

"So what have I missed over here?" she asked as she sat down on the bench next to Dolan. It had been a month since she'd been on Beaver Island. She'd been busy on Garden Island with the planting of corn and potatoes.

"Well, let's see," Dolan said. "The sheriff seized McKinley's and Tom Bennett's property for back taxes. Sam and Julia tried to pay for Tom's taxes, but the sheriff said it was too late. They were told they could try to buy the property at the sheriff's sale. They don't want the property if they have to buy it outright – they just wanted to keep it in the family by paying the back taxes."

"That hardly seems fair," Gwen said, her stern, broad brow furrowing.

"Maybe not fair, but apparently quite legal. There's going to be a sheriff's sale this week."

Bennett's and McKinley's properties covered about two-thirds of Whiskey Point. Gwen wondered who would buy it and what would happen to it. For so long it had been an unofficial gathering place for Indians, fur trappers and fishermen.

"I heard a rumor that Strang is going to buy it all for the church," Will said.

"If that happens, we'll be surrounded by Mormons on all sides," Teddy said. His little cabin sat on the back side of Dolan's property, which was on the south side of the harbor. Mormons had built their homes farther south and west of Dolan. They owned most of the property along the harbor; if they acquired Whiskey Point, they would control almost all of the land around the north side of the harbor.

"Let's hope it's just a rumor," Dolan said. But he didn't have much hope.

The sheriff's sale four days later went perfectly for Strang. With no Gentiles interested in the property and no Mormons daring to bid against Strang during the auction, he was able to buy Bennett's 140 acres for $71. He then snapped up McKinley's 39 acres for $54. After making his purchases, he headed to the newspaper office to write the story that would appear in the next issue, above the fold. He was going to let everyone know the Mormons now owned Whiskey Point and any trespassers would be fined and possibly arrested. The selling of spirits on Whiskey Point would not be tolerated. Strang finally felt he was in a strong position to crack down on the sale of liquor on Beaver Island, something that had bothered him since the day he arrived.

Archie and Dolan were in Cleary's tavern later in the week, reading Strang's article in the *Northern Islander.*

"Are we still going to be able to drink here?" Archie asked Roald.

"Yes. I have a permit to sell spirits. Strang can't take that away from me, not without a big fight."

Dolan continued to read the Mormon newspaper.

"It says here that the Gentiles are invited to celebrate the Fourth of July with the Mormons on Font Lake, since Whiskey Point will be off limits for any celebration," Dolan said.

"No point in celebrating if you have to do it with the Mormons," Archie said.

"Aren't you still a Mormon?" Dolan asked, surprised at Archie's statement.

"I suppose so, but I'm not an active Mormon anymore. I've had it with them." Archie didn't tell Dolan about having to tithe twice. He was ashamed he'd made such a stupid mistake.

The two of them continued to read the newspaper, learning that the Fourth of July celebration would be a modest one, since the big celebration was being saved for King's Day, July 8. The paper had been touting the grand celebration day for weeks.

"I'll be skipping that celebration too," Archie said.

"Gwen and I were planning to be on Garden Island on King's Day. We'd prefer to avoid all the activity on this island. Probably Will and Teddy will join us. You're welcome to come along too, Archie."

"That's nice of you, but Millie won't be in any condition to travel, and I'm not leaving her alone."

"Oh yes, of course. Then you have a good excuse for not attending the King's Day festivities."

The Fourth of July came and went without much celebration. Down on Cable's Bay, Alva Cable hosted a celebration for the Gentiles who lived in the area. Black Pete McCauley, Sam and Julia Bennett, the Whitney family and a few others came to Alva's home to toast the country's birthday with whiskey and ale that Alva was selling at his store.

In town, Frank Johnson held a gathering at his store for Mormons and Gentiles alike. It was sparsely attended. As Frank's newly appointed assistant manager, Rose served lemonade and small fruit cakes to Lucy, Will, Teddy, Dolan, Gwen, Huldy and Lorenzo, Dr. and Mrs. MacCulloch, the Wentworths, Watsons, and Bedfords, and a handful of other Mormons who attended. The celebration was subdued and ended an hour after it started.

With the Fourth of July behind them, the Mormons started working feverishly on preparations for King's Day. It was to be the first real celebration for the king's coronation, since the year before he'd been on trial in Detroit on the anniversary.

Font Lake was to be the scene of the celebration, just as it had been the location for the coronation two years ago. Strang said it was to be a day of feasting and dancing. Everyone was expected to bring a sacrifice of an animal or fowl for the feast. Mormon men dug huge pits for roasting pigs, cows, ducks and chicken; women baked pies and cornbread in preparation.

Dolan and Gwen quietly paddled off Beaver Island on the morning of July 7.

When they arrived at Garden Island, Otto greeted Dolan and Gwen on the beach. He walked with them back to the wigwam, where he had started roasting ducks over an open fire.

"Your boys coming today?" Otto asked Dolan.

"Yep, a little later. They wanted to get some fishing in."

"They'd better get here before dark. There's a big storm coming."

Dolan looked up at the cloudless sky, finding it hard to believe. "What have you noticed?" he asked.

"Frogs in the inlets, croaking louder and longer than I think I've ever heard them. And look at the birds." Otto raised a hand to the eastern sky.

Dolan looked eastward, and noticed birds flying low – very low. On clear summer days, the birds liked to soar so high in the sky they looked no bigger than mosquitos, but the flock of gulls he saw were flying just above the treetops.

Gwen, meanwhile, was poking around in her vegetable garden, looking closely at the beans and turnips.

"Otto's right. No sign of a bee or butterfly anywhere. They've taken shelter already."

"Let's hope the boys make it before the storm hits," Dolan said.

Will and Teddy sailed easily to Garden Island, arriving at dusk. The sky was still clear. Otto and Dolan met them on the beach.

"Pull the boat up high," Otto said, reaching for the bow line to help hoist the boat onto the shore. "And batten your sails down real good," Otto told them. "Storm's coming."

"You sure, Otto?" Teddy asked. Dolan gave him a dirty look.

"I can't recall a time Otto's been wrong about the weather," Dolan said.

Teddy looked chastised, but still said, as he looked at the cloudless sky, "There's always a first time."

It hit about six in the morning. Sheets of rain flew sideways in the powerful wind. Otto and Dolan looked out the front door toward the shoreline, which was no more than 30 feet from them. They couldn't see it through the torrential rain.

"This is going to put a damper on King's Day, no pun intended," Dolan said with a grin.

Dolan was correct. Back on Beaver Island, the main road through town had turned into a river from the rain water rushing to the lake. No fires could be made to roast the animals that had been sacrificed for the king. The fire pits turned into ponds within minutes.

By early afternoon, the storm still hadn't let up.

Archie was looking out the window at the ferocious display of nature's power, watching the lightning strikes and hearing the thunder almost immediately afterward. The thunder was so deafening, he almost didn't hear Millie moan.

"You okay, my little love?" he asked her.

"I'm fine, just a bit uncomfortable," she said. Then she tried to stifle another moan.

"I don't think you're okay, Millie. Tell me the truth."

She managed a little smile. "I think this baby has decided to arrive a little early," she said.

Archie paled. The baby wasn't due for a few more weeks, according to Gwen. And now Gwen and Dolan were on Garden Island, which might as well have been a thousand miles away, given the strength of the storm.

"I'll get help, Millie, just hang in there."

Millie looked frightened. "Who are you going to get?"

"Dr. MacCulloch, I suppose. There's no chance I can get to Garden Island to fetch Gwen."

Millie frowned, and then her frown turned into a grimace as another contraction overtook her.

"I don't like him," she said when the contraction subsided.

"I don't care much for him either, but he's all we have right now. And it's different this time, Millie," Archie said, remembering how cruel and insensitive the doctor had been after Millie lost her first baby. "This time, the baby's all grown inside you. All he has to do is help you get it out."

"All right," Millie said with resignation in her voice. Then another contraction hit her.

"You'd better hurry, Archie, this seems to be speeding up."

Archie pulled on his oiled cotton jacket. He grabbed his rain hat, also oiled, and pulled it down hard on his head, the long, downward sloping brim practically hiding his face. He ran out the door and kept running until he reached the home of Dr. MacCulloch.

Archie pounded on the front door for several minutes. He realized if the MacCullochs were inside, they probably couldn't hear his knocking over the sound of the thunder. He thought about bursting through the door when it swung open.

"Good heavens, what are you doing out in this weather?" Dr. MacCulloch asked as he let a soaking wet Archie into the house. Archie noticed MacCulloch smelled like whiskey.

"It's Millie, she's having her baby," Archie said.

"I thought the Indian woman was tending to her," MacCulloch said with a tone of resentment.

"She was supposed to, but the baby's coming early and Gwen is on Garden Island. You've got to help Millie, Doc."

"All right then, let me get my coat." MacCulloch took a few steps over to the corner of the room, where his coat hung on a wooden peg mounted to the wall.

Walking back to Archie's, they had the wind behind them, pushing them along. When they entered the house, they saw Millie on the bed, damp with sweat, face flushed.

"How long has it been going on?" MacCulloch asked her.

"Since early this morning," Millie said.

"This morning! And you didn't tell me?" Archie said.

"I didn't want to worry you," Millie said. Then a contraction seized her and she cried out in pain.

MacCulloch felt her enormous belly and ran his hands down her small hips.

"I need to examine you," he said. Millie nodded her consent.

MacCulloch inserted his finger into her and immediately came in contact with the crown of the baby's head.

"Shouldn't be long now, it's getting close," he said confidently. "Just keep pushing."

Millie kept pushing. For one hour, then another. She was running out of strength.

"Why isn't it coming out?" Archie asked frantically. "Shouldn't it be out by now?"

"I think it's stuck," MacCulloch said. "Her hips are so small, the baby can't get through. I might need to help it along."

Without warning, MacCulloch flung himself on top of Millie's belly. Archie heard bone crack.

"Jesus Almighty, you've broken her!" he yelled.

Millie fainted.

"I had to do it to get the baby out. The baby's life is in danger."

"I don't care about the baby's life; I care about Millie's life first!"

"Don't worry; it's going to be fine now." MacCulloch inserted two fingers into the unconscious Millie, then three. He probed around the baby's head, trying to make a path for it.

With one hand practically inside her, MacCulloch used his other hand and pushed hard on her belly.

"Here it comes," he said. Archie wasn't paying attention. He was holding Millie's head and kissing her cheeks, trying to wake her up.

"Best if she's unconscious for this," MacCulloch said. "She won't feel the pain."

In a few more minutes, MacCulloch delivered a tiny baby girl with a large head. He dangled her by the ankles and stuck a finger roughly into the baby's mouth. Then he swatted her and she began to cry.

"There you go, a healthy baby girl," he said proudly to Archie.

Archie wasn't listening. He was still kissing and stroking his wife's head.

"When will she wake up?" he asked. MacCulloch laid the baby down on the bed next to Millie and lifted her wrist. Her pulse was weak and shallow. He suddenly felt nervous.

"I've got to get her to expel the afterbirth," he said authoritatively. Once again, his fingers probed inside her. His hand was met with a river of blood. The blood spread quickly on the bed, forming a large dark pool. Archie saw it and screamed.

"My God, what is happening?!" he yelled. He looked at Millie's face, which was as pale as the blood was dark.

"I've got to stop the bleeding," MacCulloch said. Get me some clean cloths."

Archie hesitated to leave his wife's side, but did so in order to save her. He opened a trunk at the foot of the bed and started pulling out sheets, handing them to MacCulloch.

"Tear them into strips," MacCulloch ordered. Archie had no trouble tearing the worn sheets quickly and handing pieces to MacCulloch. MacCulloch took the strips and wedged them into Millie as far as he could. They quickly became soaked with blood. When that happened, he removed the bloody strips and inserted clean strips. He kept repeating the procedure until he was out of strips.

And then Millie was out of life.

The baby started to cry. So did her father. Both wailed while MacCulloch hastily made his way out the door and into the storm, leaving behind a wet coat and a broken family.

CHAPTER 50

SUMMER, 1852

The rain had let up slightly when MacCulloch found himself knocking on Lucy's door. His clothes were drenched and his sleeves were stained with Millie's blood.

Lucy answered the door, puzzled to see the doctor.

"Come in," Lucy said politely. MacCulloch didn't move.

"I'm too wet," he said. He wasted no time coming to the point. "Millie had her baby."

"Oh! She wasn't due for another few weeks! Is it a boy or a girl? What happy news!" Lucy couldn't understand why MacCulloch still had a grim look on his face. Then Lucy looked down and noticed the blood on his shirtsleeves.

"Is the baby all right?"

"The baby is fine," MacCulloch said. "But Mrs. Donnelly isn't. She didn't make it." He looked down at his shoes. The usually arrogant man was alarmingly humbled.

"What?! Millie is – Millie is dead? Is that what you're saying?"

"I'm afraid so," MacCulloch said. "Nothing I could do about it."

"Oh good Lord, how is Archie doing?"

"That's why I'm here. I think he's going to need your help. I'm sorry."

With that MacCulloch turned and walked away, his face pointed at the ground, shielded from the rain and Lucy's shocked expression. Lucy watched him walk away, still stunned at the news. Then she snapped out of her daze and grabbed her raincoat. She pulled it on and rushed to Archie's home.

When she opened the front door to the Donnelly home, what she saw broke her heart. Millie lay on the bed, bluish-white, her eyes folded closed. Archie lay next to her. In between them was a tiny baby that must have cried itself out, for now the baby's breath was ragged and weak. Archie's eyes were open, staring at nothing.

Lucy knelt at Archie's side. "Oh Archie, Archie, I'm so terribly sorry," she said as she stroked his big head. He didn't respond immediately. Then he slowly looked at her and his puffy eyes welled with tears again.

"How can it be, Lucy? How can Millie be gone? I can't go on without her." He squeezed his eyes shut and let the tears spill down the sides of his face.

The baby stirred at the sound of a new voice, and started whimpering. Lucy assumed it was MacCulloch who had taken the time to wrap the baby in a soft, small blanket. Lucy leaned over Archie and scooped the baby into her arms.

"You must, Archie, you have a baby to think about," Lucy said. She unwrapped the blanket partway and peered in. "A baby girl, I see."

"I can't raise a wee one on my own without Millie," Archie said, his voice a monotone of defeat.

"We'll figure it out," Lucy said. "Right now, this little one needs feeding. Can I leave you alone for a bit? I'm going to go to the Watsons' and get some things for the baby."

Archie didn't respond. He just continued to look up at the ceiling.

"All right then, I'll be back soon." Lucy didn't need an answer from him. She could see he wasn't going anywhere. She tucked the baby back in between the dead Millie and anguished Archie. Then she headed to the home of Wingfield and Jane Watson.

"I don't have much time," Lucy said after Wingfield and Jane invited her in. Their little girl Abby was playing on the floor with a wooden toy train.

Lucy told the Watsons what she knew – that Dr. MacCulloch had delivered Millie's baby but Millie had died, and now Archie and the baby were lying in bed next to her.

"Oh my, I'd best round up some men to remove poor Millie," Wingfield said. "We must get her out of the house."

"I agree," Lucy said. "But don't get those deputies to do it. That will only upset Archie more."

"I won't," Wingfield said. "I was thinking of Lorenzo Hickey and George Miller, the Constable's father. They're good people." Wingfield headed out the door as Lucy started spelling out her needs to his wife.

"Jane, I need baby supplies; diapers, baby bottles, clothes, whatever you can spare," Lucy said.

"I have plenty, I kept everything." Jane was hoping another child of her own would come along soon and the baby items would be needed again.

Jane opened a trunk at the foot of their bed and started laying baby supplies on the bed. "There's a sack hanging on a hook by the door, you can use that," she told Lucy.

Lucy got the sack and started filling it. When the bag was full, she started to head out the door.

"May I come too?" Jane asked. "Maybe I could be of some help."

"Of course, but what about little Abby?"

"I'll drop her off at the King's home. Elvira will watch her. Abby and Charles are friends."

"All right," Lucy said. "You do that, and then meet me at Archie's."

The rain had finally let up, but water still rushed down the road, soaking the hems of their dresses.

Lucy arrived at Archie's home the same time as Wingfield, who was accompanied by Lorenzo Hickey and George Miller. They all went in together.

Wingfield was the first to approach Archie, who was lying as still as Millie. The baby was asleep between them.

"I'm so sorry for your loss, Archie," Wingfield said. "She was a wonderful woman. God will welcome her into heaven."

"I don't believe in God anymore," Archie said. "No God would let this happen to a good woman like Millie."

"We don't know the mysterious ways of God, but I'm sure he had his reasons for taking Millie at this point in time," Wingfield said.

Hickey came to stand on the other side of the bed, by Millie. "Archie, I'm so sorry about this," he said. "We're all here to help you get through this."

Archie didn't respond.

"We need to take Millie now," Wingfield said, feeling increasingly uncomfortable in the room with a corpse.

"NO!" Archie said. "Don't take my Millie from me!" He rolled on his side and put one of his massive arms protectively over Millie's body.

"She's gone, Archie," Hickey said gently. "She's already gone to be with her Maker. This is just the empty shell she left behind. No sense in holding onto it."

"Please, don't take her away yet," Archie begged, clinging more tightly to her.

Wingfield gave Hickey a sympathetic look. "Archie, how about if we sing a hymn for her before we take her to the tabernacle? She can lie in wait there until the funeral."

Wingfield didn't wait for an answer. He cleared his throat and started singing a hymn he'd learned and loved before he became a Mormon; *Now The Day Is Over.*

"Now the day is over, night is drawing nigh, shadows of the evening steal across the sky...

"Grant to little children, visions bright of Thee, guard the sailors tossing, on the deep blue sea...

"Jesus give the weary, calm and sweet repose, with thy tend'rest blessing, may thine eyelids close..."

In a sweet tenor voice, Wingfield sang all six verses of the hymn. When he was finished, Archie let two more tears slide down his face, then he released Millie's corpse.

Lorenzo pulled the sheet up over Millie's face, and then nodded to Wingfield and George. Wingfield was already in place on the opposite side of the bed, and George came around to help him. The three of them gently lifted Millie out of bed. They made a hammock of their arms for Millie and carried her respectfully out the door.

As soon as they were gone, Lucy stepped up to the bed.

"This little girl of yours needs some clothes and some feeding," Lucy said as she reached for the baby. She carefully unswaddled her and wiped her clean with a dish cloth she'd found in the kitchen area. Then she diapered her and dressed her in a faded pink baby gown. As she was finishing, Jane came through the door, set a bottle on the table and rushed to Archie. She put her head next to his and stroked his forehead.

"I'm so sorry, Archie," she said. "I loved Millie too." Archie remained unresponsive.

"I brought goat's milk," she said to Lucy. "Elvira gave it to me."

Lucy hadn't even thought that far. She was relieved that Jane, now an experienced young mother, had thought ahead. Jane put a couple of ounces of milk into a baby bottle and handed it to Lucy.

"I'll let you," she said.

Lucy sat in a rocking chair that Millie loved and held the tiny baby in her arms. She put the nipple of the bottle to the baby's mouth. At first the baby squirmed as if to avoid the nipple, but then turned and latched onto it. She sucked hungrily and finished every drop.

"You need to burp her now," Jane said, laying a spare diaper on Lucy's shoulder. "Sometimes a little spit comes up with the burp."

Lucy put the baby up to her shoulder and patted her back as she'd seen other mothers do. The baby burped and up-chucked a portion of the goat's milk she had just consumed.

"It's okay, it's what babies do," Jane said.

Lucy had held other women's babies in her life. She'd even changed a diaper or two, but had never fed or cared for a baby. She cradled the baby and looked down at the sleeping face. The baby had Millie's coloring – a sprig of light red hair on the top of her head, and her skin was as soft and translucent as Millie's had been. Her relatively large head was the only thing that bore a resemblance to Archie. Lucy was in awe of the little creature's perfection.

"Elvira and Betsy said they'd bring goat's milk every day for the baby," Jane said. "They want to help. And they have a goat."

Lucy thought of Strang's two wives, whom she'd never cared for, and realized perhaps she'd been too harsh in her judgment of them.

"Please tell them that Archie sends his thanks," Lucy said. "I'm sure he would if he could."

"I'd better get back to Abby," Jane said. Then she knelt beside Lucy and put her lips to Lucy's ear.

"What on earth are we going to do about Archie?" she whispered. "He's in shock. We can't leave him alone with a baby."

"I'll take care of him and the baby until he comes around," Lucy whispered back.

"Maybe it would be best if he wasn't in this house, where he lost Millie," Jane said.

"Good thinking. I'll take him to my house."

"You'll need help. I'll send Wingfield as soon as he returns from the tabernacle."

Lucy smiled gratefully at Jane, then went back to the soothing task of holding and rocking the baby.

CHAPTER 51

SUMMER, 1852

It took Wingfield and Lorenzo the better part of the day to convince Archie to stand up and go to Lucy's house. The rain had stopped and a cloud-spattered sky the color of fresh bruises was on the western horizon. Archie walked unsteadily between the two men, being propelled forward by the arms the men had linked through his own.

Lucy had taken the baby to her home ahead of the men. She'd pulled a drawer out of a wooden chest in her room, put it on the kitchen floor, lined it with cotton sheets and placed the baby in it, where she was now sleeping. Her tiny mouth made little sucking motions in her sleep.

"Put him in the first room upstairs," Lucy told the men when they got Archie over her threshold. Then Lucy went to the corner cupboard in her kitchen and pulled out the bottle of scotch. She poured some in a teacup and went upstairs after the men.

"Here, Archie, this will help," she said as she handed him the cup. He was sitting on the edge of the bed, his head in his rough, brawny hands. "Nothing will help," he said, but he took the cup anyway and drank the scotch in one big gulp.

"Are you going to be okay?" Lorenzo asked Lucy, after taking a nervous look at the giant of a man who had been reduced to rubble.

"We'll be fine," Lucy said. "I'm grateful for your help. You two can be on your way now."

"If you're sure," Wingfield said, but he was anxious to be on his way. He could hardly stand the misery that filled the room.

"Yes, go," Lucy said firmly.

After the two men left, Lucy went downstairs to make soup for dinner. She had the fire in the woodstove stoked and a chicken ready to put in the pot when she heard Archie's sobs. They shook the house. She ran back upstairs.

Archie was curled up on his side in the bed, looking like a wounded bear, sobbing uncontrollably. Lucy didn't know what to do. She sat on the bed next to him and patted his head. The sobbing continued. She ran her hand up and down his arm, hoping it would soothe him. It didn't.

Ever so gingerly, she laid down next to him and pulled her body tight against his back, her long arm wrapped around him. The sobbing grew softer. She stayed there, holding the big man until she heard his sobs turn into steady breaths.

As Archie cried himself to sleep, his daughter cried herself awake. Lucy left Archie and ran back downstairs to tend to the baby, who was making a tremendous racket.

This child has a good set of lungs for an early baby, Lucy thought to herself. She poured goat's milk into a clean bottle, picked up the baby and started feeding her while she sat at the kitchen table. She heard a knock on her door.

"Come in!" she called, not wanting to interrupt the feeding process to answer the door.

Moments later, James Strang entered her kitchen.

"I heard about Millie," Strang said. "What a terrible tragedy."

Strang looked genuinely morose, his intense brown eyes soft as he gazed at the baby in Lucy's arms.

"I've come to offer my condolences to Archie."

"He's sleeping right now, I think it's best not to disturb him."

"I understand." Strang stood quietly for a minute or two. "It's a beautiful baby," he finally said. "A girl, I heard. What's her name?"

"She has no name yet," Lucy said, her eyes on the baby as it sucked contentedly.

Strang shifted his weight from one foot to the other as he watched Lucy. The sight of her feeding a baby tugged on his heart strings.

"You would make a good mother, Lucy," he said. "Archie is lucky to have you taking care of his baby."

Lucy looked up at him, then back down to the baby. "Babies are a joy, even if they come with sorrow."

Strang shifted his weight again. "I hate to bring up a tender subject, but there's the matter of Millie. She needs a proper funeral. She's the first of our island congregation to pass away. I've selected a plot of land behind the tabernacle for a graveyard and blessed it. When do you think Archie will be ready to deal with this?"

The infant finished her bottle, and Lucy held her up to her shoulder and patted her gently until she burped. Then she stood, still holding the baby to her shoulder, and looked squarely at Strang.

"I don't know when Archie will be ready to put his beloved wife in the ground. And I don't know if he'll want to put her in a Mormon graveyard. He hasn't been treated very well by the Mormons, including you."

Strang looked surprised. "What have I ever done to Archie? I've given him a lot of work and paid him fairly."

"You made him tithe twice for the school building," Lucy said bluntly. "Millie told me about it. And you protected your Doctor MacCulloch when the sheriff from Mackinac came to arrest him. Then, that very same doctor had a hand in Millie's death, somehow."

Strang resisted the urge to wrap his arms around Lucy and tell her he would undo anything he'd done if he could get back in her good graces. Instead, he simply said, "I don't recall this tithing business, but if Archie had to pay twice, I'll set it right. As for MacCulloch, my men did what they thought was right at the time. It was their decision, not mine, to prevent the sheriff from arresting him. I, in turn, protected my men. Maybe that was a mistake."

Lucy had never heard Strang come close to admitting he might have made a mistake. It softened her feelings toward him. She took a step forward and briefly put a hand on his arm.

"Thank you for saying that. I suspect your decision to harbor that fugitive MacCulloch might come back to haunt you some day."

Strang pondered her words, while still relishing the brief touch of her hand on him. "I guess I never really thought of MacCulloch as a fugitive. I think the Bennett shooting was just a tragedy that could have been avoided if the Bennett brothers hadn't started shooting at my men, and MacCulloch was one of many firing weapons back at them. There was shooting going on from both sides, I might add." Strang completely believed his words. He'd rewritten history and repeated the story of Bennett's shooting so many times that it was now absolute truth in his mind.

Such was not the case with Lucy. "I don't want to discuss Tom Bennett," Lucy said sharply. "I have my opinion, you have yours. There is no convincing one another of anything different than what we already believe." Her voice rose almost to a shout as she spoke.

Strang was suddenly distraught. How did a lovely moment with Lucy turn into a fight? Yet he wouldn't back down. "There is certainly no convincing you of the truth, because you want to believe we Mormons are a bunch of murderous thugs, and you know in your heart that isn't true!" Now Strang's voice rose to match Lucy's.

The baby on Lucy's shoulder started fussing at the tension she could feel building in Lucy's body. Then they all heard the creak of the stairs as Archie slowly made his way down them.

"Oh, dear, look what we've done," Lucy said, the fire in her voice now tamped down. "We've woken Archie."

"I'm sorry," Strang said, his voice equally low.

Archie walked past the two of them and helped himself to a seat at the kitchen table. Strang pulled a chair up next to him.

"I'm so sorry for your loss," Strang said. "I, too, have experienced the terrible loss of a family member and I know how painful it is."

Archie looked at Strang warily. "You've lost someone?"

"Yes, my first-born daughter, Mary. She was the light of my life. When God took her, I cursed Him mightily. It took me quite a while to accept that God has his reasons, and life will go on in the wake of a tragic loss."

Archie was surprised to hear Strang's story, yet he believed him. The jagged tone of his voice told him Strang was being truthful.

"I don't see how my life can go on without Millie," Archie said.

"Your life will never be the same without her, that much is true. But don't give up hope. In time, you will be able to smile again and find happiness in other ways. For one thing, you have this beautiful daughter." Strang gestured toward Lucy, who was holding the baby in her lap.

Archie put his elbows on the table and his head in his hands. Thinking about raising his new daughter without Millie made his head so heavy he couldn't hold it up.

Strang switched the subject. "Archie, I know this is difficult for you to think about, but Millie needs a proper funeral," he said. "I'd like to bury her in the new church cemetery. I've blessed it, so it's hallowed ground. I think Millie would find peace there."

"Fine, whatever you want," Archie said. He had no strength to protest anything.

Lucy was surprised. "Are you sure that's what you want, Archie?"

"Yes."

"Then it's settled," Strang said. "How about the day after tomorrow?"

"Whatever you say," Archie said, his head still in his hands.

"All right then," Strang said. "Lucy, I'll get back to you with details. I'll show myself out." Strang rose and left.

"You really want a Mormon funeral for Millie?" Lucy asked.

"What does it matter? She's gone. Gone forever. Does it really matter where her body lies?"

"No, I guess it doesn't," Lucy said, thinking of Antoine's body somewhere at the bottom of Lake Michigan.

———◆••◆———

Millie's funeral took place on a calm, sunny day, the opposite of the day she'd died. Nearly every island resident was in attendance, given their fondness for Archie and Millie. Dolan, Gwen and the boys had returned from Garden Island in time to attend the funeral. Gwen was filled with questions about the baby's delivery, wondering if Millie's death could have been avoided had she been there.

Strang delivered a moving eulogy, praising Millie's cheerfulness and generous heart. Archie stood quietly next to the pine coffin that Dolan and the Mormons had made for Millie. Archie didn't cry. He was fresh out of tears for the time being.

After the service, everyone headed to the tabernacle for food. While people offered their condolences to Archie, Gwen sought out MacCulloch.

"What happened, exactly, during the birth?" she asked him.

"It was obstructed labor," MacCulloch answered. "You know how small she was. The baby couldn't fit through the birth canal."

"What did you do to help?" Gwen asked.

MacCulloch assumed a pompous look of superiority.

"I did the logical thing. I flung myself upon her to help push it out."

"You didn't stand her up? Have her walk around? Put her in a squatting position?"

"There's no evidence that those techniques work," MacCulloch said. "I believe they are just Indian wives' tales perpetuated by the ignorant and uneducated."

Gwen bristled. She stared down her long nose at MacCulloch. "On the contrary, I have seen it help many times. I don't need book learning to know what actually works."

"It wouldn't have mattered. She hemorrhaged after she expelled the afterbirth. There was no stopping the blood. That's what she died from."

"Did you massage her womb? Apply pressure?" Gwen was persistent. "Those things help to stop the bleeding."

"I did everything that was appropriate under the circumstances," MacCulloch said. "And I will not be grilled by an Indian woman about delivering babies!" MacCulloch turned and walked away from Gwen before she could say another word.

Lucy and Archie had seen Gwen talking to the doctor. They approached Gwen as soon as the doctor had taken his leave.

"What did he say?" Archie asked. "I bet you could have saved Millie, right? That bastard killed my wife!"

Gwen looked at the fury and agony on Archie's face. She knew that speaking the truth wouldn't help him.

"I'm afraid nothing would have saved Millie," she said softly. "Birthing babies is always a dangerous business. Things happen. Things go wrong. Sometimes mothers die in the process."

"But he BROKE her!" Archie said. "He threw himself on her! I heard her bones crack!"

Gwen's jaw clenched, but she said, "Sometimes that's the only way to get the baby out. Some mothers, especially tiny women like Millie, aren't built for childbirth. I believe Dr. MacCulloch did everything he knew how to do to save Millie and the child." Gwen wasn't lying when she said that. She did think MacCulloch did everything he knew how to do. Unfortunately for Millie, his knowledge of things to do wasn't enough.

Lucy put a hand on Archie's arm and said, "Mother Nature and Father Time are always roaming the earth, walking hand in hand. Mother Nature gives, Father Time takes away. No one knows when or why. It just is."

After letting her remark sink in, she tugged his sleeve. "Let's go home," she said. "There's nothing more to do here. You've got your answers." Lucy looked at Gwen, and through the unspoken language of women's facial expressions, she had a sense that Gwen may have been able to save Millie, but it was something she would not tell Archie. He would never be able to move past his grief if he knew that.

CHAPTER 52
LATE SUMMER, 1852

Archie never moved out of Lucy's house. He needed her help with the baby, and he couldn't bring himself to return to the home he shared with Millie.

He didn't get over losing Millie, but he learned to cope with it by burying himself in his work. He rose at dawn every day and set about the business of building homes. He worked until the last sliver of daylight vanished into the lake. For 30 days and nights, Archie worked without ever taking a day off. He couldn't risk being idle with nothing but his memories to keep him company.

And then there was Lucy and the baby. Lucy bonded with the infant in a way that Archie couldn't. Every time he held his infant daughter and looked into her eyes, he saw Millie looking back up at him. It broke his heart all over again.

For Lucy, the little girl was the daughter she never had. She loved her more each day, and couldn't bear the thought that someday Archie would get over the worst of his grief and move back home with his baby, leaving Lucy to resume her life in a house with no one to love.

True to her word, Elvira came to Lucy's home twice a day, bringing goat's milk for the child.

"She's a pretty baby," Elvira said, admiring the petite, red-headed little girl. Lucy smiled at her.

"Yes, she is. She had a lovely mother and has a handsome father."

Elvira stood awkwardly for a moment, fiddling with the linen skirt of her dress. Then she spoke up.

"I know you aren't a Mormon, but do you think you should have the baby baptized in the Mormon Church? Her parents are Mormon, after all."

Lucy gave her a caustic look. "That's for Archie to decide, not me."

"Perhaps you could ask him to come to services this Saturday," Elvira continued, ignoring Lucy's remark. "The King has an important decree to make. Archie may want to hear it."

Not much chance you'll see Archie in that tabernacle, Lucy thought to herself. Archie had extricated himself from the Mormon community after Millie's death.

"I'll give him your message," Lucy said.

The following Saturday, Archie was not in the tabernacle to hear Strang's service. Not that it mattered. After the service concluded, word of Strang's new decree spread through town like a swarm of bees looking for a new home.

Strang had delivered a stern sermon about the dangers of spirits and the demons that entered the bodies of those who consumed liquor. Then Strang paused and switched topics.

"I would like to decree that the time has come to unite all the people of this island," he said, his voice ringing off the rafters above him. "Let it be known to all the island residents that we will have a baptismal service at Font Lake next Saturday for all the remaining islanders who are not Mormons. To continue to live on this island, we all need to be of one mind and one belief – the belief of the Strangite Church of Latter-Day Saints. Anyone who does not join the church must leave the island. So go forth, good members, and spread the word to all our Gentile friends that we shall embrace them and invite them into our fold, or they can leave."

Gasps and murmurs rippled through the tabernacle. Strang was actually going to force the Gentiles to become Mormons or get off the island.

When the service was over, Phebe Wentworth shot out of church with the trajectory of one of Strang's cannonballs. She found Rose Pratt sweeping the front porch of the little home she'd acquired from Nathan.

"Lucky for you you're already a Mormon," Phebe told Rose. "You'll be safe here. All the non-Mormons either have to join the church or leave the island. The King just decreed it."

Rose didn't attend the Mormon Church services. She was no more a Mormon than the possum living in her woodpile out back. She and the possum lived on Mormon property, but that's where the religious affiliation ended.

"It doesn't matter to me," Rose said. "And I can't imagine how Strang plans to force people to do something against their will." She was thinking of Frank Johnson, her boss, who was also a Mormon in name only, for the sake of his business. He never attended church services or activities. She couldn't imagine Strang compelling him to be active in the church or leave. Johnson was too valuable to the island, selling goods to Mormons and offering them lines of credit during the harsh winter months.

Phebe wasn't the only one spreading the word of Strang's new decree. Jane and Wingfield Watson stopped by Dolan's home after church to tell him of the new decree. They found Dolan in his vegetable garden, pulling weeds and picking tomatoes off plants. Will and Teddy were out fishing. Saturday was a work day for them, not a day of prayer.

"This will not be tolerated, you know," Dolan said. "Strang can't force us to join his church, and he can't force us to leave the island either."

"I tend to agree with you," Wingfield said. "But I also see how we would all live more peacefully if we were all under the same umbrella of religious faith."

"You're a good man, Wingfield, but it's a matter of principle. We won't be chased off our island and we won't be forced to join your church."

"I'll miss you if you leave," Jane said to Dolan.

"No need to miss me. You'll be leaving before I ever will. Count on that."

"What if the king finds a way to force you?" Jane couldn't imagine what her beloved King Strang would do to force people away. She believed in her tender heart that he was a man with nothing but goodness in his heart for his people. He wanted a peaceful island where they could openly follow their beliefs without interference.

"He can't force me off the island. This isn't the Spanish Inquisition."

"What is the Spanish Inquisition?" Wingfield asked. He was young, uneducated, and hadn't learned about religious wars in parts of Europe.

Dolan, on the other hand, had been brought up on stories of the Spanish Inquisition, the French Civil War, and the never-ending battles during the protestant reformation. It was why he chose not to follow any organized religion. They all seemed to lead to war at one point or another.

"The Spanish Inquisition was a time when the Catholic King of Spain said all other religions were unacceptable, and the Jews and Muslims had to convert to Catholicism or leave the country. It led to a lot of bloodshed, torture and violence. But that was hundreds of years ago, and no one in this country believes that people who follow one religion can evict people from their homes and native lands just because they don't follow a certain prescribed belief."

Wingfield looked wide-eyed at Dolan. "Goodness! I should think not! That would be most despicable behavior. I'm confident our King James has no such thing in mind."

Dolan looked at the ingenuous couple, brimming with passion for a peaceful, religious community. *How touchingly naïve they are*, he thought. *Naïve, and ignorant of the cunning means unscrupulous leaders can use get their way.*

By the time the sun was setting, most of the Gentiles living near the harbor had heard the news. Rose Pratt had gone over to Frank Johnson's home to tell him.

"You've got nothing to worry about Rose, you're already a Mormon."

"Not much of one," she said. "I hope they don't force me to start going to church. My bottom gets sore at the thought of sitting in those wooden pews for two hours."

Johnson laughed. "I'll protect you from that, I promise. Even if I have to make you do inventory on Saturdays. At least it will keep you out of the tabernacle."

"I'll take inventory over a sermon every day of the week," she said.

———— ◆◆◆ ————

The following Saturday, Strang and his apostles waited on the shore of Font Lake for the Gentiles to come for their baptism. Strang was wearing an old pair of black cotton pants and a plain white cotton shirt. He knew he'd get wet as he dipped each convert into the lake. He didn't want to ruin any of his good clothes in the process.

He needn't have worried about getting wet. No one came.

Lucy and Archie were sitting on her front porch a few days later, enjoying the warm weather. The baby had grown significantly in the past month, thanks to her healthy appetite and a steady supply of goat's milk.

Archie had brought a couple of chairs from his house over to Lucy's, so they could sit on the porch during the last of the summer days.

Lucy was rubbing the baby's face with the back of her forefinger while the baby gazed, wide-eyed, up at Lucy.

"Her skin's as soft as the petals on a day lily," she said as she stroked the baby's cheek.

Archie leaned over and stroked the baby's other cheek with his big, calloused finger. "You're right; it really is soft as a petal on a lily."

Then he had a thought. "That's what I'll name her. Lily. Rhymes with Millie. I like that."

Lucy smiled at him. She'd been waiting to see when he would be able to give the baby a name. Initially, his grief was so great that he couldn't even bear to look at his child for more than a minute without sinking into depression.

"I think Lily is a perfect name," Lucy said.

Archie smiled back at Lucy. "It is, isn't it? For a perfect little baby."

The two of them sat in companionable silence for a while, Lucy rocking the baby and Archie looking out at the lake.

"Are you happy, Lucy?" Archie suddenly asked.

"Why, I suppose so," Lucy said, looking over at Archie. She noticed the laugh lines around his eyes were less pronounced since Millie's death, and the furrows in his brow were deeper. His Irish skin never really tanned, but it was rusty from his long days of work in the sun. Freckles spilled like flecks of tobacco across his cheeks and nose. "Why do you ask?"

"You lost your husband, I just wondered if it's possible to be happy again."

Lucy pushed a stray strand of long black hair off her face and smiled. "Yes, Archie, it is possible to be happy. You'll never stop loving Millie, but you can find happiness again, in other ways, with other people. You've got Lily now; that will make you happy."

"I can't take care of Lily without you."

"You know I'm happy to help. I love this little papoose," Lucy said.

"I guess I also meant, can we be happy on this island? Strang has decreed that everyone must become a Mormon or leave. I have friends here who aren't Mormon, and I don't know if they're inclined to leave."

"I've lived here in the house Antoine built for many years," Lucy said. "I'm not leaving. I was here first. I won't be driven from my home, you can count on that."

Archie smiled at her gumption. He could see that no one, not even the king of Beaver Island, could make Lucy do something she didn't want to do.

"I've no doubt of that. But what about the others?"

"Time will tell," Lucy said with a shrug of her shoulders. As she shrugged, Lily woke up and started fussing.

"You hold her while I get a bottle," Lucy said as she stood and laid the baby in Archie's big arms. Archie looked at his daughter with the usual mixture of sadness and amazement. He often found it hard to believe he'd created such a precious little thing. He put her to his shoulder and bobbed her up and down while he sang an old Irish lullaby to her. Lucy could hear him through the window and it made her realize she was, indeed, very happy at that moment.

Her happiness didn't last long.

The deputies Pierce and Chidester arrived on her porch just as she was handing a bottle to Archie so he could feed his little girl. They had letters in their hands.

"Part of the King's decree," Chidester said bluntly. He handed Lucy a letter. She opened it and read the decree.

ALL GENTILES HAVE 10 DAYS TO JOIN THE LATTER DAY SAINTS IN A BAPTISM AT FONT LAKE, OR THEY MUST LEAVE THE ISLAND.

Lucy read the letter, then wadded it up and threw it at Chidester.

"You can tell your king the only way I'll be leaving this island is if one of his angels flies down, hog ties me and transports me to another location. And if an angel shows up here, I'll pluck him and slow roast him over the fire. I hear angels taste like chicken."

Archie couldn't help himself. He burst out laughing at Lucy's remark.

"You think this is funny, Donnelly?" Chidester said, turning his attention to Archie.

"Well, it was funny, you must admit," Archie said, still chortling. It felt good to laugh, and he was in no hurry to stop.

"It is not funny. It's deadly serious. Join the Mormon religion, or leave. You're not much of a Mormon, Donnelly. It wouldn't take a lot to convince the Circle of 12 to have you excommunicated and thrown off the island."

"Listen here, Dennis, I'm a Mormon and my beloved late wife is the first Mormon to be buried in the church cemetery. I won't leave her behind, never."

"Get off my property," Lucy told Chidester. "I'm an Indian. A Lamanite, according to your king. I seriously doubt he wants to rid this island of our noble people, as he calls us."

Chidester thought for a moment. He had been given instructions to serve letters to all the non-Mormons. It didn't occur to him that Lucy would have special dispensation for being an Indian. He decided to back down. Lucy's flashing black eyes frightened him.

"Fine, I'll leave" he said. "But all the other Gentiles must obey the king's new decree or plan to leave." With that, Chidester turned and walked quickly away from Lucy's home.

After he was out of earshot, Archie shifted his vision from Lily to Lucy. "How can he do that? How can Strang force people to leave?"

"I don't think he can, but he must have something up his sleeve that leads him to believe he can, or he wouldn't have decreed it. I know James, and he doesn't do anything without forethought."

Lucy's assessment of Strang proved to be accurate. While he couldn't literally throw anyone off the island, he could make their lives most uncomfortable.

It started with arrests. Constable Joshua Miller and his men lurked outside Cleary's tavern, and every time a boozy Gentile walked out, they arrested him for drunkenness and debauchery. They arrested other Gentiles for not paying a tithe.

Miller's father George was now sheriff of Mackinac County, and used his muscle to arrest the Beaver Island Gentiles for a host of offenses, ranging from not paying their taxes on time to charges of selling liquor to Indians.

The ensuing result was that the Indians on neighboring islands grew more sober and the Gentiles grew more incensed.

Gentiles struck back, pilfering the Mormon's vegetable harvests and stealing their cordwood. Potatoes and turnips disappeared by the wagon-load from Mormon farms. Arrests were made, and Gentiles were hauled off by the boatload to await their trials on Mackinac Island. Regardless of guilt or innocence, many of them decided not to return to Beaver Island, choosing instead to make a new life on Mackinac or in the Pine River outpost on the mainland.

There was plenty of guilt to go around. Henry Van Allen, the Gentile lighthouse keeper at the southern tip of the island, firmly believed that fishing was the territory of the Gentiles, not the Mormons. He stole 18 fishing nets from some blameless Mormon fishermen and hid them in the lighthouse.

Two weeks later, after setting his nets on Lake Michigan, a heavy wind and current swept Van Allen's own 24 nets underwater and out of sight. He promptly accused the Mormons of stealing them, believing that they knew he'd stolen their nets and had stolen his in retribution. Tired of the fighting, Van Allen suggested they all come clean and he would give back their 18 nets if they would return his 24 nets. Then the wind calmed down and Van Allen's buoys popped back to the lake's surface, revealing his 24 nets still quite intact and still in his ownership.

With his accidental confession of theft, Sheriff George Miller arrived on Beaver Island with a warrant for Van Allen's arrest. Van Allen made bail, and then took his own 24 nets, plus the 18 Mormon nets he'd pilfered, and fled the island. Rumor had it he went to Pine River, but he hadn't disclosed his plans to anyone on the island, not wanting the Mormons to know of his whereabouts.

Battling newspaper articles reflected the escalating bitterness on the island. The *Green Bay Spectator* editor wrote, "*Several families have been driven from Beaver Island in a state of destitution and misery, by the so-called Latter-Day Saints, because they refused to affiliate with the Mormon Church.*"

A decidedly anti-Strang Whig newspaper in Detroit reported that, "*The time is coming when a collision will take place on Beaver Island, unless the Mormons abandon their nefarious practices and abominable crimes.*"

Strang could never, ever let any other newspaper have the last word. He used his Beaver Island newspaper, the *Northern Islander*, to countermand every story ever written about him that cast him in a poor light. The accusations now circulating about him in downstate newspapers made him seething mad. He helped Elvira craft responses to be printed in the *Northern Islander*.

"To the charge of driving families from Beaver Island in a state of destitution, we can only say that, if any people have been driven from here in poverty, it's because drunkenness led them to poverty. There has been no driving people off the island except by sending officers of the law to arrest them for their drunkenness, perjuries and theft. If this is how you define driving people off the island, then we intend to keep at it."

———————— ◆●◆ ————————

"We've had enough, Pop," Will told his father Dolan after they learned of Van Allen's hasty departure. "We want to move to Pine River."

Dolan was stunned. "Leave here? This is the only home you've known, Willy," he said.

"I know, but things are changing here. Teddy and I just want to fish and have some fun."

Teddy was standing next to Will, nodding in agreement. His short, stocky frame next to Will's tall, lithe body made Dolan think of a young tamarack tree growing next to a mature red pine. He hated the thought of his little forest family being thinned.

"I'm not leaving," he said. "I have Gwen to think about."

Will shifted uncomfortably. "Yes, Papa, and that will make it easier for you to stay. Strang likes the Indians. He won't make them leave."

Dolan sighed heavily. He could see by the look in his son's eyes that the decision had been made.

"When were you thinking of leaving?"

"As soon as possible. We need to get a cabin built at Pine River before the winter sets in."

"I'll help you," Dolan said. "I can come over and help you build it."

"I don't think that's a good idea, Papa," Will said. "You're not a Mormon. If you leave here, you might not be allowed to come back."

Dolan hadn't thought of that. His son was right.

"No offense boys, you're great fishermen, but you don't know much about building. You're going to need help."

Teddy spoke up. "We already thought of that. We've asked Archie Donnelly to come over and help us. He's a Mormon, he'll be okay. He can come and go as he pleases."

Dolan was surprised at this news. Archie was the father of a newborn baby, and a recent widower who was still grieving over Millie.

"Did Archie agree to this?"

"Yes, as long as Lucy will keep the baby for him while he's gone."

"Well, life is full of surprises, isn't it," Dolan said, shaking his head. "That's the one thing we can count on."

Lucy was as surprised as Dolan when Archie proposed his idea to her.

"You're going to Pine River with Will and Teddy to build them a cabin?" she asked. She was standing over her kitchen table, peeling the skin off a large piece of whitefish to put in the stew pot. As she worked, she carefully removed pieces of fish from the bones, leaving behind a lacy skeleton.

"I think it would do me good to have a change of scenery," Archie said. He knew he would miss Lily and Lucy, but he wanted to get away from the memory of Millie, which was around every corner on the island. "It's only temporary. I'll be back by Christmas. And I'll only do it if you will be all right with caring for Lily while I'm gone."

Lucy wiped her hands on her worn, cotton apron. She put the fish meat into a pot on the stove and swept the skeleton off the table and into a bucket. Later, she would grind the bones into a paste and use it to thicken the fish broth.

The thought of Archie leaving suddenly made her feel alone all over again. She'd grown fond of having Archie around the house, splitting wood and bringing home rabbits he'd caught in his traps. He was an easy man to live with, always helpful, and never selfish or boastful. She loved hearing him sing Irish lullabies in his lovely tenor voice.

"If it's what you need, Archie, then I won't stand in your way. I'd be happy to take care of Lily for you." The fact that Lily would stay with her was the only solace she found in the current situation. She turned her back on Archie so she could stir the pot on the stove. And so he couldn't see the tears brimming in her eyes.

CHAPTER 53
AUGUST, 1852

Roger Nagle was tall, with a barrel chest, big shoulders and an even bigger chip on one of them. He hated Mormons. His mother, a poor Bostonian named Belinda Nagle, had been a wide-eyed, virtuous young woman who had been completely taken in by Joseph Smith, with his blonde good looks and his talk of a happy, communal way of life. Belinda Nagle devoted herself to the church as soon as she had been baptized into it. It wasn't long before a scoundrel in the church convinced her that God wanted the Latter-Day Saints to share intercourse with one another outside of marriage in order to strengthen their bonds of togetherness.

Eighteen-year-old Belinda soon found herself pregnant, and the scoundrel who was responsible had already left Boston for parts unknown.

Still naïve and devoted to the Mormon faith, Belinda raised her boy Roger in the church. She worked in a glass factory and when Roger was 10 years old, he joined his mother in the dangerous work. He was assigned the job of being a crack-off boy, carrying scalding hot glass from the blower to the annealing lehr. Transporting glass from one fiery place to another left young Roger with burn scars on his hands and wrists. His palms were shiny smooth in some places, and ridged with scar tissue in others.

Nagle had a pumpkin-shaped head and a very round face, made to look less round with a tapered beard that covered the lower part of his face. He had narrow green eyes and a hairline receding in two deep V's over the corners of his eyebrows, which, along with his sharp, curved nose, gave him a hawk-like appearance.

Nagle's best friend Kent Pentour was a feisty Welshman whom Nagle had met growing up in Boston. Like Nagle, Pentour had grown up in poverty; he'd spent his youth selling newspapers on street corners and sweeping filth and waste from the gutters. Pentour was short and scrawny, with chin-length black hair he tucked behind his ears, a thinnish face and a wide mouth that made his cheeks crease into deep dimples that spread from nose to chin when he smiled. Hawking newspapers turned out to be a benefit to the scrappy Welshman. He learned to read, and he acquired a voracious appetite for news and politics. He was Nagle's right-hand man.

Nagle was 18 when his mother died in a factory accident. He promptly denounced the Mormon faith and practices he'd endured to make his mother happy, and got a job as a deckhand on a schooner in Boston. With his friend Pentour, he was soon sailing up and down the eastern seaboard, delivering cargo and helping himself to some of the more valuable cargo along the way. When the two of them were caught stealing some of the contents of one ship, they narrowly escaped capture and prison. With pockets full of cash from the sale of stolen cargo, they fled to the Great Lakes.

In Chicago, the two men bought a 22-ton, two-masted, gaff-rigged schooner named the *Mary Clark* and immediately renamed it *The Defiance*. Nagle picked the name based on his defiant disdain for law and order.

They rounded up crewmen from dirty waterfront taverns in Chicago and Milwaukee. They were a motley assortment of men who ranged from young rapscallions to mature thugs. The one thing they all had in common was an extreme dislike of honest labor and no religious affiliation whatsoever. They all had plenty of sailing experience, preferring the dangers of sailing on vast open water to the stink and grime of factory work.

The Defiance made its way up and down the coast of Wisconsin, robbing small villages and warehouses in rough ports. Growing weary of the scenery on the sunrise side of Lake Michigan, Nagle decided to take the boat over to Grand Haven, a small town on the east side of the state of Michigan.

It was a stroke of pure luck that Pentour read about James Strang and the Mormons of Beaver Island in a Grand Haven newspaper.

"I know you hate those Mormons, and it looks like you're not the only one," Pentour said to Nagle.

"What's it say?" Nagle asked, leaning over his friend's shoulder to get a look at the paper.

"The Mormons must be stopped," the article said. *"They have gone too far. Now they are burning warehouses after robbing them and smashing store windows in senseless acts of destruction. It would come as no surprise that small acts of thievery occur on Beaver Island, as they do in any community, but now these acts are spreading to the mainland. King Strang had better get his people in line or a battle will break out sooner or later."*

It was in that moment that Nagle had his stroke of genius.

"So if we start robbing people in Michigan we can say we're Mormons and they'll take the fall?"

Pentour smiled, dimples creasing the sides of his face. "Yep. We steal, we sail from town to town, and say we're consecrating goods for this Mormon King James Strang."

CHAPTER 54

SUMMER, 1852

From Grand Haven, Nagle and his crew sailed the *Defiance* up the Michigan shoreline to the Manistee River, and then into the harbor, where they found a berth along the commercial dock. After securing the boat, they dropped the sails, and wrapped heavy ropes around the four-cornered sails to bind them to the booms and keep them in place if the wind came up. It was early evening, so the captain and crew headed to town for a night of carousing before their real work began before dawn the next day.

In the wee hours of the morning, everything went according to plan. Stealing a horse and wagon from a nearby farm was easy in the sleepy little town of Manistee. Then the men broke into the town's largest market. While some men quickly loaded barrels of salt and crates of dry goods onto the wagon, Nagle and Pentour guarded the wagon with their pistols drawn. Dazed villagers, awakened by the sound of feet scuffling and glass breaking in store windows, stood in fear as the two of them brandished their guns at them. When the wagon was loaded, one of the crew members cracked a whip over the head of the horse pulling it and steered it blatantly down the middle of the road to the dock, where the rest of the crew was waiting on the *Defiance*. Another sailor casually tossed a flaming torch through the broken window of the store and set it on fire before heading for the boat, where sails had been hoisted and dock lines cast off. A couple of sailors stood on the dock holding the *Defiance* in place while the others loaded the goods onto the boat.

Nagle and Pentour brought up the rear, jumped onboard and gave the order to cast off. Within minutes, the *Defiance* was making its way downriver to Lake Michigan.

By the time the village awoke the following morning, it was too late to catch the perpetrators. The *Defiance* was approaching the southern coast of South Manitou Island, far from Manistee.

"We could drop anchor in there," Pentour said to Nagle as South Manitou grew bigger upon their approach. "I've been told there's a sheltered bay on the east side of the island."

"Good idea. Hopefully we can make it from there to Mackinac Island tomorrow." He turned to get the attention of his crew.

"Alright, men, prepare to heave to port, we're headed to that island ahead," Nagle commanded. The men grabbed heavy lines attached to the sails and prepared to change from a leeward to a windward tack. As Nagle cranked the boat's wheel to the left, the men pulled in the lines and pushed the booms on sails to the port side of the boat. The sails slowly traveled across the boat, flapping loudly as they emptied of air, until the wind caught on the other side and they filled again with a loud snap.

The *Defiance* sailed gracefully into the crescent-shaped bay. As soon as the schooner was well inside of the crescent, out of sight from any boats navigating the water between the island and Michigan's mainland, Roger gave the command to drop anchor and lower the sails. They had arrived in their port of refuge for the night.

CHAPTER 55
LATE SUMMER, 1852

After a peaceful night's sleep in the bay of South Manitou Island, Nagle and his crew set sail for Mackinac Island. It was an uneventful trip, with steady wind out of the southwest pushing them along.

Equally uneventful was the sale of their goods. Merchants were always present on Mackinac Island, looking to broker deals for the goods that came and went on Mackinac. Nagle and Pentour had no difficulty selling their cargo.

With their pockets bulging, they headed to Jillet's Tavern for drinks. The crew split up, with some going to Jillet's and others heading further inland to the French Outpost, where beer was cheaper and women were looser.

The two men wasted no time tossing back a few whiskeys and talking loudly about the 'consecration' they'd committed at Manistee for their prophet, James Strang.

After they were sure the blame had been firmly laid at Strang's feet, Nagle and Pentour left the tavern and started walking back to the *Defiance*.

While they walked casually down the dirt road, Nagle and Pentour didn't notice the man who was following them. The man had also been in Jillet's, and had overheard their conversation. He was also a Mormon – at least he was once a Mormon, about as dedicated to the cause as Nagle appeared to be. He caught up with them just as they were about to board the *Defiance*.

"Excuse me, I couldn't help overhearing you at the tavern," the man said to Nagle when he sidled up to him. He was exceptionally filthy and smelled of body odor and bad fish.

"What do you want?" Nagle said gruffly.

"I want to join you," the man said.

Nagle wrinkled his nose at him. "Why would you want to do that?"

"Because I am a Mormon – or at least I was a Mormon – and I hate them, just like you."

Pentour's eyes narrowed. "Wait a minute. We are loyal Mormons and—"

The grimy man laughed. "I know the ways of Strang's Mormons and you don't act like them. I may not know you or exactly what you're up to, but I wish to join you. I could be of great help."

Nagle's green eyes lit up. "Do tell," he said.

"I was a good Mormon, working as a deputy constable for the king. I did everything asked of me. I even took a second wife, at the king's request, to strengthen the king's position on polygamy." The man paused. "But Strang set his sights on my lovely second wife, and made up terrible lies about me so he could pursue my wife. He had me beaten to a pulp by one of his men and cast me off the island. I have been near starved to death since it happened, and have been forced to work with unsavory fur trappers. "

Pentour gave the man a sideways glance, not entirely believing his story, but Nagle was fascinated.

"What is your name?"

"I am Nathan Bowman, former deputy constable and former apostle in Strang's Circle of 12."

"And you lived on Beaver Island?" Nagle asked.

"Yes, I did, for several happy years until Strang viciously turned on me," Bowman said. "I know a lot about Strang, and I know the island like the back of my hand. I can help you."

Nagle didn't have to think long about Bowman's proposition. He could take him on as a crew member, and if he turned out to be helpful, he could remain. If he turned out to be a liar or a spy, Nagle could throw him overboard. There didn't seem to be much of a downside to the proposal.

"Fine, you can join us. But you had better prove yourself to be useful or you'll find yourself taking a very long swim in Lake Michigan."

Bowman smiled for the first time in seven long months. "I believe we share the same goals, and in reaching those goals, I shall prove myself to be most useful."

The following day, the *Defiance* set sail for Grand Traverse Bay, charting a course that took them near Beaver Island so they could get a good look at the harbor entrance and see the homes and businesses lining the bay.

While Bowman identified landmarks for Nagle from the prow of the boat, Strang was in his newspaper office reading an assortment of Michigan newspapers, completely unaware of who was sailing past his harbor.

He focused on the Allegan newspaper account of Mormon pirating:

"The people along Lake Michigan, from Allegan north to Manistee, have been thrown into a state of the most intense excitement by a gang of marauders, who are reported to be Mormons from Beaver Island, and who have carried on in their operations with a boldness, coolness and desperation rarely equaled in the annals of highwaymen.

"They have burned saw mills and robbed stores north of the Grand River. At Grand Haven they made repeated attempts to break into stores and shops… They sail one small schooner of 20 or 30 tons. There seems to be no question as to the identity of the robbers or their hailing place. They are emissaries from King Strang's Realms."

Strang stood up, closed the paper and slapped it down on his desk while his hackles rose.

"Damnation!" he exclaimed, talking only to himself. "They're doing it again! Always blaming the Mormons for any wrong doing. I am fed up with this blasphemy! What will it take to get them to stop?!"

Strang sat back down and grabbed a sheet of paper and pen. He began writing a letter to the editor of the *Detroit Free Press*, the paper that had given him good press coverage of his trial.

"Dear Editor," he wrote rapidly. *"Once again, the poor, persecuted Mormons in Michigan are being maligned in the newspapers that hate us and want to see us fail.*

"No matter what the crime, large or small, no matter what the evidence, great or little, the blame is always attributed to the Mormons. Now some band of pirates is plundering towns along the coast of Lake Michigan and the Mormons are getting the blame.

"There is no evidence whatsoever that these pirates are a part of the Mormon community. From what I read and hear, there is no evidence at all as to the

identity of the marauders. And yet, for lack of a better target, it is always the poor, hard-working Mormons on Beaver Island who take the blame.

"I can assure you that my people have more than enough to do with harvesting our crops and legally logging our timber. We have neither the time nor the inclination to go sailing about Lake Michigan and robbing people. We also have no need to do so, as our community is thriving from our honest hard work.

"I can only pray that God will expose the true villains in this criminal activity and we Mormons can continue to conduct ourselves in our Saintly manner without interference and slander. I look forward to the day when the lawmen of Michigan capture the true pirates and they will feel the full force of God's wrath for their ruinous behavior.

"Most sincerely,

"James J. Strang, Prophet, the Latter-Day Saints"

After finishing the letter, Strang had one pressing concern: Would the bad press about the Mormons have an impact on the upcoming election?

CHAPTER 56
FALL, 1852

"Strange, isn't it, how in some ways I feel like your elder sister due to my age, but you're the elder wife," Betsy McNutt Strang remarked to Elvira. It was late September, and the two women were in the kitchen, making supper while little Charlie scooted around on the kitchen floor, occasionally discovering a dead fly and popping it in his mouth before his mother could stop him. He was a sturdy little boy, with his mother's dark hair and his father's intense brown eyes.

Elvira smiled at Betsy. She had come to like the woman who was gentle and warm-hearted. The older woman was no threat to Elvira, who was still young and pretty compared to the aging Betsy. Elvira noticed the elder wife was also developing a pot belly, which made her even less attractive. Elvira knew that her husband slept with Betsy out of a sense of duty, but that it was Elvira he craved under the covers.

Since Strang was increasingly busy with mission trips away from the island, Elvira and Betsy had no one to turn to but each other, so they had become friends. Even so, Elvira never let Betsy forget she was the senior wife of the king. When they did household chores, Elvira was the one to assign the tasks, usually giving Betsy the less desirable work of emptying chamber pots and milking the goat. Betsy had never even known Mary, the first and only legal wife of Strang's; Elvira was more than happy to pretend Mary never existed.

"We are like sisters, aren't we?" Elvira said. "I might be the younger, but I'm still the boss," she said, but she was grinning when she said it.

"When do you think James will return?" Betsy asked, switching the subject. Strang typically confided more in Elvira than in Betsy about his work and whereabouts.

"I have no idea," Elvira said. "I know he is gathering more people into our fold, but they won't be settling here. James wants to spread the Latter-Day Saints onto the mainland, to help our flock spread and grow."

Betsy looked confused. "I would think it would be in our best interests to have all of our people on the island," she said.

Elvira stopped peeling the potato she was working on. She turned sideways to look at Betsy.

"James says it's necessary for us to have our people spread out and multiply, in order to spread the word of our faith more effectively," Elvira said. "He's planning to start Mormon outposts on Drummond Island, Pine River and in Grand Traverse Bay. I think it's quite exciting."

"But will he be back soon?" Betsy was getting anxious. "I have news for him."

"And what might that be?" Elvira had returned to the business of peeling potatoes, not thinking Betsy could have any news of import.

"I'm with child!" Betsy beamed as she said it.

Elvira once again stopped what she was doing, stunned with the news. She didn't even know it was possible for women in their thirties to conceive a child. She didn't know how she felt about this news. It would certainly elevate Betsy's status in the eyes of their shared husband.

"I guess congratulations are in order then," Elvira said. When she saw the glow of happiness on the older woman's face, she softened. "Come then, give me a hug, sister." She gave Betsy a hug, who returned the hug gratefully.

"Please don't tell anyone until I've had the chance to tell James myself," Betsy said, and then paused uncertainly. "Do you think he'll be happy?"

"Yes, he'll be pleased," Elvira assured her. "That is one of the reasons James believes God wants us to practice polygamy, so we can multiply our numbers faster than we could if our men took only one wife each." Elvira believed in the words she was saying. She believed in her husband. What she didn't tell Betsy, because she didn't want to ruin her moment, was that she believed she was pregnant as well.

The Lord works in mysterious ways, she thought to herself. Then, with wifely resignation, she went back to the potatoes.

CHAPTER 57
FALL, 1852

Archie, Will and Teddy weren't the only ones to leave Beaver Island. Alva Cable, his brother James Cable and Walter Whitney had also taken their families to Pine River. Cables' Bay was renamed the Bay of Galilee by the Mormons who moved there. By October, the island had over 900 Mormon residents and only a handful of Gentiles standing their ground and remaining on the island.

Lucy was walking through town on a late October day, headed to Jane Watson's home to borrow more baby clothes. Lily was rapidly outgrowing everything Jane had originally loaned her. Lucy paused at the harbor's edge. She looked out at the trees on the south shore, where a few remaining leaves of orange and red clung stubbornly to the branches. Most of the leaves had given way to the winds of October and now blanketed the ground.

While she watched, the wind shifted and started blowing hard out of the southeast. Swells built quickly and rolled out of the harbor. The wind created swirling patches on the lake's greenish-gray surface. Lucy watched, mesmerized at the patterns the wind formed on the surface.

Then the rain came. Fat, heavy drops splattered back up into the air after hitting fallen leaves on the ground, as if the drops were wet rubber balls that could bounce.

It stopped as quickly as it started. Sunlight found its way through cracks in the dark clouds and briefly illuminated golden trees before hiding once more behind the wind and rain.

Mother Nature acts like a woman going through the change of life at this time of year, Lucy thought to herself. *She just can't seem to make up her mind whether she wants to be wicked or wonderful.*

As soon as the thought went through her mind, she was reminded of Strang. His behavior had been strangely mercurial that autumn. He'd been relentlessly traveling on his mission work, recruiting more Mormons to Michigan. In anticipation of expanding his territory, Strang had started to build Mormon outposts in other northern Michigan locations. He placed 20 or so new converts on Drummond Island, northeast of Mackinac Island. He liked the idea that Drummond Island was the same distance from Mackinac as Beaver Island was, but in the opposite direction. It left Mackinac flanked by Mormons. Another 20 new Mormon families had been moved to Grand Traverse Bay, on the mainland southeast of Beaver Island. A handful of Mormons he placed on a tiny island in Pine Lake, which was connected to Pine River, and named it Holy Island.

When Strang wasn't doing mission work, he was on Beaver Island being a jovial king. He visited the homes of Mormons and spoke to them encouragingly.

"You are the backbone of a great society we're building," he told Phineas and Amanda Wright. The Wrights were among the Mormons who lived near the Bay of Galilee. They were all sitting in their small cabin with Strang, their daughter Sarah and her cousin Phoebe, drinking hot tea in front of the fireplace. Strang's brown eyes glowed in the flickering firelight as he spoke. "It is brave people like you who make this possible. I'm but a common laborer, doing the work of God as He sees fit for me. But you are the ones who do the real work of building the Lord's foundation here on Beaver Island."

The Wrights, like most good Mormons on the island, found strength in Strang's passion and humble words. The oldest daughter Sarah was enamored with her king. Her cousin Phoebe was bored by all the grown-up talk, and was idly picking at a stray woolen strand dangling from her shawl.

"It is my duty to do what God asks of me, as it is your duty to support God's decisions. If God asks me to do something I find unpalatable, but I know it's for the greater good of mankind, I shall do it. I shall not question His wisdom."

Phineas rubbed his long jawbone as he listened to Strang.

"What would God ask of you that might be unpalatable?" Phineas finally asked.

Strang sat up straighter and looked toward the heavens.

"God has spoken to me," he said, "and told me that in order to protect our island and our people, and to help all of the good people in the great state of Michigan, I may be asked to serve our people by entering the political fray," Strang said. "Although I would prefer to live my life peaceably on this island and go about my daily life in the serenity of this place, I may need to throw myself in with the political wolves in Lansing, our state capitol."

Strang then looked sadly into the fireplace, flames reflecting in his coppery eyes, as if the task ahead of him was so unsavory that he couldn't meet the glances of Phineas and his wife. Daughter Sarah gazed at him with awe.

"You would do that for us?" she asked, her blue eyes wide with wonder at Strang's noble sacrifice.

"If it's God's will, then that is what I shall do, young lady," Strang told her somberly. "So, if I am called upon by the Lord, then I, in turn, must call upon you to support me."

"Why, yes, of course," Phineas said. "We must all obey the Lord, whatever He asks of us."

"I'm so glad you understand," Strang said as he rose. "I am most grateful for your hospitality and devotion to our cause."

Strang bid them farewell and walked through the rain to the next Mormon home, where he made a similar pitch to his followers. During the month of October, Strang visited every Mormon home on the island and carefully solicited their support in the event that God called upon him to run for office. What Strang didn't tell them was that the decision had already been made – he was going to run for State Representative, with every intention of serving in the Michigan State Legislature. It was a position of power he'd craved since he was a teenager in New York. He'd attempted to run for constable in Hanover, New York, and had lost by five votes. The humiliation of that failure never left him.

Beaver Island was in a curious place when it came to political lines. It was part of Mackinac County and its residents voted in those county elections, but for state and federal elections, it was assigned to the District of Newaygo County, a fact that few people in Michigan knew.

Strang was one of those few people. So was Dennis Chidester, who, with Strang's influence and help, had gotten himself appointed to be the official canvasser for the Newaygo District for the 1852 election.

On November 1, the day before the election, Strang filed to run for State Representative for the Newaygo District. Twenty-four hours later, every Mormon on Beaver Island, and every Mormon on Holy Island, and every Mormon in Grand Traverse, turned out and voted for their king.

Strang won the election easily.

His main opponent, James Barton, immediately cried foul and declared that Strang had no right to run for state representative in the Newaygo District. Election officials poured over the records of district boundary lines and decided Strang was, indeed, perfectly entitled to the office. Chidester, as an official canvasser, traveled to Newaygo to certify that Strang had received 116 more votes than his opponent. On November 16, Strang was declared to be the winner.

On Mackinac Island, the locals were in an uproar about the election. It wasn't possible, they believed, that the Mormon king was now going to be their elected representative in the state capitol of Lansing. Many of them shamefully cursed themselves for not bothering to vote. Half the island residents on Mackinac slid into dismal, drunken stupors at Jillet's Tavern, unable to wrap their heads around the idea that the powerful little Mormon had outsmarted them. The other half sprang into action, conjuring up ideas about how they could prevent him from taking his seat on the legislature.

A small group of men sat in Jillett's on an icy mid-November day, discussing the possibilities. Outside, sleet pelted the window of the bar, sounding like buckshot peppering the glass. The damp cold slipped into the bar as the wind whistled through the cracks in the log walls. Constable Granger, a Gentile, sat with the mayor of Mackinac and one of his councilmen. Mayor Ralph LaFreniere was a middle-aged balding man of French-Canadian descent. His councilman Fred Gibson was much younger; a skinny fellow who barely looked old enough to drink. Gibson had pale, fuzzy hair growing on his face, a clear attempt to look older than he was. It also served to hide the pimples that still plagued him at the age of 23. Gibson was young, but he was no fool.

"We could arrest him," Gibson said as he sipped his beer. "He can't serve in Lansing if he's sitting in jail on Mackinac."

"Arrest Strang? On what charges?" It was Constable Granger questioning him. The constable had a few years on Gibson, and while he liked the young man, he was wary of his politics, which sometimes seemed to be too radical for his taste.

"We could bring up that old mail fraud charge," Gibson said.

"That was decided in federal court. Strang was acquitted," LaFreniere said. He had followed Strang's trial closely, and remembered most of the details.

"We could bring up a new charge," Gibson said. All the men turned to look at him.

"Remember back when the old sheriff went to Beaver Island to arrest Dr. MacCulloch? The man who allegedly killed that fisherman, Tom Bennett?"

"Go on," Granger said.

"Well, the sheriff went to arrest MacCulloch, and the constable and his men down there blocked the arrest. They spirited MacCulloch away to Strang's house. When the sheriff went to Strang's house, he was told MacCulloch wasn't there, and he didn't have a warrant to search Strang's house. Those hothead deputies down there were armed to the hilt, as I recall, and the sheriff didn't want to get into a gunfight. He gave up and came back here."

"I remember that!" the mayor said. "Two men on Beaver Island wanted to see justice served for Tom's death. They brought evidence to the sheriff here to have MacCulloch arrested."

Constable Granger smiled. "Gibson, I do believe you're onto something! Strang could be arrested for obstruction of justice and harboring a fugitive." He sat back in his chair and rubbed his face while he thought about the potential arrest.

"But we can't storm down to Beaver Island and arrest Strang," Granger said. "Now the sheriff is Mormon, and it's not in my jurisdiction."

"How will Strang get to Lansing in January?" LaFreniere asked. "He'll have to go by boat, from Beaver Island to Mackinac Island, then down Lake Huron to Detroit. All boats from Beaver stop here to take on supplies. We could arrest him right here!"

"Gentlemen, I believe we have a plan. Let's keep it to ourselves. The fewer people who know, the better," Granger said as he drank the rest of his beer.

Archie Donnelly was chinking a log in the cabin he was building with Will and Teddy in Pine River when they got the election news. The cabin sat on a bluff on the north side of the Pine River, angled to face Beaver Island to the northwest. Even though they couldn't see the island, it made them feel good to have the front of their cabin facing home. Farther up the shoreline from the cabin were magnificent sand dunes, where gulls and cormorants swooped and shrieked. Teddy, Will and Archie camped in the hollows of the dunes, protected from the wind, while the cabin was being built. Unbeknownst to them, it was the same spot where Nathan Bowman had first slept when he arrived at Pine River.

Walter Whitney, another builder who had left Beaver Island with his family and settled at Pine River, approached Archie and the boys while they were working.

"Did you hear the news? King Strang won the election for our district. He'll be our state representative in the capitol," Whitney told them.

Archie, Will and Teddy all stopped what they were doing to look at Whitney. Each had a look of disbelief.

"Strang will be our state representative?" Archie asked, hoping he didn't hear Whitney correctly.

"That's right. He'll be representing all of us who live northwest of Grand Rapids, basically," Whitney said.

"This is bad," Archie said. "He'll have the power to write laws that will affect all of us."

"But he's only one of many representatives, right?" Will asked. "He's got to get a whole bunch of people to agree with him in order to write laws."

Archie looked at Will with sad eyes. "I think we've already seen how persuasive Strang can be. Hard as it is for us to believe, he could persuade those fellows in Lansing to go along with his desires."

Archie, Will and Teddy lapsed into silence, staring out at the lake. They'd left their beloved home on Beaver Island to escape Strang's rule. They'd gone to the trouble of building a cabin at Pine River and now, through the perils of election trickery, were once again under the control of a Mormon king.

CHAPTER 58
DECEMBER, 1852

Phineas Wright moved his family from a farm near the Bay of Galilee into the former home of the island's one-time store owner, Pete McKinley, on Whiskey Point. Strang had given the land to Wright after acquiring it at a sheriff's sale. Phineas had been one of the men who made sure all Mormons got out and voted for Strang in the November election, and Strang owed him a considerable debt of gratitude.

The home had fallen into a state of disrepair after Pete McKinley left the island. Phineas enlisted the help of his brother Benjamin, another recently converted Mormon, to fix the property with him. They started the work in September and by the time winter was approaching, the home was once again habitable.

"It gladdens my heart to have such upstanding Saints living on this point, which was once the site of drunkenness and beastly, immoral behavior," Strang told the Wright brothers. One week earlier, he had promoted the two brothers to the Circle of 12, knowing they would act in his best interests while he was in Lansing.

With Whiskey Point under Mormon control, the city of St. James almost entirely Mormon, and the south shore of the harbor down to Luney's Point occupied by Mormons, Strang felt his flock was secure on Beaver Island. He would be able to attend the 40-day long legislative session in Lansing without fearing for the lives of the Saints on Beaver Island from the straggling Gentiles who had yet to convert or leave.

As a nasty squall sent pellets of snow flying sideways onto the island during the first week of December, Strang sat in his home in front of the fireplace, writing a letter to his brother.

"Frankly, my brother, I intend to rule this country one day and I will be extremely disappointed in myself if I do not make myself one of the State Supreme Court judges within a year," he wrote. He was still savoring his victory when he continued, *"I have made my mark upon the times in which I live, and the wear and tear of time cannot obliterate it. Like Moses of old, my name will be revered, and men scarcely restrained from worshiping me as a God."*

It never occurred to Strang that his opinion of himself might be far greater than that of the people around him. When Strang finished the letter, his wife Betsy entered the room with a cup of tea for him. He patted her belly affectionately, which was now protruding with the growing baby inside her.

"What will you be giving me, a boy or a girl, Betsy?" he asked playfully. "Elvira gave me a boy, so perhaps it's time for a girl."

Betsy blushed. "If I had it within my power to determine the gender of our child, I would do as you wish, James," she said. "All I can do is pray that it will be a girl, if that's what you want."

"Then it will be a girl, because I always get what I want, don't I?" His glowing brown eyes were focused on hers.

"Yes, of course, James," she said before heading back to the kitchen. Sometimes her powerful husband scared her. This was one of those times. She immediately started praying for a baby girl, so as not to incur the wrath of her husband with a child of the wrong gender.

◆▪◆

Lucy looked out her window toward the harbor, watching the snow squall build momentum. She held five-month-old Lily facing forward against her chest, so she could watch the storm. Lily was proving to be highly inquisitive and rarely laid her head to rest on Lucy's shoulder, preferring to bob her head this way and that while she looked at her surroundings. Her fine red hair formed curls around her pale face.

"I don't know if your daddy is going to make it home for Christmas if this keeps up," Lucy said to the baby.

The December wind hadn't breathed a calming sigh of relief in over a week, so the lake had no chance to settle down. Huge waves formed and crashed into one another as squalls from different directions met and formed mountains of exploding water. There was no way Archie could make it back to the island with Will and Teddy in their little sailboat.

Knowing chores wouldn't wait for the weather to change, Lucy wrapped Lily snugly in a blanket, then lifted her into her papoose carrier. It was made of deerskin and lined with rabbit fur. The long, rectangular frame was made of cedar poles; two short ones at the bottom and top, and two longer ones running vertically on either side of it. Leather straps held the carrier in place. A deerskin arch like a hood covered the top and protected Lily's head from the elements. Lucy had trimmed the opening for Lily's face with fox fur, which allowed Lily to look out but prevented snow from blowing in.

After donning her own coat and boots, Lucy swung the carrier onto her back and attached it with straps that ran over her shoulders and around her waist. She headed across the prairie grass to run the trap lines she'd set the day before.

Several rabbits and one raccoon had fallen victim to her trap line. As she carefully extracted them from the traps and put them in her burlap sack, she noticed someone crossing the field. As he got closer, she could see it was Lorenzo Hickey. She waved him over.

"How are you, Lorenzo? It's been awhile," she said to him when he got close enough to hear her speak over the wind.

"I'm well, thank you," he replied.

"I'm guessing you're on your way to Huldy's?" Lucy was well aware of how enamored Lorenzo was with Huldy Cornwall.

"Yes, I am. If you can keep a secret, I'm planning to ask her to marry me. Today, if I can get my nerve up." He bit his chapped lip nervously.

Lucy didn't know what to say. She believed Lorenzo was a good man, but he was still a faithful Mormon. He'd begged Strang to take him back after he'd lost faith years ago; for some reason Lucy couldn't fathom, faith had been an important anchor for Lorenzo. Huldy had no love for Mormons as a whole, but was fond of Lorenzo as an individual. Lucy wondered if Huldy would be willing to marry a Mormon.

She smiled graciously. "I wish you the best of luck, and give my love to Huldy. I have to keep moving or Lily will start fussing." Lucy returned to the business of re-setting her traps so she didn't have to get into any further conversation with Lorenzo.

As she worked, Lorenzo walked slowly away, frequently looking back at Lucy and Lily. It filled him with a desperate longing; he wanted a wife and he wanted children. He'd had that once, and he wanted to have it again.

Lorenzo's proposal of marriage to Huldy got off to a rough start. In awkward sign language, he first asked her to join him. Join him for what, Huldy had signed back.

He finally made his intentions clear when he got down on one knee, held her hand and proffered a ring for her left hand. Huldy's expression went through a range of emotions: surprise, delight, and then doubt. She had always assumed that she would never marry, because no man would want a wife who neither heard nor spoke. And now here was a kind, decent man, down on one knee asking for her hand in marriage. But she didn't know if she could marry someone of the Mormon faith. If he chose to leave the faith, she would marry him in an instant, but if he wanted her to convert to his faith, well, that was an entirely different matter.

"I must think about it, Lorenzo," she signed, but then gave him a warm kiss, which filled him with hope.

"I'll give you all the time you need," he signed. "As long as you don't make me wait too long. I want to start a family with you, Huldy."

After he left, Huldy sat at her little wooden table in front of the fireplace. Should she accept him as her husband? Would he require her to become a Mormon? That was something she didn't think she could do. The Mormons had deceived her sister and allowed her husband to take a second wife. It was their fault that Eliza had left Beaver Island. Lorenzo didn't seem like the type of man who would want more than one wife, but what if he tired of the silence of a mute wife? What if Strang coerced him into taking another wife?

No, Huldy realized, she could not become a Mormon. Not even for the love of Lorenzo Hickey. She would marry him, but only if he would leave the Mormon faith.

<hr />

For the rest of December, the winds raged steadily on, but the temperatures never dropped below the freezing mark, keeping the ice off the lake. On the day before Christmas, a feeble sun broke through the veil of snow clouds and the wind died down. Lucy could actually see schooners sailing past the harbor again. She saw one schooner pull into the harbor and start to lower its sails as it approached the dock. She couldn't be sure, but she thought it was the *Wisconsin*, a sturdy, two-masted schooner that routinely made round trips between Green Bay and Mackinac with a stop at Beaver Island.

A handful of men disembarked, one of whom was Galen Cole, a Mormon who had recently moved to Pine River. It was he who arranged for the *Wisconsin* to stop at Pine River on its way from Mackinac to Beaver Island and give him passage. He had an important meeting with the king.

Lucy watched the activity, welcoming the familiar sight of a schooner being tied to the dock, passengers disembarking and going their separate ways. One of the passengers seemed to be heading her way. *Perhaps a new boarder,* she thought. He was quite tall and broad-shouldered, but she couldn't see his face because of the woolen scarf covering it.

Then she looked more carefully. It was Archie!

With almost frantic movements, she pulled off the stained apron she had been wearing while she skinned rabbits, and then smoothed her hair. Then she lifted Lily out of the crib and fluffed her curls. Carrying her on her hip, she headed to the door to wait for Archie.

She didn't wait for him to knock. She threw open the door as soon as he stepped onto the porch.

"Archie!" she said. "You made it back!"

Archie gave her a big bear hug and then lifted Lily from her arm.

"Of course I did, I couldn't stay away from you ladies," he said. His face was rough and red from the boat ride, his dark hair longer than usual from months of bachelor living at Pine River.

"You must be starving. Let me fix you something," Lucy said. She took Lily back so he could get out of his coat, boots, hat and scarf. When he was standing in his stocking feet, dirty trousers and worn flannel shirt, she handed Lily back to him.

"She's gotten so big," Archie said with amazement. "You must be feeding her well." Then he added, "I'm so thankful. Whatever would I do without you?"

Lucy just smiled. She found herself wanting to tell him that he didn't have to ever make do without her, but didn't want to overstep her boundaries.

Archie sat at her kitchen table with Lily propped on his leg while Lucy cooked strips of rabbit in a frying pan. She added chopped onions and potatoes to the pan. Archie watched her appreciatively.

"So, you made it back just in time to say goodbye to 1852," Lucy said while she cooked. "What a year we've had! I wonder what 1853 will bring?"

Archie was stroking Lily's soft hair, looking pensive.

"I hope it will be a good year, but I'm not feeling optimistic," he said. "The people who are settling in at Pine River have a deep distrust of Strang. Now that he is our state representative, he holds a lot of political sway over us."

Lucy turned from the stove to put a heaping plate of food in front of Archie, a smaller plate in front of her chair, and a small bowl of potatoes and onions that had been ground into mush for Lily, to the left of Archie's plate.

"I don't want to think about it," Lucy said as she sat down. "You know, I thought Strang was a good man when he first came here. I think a lot of his followers are good people. But things keep changing, and Strang keeps doing things that only serve to anger the non-Mormons." Lucy picked up her fork. "Let's not talk about it; I don't want to spoil my meal."

When they finished eating, Lucy took Lily from Archie's lap, changed her diaper and put her to sleep in her crib. She and Archie sat at the kitchen table, keeping warm from the heat of the woodstove. Archie put another log in the stove and stirred the embers.

"How are Will and Teddy doing?" Lucy asked.

"They're sturdy young lads, they'll be fine. Made some friends over in Pine River. They seem to be happy to be away from the Mormons."

"And how are you doing?" Lucy said it with concern in her voice. "Is it hard, coming back here where your memories of Millie are?"

"I think about Millie every day, whether I'm here or in Pine River," Archie said. "Some days the memories feel like waves on the lake, about to overtake me and drown me. Mostly I'm able to keep my head above water and remember that there will always be a calm place in between the waves."

Lucy reached over and put a hand on Archie's arm. "I know what you mean," she said. "When I lost Antoine, I felt the same way. Eventually, you learn to live with the feeling; the waves get smaller and the calm in between them gets longer."

"Today seems to be a calm day," Archie said, smiling warmly at Lucy.

The two of them sat up and talked until Christmas Eve turned into Christmas day. Then Archie stood, gave Lucy a friendly little kiss on the cheek and went to his room on the second floor, while Lucy retired to her room on the first floor off the kitchen.

They both fell asleep alone, wondering if their Christmas wishes would come true.

CHAPTER 59
DECEMBER, 1853

Lucy's involvement with Archie didn't go unnoticed by James Strang. He saw the two of them walking through town together with Lily strapped to Lucy's back, talking and laughing. They appeared to be a couple, although Strang had no way of knowing what intimacies they had shared, if any. Nonetheless, their togetherness provoked him.

On a rare occasion when he found Lucy shopping alone at Johnson and MacCulloch's store, Strang approached her.

"You really shouldn't be cavorting with a widower," Strang said to her. "His late wife hasn't even been in the ground for a year, and it's plain to see you're throwing yourself at him." His penetrating gaze was met with Lucy's equally powerful stare.

"How dare you suggest such a thing?!" she exploded. "Archie and I are friends. I am helping him take care of his daughter. There is nothing improper going on between us, not that it's any of your business!"

Strang secretly enjoyed raising her ire. She was her prettiest when her black eyes flashed and the color rose in her cheeks.

"It just doesn't seem appropriate for a single woman such as yourself to be living under the same roof with a widower. It's clear that he is more than just a boarder to you."

"Appropriate? What do you know about appropriate living arrangements? You are living with two women, neither of whom is legally married to you!"

"They are my legal wives in the eyes of our God," Strang said. "That is all that matters to us."

"And Archie and I are legal friends behaving in a most appropriate manner in the eyes of OUR God, who apparently has different standards than your God."

Strang bristled. "Are you saying Archie is praying to a different God than the rest of us Latter-Day Saints?"

Lucy was too angry to sense a trap. "Archie quit praying to your God when He took Millie from him, with a little help from your incompetent Dr. MacCulloch!"

"So Archie no longer considers himself a Mormon in good standing? Then he must be excommunicated," Strang said, the threat in his voice undeniably clear.

"Do whatever you want, James, I don't think Archie cares one half-penny about you or your church anymore!"

Lucy stomped off without making any purchases at the store. She was too upset by Strang's accusations to think clearly about the need for flour and lard.

Strang left the store empty-handed as well, making a mental note to have Archie ex-communicated. Then, without the protection of the Mormon Church, Archie would be susceptible to the punishments and arrests that the church doled out to non-believers. Strang smiled inwardly. If there was something going on between Archie and Lucy, Strang would do whatever he could to thwart it.

After his encounter with Lucy, Strang had a meeting with Galen Cole, the new Mormon Strang had placed on the mainland.

"How are things going at Pine River?" Strang asked Galen as they sat in his newspaper office and watched the snow fall outside. It had started as a light dusting, but was now growing thick and heavy.

Galen was a stern man with black hair, a long, narrow face and protruding teeth. He saw the world in terms of right and wrong, black and white. Strang liked that quality about him. Galen was not a man to waffle in his decisions.

"It's a rough community, I must say," Galen told Strang, slurring words that contained the letter 's' due of his prominent overbite. "A few fur trappers in the area, but mostly fishermen and some farmers. And as you surely know, a few of the former Beaver Island residents have settled there as well."

"Yes, I'm aware of that," Strang said. "My sworn enemies, no doubt."

"Some, perhaps, but mostly the people are heathens who don't want to live a pure, Saintly life."

"I'm hoping that we can change that in time," Strang said.

"I don't think you can convert those people to our ways," Galen said.

"Yes, you're quite right. But we can find other ways to make it a God-fearing, law-abiding community," Strang said with confidence.

Galen looked confused. "I don't see how, without actually going to battle with them."

"I have plans, Brother Galen, and you shall be among the first to know."

Strang then went through the motions of dismissing Galen with a firm handshake and a quick goodbye.

"There's one more thing you ought to know," Galen said before leaving. "I heard talk in Pine River that the Mackinac men want to arrest you on your way to the state capitol."

Strang had his coat on and was about to wrap a scarf around his neck, but Galen's offhand remark stopped him in his tracks.

"Arrest me? This again? On what charges?"

"I don't know, but I just thought you should be aware. I'm sorry to be the bearer of bad news."

"The bad news will be for them. I shall outsmart them once again." Strang wrapped his scarf around his neck and gave it a strong tug. Then he walked home. He hoped Elvira was finished packing his suitcase for his trip to Lansing. It was definitely time for him to set sail for his first term as State Representative.

◆◆◆

On Mackinac Island, Constable Granger was at the ready.

"He's going to be on one of these steamers," Mayor LaFreniere told Granger. "It's the best way to get to Lansing. Keep checking the boats every day. When he turns up, have him arrested."

The men were waiting for James Strang to make his way from Beaver Island to Lansing. He would undoubtedly sail by way of Mackinac Island, the most desirable route to Detroit, where he would disembark and then ride by carriage to the state capitol of Lansing.

Every day, they checked the steamers and schooners that stopped at Mackinac Island. And every day they were disappointed.

"Damn him, where is he? If he isn't on one of the boats today, then we've missed him. It would be too late for him to make it to Lansing." LaFreniere was feeling increasingly frustrated.

While the men on Mackinac Island fumed and fidgeted, Strang had already sailed to Michigan's mainland by way of Milwaukee, Wisconsin. It was a much longer trip on a cold, rough lake, but it allowed him to evade arrest. He came ashore at Grand Haven and took a long carriage ride to Lansing, where he checked into the Benton Hotel. It was a grand, three-story brick building with a ballroom and meeting rooms on the first floor. Strang thought he deserved to spend his time in Lansing living in plush surroundings befitting a king and legislator.

He woke early on the morning of January 5, 1853, and made careful preparations for his first day on the job. He combed his wavy hair straight back from his receding hairline and smoothed his red beard into place. He put on a dark topcoat and tied a white silk tie around his neck.

After breakfast, he stepped out of the front door of the Benton hotel only to find an officer of the law waiting for him.

"I'm Undersheriff Tuttle, sir. I am here to arrest you on the charges of harboring a fugitive and obstruction of justice. I have a warrant here, which was sent to the Wayne County Sheriff's department from Mackinac Island."

Strang maintained his composure. "Since you seem to have learned of my travel plans and whereabouts, I assume you also know that I am due to present myself at the opening of the state legislature in one hour," Strang said.

Officer Tuttle twitched slightly. "Yes, sir, but I am here to arrest you and take you to the county jail, even if I must take you by force." Tuttle was a young man who was physically able to take on Strang, but was feeling intimidated by the man's aura of power.

"If you take me by force, I will consider it to be an act of unprovoked assault and will have you fired from your job and your entire sheriff's department put under investigation," Strang countered. "Now, if you don't mind, I am on my way to the state capitol."

Tuttle was stumped. He let Strang go, deciding to let his superiors deal with the man. As a junior officer, he was no match for the wits of James Strang.

Strang walked the few blocks to the state capitol building and stood outside for a moment, taking it all in. The building was large; a long, rectangular shape, two stories high, with green shutters around the windows. On top was a cupola with six narrow, rectangular windows. The entire building was painted white. Strang thought it looked rather pedestrian for a place where august men would be making important decisions about the state's future.

He entered the building and found his way to the large room where 70 representatives were preparing to start the new session. He took his seat and answered the roll call when "Representative for Newaygo and attached counties," was called.

After the roll call, a speaker for the house was elected. Democrat Daniel Quackenboss of Lenawee County won the position. He wasted no time getting down to the business of planning the legislative agenda. Strang cleared his throat and asked the speaker for permission to speak.

"I have some business of a more personal nature that needs to be resolved," Strang told the members of the house. "I was arrested this morning in front of Benton House by an Officer Tuttle. It was based on a charge from an old indictment issued in Mackinac County.

"When Officer Tuttle threatened to take me to jail by force, I informed him that I had a duty to serve in the venerable House of Representatives and he could not take me without your permission." Strang paused, holding his head up high in a dignified manner.

"Well my goodness, I don't believe we've ever had such an interesting start to a legislative session," Speaker Quackenboss said with a chuckle.

"I can assure you that this action was taken purely out of malice for me and the people of my faith," Strang said. "But I think it is up to the House to decide who has privilege here; the House or the sheriff of Wayne County?"

There was lots of murmuring among the Democrats.

"I think we should table this matter until we can study it more thoroughly," Quackenboss said. "I will appoint a committee of five men to study this matter, and soon enough we can make a decision. In the meantime, Representative Strang, please consider yourself under house arrest and remain either at the Benton House or the Capitol Building."

"Thank you, Mr. Speaker," Strang said respectfully, and then sat back down.

During their first break, Quackenboss selected five house members for his committee to look into the Strang situation. He appointed three Democrats and two Republicans, assuring that the decision would favor the Democrats.

Two days later the committee came back with their findings.

"The officials in Mackinac County should be officially rebuked for attempting to turn the law into a vehicle for oppression and persecution," the committee chair said to the House members. "This trumped up arrest was designed to deprive Mr. Strang's constituents, and the House itself, of his services. Therefore, we recommend that the House adopt a resolution finding the arrest of James Strang to be an infraction of House privilege."

Strang breathed a sigh of relief.

"Now then," Quackenboss said, "Can we get back to business?"

After the lunch break at 11:30 a.m., with all members back in their seats, Speaker Quackenboss was handed a petition from a process server.

"Confound it!" Quackenboss erupted. "Another problem has been handed to us, and once again, it has to do with our new Representative Strang.

"James Barton is contesting Representative Strang's right to serve." Quackenboss scanned the petition written by the man who had been defeated in the election by Strang. "Mr. Barton says that Strang is not a resident of Newaygo District. He is further charging that Mr. Strang only got himself elected with the help of his Mormons. I don't have time for this. I'm referring it to the election committee. Debate for this in the full House will take place January 11 at 2 p.m. That gives the committee enough time to make its recommendation."

With a bang of the gavel, Quackenboss moved on to other matters at hand, which included a bill to build a shipping canal and locks in the St. Mary's River at Sault Ste. Marie.

When the day's work was over, Strang returned to Benton House, where he immediately sat down at a desk in his room and began to write notes for himself. He was not going to be unseated by James Barton, the sore loser who lost by 116 votes.

When January 11 arrived, Strang felt ready to defend himself.

"Mr. Speaker, I am well aware of my inability to do justice to this question in which not myself, a humble individual, but democracy and the right to self-government have so deep an interest." Strang was in full voice, his rich baritone blanketing everyone in the room. His eyes were piercing James Barton at some times and looking trustingly at the Speaker at other times.

"Mr. Barton's lawyer has shown with great skill that the House is omnipotent in its ability to make a decision that cannot be appealed. But he has not shown that you have a right to reject the member who was duly elected for the purpose of choosing one who was not elected. Especially when the challenge is really about religious faith."

The hearing, which started at 2 p.m., continued until 9:30 that evening, when Strang finally made his closing arguments. He produced canvassing election maps showing districts that clearly put Beaver Island in the Newaygo District.

The following day, the House voted 50 to 11 to accept Strang as the duly elected representative.

Believing that every crisis comes with an opportunity, Strang seized the momentum he built and the focus that had been directed to himself to introduce a bill that week.

"In light of the confusion over election districts and counties, I am proposing to organize Emmet County and make all of the islands in northern Lake Michigan a part of that county," Strang told his fellow legislators.

Up to that point in time, Emmet County was a county in name only – it hadn't been legally organized into an official entity. As an unorganized county, it covered a great deal of territory, from the tip of the northern part of the state almost all the way down the west side to Grand Traverse. When it came to matters such as voting for county officials and law enforcers, the unofficial Emmet County had been under the control of Mackinac County – a county Strang loathed for its selling of liquor, its nefarious attempts to have him arrested, and for its persecution of his people.

Strang's bill was genius. It stripped Mackinac County of at least half of its territory, leaving it with nothing but Mackinac Island and a strip of land along the shore of the Upper Peninsula. And it gave Strang considerable influence in Emmet County, a county that was almost entirely comprised of Mormons, free from the Gentiles on Mackinac Island.

Having been so impressed by Strang's logic and mastery of the law when he defended himself against Barton, the House needed very little convincing to go along with Strang's bill. It passed by a huge margin. Strang smiled in humble gratitude toward his fellow House members after the bill was passed. It wasn't until that evening, when he was alone in his room at the Benton House, that he indulged in a self-congratulatory grin. He had just quadrupled the amount of land under his control and rid himself of Mackinac County's ability to meddle with him. His first two weeks in Lansing serving as a state representative had been very challenging, but ultimately, he had come out on top.

CHAPTER 60
EARLY 1853

"Maybe it won't be as bad as we feared."

Dolan and Archie were sitting in Roald's tavern reading the newspapers on a brutally cold, sunny January day. The sun shone brightly because the air was so dense with cold it couldn't hold any moisture in the form of clouds. Even the short walk from Dolan's house to Roald's tavern made for difficult breathing in the biting air. Both men held scarves tightly across their noses and mouths on their walk to the tavern.

"Why do you say that?" Archie asked Dolan.

"Here's what the *Detroit Daily Advertiser* said about Strang... *'The Prophet demonstrates great reasoning ability, energy and eloquence when he addresses his fellow members in the House of Representatives. He has certainly earned his right to serve.'* So maybe he will be a decent representative after all."

Archie looked doubtful. "He is a good talker, that's for sure. Talked me and Millie into coming here. But I don't trust him any more than I can swing a dead ox by the tail."

The two men moved on to reading an issue of the *Northern Islander* while they sipped their ale.

Archie looked at the back page of the *Islander* first, and abruptly stopped what he was doing, his beer mug poised midair. "Did you see this little notice on the back page of the *Islander*? Says there's going to be a special election in St. James next week. Strang has nominated Joshua Miller to be the sheriff of the new Emmet County! He's also nominated three township supervisors; Phineas Wright, Benjamin Wright and Galen Cole! Apparently, we now live in a new county with new townships."

"Where's the rest of the story? Give me the front page," Dolan said, reaching for a section of the newspaper. He read the main story out loud, while Archie and Roald listened.

"Our Prophet has had his first major victory in the Michigan House of Representatives. A bill introduced by James Strang passed in the House by a margin of 50 to 7. Beaver Island and all the other islands in northern Lake Michigan will be part of the newly organized Emmet County. Beaver Island will be comprised of two townships, one being St. James Township on the northern end of the island, and the other being Galilee Township, which will comprise the southern two-thirds of the island. On the mainland, Pine River will become part of the newly organized county and will be the seat of a new township which will be called Charlevoix.

"Emmet County will be a separate and distinct county from Mackinac County, and will no longer answer to the laws and regulations imposed by that county.

"With this new Act of redistricting, Mackinac County lost at least half of its land holdings. Their loss is our gain, for the glory of God."

Dolan quietly folded the paper and set it down on the bar. Then he took a long swig of beer.

"Strang and the Mormons now have complete control over us, and over every single office in our area. We will no longer have the recourse of requesting help from Mackinac, since we are no longer part of their county."

Archie and Dolan finished their beers, bundled up in heavy layers of wool sweaters topped with coarse woolen coats, and wrapped scarves around their faces before heading out the door to their homes.

As Archie approached Lucy's home, he could see her out back, splitting wood. He felt a pang of guilt for going to the tavern with Dolan when he should have been splitting more wood. He hadn't calculated correctly how much wood they would need to survive the achingly cold days.

"Here, let me do that," he said, taking the splitting maul from her as she turned to greet him. But as soon as he saw her face, he dropped the maul. He jerked his scarf away from his mouth and nose and immediately put his mouth over her nose and exhaled mightily.

Lucy was completely taken aback by his actions.

"We have to get you inside now!" Archie said, panic rising in his voice. "You've got the frostbite!"

Lucy's nose and part of her cheeks were the bluish white of thin lake ice. On the tip of her nose, tiny blisters had started to form. The undamaged skin on her face was in sharp contrast, red as a ripe tomato.

Archie hurried Lucy into the kitchen and threw open the woodstove door, shoveling pieces of wood from the bin next to it as fast as he could. Then he came around to Lucy again and put his mouth over her nose and cheeks, exhaling warm, moist air.

Lucy was dazed. "I've been spending winters outside my whole life and this never happened," she said when Archie paused to take a deep breath. He checked her nose to see if it was pinking up at all. It wasn't.

He continued to cover her face and breathe warm air on her, checking every few seconds to see if the skin was coming back to life. After what seemed like an hour but was really only a few minutes, her nose started to turn back to the color of living flesh.

"Oh, thank God," Archie said. His mouth was just inches from hers, hovering over her nose. Without thinking, his mouth moved to hers and he kissed her. She kissed him back.

Archie pulled away and started stammering. "I'm just so glad you're okay, I wasn't thinking, I was worried – "

Lucy reached up and took his face in her hands. "Archie, you don't have to make excuses," she said and brought his face back to hers, where she kissed him again, this time for a long time. When she finally tilted her head back a few inches to look at him, she smiled.

"Ouch!" she said as her smile tugged at the skin around her cheeks and nose. "Ow, ow, ow! This hurts!" Sharp, tingling needles were taking the place that was previously occupied with the warm, dead numbness of early frostbite.

"I'll kiss it and make it better," Archie said as he very tenderly kissed the tip of her nose. Then he straightened up, feeling a bit awkward.

"I'd better go finish what you started and get some more wood split. You just stay where you are."

"Yes, Archie." When he left the kitchen, Lucy found herself sitting completely immobilized, grinning idiotically in spite of the pain in her face.

They ate an early supper as soon as Lily woke up from her nap. Feeling happy and a little foolish, they stole glances at each other while they ate, taking turns to feed Lily. Archie finally screwed up the courage to say something.

"Is this wrong, how I'm feeling?" he asked Lucy as he took her hand. "Millie hasn't been gone for even a year. I thought I could never feel this way again. Am I a bad person for feeling this way? So soon?"

Lucy gazed at him, her eyes the color of dark mink and looking so warm Archie wanted to dive into them. "I don't think there's a prescribed amount of time it takes to get through the grieving process," she told him. "I think it varies on the person's spirit and attitude toward life. Those who embrace life seem to move through the process more quickly."

"You're not just saying that to be nice?"

"No, I'm not. And I also think that the depth of the love for the person you lost actually makes it easier to love again. People who have opened their hearts to great love have the capacity to fill their hearts once again."

Archie leaned forward to kiss her. "I think that's how I feel. Millie left a big hole in my heart, but it was a hole carved out by love, and it needs new love to fill it." Archie blushed. "I guess these feelings for you have been coming on me for a while, but I was trying to deny them out of respect for Millie."

That night, Archie moved Lily's crib from its place right next to Lucy's bed and put it just outside the door. When they made love for the first time, Archie was dumbstruck. He'd never been with any woman other than Millie, who was a fragile, tiny creature. Lucy was long and strong and capable of countering his thrusts with parries of her own. Being with Millie was always a balancing act for Archie, trying to satisfy his desires without hurting her. Lucy gave him physical passion blended with strong, fiery abandon.

Lucy and Archie spent the next week blundering around in a state of euphoria. It had been only a short time since Archie had loved and lost someone, but Lucy had spent more than a decade alone. She wanted to make up for lost time. Archie was happy to oblige. They stayed holed up in Lucy's home, venturing no farther than her shed to fetch a deer haunch or a gutted rabbit hanging from the rafters. They needed sustenance to maintain the level of energy they were expending.

When they emerged from Lucy's house, they walked boldly hand-in-hand to Johnson and MacCulloch's store, not caring who might learn of their newfound love. When they got within 50 feet, they saw a line of people waiting to get into the store.

"Why on earth would the store be so busy on a gray winter morning?" Lucy mused. When they got closer, they learned the answer. Wingfield Watson was in line, along with fellow Mormons Tom Bedford and Alex Wentworth.

"What's going on?" she asked.

"Election day, didn't you know? Voting for the new sheriff and the new township supervisors. Strang said to hold the election here at the store, seeing as it's the most convenient location."

Lucy looked puzzled. Archie blanched.

"Oh good Lord in heaven, I forgot to tell you," Archie said. "What with uh, ah, all that's been going on this past week, I forgot to tell you about the new county and the new townships."

He pulled Lucy aside and quickly told her what Strang had achieved in Lansing within his first two weeks of becoming their state representative.

"So we live in a newly formed county now? We are no longer a part of Mackinac?"

"That's right," Archie told her. "And I'm worried about Will and Teddy. They now live in a Mormon township, where they will once again have to abide by Mormon rules."

"But the Mormons must be in the minority at Pine River," Lucy said. "Surely they can't throw their weight around!"

"If they have the law on their side, I'm afraid they can," Archie said.

There were no surprises when the election results were announced a few days later. Galen Cole was Supervisor of the new Charlevoix Township. Joshua Miller moved up from being the constable of Beaver Island to the Sheriff of Emmet County. Phineas Wright became the supervisor of St. James Township and his brother Benjamin became the supervisor of the Township of Galilee on the south side of the island.

Every aspect of the law and county politics was now under Mormon control.

The pseudo-Mormon pirates Roger Nagle, Kent Pentour and their new confidante Nathan Bowman were holed up in the rowdy, thriving community of Northport when they heard of the new Emmet County that Strang had created with the help of the Michigan legislature. They were in a dim little tavern on the tip of the peninsula, playing cards and getting drunk when they overheard some locals discussing it.

"What does that mean for us?" Pentour asked as he fingered a worn playing card in his hand.

"Not much," Nagle replied as he contemplated the cards in his hand. "We keep doing what we're doing, and keep blaming the Mormons for it. Actually, it might make it easier for us, since this is going to make a lot of people mad. They'll be more than ready to believe that the Mormons are running amok, now that they have an entire county to themselves."

Bowman wasn't playing cards with them, since he wasn't very good at it. He just looked out the window at the dismally gray day, hoping for a flash of sunlight. He had cleaned up somewhat since he joined Nagle's crew, but his teeth were still broken and chipped from rough living, and his nose, which had been broken by Archie Donnelly a year ago, was now unattractively crooked. Due to a lack of proper hygiene, his face had erupted with boils. People who had known him a few years ago would find it hard to believe he was the same man as the vain, handsome person he'd once been.

As Bowman gazed out the window, ignoring the conversation his friends were having, he saw a slim, well-dressed woman walking down the other side of the road.

"Eliza!" he yelped, and ran out the door without bothering to put his coat on. "Eliza!" he called again when he got outside.

Eliza glanced over her shoulder at the man calling her name. At first, she didn't recognize Nathan, but when she did, she started running.

Nathan didn't pursue her, not being in a mood to expend a lot of energy chasing down his former wife on a wickedly cold day. Instead, he went back into the bar.

"I just saw my first wife outside," he told Nagle and Pentour. "I never did know where she got off to, but now I do."

This was news to Nagle and Pentour. Bowman had never told them the story of his first wife, ashamed to admit he'd lost her. But now he told them his version of the story; that Strang had forced him to take a second wife, and his first wife had run away and somehow gotten off Beaver Island.

"How did she escape the island, if you had a posse of Mormons keeping watch?" Pentour asked.

"I don't know, but I suspect it was with the help of the local Indians. She was friends with the squaws."

"How many Indians live on Beaver Island?" Nagle asked. He'd been unaware that the island was home to Indians as well as Mormons.

"Not many. A medicine woman lives there on and off with one of the Gentiles. And then there's Lucy LaFleur. She's half Indian. Runs a boarding house." Bowman paused for a moment, his mind rolling back to the time when Eliza had made her escape.

"I bet Lucy helped Eliza get off the island. She was friends with Eliza. Damn half-breed, it was probably all her doing that I lost my wife!"

"Do you want your wife back?" Nagle asked, a wicked glimmer in his eyes.

Bowman thought about the question for a moment.

"Actually, no. She was more trouble than she was worth. Always griping and complaining. Good riddance to her. But as for that Indian Lucy LaFleur, if I ever got my hands on her, I'd like to punish her properly for ruining my life." Bowman loved to have other people to blame for his problems. Strang was always a good target. Now Lucy could join Strang as a culprit in Bowman's undoing.

Bowman started warming to the idea of punishing Lucy.

"She was the bitch who told Strang evil stories about me. She's the one who reported to him that I was treating my second wife poorly – a total lie! – and he believed her. She's the one responsible for me getting banished from the island. She should pay."

Pentour listened to Bowman with a half-cocked eyebrow, not entirely believing Bowman's side of the story. He was adept at smelling a skunk in the woodpile, and was pretty sure Bowman had a broad white stripe down his back. Nagle, on the other hand, didn't care if Bowman was being entirely truthful. Vengeance ran in Nagle's blood. If Bowman had been wronged by Strang or the Lucy person he spoke of, then Nagle was ready to avenge the wrongdoing.

"Someday we will visit Beaver Island, and you shall have the revenge you want," Nagle told Bowman.

CHAPTER 61

SPRING, 1853

Strang found himself thoroughly enjoying his work as a state representative. He missed his wives and little son Charlie, but the challenge of writing laws for the state and the opportunities to espouse his knowledge in front of the House was invigorating.

At nearly every turn, Strang surprised his fellow state representatives. They had heard that he ruled Beaver Island like a tyrant, with little regard to the needs of the non-Mormons. But when he was giving his input to potential new laws, the House members found Strang standing up for the common man time and again.

By the time the first legislative session of 1853 drew to a close, Strang was getting praise in a wide variety of newspapers. The *Detroit Daily Advertiser* said of him, "*Whatever may be said or thought of the peculiar religious sect of which he is the local head, throughout this session he has conducted himself with a degree of decorum and propriety which have been equaled by his sagacity, good temper and apparent regard for the true interests of the people. His integrity is second to none.*"

While Strang basked in the limelight of his success in Lansing, some residents of Mackinac Island were roiling like a river inlet during a salmon spawn.

"Strang's pulled off the ultimate consecration," Mayor LaFreniere said to his companions. They were sitting at Jillet's on a cold day in early April, discussing the latest politics. "He's consecrated half of Mackinac County's property for himself, and managed to do it with the blessing of the state legislature!" LaFreniere slapped his balding head.

"I wonder how the people at Pine River are going to feel about this," the young councilman Gibson said. "A lot of them are people who left Beaver Island to get away from Strang. Now they're back under his control, at least politically speaking."

"I should think the residents of Pine River will be duly concerned for their safety and freedom now that they're in Mormon turf," LaFreniere said. "I imagine Strang will somehow spread his tentacles to reach the mainland."

"He's certainly spread them all over the lake like a freshwater octopus," Gibson said.

The worst thing Strang threatened to do to the people of Mackinac Island was to crack down on liquor trafficking. Through his newspaper, the *Northern Islander,* Strang made it clear he would not tolerate liquor transportation and sales.

"All the counties contiguous to the lake have concurrent jurisdiction of of-fenses committed on the waters within the state. The officers of Emmet County will conscientiously do their duty to uphold the state's liquor laws, while the officers of Mackinac are unblushing in their violation of their oaths to enforce the law," the *Islander* reported.

For Mackinac, revenue from the sales of liquor far exceeded the combined revenue from fishing and all other trades on the island. The island's residents were not going to easily give up the lucrative business.

When the lake thawed in early April and boats started plying the waters of northern Lake Michigan, it wasn't long before the Mackinac liquor purveyors discovered what Strang's men had in store for them.

Wasting no time, Emmet County built an unofficial navy of three schooners — The *Dolphin, Emmlin* and *Seaman* — and they sailed the fishing grounds looking for suspicious boats that weren't fishing. The Mormon law enforcers boarded the boats and confiscated any liquor they found on board. The men of Mackinac claimed the Mormons did more than confiscate liquor.

"They took all our supplies, our nets, even our spare oars," one Mackinac man told Granger.

"They're getting quite emboldened," Granger now said. "And why shouldn't they? If they board our boats and steal from our men under the guise of looking for liquor, who's to stop them? They are in their own juris-diction, where they will have a Mormon judge and jury."

"At least we're rid of the Mormons here," LaFreniere said. "We can elect our own sheriff and our own judge. Sheriff George Miller can go back to Beaver Island and take his ugly wives with him." Miller's wives weren't really ugly; LaFreniere was simply jealous of Miller's three wives, when he was restricted to just one who had grown sharp-boned and cantankerous with age.

"I'd take George over his son Joshua any day of the week," Gibson said. "At least George is a decent fellow, even if he is Mormon. I can't say the same about his son Joshua. He's a brute."

LaFreniere thought about Gibson's remark. He had met George's son Joshua Miller once, when he had escorted Strang to Mackinac Island for a township meeting. He remembered him as a surly man with a menacing glare who never smiled.

"Those non-Mormons at Pine River could be in for a bad time if Joshua decides to exercise his authority over there, and I imagine he will, since he's now the sheriff of that county," LaFreniere said.

"We should be prepared to help the Pine River residents if it comes to that," Granger said. "Sooner or later, these Mormons must be stopped."

⬥✦⬥

Strang made it back to Beaver Island in time to see his wife Betsy deliver a baby girl to him on April 1, 1853.

"Just what I wanted," Strang said as he stroked the newborn girl's soft head. "What would you like to name her?" Strang asked Betsy, who was lying in bed, holding the baby to her breast.

"I've always been fond of the name Evangeline," Betsy said, still feeling proud that she had delivered a healthy baby girl to her husband, just as he had requested. "We could call her Eva."

"Then that is what she shall be named," Strang said. "Charlie and Eva, my two progeny born on Beaver Island."

Not to be outdone, Elvira gave birth to a girl eighteen days after Betsy had little Eva.

"I'd like to name her Evaline," Elvira told her husband.

"That's awfully similar to the name Betsy has given to our daughter," Strang told her, wondering what his second wife was up to.

"Well, Betsy wants to call Evangeline 'Eva,' so we can call my daughter Evaline." Elvira was digging in her heels.

Strang gave his wife a bemused smile. He could see that Elvira was worried about keeping her place as the first, most important wife on Beaver Island. By giving her daughter a similar name and no nickname, her daughter's longer name subtly carried more weight than Betsy's.

"If that's what you want, then that's fine with me," Strang told her. Elvira smiled smugly.

With new babies and months of church business to catch up on, Strang delegated the work of law enforcement to his subordinates. He was pleased to hear from Joshua Miller that many liquor trading vessels had been boarded and the liquor seized. Miller didn't bore Strang with the details of other items that might have been consecrated while onboard the Gentile boats.

The Mackinac men claimed the Mormons had turned into pirates who were stealing everything worth taking on the lake. When Strang learned that the *Detroit Daily Advertiser* ran an article accusing the Mormons of pirating and looting Mackinac fishing boats, he struck back in his own newspaper.

"If the liquor trade persists, the sheriff will go out with sufficient force and make arrests in all such cases," the Islander reported. *"The law will be enforced whatever the cost. He is a fool who thinks he can defeat us by crying pirates and robbers. That accusation has been raised once too much."*

At the urging of their constituents, Mayor LaFreniere and Councilman Gibson decided something had to be done.

"We have to have a general meeting with all our island residents," LaFreniere told Gibson. "We need to devise ways to deal with these Mormons."

Almost every able-bodied man on Mackinac attended the meeting, held one week later. Only the ones who were deathly sick or crippled with chilblains from a late blast of cold weather missed the gathering, so strong was their hatred of Mormons.

"The reports of theft and arson are coming in from all over northern Michigan," LaFreniere said as he opened the meeting. "Gull Island and

Grand Traverse have been attacked, robbed and had barns and sheds burned down. This is intolerable. These outrages must be stopped!"

All the men shouted and nodded in agreement.

"What can we do?" asked Gerald Greene, also known as Boozy Gerry, who was in the front row of the meeting. He was well-known as a maker of whiskey for the Indians. His recipe was to mix two gallons of alcohol for every 30 gallons of water. Then he added tobacco to give it strength and cayenne pepper to give it a fiery kick. Then end result was even stronger than pure whiskey, leading to rapid inebriation by whoever consumed it. Boozy Gerry made the firewater at a cost of six cents per gallon and sold it for 25 cents a quart – an enormous profit, some of which he used to pay the sailors who distributed his cargo throughout the lake's towns and outposts.

Gibson, who was seated at the front table with LaFreniere, spoke up. "I propose that we write a declaration of our intentions and send it to the governor; maybe even send it to the president. We must make it clear that we will not tolerate any more of this Mormon piracy."

Gibson had come prepared. He read a list of ideas he thought should be included in the letter. Within an hour, a rough draft had been composed. The letter Gibson prepared for the governor and president was well-written. It said, in part:

"We people of Mackinac County will no longer tolerate the outrages that have been visited upon us by the Mormons. We request the strong arm of the law to quell these illegal activities. If the law doesn't step in to stop this behavior, you can be assured that the Mormon activities will be met with our own most determined resistance."

Fearing that the governor and the president would do nothing without additional pressure, Gibson also sent his letter to every newspaper in Michigan, including the *Northern Islander*. Since writing about the conflict between Mormons and Gentiles always sold newspapers, many downstate newspapers were happy to reprint Gibson's letter.

The *Northern Islander* had its own response: *"Let words cease and deeds begin. We prefer peace, but if war must come, let it be upon us and not upon our children."*

LaFreniere read the Mormon newspaper with growing concern. "We should get word to our friends at Pine River that trouble is brewing," he told Gibson. "Can you draft a letter for us?"

"Happy to do so," said Gibson, who prided himself on his prowess with a pen. He titled the letter, *"Address to the Inhabitants of Pine River."* In it, he offered the support of Mackinac Island. He also urged them to take action against the Mormons. *"We feel that the time has come when something must be done… to resist their practices, and if need be, to banish the Mormons from the land.*

"This is a strife in which there can be no reconciliation and no compromise; it may require violent measures, and may terminate in bloodshed. But there is no other alternative and you must be prepared. These people are rapidly increasing and it will be easier to crush the serpent in its weak infancy than to wait until the passing years add to his venom and strength."

"Beautifully written," LaFreniere said after Gibson showed him the letter. "Maybe the brawlers in Pine River will do our dirty work for us and fight the Mormons."

The end of the letter included instructions for the Pine River settlers to organize a company of reliable men who can be depended on to do the right thing. *"Admit only those who are prepared to go to all lengths when called upon. Arm yourselves as well as you can for the present, and make sure your guns are always loaded and convenient for immediate action."*

"I'm hoping this will goad them into action," Gibson said. "Action I would prefer our Mackinac men to avoid. Fear of Mormons taking over their outpost and forcing them into a Saintly life ought to do the trick." He smiled at LaFreniere, who was smiling back.

CHAPTER 62
JULY, 1853

Roger Nagle, Kent Pentour and Nathan Bowman were laughing so hard they had to hold their stomachs for fear of getting a cramp. They were all drunk, having consumed a great deal of the liquor they had just confiscated from a Mackinac boat, so everything seemed funnier by a degree of ten.

"I don't know how you kept a straight face when you told their captain you were Sheriff Joshua Miller," Nagle said to Bowman. "What a whopper! Quite bricky of you, I must say."

Bowman grinned, showing his grimy teeth. "Well, I doubt if any of those fellows has met Joshua Miller."

The men were sprawled on the beach of South Manitou Island. It had become one of their favorite hiding spots after they'd committed a crime. They had just robbed another boat, taking with them all the liquor on board, plus anything else they found of value. But they'd added a new twist to their acts of plundering; they pretended to be Mormon law officers, searching for liquor being illegally transported on the lake. They'd even gone so far as to having a corrupt cooper in Grand Traverse make them forged sheriff's badges.

"Our exalted prophet couldn't have done us a bigger favor than he did by sending his men out onto the lake to halt the transport of spirits," Nagle said. "Gives us the perfect cover."

As soon as the men had heard about Strang's proposed crackdown on liquor trafficking, they scratched the name *Defiance* off the transom of their boat and painted on a new name: *Seraphim*.

It was Pentour who came up with the new moniker. "It means to be among the highest order of angels," he told Nagle and Bowman. "Unlike you two, I was raised Catholic and had to learn a whole lot of religious hogwash."

The crew of the *Seraphim* had been on a robbery spree that stretched across Lake Michigan. They stole from stores and trading posts; they robbed small fishing villages and major markets, burning and destroying almost everything in their wake. Then, when they got into a port of call, Pentour always bought a paper to read about their escapades. Without fail, their thievery was blamed on the Mormons.

Nathan Bowman wasn't much of a sailor, but he made up for his lack of boating skills with an abundance of local Mormon knowledge. It was he who suggested they use the names of Joshua Miller, Jonathon Pierce and Dennis Chidester when they boarded boats.

"Someday we're going to Beaver Island," Nagle said repeatedly. "Someday I want to meet the king who is perpetuating this Mormon treachery."

Nagle was obsessed with Strang, even though Strang wasn't even a Mormon when Nagle's mother became pregnant with him. But Strang was a follower of Joseph Smith, and Strang claimed to be the rightful successor to Smith. In Nagle's mind that made Strang as guilty as Smith. Nagle fantasized about meeting Strang and then killing him with his scarred, bare hands.

"Someday, but not today," Nagle said as he took another swig from the whiskey bottle he was holding. "Today, we drink and celebrate!"

———— ◆◆◆ ————

Archie opened the letter that was hand-delivered by Jonathon Pierce at Lucy's home. It had Strang's wax seal on the back. Lucy came up from behind him and put her arms around his waist and her head in between his shoulder blades.

"What is it?" she asked, nuzzling him in the back. She loved his broad, strong back. It made her feel safe and secure.

Archie scanned it, then handed it to Lucy. He was chuckling lightly as he did so. "It seems I've been excommunicated from the Strangite

Church of Latter-Day Saints," he told her. "And my crime is committing adultery. That's enough to make a stuffed bird laugh." He continued reading.

"I'm being excommunicated for 'Being the widower of a fine Mormon woman, flagrantly disregarding the known Mormon practice of spending an appropriate year in mourning, and committing lewd acts of fornication and adultery with a single woman known to be a heathen.'"

Lucy bridled at being called a heathen, but quickly got over it when she saw how ludicrous Strang's letter was.

"Yes, that's right, I'm a heathen, but he's a Saint, living a stone's throw away from here with two illegal wives, and having banished his only legal first wife to Wisconsin."

Archie was still laughing. "Ah, yes, but an angel told him to do it, so it's perfectly all right! Well, to hell with them, and good riddance!"

Archie danced Lucy around in a circle to celebrate his being free of the Mormon religion. "Since we're officially scorned sinners now, how about we go to the bedroom and sin some more?" he asked Lucy.

"Nothing would make me happier," she replied.

After they made love, they snuggled in each other's arms and talked. It was a habit of theirs that Lucy adored, to discuss the daily snippets of things to do and decisions to make while entwined together.

"I'm going to go back to Pine River for a bit," Archie told the top of Lucy's head. She was burrowed into his shoulder. "Will and Teddy need me to help them finish that cabin we started last fall. It got them through the winter, but some of the things I did were temporary until I could go back and finish it properly."

Lucy tilted her head back to look into Archie's face. "If you need to do that, then you should," she said. "I can take care of Lily by myself, although if she starts walking while you're gone, I can't promise that she won't try to walk right onto a boat to come see you."

Lily had become very attached to her gentle giant of a father in the five months since he'd returned to Beaver Island. And Archie doted on her as much as he doted on Lucy.

"If she's as headstrong as you, she will probably do just that, and sail the boat over to Pine River by herself," Archie laughed.

"When will you go?" Lucy asked. She tried to keep the concern out of her voice, but a quivery note crept in. Archie knew of Lucy's fear of the lake and losing loved ones to it.

"Soon, but not until we get a nice, easy northwesterly wind so you won't have to worry." Then he kissed the top of Lucy's head and held her tight.

Dolan had offered to take Archie to Pine River. He wanted to see his boys, and jumped at the opportunity to have a reason to sail over. The boat he'd built when he'd first arrived on Beaver Island had held up well over the decades and could make the trip across the 32 miles of open water if the weather was light.

On the day of his departure, the sun was shining and the breeze was blowing steadily but lightly out of the northwest. It was a perfect day to head to the mainland. Lucy walked with Archie hand-in-hand down to the dock, where Dolan was waiting for Archie.

"Take good care of my man," Lucy said to Dolan, jokingly wagging a finger at him.

"Indeed I will, Lucy," Dolan said as he gave her a salute.

"And you take care of yourself," Lucy said to Archie as she put her arms around his neck.

"You as well," Archie said, then kissed her passionately for several minutes.

"All right then, time to shove off," Dolan said, feeling a little embarrassed by their affectionate display, even though he was very happy for the two of them. Then he remembered that he and Gwen often couldn't control their urges in the early years and were guilty of the same public kissing.

Lucy waved goodbye and watched the boat sail out of St. James Harbor. She waved until her arm ached.

Strang watched the whole scene from his parlor window. He had just eaten a breakfast of sausage, gravy and eggs and now it lurched in his stomach. Archie Donnelly had acquired the one thing Strang had been unable to get for himself – Lucy's love. That thought turned the fire in his belly to acid. *That bumbling bear of a man will have to be punished*, Strang thought to himself. *This is my island, and that man is a sinner. He deserves the buffetings of Satan.*

As a man who never made any moves in haste, Strang didn't know how he would punish Archie, but he knew the opportunity would come, and when it did, he would recognize it.

A few weeks later the seed of an opportunity arrived in an official letter from the governor. It told Strang that Emmet County needed to form its own judicial court. Strang was told to organize an election for judges and court clerks to be held as soon as possible.

Strang called a meeting with Sheriff Joshua Miller, his deputies and the township supervisors. "We need to announce a special election to be held in two weeks," he told them. "We will be electing a judge for Emmet County. Nominations are to begin immediately. The court will be located in the Emmet County seat, which is St. James. You men must post this in locations here on the island and also on the mainland." Then Strang handed them a piece of paper with all the relevant information printed on it and told them to make copies of it and post it forthwith.

The election went smoothly. A Mormon judge was elected in Emmet County. Even with an estimated 70 Gentiles now living in the Pine River area, it wasn't enough to turn the tide against Mormons, who greatly outnumbered them on Beaver Island.

"Our next order of business is to hold court," Strang told Miller after the election. "We have many pending charges against people that stem from arrests made on Lake Michigan for illegal liquor trafficking. Any arrests and ensuing cases made by our law enforcers will be heard in the Emmet County Court, regardless of the county residence of the alleged perpetrators."

Strang's intense eyes burned ferociously for a moment, causing Miller to reflexively jump backward. Then Strang's gaze returned to normal.

"We'll need a jury of 12 to hear cases. I think it would be a grand gesture on our part to have some of our jury members come from Pine River, to demonstrate our interest in giving them fair representation." Strang's eyes burned again.

"I was thinking perhaps Archie Donnelly, who is no longer a Mormon and is currently living in Pine River, would be a good choice," Strang said, waiting to see what Miller's response would be. Judging by the malevolent look in Strang's eyes, Miller could guess where Strang was going.

"Yes, an excellent choice," Miller said. "And how about Henry Van Allen, another Gentile living in the Pine River area?" Miller still carried a grudge against Van Allen, who had accidentally confessed to stealing

Mormon fishing nets, but then posted bail and snuck away to Pine River before he could be tried, taking the stolen nets with him.

"Fine with me," Strang said. "And if we need an alternate juror from the mainland, I would suggest one of Dolan's boys, Will or Teddy." Dolan was another person on Strang's black list. Dolan had the respect of everyone on the island, Mormon and Gentile alike, and it made Strang want to punish him as well.

"Then that's settled. You can go over to the mainland and serve these jurors their summons, then bring them right back here. In the interest of sequestering our non-Mormon jurors, perhaps we should put them up in our new jailhouse," Strang said.

"Of course, in the interest of a fair and impartial jury, the Gentiles should most definitely be sequestered," Miller said. He wanted to give Strang a sly wink, but he knew that would be going too far with his leader.

"Our first session of the circuit court will be July 19," Strang said, ready to dismiss Miller and move on to other pressing matters. "Make sure you get our jurors here in plenty of time."

"Yes, King James," Miller said, and then he turned and left the prophet to himself.

It was an uncharacteristically hot, muggy day in July when Lorenzo called on Huldy, bringing gifts of raspberry jam and bread he'd made himself. Lorenzo prided himself on being a self-sufficient bachelor and had learned to cook and bake. Huldy was touched by the homemade gifts and gave Lorenzo a lingering hug and kiss.

"If you marry me, I can make jams and bread for you every day," Lorenzo signed to her. It had been half a year since he had first proposed to her, and yet she still resisted giving him a definite answer of yes or no. Not wanting to hear her turn him down, Lorenzo had simply continued to court her patiently without bringing the subject up. But his patience was wearing thin.

"I do love you, Lorenzo," Huldy signed. Then she took his face in her hands and kissed him, more passionately than she had ever done in the past. Her tongue explored his lips and mouth. Lorenzo was overcome with excitement, and started running his hands over her waist and hips. When his hands explored her small breasts, Huldy let out a little gasp of pleasure.

Emboldened, Lorenzo reached behind her and fumbled with the buttons on the back of her dress. Huldy made no move to resist; instead, she kissed him more urgently. The combination of the summer heat and sexual desire had brought a deep, damp flush to Huldy's face. She slowly broke free of the embrace and turned her back to Lorenzo, pointing at the buttons on her dress. He couldn't believe it was finally happening. He carefully unbuttoned her dress and let it fall to the floor. She turned back to him to kiss him again, wearing just her flimsy underclothes. Then she started working the buttons on his shirt. He stopped kissing her long enough to help her unbutton his shirt and trousers. He wasted no time flinging them aside and was about to pull Huldy to him again when he saw her staring at him.

Huldy had only been with one other man in her life, when she was 17 years old. She had thought he loved her, but she had been young and inexperienced and didn't realize he had merely wanted to do his sexual experimentation with a woman who couldn't talk about it later.

He had broken her heart, but at least she'd learned something of the ways of men from the event. Among other things, she learned that when the weather was extremely warm, men wore nothing under their outer clothes.

Now she was staring at Lorenzo, who was wearing odd-looking underwear that covered his whole body from his wrists to his ankles. It appeared to be one-piece and made of tawdry muslin. It was clinging to his sweaty body.

"Why do you wear such a thing?" she signed, puzzled by the piece of unnecessary clothing.

"Oh, this," Lorenzo signed awkwardly, plucking at the fabric. "It's our magical garment. It keeps the Devil from sneaking into our souls. We Saints wear it day and night, all year long, to keep Satan out."

Huldy looked incredulous. "You think a cheap piece of muslin is going to keep the Devil out of your soul? What foolishness!" She bent to the floor to pick up her dress and started to pull it back on.

Lorenzo was distraught. "But the Prophet James blesses all our garments to ensure that we will be protected from Satan," he signed.

Huldy already had her arms behind her back, buttoning her dress up. Her sexual desires had been squelched by the sight of Lorenzo's 'magical' underwear.

"Please, Huldy," Lorenzo signed, trying to pull her back to him and reignite her passion. But Huldy was no longer in the mood. She was trying to dispel an image in her head of Strang in the tabernacle, with dozens and dozens of undergarments lined up on the altar, waiting for him to bestow them with magical powers to keep the devil from penetrating them. It was utterly ridiculous.

"No, Lorenzo," she signed. "I need some time alone to think about this."

Knowing he was temporarily defeated, Lorenzo got dressed and quietly left.

Wanting to allow time for unpredictable weather, Joshua Miller left St. James Harbor on July 12 and began his trip to Pine River with three jury summonses in his breast pocket. He had originally planned to row over with a crew of five men, but after hearing that trouble might be waiting for him at Pine River, he rounded up another boat and nine more men, for a total of fourteen men in two rowboats.

The Mackinac boats were designed for the rough waters of Lake Michigan, with a high, pointed bow and narrow stern. Oar locks were mounted on the sides to keep the long, heavy oars in place. The men sat on wood benches running from the port to starboard side of the boat at evenly spaced intervals.

Lorenzo Hickey, Alexander Wentworth, Jonathon Pierce, Dennis Chidester and Frank Johnson found themselves rowing together in the smaller of the two boats.

"This is going to be a long trip," Hickey said dismally. He didn't particularly enjoy being out on the lake where the threat of a storm lurked in every wayward puff of wind. In spite of Huldy's opinion, he was glad to be wearing his magical undergarments that would protect him from the Devil if the Devil decided to disguise himself as a giant wave on the water.

"Calm down, Lorenzo," Pierce said as he pulled on his oars. "We're just rowing down the east side of the island to the Bay of Galilee today. Then we'll head over to Pine River tomorrow."

The 12-mile trip down the side of the island was easy enough, with the two boats always staying close to shore. When they reached the Bay of Galilee, Miller jumped out of the lead boat, grabbed the bow line and started hauling the boat ashore while the rest of his crew jumped into the shallow water and held onto the gunwales so they could push the boat onshore.

Pierce followed Miller's lead and in moments the two boats were securely resting on the beach. Benjamin Wright, who lived near the Bay of Galilee, met them with food and provisions for the night.

After eating, Miller stood up to address the men. "I've heard from the Indians who traverse these waters that we might be met with a hostile reception at Pine River," he told them. "But we must remain calm and maintain the upper hand. We are going there only to summon jurors to jury duty. We have God and the law on our side, and He will protect us."

Hickey and Johnson were unwilling participants in the journey. They were strong-armed into making the trip by Miller and Strang himself. After dark, the two of them walked along the beach until they were out of earshot of the others.

"This doesn't feel right," Johnson said. "Why does it take so many of us to serve a few summonses for jury duty?"

Hickey was rubbing his left shoulder that was already sore from rowing. He dreaded the next day, when they would be required to row 20 miles to the mainland and then 20 miles back. He was getting too old for such physical work.

"Good question, and I have no answer," he said to Johnson. "But I agree that something doesn't feel right."

"Just in case, I brought a couple of guns. They're under the coats in the bottom of our boat."

Hickey looked alarmed. "You think we'll need guns? I'm not much of a shot, I'm afraid."

"Hopefully we won't need to do any shooting, but if we need to point them at people, it usually gets their attention."

Johnson wasn't the only one to think of bringing guns. Miller had also stowed a few guns under the gear in his boat, just to be on the safe side.

When dawn broke the next morning, the band of 14 men ate a quick breakfast of cornbread and salted pork, then climbed into their boats for the trip ahead. The lake was smooth as a puddle of melted butter. They knew the wind would pick up in a few hours, and wanted to make as much headway as possible before then.

—•◆•—

At Pine River, Walter Whitney's nephew Lewis Gabeau was standing watch on the north bluff along the Pine River, holding a spyglass to his right eye. When the warning letter had come from Mackinac, Whitney, a former Beaver Island resident and respected builder within the community, had suggested the settlers at Pine River post someone to keep watch every day.

Gabeau was thrilled to be given such an important job. At the age of 16, he was a gangly, awkward boy, rapidly growing into his man-sized body. His feet were growing so fast he didn't bother to wear shoes in the warm weather. His large hands with long, bony fingers felt too big for his pockets when he went digging in them for a marble or half-penny.

It was a warm day and Gabeau was happy to be sitting on the bluff, looking out at the lake. His eyebrows and eyelashes were bleached golden-white from being outside in the summer sun every day, and his nose was dotted with freckles. He sat with his elbows on his bent knees, balancing the spyglass to his eye.

Then he saw it. Two specks on the horizon. Two boats. One larger than the other. He stood up, nearly tripping on his own feet as he scrambled a few feet higher on the bluff to get a better look.

Yes, it was two boats, he could see now, coming from the direction of Beaver Island. He ran as fast as he could to his uncle's house.

"Uncle Walt! They're coming! The boats from Beaver Island are coming!" Walter Whitney took the spyglass from Lewis and pointed it out toward the lake to see for himself.

"Good work, Lewis," he told the boy. "Now, we must tell everyone in town to be prepared for battle. You go across the bridge and tell the people on the south side to get their weapons and gather on the south bluff. We'll meet them over there."

Whitney grabbed the boy by his arm and stopped him for a moment. "Wait. You'll need a weapon. Let me get you a gun."

Lewis couldn't believe his good fortune. His uncle was going to entrust him with a gun!

Whitney went to his toolshed and returned with a Colt Baby Dragoon, a lightweight pistol that Whitney thought would be manageable for the boy. He handed it to him and said, "Be careful. Don't point it at anyone unless you absolutely have to."

Lewis clattered over the rough wooden bridge that connected the south and north sides of the Pine River channel. He pounded on doors and shouted at men working outside. "Grab your weapons and meet on the south bluff! The Mormons are coming!"

By the time the two approaching boats were fully visible, a band of sixty men had spread out on the south bluff, armed with pistols, rifles and shotguns. They hid behind trees, waiting to see what the Mormons were up to.

Archie, Will and Teddy abandoned their work on the cabin and joined the men on the bluff. They stayed back from the rest of the group, since they were unarmed and had no interest in doing battle with the Mormons.

When the Mormon boats landed, Archie could see Joshua Miller leading the posse. He could identify Hickey, Johnson, Pierce, Chidester, and a few other Mormons he had occasionally worked with.

"Halt!" Walter Whitney yelled to the Mormons. He and a few other men had stepped out from the hiding places behind trees. "What is your business here?"

Miller looked up the hill at Whitney. "We're only here to serve summonses to a few of your people for jury duty on the island," he shouted. "We have orders to bring the jurors back to Beaver Island for the court session starting next week." The wind was picking up and he had trouble keeping his words from blowing away.

"I don't believe you," Whitney yelled. "Who are you summoning?"

"We have summonses here for the ex-Mormon Archie Donnelly and Henry Van Allen," Miller shouted, trying to be heard over the wind and the waves which were now pounding the beach. "If one of them is not available, we have a summons for an alternate juror – Will MacCormick."

Archie and Will exchanged fearful glances. "Why do they want us?" Will said to Archie.

"I don't know, but it sounds odd to me," Archie replied. He moved up to stand behind Whitney.

"Ask him what they want with us," Archie whispered to him, although no one except Whitney could have heard him over the wind.

"Why have you chosen those men?" Whitney shouted.

"In the interest of fairness, we thought it would be beneficial to have some Gentiles on the jury. King Strang recommended it."

The men with weapons staring down at the Mormons were getting fidgety. "You're lying!" one of the fishermen yelled at Miller. "You're a pack of lying scoundrels!"

"No one here is leaving with you," Whitney called out. "Leave us in peace."

"We're not leaving without the jurors," Miller called back.

Lewis Gabeau could hardly contain his excitement as the tension mounted. He fingered the trigger on the gun his uncle had given him. His palms were sweaty, and the sweat trickled down to his fingertips. He kept the gun pointing downward, away from the men around him so he wouldn't accidentally shoot one of his own.

Then the gun went off. Lewis howled in pain. Blood spurted from his calf as he fell to the ground.

"They're shooting at us!" one of the Pine River men yelled. "They've shot young Lewis!"

Then the shooting began in earnest. The fishermen charged down the bluff, shooting at the Mormons.

Frank Johnson and Lorenzo Hickey were glad to be holding concealed weapons in the waistbands of their pants at that point. They pulled them out and started shooting back. Hickey aimed for the treetops. He prayed that he wouldn't actually hit anyone. He just wanted them to stop shooting at him.

Miller scrambled back to his boat and pulled a tarp aside to get to the weapons he'd brought. "Pierce! Chidester! Grab a gun!" he called to his men. They didn't hesitate to grab weapons and start shooting back at the fishermen. But as the 60 or so fishermen drew nearer, they knew they were outmanned and outgunned.

"We've got to go!" Miller said as a volley of bullets whizzed around him. The Mormons shoved their boats into the waves, got them turned bow out and started rowing for their lives. Six of the men had been hit by bullets, making rowing impossible. The other men pulled harder on the oars to compensate for the wounded men.

Bullets kept coming at them, so the Mormons rowed with everything they had, hoping to put enough distance between them to be out of the range of the pounding gunfire. Then they saw the worst possible sight.

The Gentiles were launching large pulling boats, double-banked with oars and oarsmen on each side of the wide vessels. In the narrow center aisle between the oarsmen stood men with guns and rifles who continuously shot at the Mormons.

"Shoot back at them!" Miller commanded his men, but it was futile. They couldn't row and shoot at the same time. If they stopped rowing to fire their weapons, the Gentiles would close the distance between them.

Hickey was feeling panicky, thinking his life might soon be over. He wondered if he would die from drowning or from a gunshot to the head. Neither option appealed to him. He prayed for his magical underwear to keep him safe.

"Keep rowing, Lorenzo!" Johnson called to him as he heaved mightily on his oars.

Miller spotted it first. The barque *Morgan* was coming toward them under full sail. Chidester saw the boat a few seconds later.

"Help, help!" both men yelled to the *Morgan*. The other Mormons quickly followed suit, and soon all fourteen men, even the injured ones on the verge of passing out, were screaming for help.

The *Morgan's* Captain Stone picked up his spyglass and looked out over the water. He saw two small Mackinac boats being pursued by larger boats. Smoke from gunfire hovered in the air over the water. He could hear shots being fired.

"Fall off, and head 10 degrees northwest," he commanded his crew. "We need to get to those men."

When they were close enough to hear what the Mormons were saying, Captain Stone asked them what was going on.

"For God's sake, take us on board and save us from being murdered!" Miller shouted to him. "The heathens from Pine River are trying to kill us!"

Stone wasn't sure what exactly was going on, but he knew he couldn't turn down a request from men who were clearly under fire. He could see the Mormon men were completely exhausted and could hardly lift an oar out of the water.

Stone's crew helped the Mormons onboard, and then tied their boats to the stern of the *Morgan* so they could tow them back to their home port.

Chidester and Pierce had both been shot, along with Alexander Wentworth. Chidester had been shot through his elbow, and Pierce had taken a bullet to the hip. A bullet made its way clean through Wentworth's upper arm. Three other Mormon men had minor wounds.

Blood stained the Mackinac boats and turned the bilge water pale red.

Out on the water, the Gentiles from Pine River saw the Mormons getting rescued by the *Morgan* and realized the fight was over. They rowed back to Pine River, where they proceeded to celebrate their victory well into the night.

The next morning, Lewis Gabeau was lying in bed, recovering from the wound to his leg. Walter Whitney went in to check on him.

"Uncle Walt?" Lewis said tentatively. "Can I tell you something and you won't get mad?"

"Of course, Lewis."

"I think I may have shot myself in the leg. I was feeling awful nervous, with all those Mormons and all our men ready to do battle."

Whitney gave a small, gentle smile to his nephew. "As soon as I saw your wound, I suspected that was the case," he said. "The bullet entered the top of your calf. It would be pretty hard for a Mormon down on the beach to shoot you like that."

"You're not mad at me? It is my fault that all the fighting started."

Whitney laid a hand on Lewis' good leg. "All those men were itching for a fight," he said. "If it hadn't been you, it would have been someone else to fire the first shot. It was bound to happen."

Lewis leaned back in his bed. "Thank you, Uncle Walt."

CHAPTER 63
JULY, 1853

Strang was irate the next day when he learned about the attack at Pine River.

"I'll strip that Pine River settlement as bare as the palm of my hand," he told Miller. "There won't be a single vagabond or thief living there when I'm done."

Strang was particularly peeved that Archie Donnelly had not been brought back to Beaver Island. Strang had planned to house him indefinitely in the new jail. He and Miller had gone through old paperwork and discovered Archie never paid his tithe from his income on the schoolhouse. Strang planned to resurrect the warrant Miller had given Archie years ago and hold Archie under arrest until he paid his old tithe. Since Archie was no longer building homes for Mormons, Strang doubted he had the money to pay, which would ensure Archie would enjoy a nice, long stay in the new jail.

Then there was the very large matter of getting back at the settlers in Pine River. Strang decided the best way to rid the area of the fishermen was to do so through legal channels. He would order Galen Cole, the Mormon township supervisor, to collect income taxes and property assessment taxes from everyone living at Pine River.

While Strang was rolling vengeful ideas around in his mind, the men of Pine River were already anticipating his actions.

"We've got to get out of here," Archie told Will and Teddy. "Strang is going to come back for us, and next time he'll bring an army. We're not safe here anymore."

Other fishermen came to the same conclusion. "Maybe we should head down the coast to Grand Traverse," one of them said at a hastily arranged meeting.

Within days, all the fishermen loaded their gear, boarded fishing boats, and headed for Grand Traverse. Archie, Will and Teddy were among them. Whether they liked it or not, they had become some of the vagabonds Strang talked about in such demeaning terms.

A few days after the land and sea battle, Lucy was cleaning berries with Huldy at her little cabin when Lorenzo Hickey came to visit. He was hoping Huldy had overcome her doubts about his magical garment. The women took a break from washing berries and removing stems to chat with Lorenzo.

He told them of the trip he'd taken with the other men to Pine River and their harrowing escape. "It's a miracle I didn't get shot," Hickey said. "I guess I need to thank the Lord for keeping me safe."

Hickey had become fairly adept at sign language, so Huldy understood most of his story. She grew increasingly angry, as did Lucy.

"The Lord didn't keep you safe, the captain of the *Morgan* kept you safe," Huldy signed scornfully at Hickey. "The Lord is the one, through your prophet, who led you into trouble."

Before Hickey could respond, Lucy spoke up.

"You went there to get Archie? Why would you do such a thing?" Lucy asked.

"It was innocent," Hickey protested. "We were just getting them for jury duty. King James thought it would be more fair if the jury had a few Gentiles serving on it."

"And you believe that?! Really, Lorenzo, can you possibly be that gullible? James obviously had other reasons for wanting to bring those men back to the island." Lucy was remembering Archie's letter of excommunication from Strang, wondering if that had something to do with it.

Up until that day, Huldy was still waffling about whether or not to accept Lorenzo's proposal of marriage. But this information, along with the bizarre undergarment he wore to protect himself from Satan, guided her decision.

"You're telling me you carried a gun and shot at innocent people and tried to force Archie back to the island," she signed to Hickey. "There is

379

nothing decent or honorable about that. I cannot continue to entertain any thoughts of marriage to you, Lorenzo."

"But Huldy, I didn't want to go! I was serving under the king's orders!" Hickey's face and shoulders sagged.

"Has it ever occurred to you that your king's orders are bad orders?" Huldy signed. "If you choose to side with him, you should take the time to figure out whether or not his intentions are noble."

Huldy turned her back on Hickey and went back to the table covered with berries.

Defeated, Hickey headed for the door. Lucy stopped him.

"Did you see Archie? And Will and Teddy? Do you know if they are all right?"

"I'm sure they're all right, because I'm pretty sure we didn't hit anyone with our bullets. I was aiming for the trees because I didn't want to hurt anyone. I just wanted to keep them at bay long enough for us to get away. But I didn't see any of your fellows."

Lucy left right after Hickey. She didn't completely understand what had happened between Huldy and Lorenzo, but she was fairly certain Huldy wanted to be alone with her thoughts.

Tears came to Huldy's eyes as she sat alone at the table covered with berries. *Why is it that I finally find a good, decent man who loves me, yet he has already given his heart and soul to a belief I cannot share?* she thought. *And why can't he see that choosing a faith based in fallacy is far worse than choosing a flawed woman based in reality?*

It was August when Lucy got a letter from Archie. The postmark said the letter had been mailed from the Grand Traverse post office.

"My Dear Lucy and Lily," it began. *"First off, don't worry about me or the young lads. We are all fine. We left Pine River the day after the battle, fearing that Strang would be coming back for us.*

"I don't know why he's after me in particular. I don't believe it's for jury duty. Now I fear that returning to the island could put my freedom or even my life in jeopardy.

"As much as I am missing you, I think it's best if we stay here in Grand Traverse for a while. I don't think Strang can come after us in this county.

"All my love, and kiss little Lily for me, Archie."

Lucy's heart caught in her chest. Archie was gone, and not planning on returning any time soon. And James Strang was behind it. In a swift motion, Lucy scooped up Lily, who was wobbling around the parlor. She had started walking a month ago, but was still unsteady on her tiny, cube-like feet.

Lucy carried Lily on her hip as she marched down the hill to Strang's home. Betsy was sitting in a rocking chair on the front porch, rocking with her baby Eva. Normally Lucy would have put on a pretense of social nicety and chatted with Betsy, but she was in no mood for it.

"Where is your husband?" Lucy demanded.

Betsy looked up from her baby. "He's inside, actually. He came home for lunch."

"I'm going in," Lucy said, not waiting for an invitation. She opened the door and strode into the house. Peering into the dining room and seeing no one, she headed back to the kitchen. There she found Strang at a table, eating whitefish and green beans.

"What do you want with Archie?" she said, stamping her moccasin.

Strang looked up at her languidly. "I don't want anything with Archie, per se," he said. "I merely wanted to summon him for jury duty. That's well within my rights as the head of this circuit court." Even though he was seated and she was standing, Strang managed to give her a superior, righteous gaze.

"You expect me to believe that? You have an ax to grind with Archie, but I don't know why." Lucy clutched Lily tighter to her side as the girl tried to wriggle free.

"I have no disputes with Archie," Strang said. "He is no longer a concern of mine. He is an adulterous, excommunicated person of no interest to me."

It was the way that Strang emphasized the word 'adulterous' that caught Lucy's attention.

"Why, you're jealous of him! I wouldn't give myself to you, but I've given myself to Archie, and that is a bramble in your boot!"

Strang's eyes narrowed and stared piercingly at Lucy. "I don't care one iota whom you choose to fornicate with. I just find your behavior to be distasteful and abhorrent." He looked Lucy straight in the eyes, then looked at Lily on her hip. The sight of Lucy with a beautiful little girl gave him a pang of envy. He had an urge to jump up and kiss her and hug both her and the little girl.

"You don't fool me, James Strang, not one bit."

"There is no foolery here. But for your information, Archie has broken more than one law and if he returns to Beaver Island, he will be apprehended."

"Archie has broken no laws; you know that's not true!"

"I'll discuss this no more with you. This is a matter for our law enforcement officials and Archie."

Lucy whirled around in a semi-circle to leave. Lily thought it was fun and squealed with delight. "Not now, Lily," she said under her breath. "There is no joy in this house."

Two months went by without hearing any word from Archie. Lily had progressed from wobbling slowly to scampering rapidly through the house. The child was prone to sprint away from Lucy and toward mischief whenever she had the chance.

As Lucy walked across the road to Johnson and MacCulloch's store on a pleasant day in early October, she held Lily's hand with an iron grip. Wagons loaded with hay bales and mountains of corn, turnips and sweet potatoes rumbled down the main road as farmers made their way from their inland farms to the old barn Pete McKinley had left behind on Whiskey Point, where the Mormons were now storing their hay, grains and root vegetables. Phineas Wright, who lived there now and was the recently appointed supervisor of St. James Township, directed them to different spots in the barn and held the horses while farmers unloaded their carts.

Dolan and Gwen were leaving as Lucy arrived. Gwen looked the same as ever, wearing her doeskin tunic with beads running down the sleeves. Dolan looked older. Concern for Will and Teddy had added worry lines to his brow.

"Did you hear about what happened at the Mormon harvest party last night?" Dolan asked.

"No, something out of the ordinary?"

"Lorenzo Hickey got married. They had the ceremony right there in the barn."

"Oh my goodness! Who is his bride?"

"Sarah Linnell," Dolan said. "New convert to the church."

"I think I've met her," Lucy said. "Young, moon-faced girl?"

"Yes. I think I heard she's 20 years old."

"A bit young for him, wouldn't you say? Lorenzo must be at least 40."

"I guess so, but he wants children, so he had to marry someone young."

"Does Huldy know?"

"I don't know if Huldy knows. I haven't seen her in a while."

"I think I'd better go find her. My shopping can wait." Lucy left Gwen and Dolan in front of the store and turned to go visit Huldy.

As Lucy walked to Huldy's she admired the tree boughs with their golden and red leaves swaying in a soft, cool breeze. *Beautiful day,* she thought, *too beautiful to be bringing bad news to Huldy.*

She needn't have worried about being the bearer of bad news. Huldy already knew. Lorenzo had gone to her a week earlier to let her know he was taking a wife. He desperately missed his children from his first marriage, but since he couldn't find them, he wanted to start another family. Huldy wouldn't marry him for her reasons, so he found someone who would; a young Mormon woman.

Huldy conveyed the information to Lucy through signs and motions.

"Are you sad?" Lucy asked her. Huldy was a hard one to read. She'd learned at a young age to hide her feelings. Most people, she'd learned, didn't care much about the feelings of a deaf mute. Lorenzo was one of the exceptions.

Huldy shook her head no, then paused, shrugged her shoulders and nodded yes. Then she held her fingers apart about an inch.

"So you're a little sad," Lucy said. "I understand that. I know Lorenzo meant a lot to you."

Huldy pantomimed a person rocking a baby.

"Yes, he wants children. That's why he took a young wife."

Huldy signed something that Lucy could understand. "I hope he's happy."

Lucy didn't know if Lorenzo was happy, but in a few months, she knew he was on his way to getting what he wanted – a family. Sarah Linnell Hickey announced that she was with child on January 15, 1854.

CHAPTER 64

EARLY 1854

The letters from Archie continued to reach Lucy.

"My dearest Lucy," Archie wrote. *"The lads and I made our way to Northport. It's a nice little fishing town and we feel comfortable here. We ran into Eliza Bowman, who is doing quite well for herself. She has a dress shop in town. For the time being, she is letting us live in the rooms above the dress shop. It's a little cramped, but I've suffered far worse in my day.*

"I don't know when we'll be able to return to Beaver Island, or even Pine River, for that matter, since it's now under Mormon control. We've heard that Strang intends to arrest me if I return. I'll not give him the satisfaction.

"I miss you and Lily so much. Stay strong and know that someday I will return to you.

"All my love, Archie"

Lucy fell into a state of despondency that winter, managing to take care of Lily and keep the house running, but doing little else. Dolan and Gwen shared food with her, since she'd lost the pluck to go out and hunt for herself.

After all those years of missing Antoine, she had finally fallen in love again and now was deprived of the one she loved. Life was cruel. She knew she was regarded as a strong, self-sufficient woman, but sometimes she hated living up to that image. Sometimes she just wanted to lie down and let someone else take care of everything. But then she would hear Lily cry out to her, calling, "Lulu!" or see that the wood needed splitting, and, knowing that she had no choice, she would pick herself up and get back to the business of life.

———•••———

Unlike other islanders who got cabin fever, Benjamin Wright, another of the newly appointed town supervisors, enjoyed the winter, and spent most of it outside. He was one of many Mormons living in the settlement near the Bay of Galilee. In spite of the biting cold days that could freeze drops of water midair if it spilled from a bucket, the men had gone out each day through the winter and chopped cordwood for the upcoming shipping season. Wingfield Watson was one of the men who chopped wood for Wright. It was highly profitable, and Wingfield was hoping to earn enough to be able to afford another child.

By April, Ben Wright reported to Strang that he had 3,000 cords of beech and maple piled up near his docks and could provide 30 cords of wood per day to steamers stopping at Beaver Island.

"If prices hold, which they should, I'll be able to clear $51 dollars a month," Wright told Strang.

"My heavens, that's a fortune!" Strang said. "We must put this in the paper, so everyone knows what money and opportunity await those who convert to Mormonism and join us on Beaver Island."

Strang called on Wingfield to write an article for the *Northern Islander* to encourage people to move to the island.

"*We grow potatoes, and corn, and squashes and pumpkins, rutabagas, turnips and cabbage and other things among the logs,*" Wingfield wrote. "*They all grow fine. Potatoes need only a hole made and the sets put in, and covered up with dirt and they need nothing more done until harvest time, when you can dig up the finest potatoes than you've ever seen.*

"*A hoe and an axe are all a man needs to get started on Beaver Island,*" he continued. "*You can clear land for farms by chopping wood and selling it, then walk home with 70 pounds of flour and a chunk of pork for your family.*"

It was just what Strang wanted. He took the newspaper article with him when he headed east on a mission trip. Strang boarded the schooner *Morton* at Beaver Island on a crisp day in May, looking forward to doing more mission work in New York.

In West Seneca, New York, Strang had no difficulty rounding up new converts to his religion, largely because of the newspaper article he brought with him and read to the people who attended his meetings.

In addition to Wingfield Watson's article in the *Northern Islander*, Elvira wrote an article under a pen name, saying, *"On Beaver Island, an industrious man with a good span of horses can do better at teaming than he can in the learned professions elsewhere. Every kind of business is prosperous at this place. Money was never as plenty as at this time. In fact, one of our island employers is currently away on a trip to New York to hire more help."*

When Strang spoke to the good people of New York who were disheartened at their inability to earn a decent living, he made grand promises to them that no law-abiding county spokesman could match.

"If you convert to our faith and come to Beaver Island, you will inherit the land that is ours through the gift of our Almighty," he told the listeners. "After you pay your first tithe to the church, a piece of land will be yours, for farming or lumber. All you need to do is come prepared to make an honest living and live a wholesome life."

The truth of the matter was that the Mormons owned less than 1,000 acres of the 33,000 acres on the island. The government owned it, and it was for sale, but rarely did a Mormon ever bother to actually buy their property. After Strang's trial, federal officials didn't have the stomach or inclination to visit Beaver Island and check to see who was logging on government property.

The promise of fertile farmland and plenty of money to be made off cordwood was enough to convince even the least religious people to join the Latter-Day Saints. By the end of his mission trip, Strang had baptized another 200 people into his faith.

CHAPTER 65

SUMMER, FALL, 1854

Will, Teddy and Archie decided to move to Mackinac Island. There wasn't anything in particular they didn't like about Northport – they just felt a greater kinship to Mackinac, which, for all of the boys' youth, had been a friendly, familiar island to the northeast of them.

They sailed north on a breezy summer day, passing by Cross Village as the sun began to set.

"I smell fire," Archie said. The westerly wind carried the smell of smoke to their nautical position a quarter-mile offshore. He looked toward land and saw billows of smoke rising from the little village. "Think we should see what's going on?"

"I'd rather not," Will said. "Could be trouble, and I think I'd like to steer clear of trouble for a while."

They sailed on. It was dark when they dropped anchor in Sturgeon Bay, where they could sleep onboard, protected from the wind and wave action by Waugoshance Point. When they woke at dawn the following morning, they discovered they weren't alone in the bay. A large schooner was anchored nearby.

"The *Seraphim*," Will said as he read the name on the schooner's transom. "Never heard of it."

They heard of it soon enough.

When the trio arrived on Mackinac Island, the bigger, faster *Seraphim* was already in port.

It still meant nothing to them until they went to Jillet's for an ale and ran into the crew off the schooner.

"My God, it's Nathan Bowman!" Will said as they elbowed their way into the crowded bar. Bowman was sitting at a table with Nagle and Pentour.

Archie glared at him. "I'd like to break his nose all over again," he said to his companions. "Although from the look of it, I'd say I did a pretty good job of it the first time."

"Well, if it isn't Archie Donnelly," Bowman said when he spotted him. "What brings you to Mackinac Island?"

"I could ask you the same question," Archie said, not wanting to give Bowman the satisfaction of an explanation.

"I'm just being a good Mormon with these other fellows, consecrating from the Gentiles along the coast."

Archie thought of the fire he'd smelled coming from Cross Village.

"Did you have anything to do with the fire at Cross Village?"

Bowman smiled. "Perhaps we did. We might have burned a few buildings after we emptied them of their contents."

"So now you're a common thief, I see," Archie said.

Nagle jumped into the conversation. "We're not thieves, we're Mormons. We're consecrating items for our good King Strang."

Archie looked at Nagle, who appeared to be almost as big as himself, although it was hard to tell while he was seated. The man had a mean, hard look to him that immediately put Archie on edge.

"The Mormons were foolish enough to be taken in by Nathan, but I doubt they'd ever accept the likes of you," Archie said to the rough-looking man.

Nagle sprung out of his chair and went nose to nose with Archie.

"Just shows how little you know," he hissed. "I've been a Mormon since I was a baby. I'm guessing you can't say the same."

Bowman rose and stood next to Nagle. "This is the bastard I told you about. The one that broke my nose." Reflexively, Bowman's hand went to his crooked nose and he rubbed it. "He and that Indian bitch Lucy were the ones who ruined me on Beaver Island."

Archie lunged toward Bowman, ready to break a different bone on his face, but Will and Teddy stopped him.

"Don't be talking about Lucy that way," Will said. "She's Archie's woman now, and if you insult her again, we can't be responsible for what Archie does to you."

A glimmer came to Nathan's eyes. "So, you're with Lucy now," he said. "What happened to your wife Millie? Or are you being a good Mormon now and taking more than one wife?"

Archie resisted the urge to flatten Nathan. "Millie's dead. And both your first and second wives are doing very well without you, in case you wondered. Couldn't be happier without you."

This time it was Bowman who was ready to lunge, but Nagle stepped in between them.

"I think we should take our business up to the French Outpost," Nagle said while he maintained a firm grip on Bowman's arm. "We have personal matters to discuss."

Pentour, who had remained silent throughout the exchange, had already paid their bill and was waiting for them by the front door. The three men left, but not without giving Archie one last menacing stare.

When the three men arrived at the French Outpost, Pentour spoke first.

"I take it you hate that fellow Archie," Pentour said to Bowman.

"Of course I do."

"Then you can ruin him without laying a finger on him."

"How?" Nathan perked up at the thought. He knew from experience he'd lose a fistfight with Archie.

"While we're here, we'll just tell everyone that Archie is part of our crew and it was his idea to plunder and burn Cross Village. When word gets back to Beaver Island, I imagine Strang will be quite angry with him."

Bowman smiled. "Strang will have him beaten to a pulp when he finds out. Excellent idea, Kent."

The crew of the *Seraphim* wore out their welcome on Mackinac within 24 hours and set sail before the sheriff caught up with them, but not before telling everyone they came across that they were Mormons and had just robbed the people of Cross Village with the help of Archie Donnelly.

It didn't take long for the story to work its way back to Beaver Island.

"I am surprised, I must say," MacCulloch told Strang when he heard the news. "I never figured Archie to be a pirate and a thief."

"If he ever tries to set foot on this island again, I'll see to it he's jailed and whipped until his skin is blowing in the wind like sheets on a clothesline," Strang said.

Strang and MacCulloch were sitting in the back room at Johnson and MacCulloch's store. A bottle of whiskey on the back shelf didn't go unnoticed by Strang. MacCulloch's appearance was pasty, with bags under his bloodshot eyes and red veins springing from his increasingly bulbous nose. Strang was starting to think MacCulloch was more of a nuisance than a help. It was because of MacCulloch that any trip he made by way of Mackinac Island would result in a possible arrest, all because he'd helped MacCulloch avoid the law when the sheriff tried to arrest him for shooting Tom Bennett. *I should have just let him get arrested then and been done with him,* Strang thought. *But unfortunately, I still need him.* MacCulloch had gotten himself elected to powerful positions in the county, including county clerk and chairman of the Newaygo District Board of Canvassers. Fortunately, his headstrong wife Sarah managed to keep him in check most of the time.

"Hezekiah, you'd better not be consuming spirits," he told him. "That is not allowed in our religion."

MacCulloch didn't react. Over the years, he'd gotten more brazen about his drinking, believing that Strang had no business interfering with his private life. He knew Strang needed him more than he needed Strang.

"Whatever you say, Brother James," he said noncommittally. Strang let out a disappointed sigh. He knew MacCulloch was being disrespectful, but at the moment, he couldn't come up with a plan to punish him. Besides, he didn't want to waste any more time talking to MacCulloch. He wanted to get to Lucy's house and tell her the latest news about Archie.

Strang left MacCulloch sitting at the backroom table and strode briskly up to Lucy's house. He found her sitting on the front porch, amusing Lily with a little dog figure she'd made with sticks, twine, and a pine cone for a head.

"What brings you here?" Lucy asked coolly.

Strang spent a moment just looking at Lucy before speaking. He wanted to soak in her beauty on that warm summer day. Her black eyelashes waved like summer fans as she blinked impatiently.

"I thought you should know about Archie Donnelly," Strang said.

Lucy eyes widened, first with eager anticipation, then narrowed with worry. "Did something happen to Archie? Oh please, don't tell me something bad happened to him!" The look on her face, so filled with love and concern, initially melted Strang's heart. Then he remembered her love and concern were for another man, not himself. His heart hardened.

"Nothing bad happened to Archie, but something bad happened to many people at the hands of Archie," Strang said. "He has joined a band of pirates who are sailing Lake Michigan and robbing people and burning villages. They just destroyed a good portion of Cross Village. Now they're holed up on Mackinac Island."

Lucy's jaw jutted out defensively. "That's not true!" she exclaimed. "Archie would never do such a thing! He's a good man and you know it!"

It irked Strang even more to have Lucy defend Archie so vigorously. "It is absolutely true; I learned it from the captain of the *Morgan,* who was just on Mackinac Island. He saw Donnelly with the other criminals, drinking in some unsavory tavern."

"There must be some explanation," Lucy said. "Archie would never be involved with pirates and looting."

"I'm sorry but he was, and is. And if he ever comes back to this island, he will be met with the full force of the law, I'll see to it."

Fear spread across Lucy's face, which switched into anger. "You would just love to get hold of him and punish him, wouldn't you?"

"I love to see the wicked punished, as they so rightly deserve," Strang replied.

"You know damn well Archie isn't wicked. You're just jealous of him because I love him, not you." Lucy could hardly believe she spoke the words as soon as they left her mouth. She knew she'd crossed a line and Strang wouldn't soon forget it.

Strang's complexion grew dark and his eyes burned. "I am not jealous of an adulterer and a fornicator who has turned to a life of crime. Don't be ridiculous."

Before Lucy could say another word, Strang turned and left, stomping his way down the hill to his own house, leaving Lucy speechless and more worried than ever. She couldn't remember when she'd seen Strang that angry.

Archie, I love you, but please, please don't come back here, she thought. *I'm afraid of what James might do to you.*

Archie, Will and Teddy found work on Mackinac Island building warehouses and docks. The younger two men also found employment at the local distillery, where they were allowed to sample the product at the end of their shifts.

Archie wrote letters to Lucy whenever he could and was dejected when he got her letters back.

"You must not return here, Archie," Lucy wrote. *"Strang will have you whipped and jailed, or worse. He will never accept that you weren't part of the thieves ruining towns along the lake."*

Archie begged Lucy to move to Mackinac, but it was futile. She would never risk her life and Lily's on a boat. No amount of cajoling or reassuring her that the lake was perfectly safe at certain times of year would convince her to take that chance. She was implacable.

Any slim hope Archie had of talking Lucy into moving to Mackinac Island entirely evaporated with the departure of summer. Soon it was autumn and the weather became fickle; sunny and mild one day, then wet and angry the next. There was no possibility Lucy would get on even the biggest and safest of steamers in that type of weather. Her fear of dying in a shipwreck ran as deep as the lake itself.

Strang had no such fear of traveling on the water. His only fear was losing his upcoming reelection bid. He made numerous trips from Beaver Island to the mainland to speak to his constituents and make promises he couldn't keep. He promised rail lines from Lansing and Detroit to northern Michigan. He swore he wouldn't sleep until he got funding to build roads and bridges in the remote parts of his district. He even talked of someday having a great, long bridge built to connect the lower peninsula of Michigan with its upper Peninsula at the Straits of Mackinac. He knew it was a ridiculous pipedream, but it was of the magnitude and scope that dazzled his mind.

On November 7, his efforts were rewarded. He easily won reelection, garnering all 695 votes that were cast in Emmet County. He also got 19 votes in Cheboygan County to the north, for a total of 714. Strang's primary opponent, Albert Lay, who was a lumberman from Grand Traverse County, received 367 votes in his own county.

Unlike 1852, Strang had no concerns about his victory being challenged by the board of canvassers. Strang was chairman of the Emmet County board of canvassers, which was also comprised of three other Mormons.

MacCulloch, as chair of the Newaygo District board of canvassers, certified that 1,374 total votes were cast in the district. Strang had won again.

CHAPTER 66
LATE 1854

Lucy was carefully making her way to Johnson and MacCulloch's store, holding Lily by a mittened hand, making sure the child didn't fall on the icy path that was covered by a light layer of snow. She was too busy concentrating on the path to notice Lorenzo Hickey and his new wife Sarah in front of her.

"Hello, Lucy," Hickey said politely.

Surprised, Lucy looked up to see the couple. Hickey was carrying their new baby who had been born in July. He looked like a proud, loving father, but there was something missing in his demeanor. He wasn't glowing with the happiness Lucy had seen when he was with Huldy.

"Hello, Lorenzo. Hello, Sarah," Lucy said, then took a peek at the baby, who was heavily bundled in blankets. "My, what a beautiful child." It was Lucy's first look at the infant. She knew Lorenzo's new wife had given birth, but she and Lorenzo had become distant after he and Huldy parted ways.

"Thank you," Sarah said, her moon face alight.

"You both must be enjoying parenthood."

"Yes, we are." This time it was Lorenzo who spoke up. "I just love children."

Lucy studied the couple for a moment while Lily stood on her tiptoes to peek at the baby, whom Lorenzo held lower for her.

Proud, beaming mother. Loving, happy father. It should have been a picture of total happiness, but it wasn't.

It also wasn't any of Lucy's business, so after making small talk about the weather for a few minutes, Lucy bid them farewell and continued to Johnson's store.

Lucy stepped over the threshold and shook some of the newly fallen snow off her coat. She tugged Lily's mittens from her hands and tucked them in her own pocket, knowing Lily would lose them in a matter of seconds if left in charge of them.

Rose Pratt Bowman was behind the counter, straightening shelves of canned goods. It had been a good harvest that year, and many of the Mormon farmers sold their surplus canned goods to the store, where they would be resold at a profit during the harshest months of the winter.

"Hi Lucy," Rose said cordially. They had formed something of a friendship after Nathan had been banished from the island.

"Hi Rose," Lucy said. "How is everything going?"

"Quite well, actually. Frank is practically overwhelmed with all the newcomers. He wants to build an addition to the store to double the size. He went to Baltimore last month to hire an architect to draw plans for him."

There was something intimate about the way Rose spoke of Frank Johnson. Lucy briefly wondered if there was something going on between them, then quickly dismissed the thought. They were both single adults, free to do whatever they wanted.

After making her purchases, Lucy went home and put Lily down for a nap. She'd already decided to visit Huldy after Lily woke up. She couldn't help wondering how Huldy was handling the news about Lorenzo and the new baby.

Two hours later, Lucy was making her way to Huldy's with Lily running ahead, kicking and dancing in the few inches of snow that had accumulated.

When Lucy approached the tiny cabin in the woods, she noticed footprints in the snow. Big footprints. Men's footprints. Curious, she peered in the window before entering the cabin. She could see Huldy sitting at her little wooden table, and could see the back of a man. Perhaps one of the neighboring Mormons had come to help chop wood for Huldy, Lucy imagined.

Normally, Lucy would simply enter Huldy's cabin, since she couldn't hear knocking. But with another person there, Lucy thought twice. She knocked on the door, waiting for the man to open it.

Lorenzo Hickey was not the man she expected to see when the door opened.

"Please don't get the wrong idea, Lucy," Hickey quickly said. "Huldy and I are just friends. We would never sin, and I would never betray my legal wife. But…"

Lucy glanced past Hickey at Huldy, who had an awkward, embarrassed look on her face.

"Hi Mister," Lily said cheerfully as she looked up at Hickey. "You're the man with the baby."

"Yes, I am," Hickey said as he bent down to offer Lily his hand to shake. "Maybe someday, when my baby's a little older, you can come over and play with her."

"Maybe," Lily said, suddenly feeling bashful.

"I should go," Lucy said. "I just wanted to stop in and check on Huldy, make sure she has everything she needs and wants." She gave Hickey a withering look. "Which I guess she does."

"It's not that way Lucy, I swear on my mother's grave." Hickey's face was puckered with consternation.

"If you hurt Huldy, if you draw her back into a relationship that you can't manage, then I will skin you alive," Lucy said under her breath so Lily couldn't hear.

"I won't, I promise. Huldy understands the situation as well. Probably better than I do."

After giving Huldy a quick hug, Lucy and Lily let themselves out and walked home. While walking, Lucy tried to figure out what she'd just seen. Huldy was one of the strongest women she'd ever known, but was she strong enough to resist romantic gestures coming from Hickey, if he made them? Was he telling the truth? Were they just friends? Clearly, Hickey's wife didn't make him happy the way Huldy did, but he'd made his choice to marry and have children, and that was a commitment he had to honor. *He can't have his new wife, his baby, and Huldy too,* Lucy thought.

Lucy had barely made it home with Lily and gotten their boots and coats off when she heard a knock at the door. It was Betsy Strang, heavily pregnant and looking as if her baby might drop out of her at any given moment if she moved too quickly.

"It's Elvira," Betsy said after Lucy opened the door for her and ushered her in out of the cold. "She's having her baby. Dr. MacCulloch is, um, under the weather and can't help with the delivery, and Gwen isn't on the island. I hoped maybe you could help. In my condition, it's hard to move about very well."

It wasn't hard for Lucy to figure out just why MacCulloch was under the weather. He was most likely under the influence of liquor. His drinking had become blatant over the past year, and he was often seen staggering through town in the middle of the day.

Lucy could just imagine the scene at the Strang household. James was on one of his final mission trips of the year; little Charlie was no doubt tormenting his one-year-old sisters, Evangeline and Evaline; and Betsy was probably doing her best to keep the kids out of mischief while her sister wife was having another baby.

"Yes, I'll come right away," Lucy said, putting on the coat and boots she'd just removed. "I'll have to bring Lily," she added.

"That's fine," Betsy said. "What's one more child to watch? I'm already tending to three others."

Elvira's delivery was simple. She was a sturdy young woman for whom labor and delivery came easily. And so, as the snow continued to build up outside and the day turned into night, Clement James Strang came into the world on December 20, 1854.

After Lucy cleaned up the baby, swaddled him and gave him to Elvira to nurse, she went back downstairs and turned her attention to Betsy, who was in the main room with the children.

"It can't be too much longer now before you're doing the same exact thing," Lucy said, nodding up toward Elvira's room.

"Yes, I'll be giving birth any day now," Betsy said. "I can only hope my birthing process goes as well as it did for Elvira."

"You didn't have any problems with Eva, did you?" Lucy asked.

"No, thank the Lord."

"I've been told the first ones are the hardest, and the babies that come after are easier."

Betsy patted her enormous belly. "I certainly hope that's the case, but I'm not getting any younger."

"I'm sure you'll be fine," Lucy said, although she wasn't sure of any such thing when it came to having babies. Too many things could go wrong; especially on an island with only one doctor who, more often than not, was falling down drunk.

Betsy got lucky. When her labor contractions started three days later, it was early in the morning and MacCulloch was sober. David Strang was born December 23 without any complications.

James Strang was now the father of five children by his second and third wife; and the father of three children by his first wife. His kingdom was definitely growing.

Part 5

1855 TO 1856
THE TURNING OF THE TIDE

CHAPTER 67

EARLY 1855

The mood in the Michigan legislature when the session opened in January, 1855, had changed since the time Strang had first stepped into the capitol building two years ago. There were more Republicans serving in the house, and, as reports of Mormon thievery and polygamy made their way downstate, there was less tolerance for Strang and his island kingdom.

The legislator from the district of Mackinac was particularly eager to rein Strang in. His voters had not forgotten how Strang cleverly organized Emmet County to give his kingdom a bigger foothold on the mainland, and in the process, stripped land from the Mackinac voting district.

The Mackinac legislator wasted no time proposing a bill that called for more redistricting. He proposed that a new county be formed and called Manitou County, and that it be comprised of the Manitou islands, the Fox islands and the Beaver Island archipelago. No property on the mainland would be under Strang's jurisdiction.

Strang spoke against the bill, claiming it was a land grab by the people of Mackinac so they could run their liquor trade on the mainland, but his speech impressed no one. The bill passed with a vote of 60 to 4. The Senate followed suit. Strang was defeated.

The *Detroit Daily Advertiser* summed up the passage of the bill neatly. *"Strang will be the monarch of all he surveys on the islands, but he cannot command on the mainland."*

The rest of Strang's time spent on the legislative session of 1855 was a waste, in his opinion. He was unable to pass any meaningful bills to help the people in his territory.

That spring, Strang went back to Beaver Island in need of an ego boost. He was 42 years old and starting to feel his age. His hairline continued to recede and gray hair was starting to sprout in his red beard.

On one of his walks through town when he was feeling sorry for himself, he came across Sarah Wright, Phineas Wright's young daughter. He recalled that evening several years ago when she sat on the floor of her family's cabin, listening to Strang talk about his need to serve God by serving in the State Legislature. Strang noticed how the girl had bloomed into a lovely young woman since that event. Sarah was heading home with an armful of wildflowers she'd picked in a nearby field. *She must be about 18 years old now*, Strang thought to himself.

"Good morning, Sarah, how nice to see you," Strang said cordially.

Sarah looked up at Strang, her wide, clear blue eyes lighting up at the mention of her name.

"King James, it is my honor," she said, somewhat bashfully.

"Those flowers are lovely, just like you," Strang said. Sarah blushed.

"Thank you, King James." She blushed again.

"I would consider it a privilege if I could call on you and your family later today," Strang said. "Perhaps we could share some apple cider and you can catch me up on all that has been happening on the island in my absence."

"Oh my, that would please my family – and me, of course – very much. I'll go home straightaway and tell Mama and Father."

"Until then," Strang said as he tipped his hat flirtatiously at the young woman. Sarah scurried off, her long calico dress swishing back and forth with each step. Strang watched her backside move gracefully until she was out of sight.

As promised, Strang went to visit the Wrights later that day. He was on his best behavior, looking dapper and neatly groomed. It was not unusual for him to discuss business with Phineas, since he was the township supervisor, but seldom had he visited them socially. Sarah couldn't believe her good fortune when most of Strang's conversation was directed at her, not her parents. Her parents noticed as well, and Phineas began to feel uneasy. Was the king really courting his daughter?

The courtship continued on a daily basis, with Strang taking Sarah on walks along the beach and impressing her with tales of his many prophesies and revelations from angels. It didn't take long for young Sarah to become completely enamored.

On July 8, the Mormons on Beaver Island celebrated King's Day, in honor of Strang's coronation five years ago. The 40 or so Mormons who had settled at Pine River made the trip to the island to join in the celebration with the 1,500 Mormons now living on Beaver Island.

After a short ceremony at Font Lake, the festivities moved to the tabernacle where wide pine boards stretched across sawhorses sagged under the weight of roasted pigs, ducks and cows. Home baked pies and fruit tarts lined another table.

"Long live King Strang!" the faithful called out over and over, to Strang's pleasure. He smiled and waved to the crowd in the tabernacle. His wives Elvira and Betsy dutifully stood by his side when they weren't busy taking care of their five children.

Strang stood up and pounded on the pulpit to get everyone's attention after they had eaten.

"It is a fine thing to be gathered here with all of you to celebrate King's Day," he said, his voice carrying easily through the enormous room. "I'm happy to announce we will have reason for another celebration in the very near future. On July 21, I plan to wed Sarah Wright."

Sarah, who was standing five feet away from Strang when he made the announcement, curtsied to her future husband and then smiled at everyone in the room; all except Strang's wives, who intimidated her.

Elvira and Betsy gave each other a dumb-founded look. Another wife! This would upset the balance of their home, undoubtedly. The new wife-to-be was a very pretty girl. They both were intimately aware of Strang's sexual appetites. He would be feasting on tender young meat for some time to come, and probably neglecting the tougher, older birds in the process.

Phineas Wright was no happier to hear Strang's announcement than Elvira and Betsy. He pulled his wife off to the side of the room.

"I don't want our only daughter to become one of Strang's harem," Phineas said, speaking ill of the king for the first time in his life.

"I don't either, but what are we to do? Sarah obviously loves him." Amanda twisted her handkerchief in her hand.

"Is there no way to stop it?"

"I don't think so, dear. It's the law of our church. I just didn't think the peacock of polygamy would come to roost in our own home."

Phineas and Amanda kept their objections to themselves, knowing that to voice them was to risk Strang's ire and punitive retaliation.

Filled with sad resignation, they attended the wedding ceremony, along with the other Mormons. Betsy and Elvira maintained stiff upper lips.

It was fortunate for the three wives that Strang did have an enormous sexual appetite. He rotated from bed to bed every night of the week, keeping his wives reasonably contented with his interest in them. Sarah thrilled him with her firm flesh and made him feel like a young man again. Elvira delighted him with her cleverness and quick mind, which never failed to arouse him. And Betsy, although she was the oldest and the least attractive, knew secret ways to please him that made him flush a deep red at the thought of what she was about to do when he entered her bedroom.

Getting his sexual needs met on a nightly basis made Strang feel robust and powerful. It was a hunger that grew and cried out for more.

He fed it with yet another new wife, Sarah's cousin Phoebe, who was the daughter of Benjamin and Margaret Wright. Eighteen-year-old Phoebe wasn't as smitten with Strang as her cousin was, but she craved the prestige that she would get as one of the king's wives.

Benjamin and Margaret were no happier about the wedding than Phineas and Amanda.

"I guess we should look at the bright side, knowing that our daughters will always be provided for," Ben said after the wedding ceremony.

"Not much of a consolation, if you ask me," Margaret said. She was especially crushed to see her tall, graceful daughter marry a short, balding prophet.

"It's done now, so it's the Lord's will," Phineas said to his brother's wife.

"Yes, the Lord's will," Amanda echoed without feeling. Her heart had gone numb ever since her own daughter's wedding to the king. She rarely saw Sarah now that she had moved into Strang's home. Sarah was kept impossibly busy with cooking, cleaning, and performing other demeaning household chores while helping take care of five children. The first two wives assigned her the unsavory tasks of washing diapers and cleaning baby bottoms.

As the weather grew cooler, Strang found himself inside more frequently, reading newspapers from around the country. He came upon an article in the *New York Sun* about a woman named Amelia Bloomer, who had invented a new, practical style of clothing for women. Strang thought it made perfect sense. He tore the article out of the newspaper and asked his wives to sew some of the new outfits for themselves.

After the women sewed their new outfits, Strang had them wear the creations to Saturday services a week later.

"I'd like to draw all of your attention to the wonderful new outfits my wives are wearing today," he said after delivering his sermon. Betsy, Elvira, Sarah and Phoebe rose and took their positions in the front of the church.

MacCulloch's wife Sarah was seated in a pew next to Ruth Ann Bedford. They both looked up at the wives and surveyed the outfits slowly. They wore pantaloons, which were full and baggy from the hips to the calves, then tapered quickly to the ankle, where they were securely snugged. The dresses on top of them were drab and loose and stopped at their knees. Sarah elbowed Ruth Ann to see what her thoughts were.

"Hideous," Ruth Ann whispered to Sarah.

"My thoughts exactly," Sarah whispered back.

"Ladies, this is the newest style coming out of New York," Strang told the parishioners. "Women should wear practical, utilitarian clothing instead of being strangulated in long bustles. They will be more able to keep their homes clean and disease-free by wearing garments that don't get dragged through maggot-ridden dung heaps. Our women will live a more healthful existence in this apparel. And that, in turn, will benefit all of us."

As the congregation took in the information, Strang's wives shifted back and forth self-consciously.

Strang cleared his throat and continued. "Bloomers are progressive, and infinitely better for a woman's well-being. How can a woman tend to children, work on the farm or cook meals properly when she is dragging a germ-infested skirt around with her? Therefore, I am decreeing today that the bloomer outfit will be required attire for all island women."

Groans of protest rippled through the tabernacle.

"You'll never see me in that wretched attire!" Sarah MacCulloch shouted at Strang.

"Now, Mrs. MacCulloch, it will just take some getting used to, but I'm sure you will find it a most comfortable and practical type of garb," Strang said glibly.

Sarah stood up in her pew and pushed her way past the others until she got to the center aisle where she turned and headed out the door. Ruth Ann Bedford followed her. Their husbands Tom and Hezekiah sat silently, not knowing what to do.

Strang chose to ignore Sarah and Ruth Ann's little act of protest.

"Ladies, feel free to come to our house where my wives can show you how to make your own bloomer costumes," Strang said. "As soon as possible, I expect all women to be properly attired. I have informed Mr. Johnson of this plan and he has assured me he has put in orders for plenty of fabric for all of you."

All four of Strang's wives wore the bloomer costume everywhere they went. Jane Watson quickly adopted the costume, finding it practical. Even if she hadn't liked it, she had little choice in the matter. Her husband Wingfield had informed her that she would dutifully accept the king's decree. Jane had another secret reason to like the costume – she was with child again, and the new outfit didn't bind her swelling belly.

It wasn't long before Lucy became aware of Strang's latest dictum. She was in Johnson and MacCulloch's store one day when she heard Sarah MacCulloch and Ruth Ann Bedford talking to Rose Pratt.

"I haven't decided if I like them or not," Rose told the two women who were explaining Strang's decree and the ugly pantaloons that went with it.

"It doesn't matter if you like them, the king has said we all must wear them," Sarah said.

"What's the king going to do, come over himself and dress me every morning? I doubt that," Rose said.

Sarah liked Rose's words, even if they were coming from the mouth of a lowborn woman. "You have a good point, Rose. The king can hardly come over and stuff us into those puffball mushroom pantaloons every morning. I guess we could all protest and not wear them."

"I'm not saying I will or I won't," Rose said, not wanting to get inextricably bound up in a protest group with Sarah and Ruth Ann. "I'm just saying no king is going to decide how I dress myself."

Lucy walked up to the counter with her basket of dry goods. She set them on the counter for Rose to tally.

"What do you think of the new bloomer outfits, Lucy?" Sarah asked.

"It makes no difference to me. I wear white women's dresses when I'm home, but if I go out hunting or foraging, I wear my Indian tunic, which is essentially the same concept as the dress that goes with your bloomers. A loose tunic that doesn't bind at the waist and doesn't drag along the ground."

"Don't you find the bloomer get-up to be unattractive?" Sarah asked.

"Perhaps," Lucy said, thinking about what Betsy and Elvira had been wearing last time she saw them. "I guess it does bear a resemblance to an upside-down turnip."

Sarah laughed. "Oh, that's wonderful, Lucy! I'm going to remember that, and tell the king's wives that next time I see them!" Then Sarah had a new thought: "If we organize a protest, will you join us, Lucy?"

Lucy shook her head. "It's not my battle," she said. "I'm not a Mormon, and I will not follow any of your king's decrees. But I wish you the best of luck if you choose to stand up to your prophet."

Lucy's encouragement made Sarah feel like she'd just earned a prize.

"Then that will be that," she said. "Ruth Ann, you and I shall organize a protest. We will not let King James start dictating our apparel."

———◆◆◆———

Back at home, Lucy thought about the conversation she'd just had with Sarah MacCulloch. Lucy had never cared much for the high-handed wife of the drunken doctor. Sarah was always putting on airs, a relentless effort to remind the other Mormons of her former high social standing in Baltimore. The hard-working Mormons weren't impressed with Sarah's former life. Neither was Lucy.

Yet Sarah MacCulloch was perpetually trying to ingratiate herself to Lucy, which Lucy found amusing. Sarah still regarded Lucy as some sort of Indian princess, given her relationship to Chief Peaine. She gave Lucy gifts on her birthday and at Christmas, gestures Lucy didn't return. She brought Lucy jars of homemade jam and preserves, none of which Lucy needed. Lucy simply turned around and gave the gifts to islanders who were more in need than she.

There was no doubt in Lucy's mind that Sarah's acts of generosity were motivated by her desire to increase her standing in the island community, where Lucy was considered to be a leader. The efforts to garner her affection with presents galled Lucy. She would never like or trust Sarah MacCulloch. Lucy couldn't abide people who cloaked themselves in religion and pretended their good deeds were done to serve their God, when in truth, they were only trying to serve themselves.

Lucy hadn't forgotten the testimony Sarah MacCulloch had given at Strang's trial where, under oath, she had sworn that she had witnessed Strang speaking in tongues that the angels had given him, and had sworn she'd seen his prophesies come true. In Lucy's opinion, Sarah had perjured herself to earn Strang's indebtedness.

But Lucy did grudgingly admire Sarah's outspoken refusal to wear bloomers. The mighty Mrs. MacCulloch had demonstrated she could stand up to her king instead of groveling for his favor in exchange for rewards. It made little difference to Lucy what Sarah's true motives were. And Lucy suspected her motives were simply that the bloomer outfit was unflattering to Sarah's overly large behind.

CHAPTER 68
WINTER 1855, SPRING, 1856

Even though Strang no longer officially represented the mainland community of Pine River, it didn't deter him from expanding the Mormon settlement there. A new Mormon convert, George Preston, had moved to Pine River and become fast friends with Galen Cole, the Mormon township supervisor. They encouraged more Mormons to settle in Pine River. All told, there were nearly 3,000 Mormons living on Beaver Island and in the surrounding areas on the mainland.

Since he'd lost his own ability to govern on the mainland, Strang suggested Preston run for county clerk. Then he sent his favorite deputy sheriff, the strong-armed Jonathan Pierce, to campaign for Preston on the mainland. It wasn't an uphill climb. The Mormons voted for whomever the king suggested; they were also terrified of Pierce and would do as they were told by him.

On November 7, George Preston was elected county clerk. The Gentiles in Pine River were disheartened to see that the Mormons would likely maintain considerable control over Emmet County even though it had been politically severed from the Mormons on Beaver Island.

Preston was delighted with his victory. He had ambitions to run for state representative when Strang was ready to step aside; to win his first race was an auspicious beginning. Strang personally congratulated the young, eager Preston when Preston visited the island to arrange for supplies to be delivered to Pine River.

"Your victory assures us that the Mormons on the mainland will continue to get treated decently," Strang said to Preston when they met in the newspaper office.

"I will do my best to serve the county fairly and honestly," Preston said. Even though he would now be serving the new Emmet County that didn't include Beaver Island, he knew Strang would value him as a Mormon with influence on the mainland.

After a few minutes of polite conversation, Preston excused himself to make arrangements for the supplies that needed to be ferried from Beaver Island to Pine River. He went to see Jonathan Pierce, who owned a small boat called the *Maid of the Mist*. When Pierce wasn't working in the service of Strang as one of his deputies, he enjoyed making money on the side with his utilitarian boat, delivering goods to nearby islanders. It was easy money and allowed him to get out from under the constant demands of his king for a few hours.

"Is your boat large enough to carry all these supplies back to Pine River?" Preston asked Pierce after running down the list of goods that needed to be transported; barrels of flour, sugar, salted fish, and coffee.

"Of course," Pierce said gruffly. "My boat is more than ample to handle your needs."

"Then can we leave tomorrow?" Preston was eager to get back to the mainland and prepare for his work as county clerk.

Pierce looked at the darkening sky. "I don't know. Let's see what the weather is like tomorrow and decide then."

By the next day, November 25, the weather had taken a turn for the worse. Whitecaps rolled into the harbor and a mixture of snow and rain battered the *Maid of the Mist* where she pulled fitfully at her dock lines.

Preston met Pierce at the boat, which they had loaded the day before.

"Let's go," Preston said.

"It doesn't look good out there," Pierce replied.

"I thought you said your boat was more than ample to handle my needs," Preston chided him.

Pierce was a proud man who didn't take well to taunts.

"Of course my boat can handle your needs. And my boat can handle this weather. Fine then, prepare to cast off."

The flour, sugar, salted fish and coffee never made it to Pine River. Neither did Pierce and Preston.

Lake Michigan has a ferocious appetite for foolhardy people. It swallowed up Pierce, Preston and the *Maid of the Mist* in one gulp, never to be seen again.

Strang took the loss hard.

"I've lost my best deputy and the new county clerk in one fell swoop," he told the Circle of 12 at their December meeting. "This is a bad blow. It's going to be more difficult to rule my kingdom without them."

It didn't go unnoticed by Phineas and Benjamin Wright that Strang seemed more concerned about how the deaths of two Mormons would affect his political power than the loss of human life. But they said nothing.

Although Lucy had never met George Preston and had no fondness for the bully deputy Jonathan Pierce, she still mourned their deaths. *No one should have to die in Lake Michigan,* she thought.

The sinking of the *Maid of the Mist* steeled Lucy's resolve to never go in a boat on the open waters of Lake Michigan, which was disappointing to Archie. He kept writing her letters, begging her to come to Mackinac Island, but she was unwavering in her refusals.

"Dearest Lucy," Archie wrote in January of 1856. *"The ice is forming on the lake, and will soon be over a foot thick. Surely you and Lily could come to Mackinac by dogsled? The boys and I are doing well. We built ourselves a cabin and are finding work with other building projects on the island. Will and Teddy are earning extra income working at the liquor distillery.*

"How I miss you and Lily and Beaver Island! It's nice enough here, but it's not the same as the beautiful Beaver Island I fell in love with at first sight. I miss the endless miles of tall trees and the sunsets over Pisgah Bay.

"I can't go on without laying my lonely eyes on you and Lily once again. I am starved for your touch. Please don't let me waste away here without seeing you soon!

"All my love, Archie"

Tears came to Lucy's eyes when she read the letter, but she knew what her answer would be.

"Archie, my love, you know my answer is no, as much as it breaks my heart to say so. I would risk my own life to see you, but I can't risk Lily's.

"I truly believe that something will change soon – James Strang can't keep going on the way he is. He's making too many enemies. I am hopeful that he will see the error of his ways and make peace with those he battles, so you and others like you can return to Beaver Island.

"My thoughts and my love are with you, Archie.

"Yours, Lucy"

Archie didn't share Lucy's hopefulness. Living on Mackinac Island, he'd seen that the hatred for Strang and the Mormons was palpable. Even if Strang tried to make some sort of peace treaty, which was unlikely, the Mackinac residents would never agree to it.

For several months after the *Maid of the Mist* went down, the weather never let up. During the months of December and January of 1856, the island went into a deep freeze.

While other islanders chopped cordwood or went ice fishing on the frozen harbor, Strang kept himself warm and busy by bedding his four wives. It was a wonderful way to pass the cold winter days.

Strang's sexual activities came to the obvious fruition; Phoebe became pregnant in January; Sarah followed close behind by getting pregnant in February. Strang was elated. He believed the number of children in his household was a direct reflection of his manly prowess. Their pregnancies also came with the unexpected bonus of making Elvira and Betsy jealous, so they laid with him all the more frequently and vigorously.

It wasn't until mid-March that the weather broke. The temperature rose to well above freezing and islanders flocked outside to breathe in the relatively warm, balmy air. Many of them made the trek to Johnson and MacCulloch's store to replenish the supplies that had dwindled in their homes during the frozen months.

Tom Bedford was moving crates of flour and sugar from the back room to the main floor of the store as a steady stream of customers came and went. Islanders were not only in need of basic staples, they were in need of comradery. They had spent too many dark, cold days in isolation, speaking only to their spouses inside and their livestock outside.

Animated conversations sprouted up in different corners of the store. Bedford was leaning on the counter, sharing stories with Frank Johnson and a few other islanders. He was smoking a cigarette, which was frowned upon by Strang, but Strang was nowhere to be seen.

"I consecrated a fishing boat from Gull Island last year, under the king's orders since one of our newcomers was in need of a boat," Bedford told the people gathered near him. "Then a month later, I read in the *Northern Islander* that a man on Gull Island was offering a $50 reward for the return of his boat. I said to myself, this could be a whole new way to make a living! Steal a boat one day; return it for the reward the next!"

Bedford laughed heartily at his own story. Johnson smiled but said nothing. The other Mormons pretended to find it amusing, but some were new converts who didn't believe in the practice of consecration. Bedford hadn't noticed Dennis Chidester lurking nearby, listening to his every word.

At the end of a long and busy day, Bedford slogged his way back home. Before the thaw had arrived, the island had been buried under six feet of snow. Now it was slowly compacting into dense, wet snow that made walking a challenge. Bedford couldn't wait for it all to melt and disappear.

Ruth Ann had supper waiting for him when he walked through the door and took off his soaking wet boots. She was wearing a spring-like calico dress of pale blue, trimmed at the neck and cuffs in yellow ribbon.

Tom kissed her lightly. "My, don't you look nice!" he said. Bedford wasn't the sort of man who gave compliments easily, although he frequently had kind thoughts for his wife. He was in an expansive mood that evening, no doubt brought on by the mild weather and a steady supply of conversation at the store.

"I'm so glad you're standing up to Strang and aren't wearing those awful bloomers," Tom said after he and his wife were seated at the table with a meal of smoked ham slices and canned sweet potatoes in front of them.

Ruth Ann squeezed her husband's hand. "Thank you, dear. Your support means a lot to me."

They were halfway through their meal when they heard a loud knocking on the door. Tom got up to answer it.

It was Dennis Chidester, the one remaining deputy sheriff who did Strang's dirty work.

"You're wanted at the newspaper office," Chidester told Bedford brusquely.

"What for?"

"The king will tell you when you get there. Now come along, you're to report to the king immediately."

Bedford pulled his boots and coat back on. He walked silently with Chidester the few hundred yards to the newspaper office and entered with Chidester prodding him through the door from behind.

Bedford saw no sight of Strang, but he did see Joshua Miller.

"What's going on?" he asked, thoroughly confused.

"What's going on is that you betrayed and shamed us with your open talk of consecration," Chidester said. "You should never be talking about consecrated property. We're here to make things right. We've been ordered to give you 75 lashes save one to teach you a lesson."

"Wait a minute," Bedford protested frantically. "I've not done anything that each and every one of you hasn't done as well!"

"Perhaps that is so, but we don't talk about it," Joshua Miller said. "Now come with us."

The men dragged Bedford out of the office and down the road toward Whiskey Point. They turned toward the lake and stopped about 20 feet from the shoreline. They stripped Bedford of his jacket and shirt. In the darkness of the evening, the temperature had dropped again and it was near freezing.

"Put your hands up against that tree," Chidester said, pushing Bedford toward a small beech tree. Knowing he was outnumbered and escape was impossible, Bedford did as he was told.

Miller pulled a horsewhip out from under his coat. Chidester picked up a switch made of beech that he'd prepared earlier by twisting it and heating it over a fire to harden it.

When Bedford saw the weapons about to be used on him, he made a break for it, but slipped in the slushy snow and went down face-first on a small boulder. Miller pulled him back to his feet and marched him back to the beech tree. He saw that Bedford's eye was bleeding and starting to swell shut.

"Serves you right for trying to escape your punishment," he said.

The two men took turns whipping Bedford, raising angry welts on his back and splitting his skin in vertical lines until his back was covered with blood. When they were finished, they left him slumped on the ground, clinging helplessly to the very same beech tree whose branches had been used to form the switch that lashed him.

———◦•◦———

Lucy woke up the following morning to an island in the grips of a gray coma. Bare tree branches drooped under the weight of dullness. The rain couldn't even work itself up to a decent shower; it just leaked from the sky in a misty curtain. Where the ice on the lake had melted near the shoreline, water wobbled a couple of inches back and forth, lacking the strength to form a proper wave.

Gray everywhere. Dead silence, except for a murder of crows cawing restlessly about something in the near distance.

After doing her chores and leaving Lily with Rose at the store, Lucy walked to the lake shore, stepping carefully through the slushy snow. She couldn't explain why she headed off in that direction, other than wanting to see if the ice was breaking up under the blanket of gray sky. She was mildly curious about what had worked the crows into a lather. They wouldn't stop their cawing. It didn't take much in the way of a keen eye to see the dark red splotches of blood screaming for attention against the monotone of the day. The snow was scuffed up, clods of dirt thrown about, showing a lot of activity. A bloodied beech switch lay discarded near the scuffled snow.

Lucy headed into town and flung the door open to Cleary's Tavern, dark eyes blazing, looking for answers. The tavern had experienced a resurgence in popularity with the newer Mormon arrivals who weren't yet intimidated into obeying Strang's anti-liquor laws. At the bar sat Dr. MacCulloch and Frank Johnson, bookends to Thomas Bedford. She didn't expect to see those particular Mormons sitting in a tavern.

Bedford was smoking a cigarette and looked like a raccoon that had fallen off a hay wagon and then gotten stepped on by a mule.

"What on earth happened?" Lucy asked, taking note of Bedford's bruised face and swollen purple eye. She also saw blood oozing through the back of his shirt.

"Bedford got whipped by Strang's strong men," MacCulloch answered.

"Why would Strang have one of his own beaten like this?" Lucy asked.

"Apparently he got word that Thomas here was bragging a bit about the Mormon laws of consecration," Johnson said. "He fessed up to stealing a boat for Strang. Strang didn't take kindly to having one of his own revealing their consecration activities, so he decided to make an example of Thomas." He then told her what Strang had ordered for Bedford's punishment.

Bedford lit another cigarette and drank more whiskey, even though lifting his arm to raise a glass to his lips made his back hurt.

"I'm gonna kill him," Bedford slurred. He had consumed as much liquor as it took to numb his pain, and his pain was extensive. "I'm gonna kill Strang, I swear it."

"You're not going to kill anyone," Lucy barked at him. "We don't solve problems that way. But I do think I'll go have a word with your king."

It was none of Lucy's business, but that rarely stopped her if she believed an injustice had occurred. Strang's increasingly tyrannical behavior was threatening the balance of life on her island. She'd heard his men had beaten a few Gentiles in the past who refused to tithe, but she'd never known if the orders had come from Strang or if his brutish men had taken matters into their own hands. But now Strang was giving orders to have his own men beaten? It was unconscionable.

Strang's newest wife Phoebe answered Lucy's knock on the door. She swept past the young woman and into the parlor.

"Where is your husband?" she said harshly to Phoebe. "I need to have a word with him."

Phoebe went upstairs to fetch her husband, who was last seen entering Elvira's bedroom.

"James, you have company. Lucy LaFleur is here to see you."

Strang got himself dressed and went downstairs. As usual, the sight of Lucy caused a lump to rise in his throat. Before he could even greet her, she was speaking.

"Have you lost your mind?!" she exclaimed. "Having one of your own men horsewhipped? I saw Tom Bedford; I know what's going on. Do you really think your people will stay loyal to you if you start beating them within an inch of their lives over some minor infraction?"

"I gave no such order," Strang said defensively. Why did every confrontation with Lucy have to be a battle? Why couldn't she come to him with kindness and affection? Why couldn't she understand his role as a leader, and know that leaders sometimes have to suppress unruly followers? Why couldn't she just take his side for once?

Lucy didn't believe him. She'd finally learned to accept that the man she once admired, even loved, was a smooth and indignant liar.

"I've heard otherwise, and I have no reason not to believe the men who informed me."

"All right, I did give an order to have Bedford punished. I told my men to punish Bedford quickly and be done with it. I didn't specify the nature of the punishment."

"I think you're lying, James. I heard you specifically ordered them to give Tom Bedford 75 lashes save one, holding one back for the next time. And I think the pile of lies you've been telling will soon collapse on top of you and you'll be finished."

Lucy didn't wait for a response. There was no point. Anything Strang said was likely to be a lie, and listening to his lies served no one.

CHAPTER 69

APRIL, 1856

Word traveled quickly about Bedford's beating. Some of the Mormons thought he got what he deserved. Others thought it was excessive, but didn't speak up for fear of having Strang dole out the same punishment to them.

Bedford couldn't let it go. He was sitting in the back room of Johnson and MacCulloch's store after work one day, with the other store manager, Alex Wentworth, and the two store owners. Rose Pratt was just outside the storeroom, pretending to restock shelves while eavesdropping. Her ears were as sharp as a freshly stropped razor. She didn't miss a word.

"I don't think it was just about my talking of consecration," Bedford said of his whipping. "I think Strang wanted to punish me for Ruth Ann's refusal to wear bloomers."

It was something MacCulloch had also thought about. His wife Sarah and Ruth Ann were increasingly vocal about their objection to bloomers. They encouraged other island women to stand up against Strang's decree. Phebe Wentworth, Alex's wife, had joined in the outcry.

"Perhaps we should speak to our wives and get them to stop this nonsense," MacCulloch suggested.

"Never!" Bedford said. "I completely support my wife. And I think those bloomers make women look like a plume-plucked turkey."

Johnson chuckled. "I'm not married, so I guess I have no stake in this issue," he said. "But I would be sad to see Rose wearing one of those awful costumes to work."

As Rose listened, she was glad she'd decided to join the other women in their protest against bloomers. It helped to know that Frank Johnson would never force her to wear them on the job. And although she was getting on in years, she knew her figure looked best in the traditional dress of the time. She wanted to look good for Frank, a man she admired and liked more than she should. She'd been careful to hide her feelings from Frank. Her experience with Nathan Bowman had taught her not to aggressively pursue a man – and certainly not to create a sexually perverted appetite she had no desire to satisfy.

The four men drank whiskey in the back room until the light started to fade outside. MacCulloch wobbled back to his own home, where he helped himself to another whiskey from the bottle on the sideboard. He poured it into a teacup and sat down with his wife in the parlor.

"I fear the king will extract revenge against us because of your bloomer protest," MacCulloch told Sarah.

"What can he possibly do to us? We're women. He wouldn't dare whip us," she said confidently.

MacCulloch took another swig of whiskey. "No, he won't punish you women. But I know Strang all too well. He'll find another way to be punitive." He was thinking of Bedford and wondering if he was correct in his assessment of the real reason he was whipped. It made him worry, which made him pour himself another whiskey. He fell asleep in his chair and had upsetting dreams about being whipped by Strang himself.

MacCulloch soon found out what Strang had in mind for him. Elections for the newly formed Manitou County were going to be held in a few weeks, and Strang nominated Dennis Chidester to run against MacCulloch for the position of clerk and register of deeds. It was a position MacCulloch had held for years, first when Beaver Island was part of Mackinac County, and then when Emmet County had been organized. He enjoyed the power that came with the job and had no desire to give it up.

With Strang's backing, Chidester had no difficulty getting elected on April 7. MacCulloch was furious. He'd heard about the campaigning Strang did behind his back, telling voters MacCulloch was becoming a common drunkard who wasn't capable of carrying out the duties of such an esteemed position. Since he didn't consider himself to be a man with a drinking problem in spite of his obvious lust for liquor, he blamed his wife Sarah's bloomer protest for his loss.

"Bastard," he said to Sarah when the election results were announced. "I told you Strang would find a way to punish us over this bloomer upheaval."

Sarah was sanguine about it. "You don't need that job, Hezekiah," she said. "You have more than enough to keep you busy with the store and your patients, which earn you money, unlike that unpaid county job."

MacCulloch didn't pursue the topic with his wife any further, but he immediately started thinking of ways he could get back at Strang. Murder came to mind, but he quickly dismissed it as an outrageous idea.

Bedford had entertained the same thought, and didn't find it at all outrageous. He was single-minded in his pursuit to murder Strang. He even sat outside Strang's house one night with a rifle jammed under his armpit, ready to shoot Strang if he appeared in one of the bedroom windows.

Strang did appear in a window, but before Bedford pulled the trigger, he realized he hadn't planned an alibi or a method of escape. Ice floes still covered the lake, so there would be no escaping by boat. The island was almost entirely inhabited by Mormons, none of whom he could trust with the exceptions of MacCulloch and Wentworth. Bedford went back home, frustrated but undeterred.

Lucy offered the privacy of her home to the Mormon women who wanted to meet and talk about the bloomer protest. They were there one afternoon in late April, with Rose Pratt, Sarah MacCulloch, Phebe Wentworth, Ruth Ann Bedford, and the sisters-in-law Amanda and Margaret Wright in attendance.

"It will be your husbands next," Sarah said. "Ruth Ann's husband got whipped and my Hezekiah got forced out of his county job, so your husbands will be punished too."

Lucy sat and listened to the women, but said nothing. She didn't agree with Sarah's belief that Tom and Hezekiah had been punished over a silly thing like bloomers, but she couldn't be sure. Strang was acting more like a despot with each new day. She sometimes wondered if his brain was becoming addled with the stress of keeping his kingdom under control while also trying to expand it.

Phebe disagreed with Sarah. She pointed her tuberous nose in Sarah's direction. "You can't deny your husband is wobbly as a wheelbarrow six days out of seven," she said. "And Ruth Ann, I was in the store when Tom's mouth was flapping. I don't agree with what they did to him, but I do agree with the charges. So I don't think my Alex will be punished on account of me."

The two women stared churlishly at Phebe.

"For once in your life, Phebe, shut up!" Sarah snapped at her.

Rose, who usually stayed on the edges of the women's frays, joined in.

"I think Strang is a tyrant whose mind is collapsing under the weight of his ego," she said. "Personally, I'm not going to wear bloomers, but I'm not going to be a rabble-rouser and try to encourage other women to do the same. It's not safe."

Lucy smiled at Rose. She admired the woman's practicality and calm, levelheadedness. Rose caught her smile and returned it. *I never imagined I'd see the day I'd be applauding Rose Pratt in my head,* Lucy thought.

"What do you think, Lucy?" Sarah asked her obsequiously while she smoothed the front of her silk dress over her chubby thighs.

"You can wear possum pelts trimmed with chickadee feathers for all it matters to me," she said. "But I agree with Rose. James Strang is becoming increasingly resolute in his determination to rule all of you without allowing anyone to voice their opinions. That seems like a pot full of trouble with the first ingredients starting to boil over."

Amanda Wright spoke up. "I was a dutiful believer in the king for a long time," she said. "But then he took my young daughter to be his fourth wife, and then took my equally young niece to be his fifth. How many wives does one man need? It's not like the first two wives were barren and he needed to add more breeders to his stable."

Her sister-in-law Margaret joined in. "We all believed in the king in the beginning, but I have trouble believing in him now. I believe in our church and our faith, but King James..." her voice trailed off and she couldn't complete her sentence. It actually frightened her to speak ill of her king out loud, as if he was omnipotent and had ears embedded in Lucy's walls.

"You all can do what you want," Ruth Ann said. "But I will not be silent about Strang's decree to wear bloomers. My husband has been grievously wronged and I refuse to live in fear of a false prophet, which, in my opinion, describes Strang."

The meeting came to an abrupt halt when Jane Wingfield knocked on Lucy's door. Lucy welcomed her in.

"I'm sorry, am I intruding on something?" Jane asked politely. All the women liked Jane, who was still as sweet and ingenuous as she'd been when she arrived on the island as an innocent young woman in 1849.

"No, of course not," Lucy said. "These women are just having a lively bloomer discussion, but it's over now."

Jane self-consciously ran a hand down the front of her bloomer dress, which was now protruding over the baby inside her.

"In your condition, I think that outfit makes perfect sense," Rose said encouragingly. She had never forgotten how kind Jane had been to her after Nathan had been banished from the island.

"When are you expecting?" Phebe asked.

"Early July, I think. That's why I'm here, Lucy. I'm trying to plan ahead, so I wondered if I could get those baby supplies back from you. Seven weeks isn't that far away."

"Of course, let me get those things while these women keep you company."

The other women made small talk with Jane in Lucy's absence.

"Is little Abby excited about getting a new baby brother or sister?" Ruth Ann asked. She was a bit jealous since she hadn't been able to conceive a child of her own, but it was impossible to dislike Jane. The woman didn't have a mean bone in her body.

"I'm not sure she entirely understands what's going on," Jane said. "But she's had Wingfield and me to herself for five years now. I hope she doesn't resent the new baby."

Lucy returned with a sack of baby items.

"Here they are, clean and folded, but a little more worn than when you loaned them to me," she said.

"That's fine, Lucy. That's what baby things are for – to be used and worn by as many babies as possible until they're all used up."

CHAPTER 70
MAY, JUNE, 1856

"I saw Elvira and Betsy Strang at the store today," Gwen said to Dolan. They were sitting on the porch and Dolan was whittling.

"Yes, and how are they?" Dolan said absent-mindedly, not really caring much for gossip about the king's wives.

"If I had to guess, I'd say they are both with child," Gwen said. "I know the washed-out look of a woman's face when she's got morning sickness. I know how a woman with child will put a hand on her belly subconsciously to protect it."

Dolan sat up and looked at Gwen. "More children? My stars, how many is that?"

"Well, if you don't count the three he had with his first wife, Mary, he now has five children by Elvira and Betsy; Sarah and Phoebe are both with child and likely to give birth in autumn; and it wouldn't surprise me if Elvira and Betsy have babies early next year. So that would make nine by his island wives, for a total of 12."

"I guess that's one way to increase the Mormon population in these parts," Dolan said as his knife made a clean swipe down the side of the piece of wood he was holding. "If he keeps taking young wives and having babies with them, he can get reelected to the state legislature permanently with the vote of his own offspring someday." Dolan grinned at his own remark, and Gwen gave him a playful kick.

Gwen was right. Elvira and Betsy told their husband that they would be giving him new heirs to the throne early next year.

Strang could hardly wait to boast about it at the next meeting of the Circle of 12, where Alex Wentworth, the Wright brothers, Chidester, Sheriff Miller and his father George, were all in attendance. MacCulloch had been relieved of his position in the Circle of 12 after he lost the county election. Strang told him it had nothing to do with the election, but rather it was because his drinking was a disgrace to the Mormon faithful. MacCulloch had been incensed over it for two reasons; he would no longer be in the loop about Strang's plans; and it was utterly humiliating to a man of his stature.

"I'm happy to announce I now have four wives with child," Strang said before they started their official church business. "Our island kingdom is growing by leaps and bounds, thanks to my unflagging efforts." His eyes gleamed as he said it; the conceit and pride were unmistakable in his voice.

"Congratulations, King James," Sheriff Miller said, and others followed suit, mumbling their congratulations. The Wright brothers sat stone-faced and silent. It was their daughters who were with child, and Strang was preening about it like he'd just acquired two fatted calves for the price of one.

Alex Wentworth was the only one to make a dissenting remark.

"I think your acts of polygamy are harming our standing in the State of Michigan," he said. "The more wives you take and the more children you have, it makes us look more and more like a bizarre kingdom with harems and concubines instead of a decent, moral community."

Strang snorted and gave Wentworth a snide look. "Oh, that's just rich, coming from a man whose father is his grandfather and whose mother is his sister." Strang laughed at his cleverness. "I know full well how those mountain men in West Virginia – that is where you're from, correct, Alex? – how they choose to breed."

Wentworth looked like he'd just been slapped in the face. "That was uncalled for, King James," he said as he stood up. "I'll not be subjected to such insults. I'm leaving." He stomped out of the room, and Strang made no effort to stop him, which was equally insulting to Wentworth.

The Circle of 12 still had a quorum present without Wentworth, so they continued with their business. Now that the weather was nice, Strang wanted more men out patrolling and looking for women who were defying his decree to wear bloomers.

"Don't think of it as punishing women and forcing them to wear something they don't like," Strang told them. "Remember that they don't understand the risks to our health that their old style of dresses creates."

Chidester and Miller brought up the rumors they'd heard about Bedford; that he was intent on getting revenge on Strang for his whipping.

"We think you should employ bodyguards to protect you at all times when you're out of your house," Miller said.

"Nonsense!" Strang said. "That impertinent clod will do me no harm. He got a fair punishment and now it's done. He'll cool down and come to his senses soon enough. But his wife still needs to be reckoned with. I hear she's still protesting the bloomer outfit quite vociferously."

"How do you propose we punish the women? It would be extremely ungentlemanly to physically harm them," Miller said.

"Of course it would be; I would never suggest such a thing," Strang said. "But you can be persuasive with your powers of intimidation, Joshua. I've seen you do it. And Dennis, the same goes for you. If you need to hold them firmly – extra firmly – by the arm while you speak to them, I've no objection to that."

Miller and Chidester weren't exactly the kindest and most thoughtful of men, but they didn't relish the thought of being rough with women. They knew, however, they had no choice.

After some discussion for the upcoming conference to be held on Holy Island in Pine Lake that summer, the meeting was adjourned.

Wentworth was already at Johnson and MacCulloch's by the time the meeting ended. He sat in the back room with Johnson, MacCulloch and Bedford, still fuming over Strang's remark.

"How dare he insult my parentage?" Wentworth asked. "I come from poor folk, but they were all decent, law-abiding citizens who never took part in any inbreeding!"

"He's more of a law breaker than your family probably ever was," Bedford said. "I guess he thinks he can insult you in front of the Circle of

12 for the same reason he thinks he can have me whipped. He thinks his position as prophet and king puts him above all laws."

MacCulloch piped in, "Why should he obey laws, when he controls the county and everyone in it? There isn't a single person who can take him to task."

Johnson, Wentworth's father-in-law, spoke up. "I'm sorry that Strang insulted you. I know your family is not guilty of Strang's accusations." He paused, rubbing his forehead thoughtfully. "From my perspective, Strang has become a liability. People are leaving the island to get away from his scrutiny and policies. He's already driven most of the Gentiles off the island. Unhappy Mormons are starting to follow. Soon, who will be left on the island to patronize our store? Alex, I pay you and Tom good wages for your work here. I'd hate to have to let you both go if I can't afford to pay you anymore."

Wentworth had been too busy stewing over Strang's insult to have considered the economic impact of the king's actions.

"But surely you wouldn't deny me a means to support your daughter, would you?"

"I won't deny you the right to earn a living, Alex, but if my business fails due to Strang, we all may have to find another way to earn a living. Chopping cordwood or fishing, perhaps."

Wentworth shuddered at the thought of returning to manual labor for his livelihood. He'd chopped wood when he first arrived on the island, and learned it was miserable, hard work, best suited to men who had grown up doing physical labor.

"So what do we do?" Bedford asked. "We can't fire him from being King and Prophet. We can't force him off the island the way he forced the Gentiles off. We're stuck with him."

"We need to kill him," MacCulloch said calmly. "But first, we have to figure out how to do it."

"Agreed!" Bedford said, delighted to hear that MacCulloch had come around to his own way of thinking.

Wentworth initially was shocked at the thought of committing murder, but it didn't take him long to warm up to the idea after he considered the alternatives – chopping wood and enduring demeaning insults from his leader.

"It's a radical solution, but probably the only one that will work," he said.

Johnson shook his head. "Gentlemen, you'll be hard pressed to find a way to kill Strang and get away with it if you don't lay the proper groundwork first," he said pragmatically. "You need to build a case for your actions. You need to plan your getaway and figure out how to escape retribution from Strang's protectors. And you need to learn how to shoot straight if you're planning to take his life with a pistol or rifle."

"He's right," MacCulloch said. "We need to do some planning. And I think the first thing we should do is to employ Strang's own methods of controlling public opinion. We need to start writing letters and articles for newspapers."

In addition to their letter-writing campaign, Johnson and MacCulloch met with the captain of the *USS Michigan* when it docked at St. James for refueling on a routine patrol. Captain McBlair was a Navy veteran who had been in command of the *Michigan* for eight months. He was a fair-minded man with trim gray hair, a square-cut beard and a taut military bearing. He also had a predilection to take the word of disgruntled Mormons over the word of their king.

After talking at length with MacCulloch and Johnson in the captain's cabin, McBlair felt compelled to get their message to Governor Bingham.

"There is a frightful disturbance occurring on Beaver Island," McBlair wrote in his letter to the governor. *"I feel it is my duty to take affidavits from two of the island's most intelligent Mormon men, a Mr. Frank Johnson and a Dr. Hezekiah MacCulloch. They have told me of the unforgiveable actions of their king, James Strang. According to them, he greatly inflated the 1854 census figures in order to receive more government funding for his county. He has been plundering the innocent fishermen and loggers in the region by demanding a tithe on their earnings, even though they are not of the Mormon faith. He even required the people of his own faith to pay a tithe on whatever booty they may have acquired through their acts of consecration.*

"It is my understanding that there are 10 or so persons who have seceded from the Mormon Church and are exposed to all the consequences of Strang's resentment. I have been given the names of Archibald Donnelly, Will MacCormick and Theodore Duffy as being among those who fear retribution so much that they are no longer living on the island, taking refuge instead on Mackinac Island.

"It is said that there are a number of others who at heart are opposed to Strang but suppress their feelings from fear of reprisal. All of these people are seeking prompt and vigorous protection by the state."

After taking the affidavits of Johnson and MacCulloch, McBlair promised that his letter would be delivered to the governor.

"I hope you can take care of yourselves until the state can step in and give you proper protection," McBlair told MacCulloch just before the *Michigan* set sail. As soon as the *Michigan* docked in Chicago on June 6, McBlair mailed the affidavits and his letter to the governor.

Michigan's Governor Bingham studied the letter from Captain McBlair very carefully before drafting a response.

"I will submit the affidavits to our attorney general, and if justice can be done, it will," he wrote to the captain. *"I regret to say, however, that the shrewdness of 'King Strang' in procuring a separate county for the Beaver Islands has made it almost an impossibility to bring him to trial."*

McBlair understood that the governor's hands were tied by the decision of the state attorney general, but he wasn't satisfied with the potential outcome.

He wrote to his superior, the Secretary of the Navy, and told him what he had in mind.

"I plan to stop at Beaver Island and render assistance to those citizens threatened by the hostility of Strang," he wrote. *"I will proceed with a cautious regard for the laws of the state and my public duties."*

McBlair wouldn't personally engage in a battle with Strang, but he could offer safe passage to frightened Mormons who wanted to leave the island. He believed it was his duty to do so.

———◆•◆———

MacCulloch called a meeting in the backroom of the store with Wentworth and Bedford.

"Frank and I have taken care of your escape route," he told them. He was sober. His need to drink was supplanted by his need for accurate assassination planning.

Wentworth and Bedford leaned in, feeling both frightened and exhilarated.

"We're really going to do this?" Wentworth said. He'd been thinking for quite some time that talking about killing Strang was as satisfying as actually killing him might be. He'd never killed a man, and wasn't sure he really wanted to start at that point in his life.

"Of course we're going to do this," Bedford said. He'd suffered more than a mere insult from Strang, and he wanted the ultimate revenge for the unjust physical assault he'd suffered.

"Frank and I spoke to the captain of the navy warship, the *Michigan*, last time he was in port," MacCulloch said. "The *Michigan* will be back here June 16. I have every reason to believe the captain will give you the protection you will need after the deed is done."

"It's really happening," Bedford said. He grinned at the thought.

"Prepare yourselves for that day. In the meantime, for God's sakes, stay out of trouble."

CHAPTER 71
JUNE, 1856

The *USS Michigan* slid gracefully up to the pier at Beaver Island in the early afternoon on June 16. After giving the orders to have the ship secured and the gangplank lowered, Captain McBlair walked over to Johnson and MacCulloch's store. The two men were waiting for him.

"Things are about the same here, Captain," MacCulloch said. "But now Strang is having his men loot and plunder from our storage buildings. He hates us, and hates our wives for defying his bloomer decree. We live in fear every day that soon he'll burn our store and finish us off."

It was an exaggeration, but McBlair was ready to believe every word MacCulloch said.

MacCulloch continued, "If you could just talk to Strang, perhaps you could convince him to call off his hounds and leave us alone. He will respect you as a decorated man of the U.S. Navy." MacCulloch gave McBlair his most respectful smile, mixed with some false humility for good effect.

"I could try, I suppose. I've got to get back to my ship, but I'll send one of my men to fetch Strang so we can talk. I can't promise you anything, however. It seems everyone is of the opinion that Strang is a very mule-headed man."

"It will be most appreciated if you could at least try," Johnson said.

"You have my word that I shall."

Johnson and MacCulloch kept the true nature of their plans to themselves. They knew Captain McBlair, no matter how sympathetic he was to them and their plight, would never sanction murder.

McBlair headed back to the *Michigan*, leaving MacCulloch and Johnson to return to the store's back room, where Bedford and Wentworth were waiting.

"It's all set," MacCulloch told them. "Later this afternoon, McBlair will send one of his men to fetch Strang. When Strang comes to the *Michigan*, that will be your chance to shoot him. Then you can jump on board and sail to Mackinac, where you'll be safe from Strang's men."

Bedford and Wentworth looked at each other. This was it. This was the big moment they'd been waiting for.

"So now we wait," Wentworth said.

"Yes, we wait," MacCulloch. "We wait, and we watch, and then you start shooting."

MacCulloch, Johnson, Wentworth and Bedford stepped out onto the front porch of the store, where dozens of people had gathered to admire the sight of the mighty *USS Michigan* as sailors loaded cordwood onto the ship. Its appearance had changed since it made its first visit to Beaver Island five years ago. It had topsail rigging instead of the more cumbersome barkentine rigging. It looked sleeker and faster, with the triangular sails pointing out over the bow. Crewmen efficiently lowered the sails and looped the deck lines around cleats while the islanders watched with fascination. Anytime a United States Navy warship sailed into port was a time of excitement.

Dolan and Gwen were among the crowd gathered on the porch.

"She's a beauty," Dolan said as he admired the ship.

"If you say so," Gwen replied. "But I don't care much for the appearance of those cannons." Gwen was averse to the sight of heavy weaponry. She had an innate distrust of the U.S. government.

Dolan put his arm around her. "Don't worry; they're not pointed at us."

Phebe Wentworth and Ruth Ann Bedford were tending to the gardens at their respective homes instead of mingling with the people at the store. Their husbands had told them not to go anywhere near the harbor that day, claiming trouble was afoot and they didn't want them to get caught up in a ruckus. The women didn't ask for details. It was a beautiful summer day and they were happy to be outside snapping peas and beans off the vines.

Wentworth and Bedford had concealed their weapons under their shirts. Wentworth was armed with MacCulloch's infamous Colt Paterson revolver, while Bedford was planning to make do with a simpler Ruger horse pistol.

They saw a smartly uniformed man leave the *Michigan* and head up to Strang's house.

"Get ready," MacCulloch whispered to them.

Strang was sitting in his parlor with his four pregnant wives when the ship's pilot knocked on his door.

After answering the door, Strang invited the man in.

"Officer St. Bernard, sir," the man introduced himself. He had the typical appearance of a Navy officer; narrow build, dressed in a crisp, dark blue uniform trimmed with shiny brass buttons that bore the naval emblem.

"What can I do for you?" Strang asked pleasantly.

"Captain McBlair has requested the honor of your presence on board," St. Bernard answered. "He has some business he'd like to discuss with you."

"Happy to accommodate the good captain," Strang said. He grabbed his new, rounded plug hat and popped it on his head, thinking he should be as dapper in his appearance as the young naval officer.

The two men headed out Strang's front door and shared light conversation about the fine weather as they made their way to the harbor.

Bedford and Wentworth knew the moment was upon them. They stepped off the store's porch and tried to walk calmly and inconspicuously to the new, long pier that had been built to accommodate large steamers. The pier stretched into the harbor, but was dwarfed by the *Michigan*, which extended far beyond the end of the pier. The two men resisted the urge to look over their shoulders at Strang and his companion, who were also approaching the pier. Sweating nervously, Bedford and Wentworth arrived at the pier just minutes before Strang. There was a tall pile of cordwood sitting on the foot of the dock; Bedford and Wentworth hid behind it, then pulled their weapons out from under their shirts.

The youngest child of George Miller was wading in the shallow water next to the pier, and saw the two men hide behind the cordwood. He also saw them pull out pistols.

"Brother Strang, they are going to shoot you!" he shouted to his king as Strang stepped onto the pier, but it was too late.

Bedford and Wentworth both leapt out from behind the stacked cordwood and shot at an unsuspecting Strang. Naval Officer St. Bernard, who had been accompanying Strang, jumped into the water to avoid being shot.

Bedford's shot whistled through Strang's round hat and grazed the side of his head.

Wentworth's shot was more effective. His bullet found its way into the lower part of Strang's back.

Strang collapsed on the dock on his left side, then turned to see who shot him. He looked up, dazed, to see Alex Wentworth running for the gangplank of the *Michigan*.

"Come back!" Bedford shouted at him. "I've got no more bullets!"

Wentworth was in a state of shock, adrenaline racing through his body, but he obeyed his friend. He returned to where Bedford was standing, breathing heavily as he watched Strang attempt to move.

"Shoot him again," Bedford said. "Kill him. He's not dead."

Horrified, Wentworth cocked his pistol once more and fired his weapon at Strang's head. From a distance of five feet, he could hardly miss. The bullet buried itself in the right side of Strang's face. Blood and shards of bone exploded from his face and sprayed onto the dock. Wentworth felt sick. He ran again toward the gangplank, leaving Bedford behind.

Bedford still wasn't satisfied. Strang was still moving, albeit very little. With no bullets left in his pistol, Bedford took the handle of his gun and clubbed Strang in the face over and over until the gun barrel separated from the handle and only a piece of the pistol remained in his hand. Then he, too, took off running for the *Michigan's* gangplank.

Several astonished crewmen saw the entire assassination attempt. As Bedford and Wentworth ran past them and onto the ship, one of them asked what the hell just happened.

"We killed the son of a bitch, that's what happened," Bedford said.

The people standing on Johnson and MacCulloch's porch couldn't believe what had just occurred barely 100 feet away from them. Some women fainted. Others got sick. Everyone ran in different directions, some to the dock to see if their king was still alive; others to their homes to hide from the horror.

Dolan looked at Gwen with a face drained of color.

"I never cared for the man, but what just happened is all wrong," Dolan said.

"I agree, that was awful. Is there anything we can do?" Gwen asked.

"I don't know," Dolan said. "There are quite a few Mormons gathered around Strang. I don't think we can be of much help."

Gwen looked at the gathering of Mormons on the dock.

"They're all crying and praying," Gwen noted. "We might be able to do something of actual use. Let's go see."

The two of them headed to the dock, bumping their way through clusters of Strang's followers.

The store owners had quietly slipped back inside and retired to the privacy of the back room, where they poured themselves a hefty shot of whiskey.

"The king is dead," MacCulloch said as he raised his glass in a toast to Johnson.

"And our hands are clean," MacCulloch said as he returned the toast.

"I do hope Tom and Alex are treated fairly."

The two men clinked glasses and downed their whiskey in one swallow.

———◆◆◆———

On board the *Michigan*, Bedford and Wentworth turned themselves in to Captain McBlair.

"We did it, we confess," Wentworth said, eager to get the weight of his crime off his chest.

"Yes, we did, and we'd do it again to protect our families and the others who have suffered at the hands of that vicious king," Bedford said.

"I'll secure you in a safe place until we get to Mackinac Island," McBlair said. "Then I'll have to turn you over to the authorities there."

McBlair's first action was to send the ship's surgeon, Dr. McClelland, to see if Strang was dead or alive. Then McBlair ordered two crewmen to escort Bedford and Wentworth to the galley. Instead of imprisoning the men in a dank, dark broom closet below decks, McBlair put the two men in the spacious galley with plenty of food and one officer to guard them.

Dr. McClelland arrived at Strang's side, checked for a pulse, and to his surprise, he found one.

"Help me! We need to move this man!" he called out. Gwen and Dolan were approaching when they heard the call, and picked up their pace to get to Strang.

Dolan was shocked when he saw the damage that had been inflicted by the attackers. Strang lay crumpled awkwardly, completely unconscious and near death in a pool of his own blood.

Gwen stepped up next to the doctor. "He's bleeding excessively from this wound," she said as she pressed her fingers to a gash above his left ear. It was from Bedford's shot, which nicked an artery. Gwen kept pressure on the gash to stem the bleeding.

"Can you help me get him to a place where I can treat him?" the ship's doctor asked.

"Yes," Dolan said. "Lucy's is the closest. Let's take him there."

Dolan and the doctor enlisted the help of Phineas Wright and Lorenzo Hickey, who had come running when they heard the gunshots. While Gwen kept pressure on Strang's head wound, the four men carried Strang to Lucy's house.

"Oh my God," Lucy said when she answered the door and saw Strang. "Bring him into the parlor. I'll get buckets of clean water and rags."

The men laid Strang down on the floor of Lucy's home, on top of a thick rag rug. Dr. McClelland began to examine Strang to assess the damage. In addition to the gash above his ear, which Gwen was still pressing, he found Wentworth's second bullet lodged in Strang's cheekbone, just below his right eye. Wentworth's first shot was embedded in Strang's lower back, just a hair's breadth from his spine.

There were cuts and bruises all over Strang's face from Bedford's repeated blows with his gun. While Wentworth's bullet had splintered his face, Bedford's pistol whipping left it completely pulverized. If it weren't for his red beard and wavy hair, Strang would have been unidentifiable.

While Lucy filled a bucket of water from her rain barrel, she fought back tears. It had been a long time since she had felt genuine affection for James, but this was an unspeakable outrage. In his mangled, unconscious state, Lucy immediately pitied the once-powerful but now-helpless man. She felt a surge of guilt for the many times she had confronted him and unleashed her harsh feelings at him, holding nothing back. Now it was too late to fix the rift that had come between them.

She carried the bucket to her parlor while she wiped away her tears.

"Will he make it?" she asked the doctor, but sensed she already knew the answer to the question. She couldn't imagine how such a broken, bullet-ridden body could survive.

"Unlikely, but you never know," McClelland said.

Gwen looked up at Lucy and shook her head no. Yet she kept her fingers on Strang's head, staunching the flow of his blood.

Strang survived the night. After the doctor determined that Strang could be moved, six strong Mormon men moved him carefully back to his own home, where his wives were frantically waiting.

Whatever differences the four sister wives may have had among themselves before the shooting, they set them aside and circled the wagons around their husband, tending to him around the clock. While one wife bathed his wounds, another would watch the children. The third wife would prepare food while the fourth kept clean linens on Strang's bed.

"Is he going to live?" Phoebe kept asking repeatedly.

"He has always lived a blessed life," Elvira said. "The angels are always watching out for him. He will survive, with the help of our prayers."

And pray they did. But if God heard their prayers, He knew they were praying for themselves as well as for their husband. They were all with child, and were terrified of what life would be like as young widows with infants to care for and no husband to provide for them.

When Strang regained consciousness, he spoke to Elvira first.

"I want to go home to Voree," he said, his speech garbled due to his shattered cheek. "I want to see my parents. I want to see Mary again before I die."

Elvira resisted an impulse to slap him. She couldn't believe the first request her husband made after regaining consciousness was to return to Wisconsin and see his first wife.

"I think that sort of travel would be very hard on you," she said, suppressing her desire to lash out at him.

"I must get back to Voree," Strang said again. "I must see Mary and my other children. I want to see my parents. I don't think I'm going to be long for this world, and I must set things right before I meet my Maker."

Elvira then understood her husband's motives, and realized it had nothing to do with any romantic desire to see his first wife. He wanted to make amends for his wrongdoings in case he died.

"All right, James, whatever you want. I'll make the arrangements for you. But I think you need to rest up a few more days before you make the trip."

While Strang kept hanging onto his life by a thread, Wentworth and Bedford were enjoying their freedom on Mackinac Island.

McBlair had fulfilled his obligation to transport the would-be assassins to Mackinac and had turned them over to the sheriff who, in turn, escorted them up to the jailhouse. Wentworth and Bedford experienced a few tense moments when they were placed in a jail cell and the iron door clanked shut behind them.

But it was temporary. As soon as McBlair had returned to his ship, the jail cell door was opened by the sheriff and the two men were walked back into the main room of the jailhouse where at least a dozen lawmen, council members and fishermen waited to greet them. The sheriff was Julius Granger, former town constable when Mackinac had been under Mormon control. He escorted Bedford and Wentworth to the county courtroom where the justice of the peace was ready to hear their case.

The hearing lasted less than one hour, and no charges were brought against Bedford and Wentworth. But before discharging the prisoners, the judge informed them that each would have to pay $1.25 for court costs.

"I'll assume you're good for it, so you don't have to pay it now," he said. "Therefore, you're free to go."

Granger then took the men down to Jillet's and asked the bartender to put a bottle of whiskey on the bar. Granger opened the bottle of whiskey, filled three glasses and handed two of them to Wentworth and Bedford, keeping the third for himself.

"Here's to the brave men of Beaver Island who have taken down King Strang!" he said, raising his glass to the men. The others in the tavern cheered.

Soon everyone on Mackinac Island assumed Strang was dead. Archie, Will and Teddy were happy to believe that was the case. They drank one ale after another as they planned their return to Beaver Island.

"We're going back home at last," Will said. "Don't tell my father I said this, but I've missed him so much I could hug him all day!"

"I won't tell if you won't," Teddy said, "But I've missed him just as much."

Archie was giddy with joy at the thought of his reunion with Lucy. He sat on his bar stool, dreamy-eyed, ignoring the boys' banter.

"Archie, you must be ready to go back," Will said. "You've got a little girl and a lovely lady waiting for you."

"Well, I suppose it wouldn't be too terrible to return to Beaver Island," he said, giving the younger men a wink. Then he finished his beer and said, "Let's get packing. I've been yearning to go home ever since I left."

As they left Jillet's, they missed crossing paths with the captain and co-captain of the *Seraphim* by about a minute.

———◆•◆———

"Well, I'll be. Somebody finally killed the bastard," Nagle said after he'd taken a seat at the bar.

"This could put a damper on our looting and raiding endeavors," Pentour said. "We can't lay the blame at the king's feet if the king is dead."

"I guess we'll just have to go back to good old-fashioned stealing then, with nobody to blame but ourselves," Nagle chuckled. "With Strang dead, I'll bet there's a lot of good stuff to steal on Beaver Island."

Nathan Bowman walked into Jillet's and joined them.

"Did I hear you mention Beaver Island?" he asked after ordering a whiskey and a beer chaser. He'd also heard the news about Strang, which made him feel somewhat vindicated.

"Yes," Nagle said. "Now that the almighty King James Strang is dead, we think it's high time we paid a visit to his island and relieve his pathetic followers of their belongings."

Bowman stroked his broken nose, remembering when Strang had banished him from the island. Then he also remembered Lucy LaFleur, who had paved the way for his downfall by telling Strang about his so-called abusive treatment of his wife. Strang was dead, but Lucy LaFleur had escaped without any punishment. So far. With any luck, that was about to change.

"I can think of nothing that would give me more pleasure than making a trip to Beaver Island and righting a few wrongs," Bowman said.

CHAPTER 72

JUNE, 1856

The men on Mackinac Island didn't know it, but they were celebrating the death of Strang prematurely. He continued to hang on, slipping in and out of consciousness in his home on Beaver Island. When he was conscious, Elvira was the one to decide who would be allowed to visit her husband. She was rigorous in her efforts to protect Strang while he was recuperating.

For nine days after the shooting, a group of Mormons gathered to pray and sing hymns in front of Strang's home. It must have been working, because Strang started to regain a scrap of his strength, although he was paralyzed from the waist down from Wentworth's bullet in his back.

Hickey and Chidester paid a visit to the house, where they begged Elvira to let them see Strang.

"We must see him, Elvira; it's church business that cannot be ignored," Hickey told her.

"Very well, but don't get him overly excited. He needs his rest." She then escorted the men to the bedroom where Strang lay.

They tried to suppress their looks of shock when they saw Strang and his fractured face.

"King James, we need to know what to do now, and what to tell your flock," Chidester said.

Strang was propped up on pillows that Elvira had put behind his head and back. He looked small and frail, which was terribly upsetting to Hickey.

"Tell our brethren in a quiet way that they need to be prepared to do whatever it takes to protect their families," Strang said. "I don't want you to start a panic, but it might be wise for people to have weapons at the ready in case the island is attacked by Gentiles while I'm incapacitated."

"That we can do," Chidester said, then looked down at his big feet and back up at Strang. "Then there's the delicate matter I don't want to bring up, but must," he said. "King James, you need to appoint a successor in the tragic event that you don't pull through."

Strang winced. "I can't think about that right now," he told them. "Perhaps, God willing, it won't be necessary." In truth, Strang couldn't abide the thought that his church might go on without him. It seemed unfathomable.

He wasn't the only person who thought the church couldn't go on without him. The editor of the *Detroit Advertiser* ran an article about the assassination attempt.

"Strang was the heart and soul as well as the intellect of the Mormon gang and it is to be strongly hoped that his impending death will break them up and scatter them abroad. There remains no man among them capable of wielding Strang's influence or of filling his place."

On June 28, Strang was carried on a mattress from his home to the *Louisville*, a steamer headed to Racine, Wisconsin. His wife Sarah went with him, along with Chidester and Sarah's parents Phineas and Amanda Wright. Elvira, Betsy, and Phoebe stayed behind, believing they had to protect their home for Strang's return, if indeed he could ever make the return trip.

"Please, King James, appoint a successor, just in case," Chidester pleaded with Strang on the trip to Racine.

"I cannot do that at this time," Strang said, choosing to ignore the unpalatable topic.

When the *Louisville* docked in Racine, Wisconsin on July 1, Strang was starting to feel better. His father and brother met him at the boat. They brought a couch from their home and laid him on the couch, then loaded it into a train car headed for Burlington. It was fortunate for Strang that the rail line had been completed the year before. A trip that long in a horse-drawn wagon would have been exceptionally painful.

When Strang was carried into his parent's home in Voree on the White River, his mother was waiting expectantly. She couldn't remember the last time she'd seen her son, and the man she looked at was hardly recognizable as her own child.

"My Lord, what have they done to you?" she cried, her hand reaching out to touch his black and blue face.

"My enemies have always been nipping at my heels," Strang replied. "They will get their proper punishment when they meet their Maker. They will be cast to Satan, and I will be a celebrated martyr who will be forever remembered and exalted."

It was a remark Strang's mother found typical of her egotistical son. Even near death, his thoughts went to his own fame.

Sarah Strang stayed by her husband's side for days, believing that he was going to get better.

"See?" she said to her mother-in-law. "He's brightening up. His face is healing. God is on his side, and he will recover from this terrible thing."

Strang's own mother had her doubts. Her son still had two bullets in his body and the gash on the side of his head looked infected. He couldn't move from the waist down, and would never walk again even if he survived. How could a king rule his kingdom from his bed?

Strang's first wife Mary was a good woman. When she learned that Strang was in Voree, she went to see him. Whatever anger she might have harbored for her husband melted away when she saw him. Her once powerful husband was now a broken shell.

Strang reached for her hand when she came to stand by his bed. "I'm sorry, Mary, I truly am. I have always loved you and our children." Tears came to his left eye, the one that functioned. His right eye was a green and purple landscape of pulp and scabs.

Mary had always wondered what she would say to her husband if she had the opportunity to talk to him again. Now, all her thoughts of scolding him and punishing him for the way he had treated her seemed pointless.

"I know that, James. And in my heart of hearts, I have always loved you."

With a clear conscience, Mary left Strang in the care of his fourth wife and his mother. That chapter of her life was officially closed.

CHAPTER 73
JULY, 1856

Without their leader, the Mormons on Beaver Island were in a calamitous state of confusion. Some decided there was no future on the island without their king, who had left them to return to his old home of Voree, so they followed suit. They boarded steamers and schooners headed for Wisconsin. They would follow their king wherever he went. Others became paralyzed by indecision, waiting for someone to tell them what to do.

They didn't have to wait long. No Mormon leader emerged to tell them what to do, but like warm air expanding to fill a vacuum, a swarm of non-Mormon bellicose voices came to take the place of Strang's once powerful baritone.

Boat after boat of Gentiles headed to Beaver Island, coming from Mackinac Island and its nearby neighbor, St. Helena Island. As word traveled, boats came from Cross Village and Pine River as well.

The waters of northern Lake Michigan churned under the movement of what became an armada of boats. Commercial steamships also made their way to Beaver Island, knowing that fleeing Mormons were going to need passage to other places on the lake.

Roger Nagle, Kent Pentour, Nathan Bowman and their crew sailed the *Seraphim* out of Mackinac harbor, along with a fleet of about 60 other boats, all headed to St. James. Archie, Will and Teddy were near the back of the fleet.

Nagle was elated to be heading to Beaver Island, where he planned to do his fair share of looting and burning. Pentour had heard the rumors about

Strang's counterfeit money operation and was fantasizing about finding the counterfeiting machine that would allow him to make as much money as he wanted or needed.

Bowman had different thoughts. Ever since he'd latched onto the idea that Lucy LaFleur was entirely responsible for everything that had gone wrong in his life, he'd been plotting his revenge.

He planned to rape her. Rape her, then kill her.

She was beautiful and well-shaped, but that wasn't what made the thought of raping her so tantalizing. She was supremely self-confident and had always treated him with arrogant disdain. He couldn't wait to strip her of her power and her clothes and see her quake, naked and fearful, in front of him.

He'd already told Nagle of his plans and explained that Lucy was a strong woman and it would take two of them to pin her down.

"Fine, I'll help you, but then I get to have a go at her as well," Nagle said.

"You can have a go at her as many times as you want," Bowman said. "We can tie her up so everyone can have a turn." The thought of the entire crew of the *Seraphim* raping Lucy gave Bowman an erection.

On Beaver Island, the ransacking and pillaging had begun with the arrival of the first boats.

Mackinac County's Sheriff Julius Granger was among the first to arrive at Beaver Island. He had a handful of warrants for the arrest of some of the Mormon members of the Circle of 12, but learned they'd already taken a boat to Wisconsin.

Wingfield Watson was walking from the store to his home three miles inland, where Jane was waiting for him. She'd just given birth to their second daughter two days earlier and Wingfield had gone into town for supplies.

The Mackinac sheriff stopped Wingfield.

"Where are you going?" he asked gruffly, recognizing Wingfield as a Mormon from earlier trips to Mackinac.

"Home," Wingfield said.

"Where's home?"

"About three miles inland."

The sheriff gave him a stern look. "Well, get your things down to the harbor by 1 o'clock tomorrow or your house will be burned over your head."

"My wife just gave birth two days ago! She's in no condition to travel!"

"Then that's a goddam mess of your own that you've gotten yourself into."

"That's pretty harsh of you," Wingfield said.

"You want harsh? You do as I say or I'll tie you to that cherry tree and whip you."

Wingfield could see that there was no point in trying to reason with the sheriff. He looked like he was ready to rip the head off a porcupine with his bare teeth.

"All right. Let me just go get some help, is that permissible?"

The sheriff nodded, so Wingfield headed to Lucy's home.

Wingfield wasted no time explaining the situation to Lucy.

"Oh my goodness, this is terrible!" Lucy said. "Of course I'll help you. Just let me drop Lily off at Johnson and MacCulloch's. Rose can watch her for a while."

Rose had taken a liking to Lily. She often amused the little girl with stories of shop elves spying at her from behind sacks of flour and dancing on the fish barrels after the store was closed. It was an unlikely friendship that Lucy couldn't have predicted, but there it was.

After depositing Lily with Rose, Lucy made the three-mile walk to the Watson's home in a little over 30 minutes. She found Jane in tears, clinging to her new baby. Little Abby hovered by her side.

"I can't believe this is happening," Jane said. "Where will we go? What will we do?"

"I don't know, but you'll be fine," Lucy said. "You're both young and strong. You'll manage."

Lucy helped pack boxes of clothing and dry goods, and lastly, a large burlap bag with baby supplies. Wingfield loaded his beloved stove onto his wagon, his most valuable possession, and then he and Lucy tossed the other items on behind the stove.

"That's that," Lucy said, giving the final box she'd loaded a pat. "Now I suggest you all get a good night's sleep and get ready for your long day ahead. I'll come tomorrow morning to help you get to the harbor."

Jane gave her a weak smile. "Thank you, Lucy. You've always been so wonderful to us."

Lucy squeezed her hand. "And you've been wonderful to me. I will miss you. But not just yet. I'll see you in the morning."

As Lucy walked back to town alone, she could smell smoke and saw flames shooting into the sky from the tabernacle. It was on fire.

She was nearing the tabernacle from a deserted side road when she saw Nathan Bowman. He was standing at the edge of the men watching the tabernacle burn.

"Well, well, if it isn't Lucy LaFleur," he said as he approached her, after nudging the big man next to him. Lucy was shocked by Bowman's appearance. He'd once been a handsome young man, but she could see he'd aged poorly, with deep wrinkles dividing his face into a crooked patchwork quilt. His teeth were chipped and pocked with black cavities, and his nose was permanently skewed to the left from the punch Archie had delivered years ago. Lucy stared at him and the big man who was walking with him. They both had guns on their hips. Lucy suddenly felt scared.

Bowman lunged first, grabbing her by her upper arms, pulling her toward the side of the road. Lucy instinctively responded by kicking at him, almost landing a blow to his groin but catching him in the inner thigh instead. The other man moved in and grabbed her around the waist. He wrapped his right leg around both of Lucy's legs, rendering her immobile.

"I'm not looking as nice as you remembered me, right?" Bowman said. His face was inches from Lucy's, and she recoiled from his horrible breath. It smelled like he'd been gnawing on a rat carcass. "And it's entirely your fault. I had a good thing going here, and you ruined it all. First, I'm pretty sure you're the one who snuck my wife off the island. Then you reported my perfectly legal activities with my second wife to King Strang. And then you got your big friend Archie to beat me up. Last, but not least, you got me kicked off the island. Now you'll pay."

The two men pushed Lucy to the ground and Nagle held her firmly while Bowman started ripping her dress.

"Might as well use your own dress to tie you up," he said as he ripped a large stretch of her hem from the rest of the skirt. Nagle helped drag her to a nearby tree, and then sat on her while Bowman tied her wrists together over her head. Then he tied her to the tree.

Tearing at her skirt again, Bowman freed another piece of fabric, which he looped under her left knee, then forced it to bend so he could tie it to her wrists over her head. He did the same for her right knee.

Lucy couldn't move, but she refused to let Bowman see her fear. She knew bullies like Bowman loved to see fear in other people's eyes. Lucy laid still, her knees bent and legs spread wide, and stared at him with narrowed, glittering eyes.

Bowman took the skinning knife that was hanging around Lucy's neck and slowly cut away the bodice of her dress. Her breasts and dark nipples were completely exposed in seconds. Bowman flicked one nipple with the tip of her own knife.

"Nice," he said, looking at her and waiting to see the fear in her face. It wasn't there.

He continued to wield her skinning knife down her front, cutting the waistband on her dress and continuing down until her skirt lay at her sides. Then her grabbed her undergarments with his right fist and jerked hard, momentarily lifting Lucy's back from the ground. The threadbare fabric ripped easily, leaving her completely naked.

Bowman pressed the toe of his boot against her groin. Then he looked again at her face, hoping to see the terror he craved.

Nothing.

Lucy just kept her eyes leveled at him, unblinking. Black fireballs burning holes into his own eye sockets. It was disconcerting to Bowman.

"Are you going to fuck her or not?" Nagle asked. "Cause if you're not, I'd sure like to."

"Of course I am," Bowman snapped. "I just want her to suffer a little longer."

Bowman began to unbutton his pants, but was horrified to see he was as flaccid as a dead tadpole.

"If you're in such a hurry, you can go first," Bowman said to Nagle, hoping that if he watched him rape Lucy, it might give him the erection he needed to take his turn. He knew Nagle well enough to know he would inflict as much pain on Lucy as possible while he raped her. Bowman felt his little tadpole awakening.

"Give me that knife," Nagle said after unbuttoning his pants. He had a large erection that curved slightly to the left.

Bowman handed him the skinning knife, then took a position standing a few feet down from Lucy's spread legs and slightly off to the side, where he would have a good view of the action.

Nagle knelt in between Lucy's legs. He stuck the point of the knife into the soft skin of her inner thigh and pulled it toward her knee, leaving a bright, shallow line of blood.

"I like to fuck women while they're bleeding," he said as he roughly squeezed her left breast with his free hand.

He inserted the knife point into her other thigh and repeated his motion, leaving a matching red line in her inner leg. He watched the line of blood pop from her light brown skin. Then he smeared blood onto his scarred hand and rubbed it in her pubic hair.

"I do believe we're almost ready," he said, then leaned forward to bite her nipple hard enough to draw a trickle of blood. Lucy gasped.

Nagle made the mistake of standing up to unbutton his pants.

The shot came from so close by that Bowman was temporarily deafened. Nagle's head snapped backward when the bullet entered his neck just below the base of his skull.

Bowman turned away from his dead friend to see where the shot came from. He saw Archie Donnelly standing there, one-hundred and eighty pounds of pure Irish rage. Bowman made a move for his gun, but he wasn't fast enough.

Archie was upon him immediately, tackling him and forcing him to the ground, as Bowman had done minutes earlier to Lucy.

Bowman tried to defend himself with Lucy's skinning knife that he grabbed from where it had fallen. He couldn't reach his gun with Archie pinning him down. He flailed at Archie with the knife, who took Bowman's hand and banged it on the hard, dry dirt until the knife came out of his grasp. Jerking his hand from Archie's grip, Bowman went for Archie's throat. But Archie moved faster. He grabbed the knife and shoved it in the side of Bowman's neck, where he struck his artery.

Bowman passed out as the blood spurted from his neck. Soon, he wasn't breathing and the blood slowed to a trickle before it stopped leaking onto the ground.

Archie jumped off him and, still holding the knife, ran to Lucy, where he cut the fabric that bound her. He wrapped the remnants of her skirt around her, and while she sat up, he peeled off his cotton shirt and gave it to her.

After she pulled his big shirt onto her shaking body, she clung to him desperately.

"Oh Archie, thank God it's you," she said, sinking against him. Then the tears came, followed by heaving sobs as the adrenaline ebbed from her body.

"There there, it will be all right my love," Archie said, stroking her head with one hand and keeping his arm tightly around her shoulders.

"How – how – did you find me?" Lucy said in between sobs.

"I went to your house, and you weren't there. Then I saw the fire and headed this way. I took the shortcut I knew you always used."

They sat wordlessly for awhile, Archie gently rocking Lucy in his arms until he felt the tension in her body loosen up.

Lucy broke her embrace from Archie, stood up and walked over to Bowman's corpse.

"You putrefying piece of peckerwood!" she shouted as she kicked his dead body. Tears were rolling down her face again, but this time they were hot, angry tears.

"You sadistic rodent!" She kicked his lifeless groin.

"You sniveling, sick-minded snake!" She kicked him again, then shoved her foot into his side and rolled him over so he was lying on his front. His head flopped, dead eyes staring at the ground, crooked nose mashed into the dirt.

Lucy kept kicking him, over and over, harder and harder, hurling insults with each kick as the tears kept coming.

Archie came up from behind and wrapped his arms around her. Gently, he spoke into her ear.

"He can't get any deader than he already is," he said.

"I know." She gave Bowman one more kick, then leaned back against Archie's chest, her arms crossed over his.

When he felt her start to breathe more slowly, Archie spoke. "Come on, let's get you home. We can cut through the cedar swamp, out of sight."

Lucy nodded, unable to find any more words. She was physically and emotionally spent.

After they got to Lucy's home, Archie carefully cleaned the blood from her legs.

"Luckily they're not deep cuts; he just scratched the surface," he said.

"I'll be all right," Lucy said as she regained her usual strength and composure. She got dressed while Archie waited for her in the kitchen, wanting to give her privacy.

"Where's Lily?" Archie asked, suddenly worried about his missing daughter.

"She's safe; I left her with Rose at the store. She and Rose have taken a liking to one another."

"Wonders never cease," Archie said as he smiled at Lucy.

They walked down the hill to Johnson and MacCulloch's store. The door was locked. Archie banged on it until Rose came to open it.

"I locked up because of all the craziness going on," Rose said. "Lily is in back, safe and sound."

The three of them went to the back room, where Lily was on the floor, playing with a doll Rose had given her. Lily looked curiously at Archie, and then the light of recognition spread across her tiny, upturned face.

"Papa?" she said, unsure if she was correct in guessing the identity of the big man in front of her.

"Yes, my little precious one," Archie said as he swept her off the floor and into his arms. Lily wrapped her arms tightly around Archie's neck and buried her head in his neck, her coppery curls tickling his chin.

The poignant reunion came to a halt after a few minutes, when Archie turned to Rose.

"What is going on?" he asked.

"The Gentiles have gone crazy," Rose said. "They've come from all over and they're kicking the Mormons off the island. I hope they don't think I'm a Mormon, because I'm not; not really."

"Where are Johnson and MacCulloch?" Archie asked.

"Protecting their homes," Rose said. "Frank said he's going to lock up his home and come back here."

Archie pulled Lucy aside and spoke quietly to her.

"We need to do something about those two dead men I left on the side of the road," Archie said quietly. "Dolan and the boys can help me."

"I'll help too," she answered quickly.

"No. You should stay with Lily."

Lucy grabbed Archie by the arm.

"I'm not leaving your side." A flicker of fear darted across her eyes.

"Okay. But I don't want Lily to see it. Do you think we can leave her with Rose for a while longer?"

When Lucy explained to Rose that they had urgent business to take care of, she was quick to keep Lily.

Dolan and Gwen were having a happy reunion with Will and Teddy, ignoring the pandemonium outside, when Lucy and Archie arrived. Archie didn't give the men any details, just told them he needed help with some heavy lifting and that shovels would be required. Dolan didn't ask questions; he went to his toolshed outside and grabbed two shovels.

The four men, Lucy and Gwen headed down the road, appalled at what they were seeing. In front of Strang's newspaper office, thousands of pages of the book he'd written, *The Book of the Law of the Lord*, were dancing in the breeze. His office had been ransacked and the piles of books waiting to be shipped for binding had been cast into the road out front. In every direction, they saw terrified Mormons carrying whatever belongings they could manage down to the harbor, where they would wait for boats to take them from the island.

Some Mormons tried to defend their homes, but the mob of angry Gentiles told them they would burn their homes down around them if they tried to stay.

Another group of wild-eyed men were shooting at Strang's home, peppering the whitewashed walls with bullets and pellets from shotguns. Strang's three wives, who had initially stayed on the island after their husband's departure, had since left with Benjamin and Margaret Wright and were on their way to Wisconsin. The home was empty.

A mob from Pine River was tearing through one home after another, tossing furniture outside, breaking dishes and then setting fire to the homes.

Archie steered his friends to the place where Nagle and Bowman lay dead.

"That's Nathan Bowman," Archie said, pointing to the corpse that already had flies buzzing around the blood-crusted gash in his neck.

"He and that other fellow attacked Lucy; I had to kill them," Archie said.

Will looked at Bowman. "Good riddance," he said.

"Who's the other one?" Dolan asked.

"A bad character. He and his crew were doing a lot of the stealing up and down the lake," Archie said. "I know the Mormons did some consecrating of their own, but that fellow was no Mormon. He just liked to burn and steal and then blame it on the Mormons."

Dolan tossed a shovel to Will, then walked 12 feet from the edge of the road with his shovel. He started digging.

"I'm guessing we're digging two graves," he said.

"I figure it's better that way," Archie replied. "Don't know what's going to happen next, but I don't want to get hauled away for murder."

"I totally agree," Dolan said. "We need you back. And these two got the end they deserved."

While the men took turns digging holes in the ground, Lucy tore herself away from Archie to go fetch Lily. She wanted her little family together in one place, and she assumed the dead men would be in the ground by the time she got Lily. Gwen walked with her. They saw marauders shooting at the chickens behind Strang's home, whooping and hollering while doing so.

"What did the chickens ever do to them?" Lucy asked. As she said it, she saw the Strang family goat succumb to a stray bullet. "I liked that goat," she said sadly.

The women stopped at Lorenzo Hickey's house along the way, worried that he and his new wife and baby might be getting burned out of their house. The house was still intact, but no one was inside. The couple was walking toward the beach, Sarah carrying the baby and Lorenzo dragging a wagon full of belongings.

"You're leaving, I take it," Lucy said, catching up to them.

"We must. We'll be killed if we stay here."

"Where will you go?"

"To Voree, where King James is," Lorenzo said simply.

Lucy put a hand on his arm and stopped him. Sarah continued to make her way to the beach with Gwen keeping her company.

"Lorenzo, it's over," Lucy said gently. "James will not survive his wounds. He will die, and his church will die with him. You could renounce your religion and stay here on the island."

Lorenzo couldn't stop his lower lip from quivering. He cupped his hand to his chin to hide it.

"No, I can't accept that," he said. "Even if our king dies, the church will go on. It only needs the faithful to stay strong."

Lucy knew there was no convincing Lorenzo otherwise. He had always been a man who needed his faith more than anything else. His faith cost him his first wife. Then it caused him to lose the chance to marry Huldy. Now it would cost him the chance to start a fresh life on Beaver Island.

"I can never be an apostate," Lorenzo continued lamely. "I tried that once, when I thought King James let me down, and I was miserable. I lost my mind. I will remain forever loyal to the prophet and the church he created."

He leaned in closer to Lucy. "I do want to visit Huldy and ask her if she'd like to go with us. Would you walk there with me? I'm afraid if I walk by myself one of these deranged people will kill me."

Lucy suspected she knew what Huldy's answer would be, but she agreed to accompany Lorenzo to the little cabin in the woods.

Huldy looked as if she'd been waiting for them. She was sitting on a tree stump outside.

In sign language and while speaking, Lorenzo said to her, "Huldy, we must go. But it breaks my heart to leave you behind. I don't think you're safe here. Why don't you come with Sarah and me? Not as my spirit wife, but as our friend."

Huldy looked at the ground, then up at Lorenzo. She signed, "I can't do that. This island is in an uproar right now, but things will calm down, and when they do, I want to be here. I can't go live with you and your new wife in some strange town. It just isn't right. And I want to see what island life can be like when it's free of religious tyranny."

Her signed comment about religious tyranny stung Lorenzo, but he took it stoically.

"I figured as much, but I had to ask," Lorenzo said. He bent and kissed her cheek. Huldy looked into his eyes one last time and then turned her face away. Her tears, sliding down her cheeks, were as mute as she was.

Since Huldy refused to leave her cabin, Lucy and Lorenzo reluctantly left her alone. They took a different path back to town so as not to leave an obvious trail through the fields and forest. On the walk, Lorenzo felt like his life was over and didn't care if the hooligans ransacking the island killed him. He changed his mind after he arrived safely at the beach, where his young bride and new baby were waiting for him. He would never have everything he wanted in life, but with any luck, he would always have a family and his faith.

Lucy left Lorenzo with his little family and went to Johnson and MacCulloch's to retrieve Lily.

"I don't want to leave you here alone," Lucy said to Rose as she took Lily's hand.

"I'll be fine, don't worry," Rose said. "And Frank will be back any moment now."

Lucy looked at the sky. The sun was low on the horizon, turning the billowing undersides of clouds a salmon pink.

"It's going to be dark soon, are you sure you'll be all right?"

Rose was touched by Lucy's concern. "Yes, Lucy, I'll be fine. I know where Frank keeps his guns, and they're loaded. Go now. You need to be with Archie."

When Lucy got home, she found Archie had made it there first.

"When will it stop?" Lucy asked Archie as they listened to the sounds of gunfire and log homes collapsing as flames crackled and consumed them.

"I don't know," Archie said. "I don't know."

Rose was still alone at the store when the sun went down. The sky became a smear of black and orange with fires streaking the night sky. She lit one small lantern and set it on the floor behind the counter, hoping it wouldn't attract looters, but she also didn't want to sit alone in a pitch-dark building.

When she heard a knock on the door, she grabbed one of Frank Johnson's pistols and took it with her. Her grip on the pistol relaxed when she saw it was Frank.

"My, I'd hate to die getting accidentally shot by my best employee," Frank said to Rose, lightening the mood. "Actually, I guess you're my only employee until Alex and Tom make it back from Mackinac. They're probably up there enjoying being hailed as heroes for shooting Strang."

"And leaving us to fend for ourselves," Rose said.

"We'll be fine, Rose," Frank said, but his eyes kept darting toward the windows. He had a lot of merchandize in the store and knew it made him a prime target for looting. He looked at the pistol that was still in Rose's hand.

"Do you know how to shoot that thing?" he asked her.

"Of course. I used to take Nathan's spare pistol and shoot at pine cones in the trees for practice, in case the day ever came that I could get a clean shot at him." Rose grinned.

"I think I'd better go to the back room and get my other pistol," Frank said. "I'd feel more comfortable if we were both armed."

He had barely left the main room of the store when a pair of burly, flush-faced men stepped onto the porch. The bigger of the two pulled out his gun and shot at the lock on the door. Rose leapt back, away from the men's line of sight, and pointed the gun at the door.

When they crashed through the door, Rose pulled the trigger. One of the two men spun around and then fell down with a cry of pain. At the same moment, Johnson came out of the storeroom, his pistol leading the way through the poorly lit room.

Rose pulled a bullet out of her apron pocket and reloaded Frank's gun. When the other intoxicated man staggered around to see where the shot came from, Rose took aim again and fired. She clipped him in the shoulder, but it was enough to knock him down. He joined his friend on the floor, where they both writhed in pain.

"Rose!" Frank said as he rushed to her. "Are you all right?" He put his arms around her and held her so close that she could only speak into his vest, where her mouth was pinned against him.

"I'm fine," she mumbled into the cloth.

Frank loosened his hold on her. "I can't believe you shot them both! You are one brave woman, Rose Pratt."

Rose's little bowtie mouth stretched to form a big, full smile, something she hadn't done in years.

"Aw, it was nothing," she said. "They made bigger targets than pine cones."

The two men on the floor began to thrash.

"What shall we do about them?" Rose asked.

"We'll tie them up and leave them right in front of the door," Frank said. "If anyone else comes in here with the notion of robbing us, these two will be an effective deterrent."

Rose noticed Frank had said 'us,' not 'me.' She felt tingly over his choice of the pronoun.

"They're not going to die or anything, are they?" Rose asked. "You never said anything about cleaning up dead bodies as being part of my job."

Frank laughed. "No, I think they'll be fine. I think you winged them. Judging by the commotion they're starting to make, I'd say the odds are very good they'll survive. Let's get them tied up."

Rose went to the side of the store where she knew loops of rope hung on the wall. She lifted one length of rope off its hook and brought it to Frank, who proceeded to tie the two men up together, their hands bound behind their backs, facing away from each other.

"I think we've had enough excitement for one night," Frank said. "Let's go home. Not your home, it's not safe to walk all the way through town. You should stay at my home tonight."

Rose gave him no argument. She slipped her arm through his and they walked away.

CHAPTER 74

JULY, 1856

After a long night of love-making and holding each other so tightly that not even a thread from the finest cotton could come between them, Archie and Lucy woke up.

They walked, bleary-eyed with arms around each other, onto Lucy's front porch where their noses were assaulted by the smell of lingering fires. Smoke still hovered in the air where cabins and homes were smoldering.

Lucy looked out at the village. The homes that hadn't been burned had been looted. Windows were broken and glass shards winked in the morning sun. Chairs and tables had been cast outside and lay upturned on the paths leading up to the houses. It looked like many battles had taken place and the victors had ruined most of the spoils.

"I have to go help Wingfield and Jane. I promised," Lucy said.

"I'm going with you."

"All right, but we'll need to take Lily with us. Will she be all right? I don't want her to see all of this destruction."

"She's going to see it sooner or later. Better to see it now, with both of us to keep her calm."

They walked the three miles inland to Jane and Wingfield's home, taking notice of the senseless damage that had been done. Fields of corn had been trampled; tomato plants ripped out by the roots; beans thrashed, and potato mounds flattened. Lucy shook her head at the waste of food.

When they reached the Watsons' home, Jane was inside nursing her new-born baby. Abby was outside with her father, who was squeezing a few more belongings on the wagon and hitching up his horse for the trip to town.

Jane could hardly stand up. Her delivery had been difficult; the baby girl was large and healthy, but had torn Jane on its way out.

There was no room on the wagon for Jane to ride. She and Wingfield decided it was imperative to fill the wagon with as many of their belongings as they could manage.

Archie held the horse's reins and led him toward the harbor, the wagon creaking under the weight of its contents every time one of the wooden wheels hit a hardened rut. Lucy held Abby's and Lily's hands as they walked; Wingfield carried his new baby girl in one arm, and put his other arm around Jane to support her.

When they made it to the harbor, no one spoke. It was too much to take in. Hundreds of Mormons lined the western shore of St. James Harbor, their paltry piles of belongings next to them, waiting for a boat to take them away. Tents had been pitched by the Saints who had spent the night on the beach, having been forced out of their homes the day before; campfires burned so breakfast could be cooked; and cattle lowed and fretted as if knowing a long, miserable boat ride lay in store for them.

After saying a profoundly sad farewell to Lucy and Archie, the Watsons boarded the *Buckeye State*, a 282-foot steamer headed for Chicago. Gentiles forced as many Mormons and their cargo onto the steamer as it could accommodate. The *Buckeye State* typically accommodated 250 passengers; on that trip, it carried 350. No one bothered to count the cattle and oxen also onboard.

More schooners came, and more Saints were forced to leave. In some cases, the Gentiles giving the orders would rush the Mormons onto a boat, promising their cargo would be loaded after them. But the boats sailed away while the Mormons looked back from the deck rail at the last of their worldly belongings still on shore, where the callous men were divvying it up among themselves.

Within 72 hours of the first Gentile boat's arrival from Mackinac Island, every last one of the 2,500 Mormons had been driven from the island. The only Mormons allowed to stay were those who had publicly renounced their beliefs. MacCulloch and Johnson were among the first to do so, followed by a few other men from the southern end of the island who were making a good living with the sawmill. They were quick to abandon their religion in the interest of keeping their businesses going and the money flowing.

Three days after the start of the uprising, Lucy said impulsively to Archie, "Let's walk over to Pisgah Bay." Lily, who had remained remarkably quiet for the past few hours, brightened. She loved Pisgah Bay. "Yes!" she shouted eagerly, bolting ahead of them in the direction of the bay. She, too, had had enough of the recent mayhem in her life.

The three of them cut through the forest over to the bay that was still and calm, undisturbed by the comings and goings of boats at St. James Harbor. They stood on the shore, looking out toward Garden Island.

"What now?" Lucy asked. "Our island is a smoldering pile of wreckage, overrun by ruffians."

"This too shall pass," Archie said. "We will start again. We'll put out the word that Beaver Island is a fine place for people who want to live in peace without interference from any religious orders. People will be allowed to follow the faith of their choosing."

"How do we do that?"

"I'm going to write letters to my people back home on Árainn Mhór Island. They're still struggling to rebuild their lives after the potato famine. They'll be happy to come to a place that is so much like home, yet offers work, food and freedom."

"If they're like you, then I will welcome them all," Lucy said happily, imagining an island filled with jovial, big-hearted Irishmen and women. Then she had a less pleasant thought.

"What about all these hedge pigs who are wreaking havoc on our island? Do you think they'll stay here?"

"I suppose a few of them will, but I think a lot of them came here to drive the Mormons out of northern Michigan. They'll take the valuables they looted and go back to wherever they came from."

Archie reassured her with a kiss. It was a delicious kiss that could have gone on for hours, but they were interrupted.

"Papa! Lulu!" Little hands tugged at each of them. "Let's catch minnows!"

They took off their shoes and, as they waded into the shallow water looking for minnows, Lucy caught sight of her reflection on the glassy surface of the water.

She started reflecting on all she had gained and lost over the past years: The arrival of Archie and Millie; the loss of Alice Bennett and her children, resting with Antoine at the bottom of the lake; Tom Bennett, finally laid to rest along the shore overlooking his favorite fishing grounds; Eliza Bowman, now living in Northport; Nathan Bowman, buried in a shallow grave along the side of a little-used road; the consummate fraud George Adams and his wife Louisa, living God knows where; Mary Strang, living in Wisconsin with her family; Millie, who was buried alone in the Mormon cemetery; Pete McKinley, who was living on Mackinac Island; Jonathan Pierce, the hard-fisted bully who had met his match with Lake Michigan's fury; and James Strang, a man who had unexpectedly come into her life and dragged her out of her self-imposed numbness, causing her to have feelings again. Sometimes it had been love she felt for him; other times it was rage and hatred. But the one thing she could always count on with James Strang was that he made her feel something all the time.

Lucy suddenly shivered.

"Did you feel that?" she asked Archie.

"I didn't feel anything, what do you mean?"

"I just got a chill, like a cold breeze off the lake."

Archie looked at the lake, which was still smooth. No breeze had ruffled its surface.

"I didn't feel anything," he said again. "I hope you're not coming down with something." He put a hand on her forehead to check for a fever.

"No, I'm fine. I don't know what it was."

It was July 8, 1856, the six-year anniversary of King Strang's coronation day. In Voree, Wisconsin, Dennis Chidester carefully closed the eyelids of his prophet James Jesse Strang, whose heart had just stopped beating.

EPILOGUE

The men who had ransacked Strang's newspaper office made use of the printing press to create their own piece of news just days after the Gentile takeover of Beaver Island.

They printed a proclamation for all to read, and nailed it to the signpost at St. James Harbor. It read:

> *EXTRA – ISLANDS REDEEMED – The dominion of King Strang is at an end. The band of marauders, once occupying the Beaver group of Islands, have fled at the approach of the Sheriff. The land is redeemed; a kingdom no longer exists upon the borders of one of our most populous states. The institutions of our country provide protection to all her citizens, especially to their religious freedom; but when its tenets are criminal and directly antagonistical to our laws and subversive of our constitution, we as citizens would prove remiss of our duties to permit a longer continuance of the evil.*
>
> *It should be a matter, therefore, of public rejoicing to all persons living contiguous to the lakes that this nest of banditti has been exterminated, and we would take this occasion to caution the citizens of Wisconsin against many of them who have fled there.*
>
> *Of this sad condition of things we are now happily set free – and we say again we have reason to congratulate ourselves and rejoice that the state has been relieved of an excrescence that had recently become intolerable.*

On July 9, *The Buckeye State* made a stop at Milwaukee, where 150 Mormons disembarked. One hundred more had decided to continue on to Chicago. Jane and Wingfield Watson were among those who stayed onboard.

When they reached Chicago, they were greeted with the terrible news that Strang had died. The faithful young couple found it impossible to believe. How could God give them a prophet to lead them out of darkness only to take him away?

The Watsons stood on the dock in Chicago with their two daughters and a meager pile of belongings. The stove was no longer with them; someone disembarking at Milwaukee had helped himself to it. The hot summer sun seeped through a hazy sky and the humidity was stifling. Other Mormons stood with them, at a loss for what to do next.

Amidst the crowd of gawkers staring at the Mormons was a tall, angular man who owned property on the wharf.

"Come on," he said to Watsons and the other Saints with them. "You need to get out of this sun. I have a warehouse across the street where you can rest until you find places to go." It was the first nice thing the Mormons had heard from a Gentile in days.

Strang was buried in the Saints' cemetery in Voree. Lorenzo Hickey opened the funeral service with a prayer that impressed even the surly Chidester.

"Such a prayer I never heard except from the Prophet himself," Chidester told his neighbors afterward. "Brother Hickey had the spirit in him, for certain."

Hickey never lost his spirit or his faith. He took another wife, had more children and continued to believe in the Strangite Latter-Day Saints.

Alex Wentworth and Tom Bedford returned to Beaver Island where they lived with their wives after renouncing their faith.

Peter McKinley returned to the island as well, opened a new store, and was elected to fill Strang's seat in the state legislature at the 1856 November election, representing the islands of Manitou County.

James and Alva Cable returned to their homes on the southeast side of the island, where they reopened their trading post and continued to sell cordwood to steamers. They changed the name of the bay from Galilee back to Cable's Bay.

After the cruelty of Roger Nagle had been excised out of his life, Kent Pentour turned out to be a decent, if rascally, fellow. While he never found any counterfeit money-making contraptions in Strang's print office, he did thoroughly enjoy making use of the printing press and wrote a book about his time on the high seas with Nagle. Being a talented storyteller, he blamed everything on Nagle, rendering himself an innocent victim under the sway of an evil man which was mostly true.

Rose Pratt and Frank Johnson unofficially exchanged vows with one another in a private ceremony in the store's back room.

Huldy Cornwall gave up her remote little cabin in the woods for an even more remote dwelling. She became the lighthouse keeper on Manitou Island, a job she adored and which suited her perfectly. She needed no gift of speech or hearing to communicate by light with boats passing in the night.

Eri Moore, who had been chased off Beaver Island by a band of Mormons on a dog sled, returned and became a profitable merchant as a wood salesman.

Sarah and Phoebe earned their place in the history books by being the first widows of Strang to give birth to more heirs. Phoebe gave birth to Eugenia Jesse Strang on October 28, 1856. She was followed closely by Sarah, who gave birth to James Phineas Strang on November 11 of that same year.

Betsy started the new year of 1857 by giving birth to Abigail Strang on January 1.

Elvira gave birth to James Jesse Strang Jr. on January 22, 1857.

The births made Strang the posthumous father of 12 children.

With the Mormons off the island, liquor sales boomed. Roald Cleary opened a second tavern on the east side of the island and hired Teddy Duffy to run it. Will continued to fish, but now it was with his brother-in-law Danny. Will had married Bridgette Greene, a new arrival from Donegal, Ireland. He moved out of his father Dolan's home and into the home of his in-laws on Pisgah Bay. As more people came from Donegal to Beaver Island and settled around the bay, it became commonly known as Donegal Bay.

Lucy was delighted to become unexpectedly pregnant after Archie's return to the island. She gave birth to a son, Antoine Archibald Donnelly, on April 15. Archie was over the moon.

WHO'S REAL AND WHO'S FICTIONAL?

REAL PEOPLE –
Women

Bedford, Ruth Ann
Bennett, Alice
Bennett, Julia
Cogswell Adams, Louisa
Hickey, Sarah
MacCulloch, Sarah
Moore, Peg
Strang, Mary Perce
Strang, Elvira Field
Strang, Betsy McNutt
Strang, Sarah Wright
Strang, Phoebe Wright
Watson, Jane
Wentworth, Phebe
Wright, Amanda
Wright, Margaret

REAL PEOPLE –
Men

Adams, George
Bedford, Thomas
Bonner, Black Jack
Cable, Alva
Cable, James
Chidester, Dennis
Cole, Galen
Gebeau, Lewis
Hickey, Lorenzo
Johnson, Frank
Kilty, Patrick
LaBlanc, Gus
MacCulloch, Hezekiah
McCauley, Black Pete
Miller, George
Miller, Joshua
Moore, Eri
Peaine, Chief
Pierce, Jonathan
Strang, James Jesse
Watson, Wingfield
Wentworth, Alexander
Whitney, Walter
Wright, Benjamin
Wright, Phineas

FICTIONAL
CHARACTERS

Bowman, Nathan
Bowman, Eliza
Bowman, Rose Pratt
Cleary, Roald
Cornwall, Huldy
Donnelly, Archie
Donnelly, Millicent
Duffy, Teddy
LaFleur, Lucy
MacCormick, Dolan
MacCormick, Will
Miigwech, Gwen
Miigwech, Otto
Nagle, Roger
Pentour, Kent

ACKNOWLEDGMENTS

Writing this book would have been a nearly insurmountable research task without the help of those who wrote nonfiction accounts of James Jesse Strang before I tackled this project. My deepest thanks go to: Milo Quaife, *The Kingdom Of Saint James: A Narrative Of The Mormons;* Roger Van Noord, *Assassination of a Michigan King;* Don Faber, *James Jesse Strang - The Rise and Fall of Michigan's Mormon King;* Vickie Cleverley Speek, *God Has Made Us A Kingdom;* Doyle Fitzpatrick, *The King Strang Story;* and Elizabeth Whitney Williams, *A Child Of The Sea and Life Among The Mormons.*

I also want to thank Allison Townsend, my location director, research assistant and unflagging supporter; Sandra Haven, the development editor who helped keep my story on track; Beth Anderson, super copy editor; Holly Eliot, my neighbor and enthusiastic beta reader; and Adrienne Malley of the Westside Writer's Group, who helped shape this story in the early stages.

Laurie Lounsbury is a national award-winning journalist and editor who spent most of her writing career covering northern Michigan, including Charlevoix, Petoskey, Boyne City, Gaylord and Beaver Island.

She has spent a portion of every summer of her life in Charlevoix, originally known as the Pine River settlement.

She currently lives in Ann Arbor, Michigan, where she sings in a girl group dance band with great enthusiasm and exceptionally mediocre talent.

Made in the USA
Monee, IL
21 July 2020